PENITENCE

BY JENNIFER LAURENS

Grove Creek Publishing

A Grove Creek Publishing Book
PENITENCE
Grove Creek Publishing / March 2010
All Rights Reserved.
Copyright 2010 by Jennifer Laurens

This book may not be reproduced in whole or in part without permission.
For further information:
Grove Creek Publishing, LLC
1404 West State Road, Suite 202
Pleasant Grove, Ut 84062

Cover: Sapphire Designs
http://designs.sapphiredreams.org/
Book Design: Julia Lloyd, Nature Walk Design
ISBN: 1-933963-83-2
$13.95
Printed in the United States of America

For Cortnie, Tiffinie, Jennifer

Heidi and Mikelynn

My sisters - I thank you

PENITENCE

- BOOK TWO -

ONE

I was awake.

But I was dead.

Was the vast gouging ache in my heart or in my soul? It didn't matter. I writhed in agony trying to escape, willing to do anything—even hurl myself from a rocky cliff or into a turbulent black sea to rid myself of the dread spreading throughout my being.

Seconds ago I'd been cradled in the arms of the man I loved. Complete comfort had surrounded me. Joy. Peace. Safety. All of those gifts eluded me now. Now, a fierce fire raced through my veins. Bruised muscles screamed. My heart pounded out each difficult breath.

Flashing images of the accident blared into my consciousness, more vibrant and real than any memory I'd ever recalled when I'd been alive. I gasped. My heart sped. I reached for Matthias.

Concern flashed over his face. "Zoe?"

"I…" I gulped for breath. Night. Pouring rain. The yellow and black truck. Scraping steel. Blinding headlights. "I see the accident."

"Look at me." His hands reached out in urgency but he was disappearing—being sucked away. "Zoe. Look at me."

I'm trying! Through the blast of crashing images, I strove to keep my gaze locked on his. I could barely see his face through the collage of the accident whirling in my mind. My body felt weighed down, as if I'd taken in a breath of leaden air. Like a tornado the sensations stormed, tearing apart the image of Matthias' face, ripping him further and further from my view until he shrunk, devoured in the vortex.

I strained, reaching. Screamed for him. Kicked and clawed as though I'd been dropped into the dark abyss of an open grave. *Please! I don't want to go. I want to stay with you!*

Slipping into the agony-drenched weight of flesh was like laboring into a two-ton wet suit. Scratchy noise filled my head. Why was mortality so… loud?

Just as I'd been unable to stop my death, I couldn't stop myself from sliding back into my body. Back to life. Wretched, fragile life.

Life without him.

Matthias.

Uttering his name didn't call upon serenity. Peace didn't bestow its tranquility over my suffering. Was I being punished? Where was he? Why was his assistance inaccessible to me now? Even through the exhaustive fight, the misery of pain, I knew as powerful as Matthias was, there was One more powerful than he.

One whose will I couldn't fight.

At that moment, I knew I was meant to return to my family. There were things I had to do. With that understanding, the scratching in my head started to subside. From the core of my being, a warm calm reverberated and spread slowly into my battered limbs.

At the same time, tears sprung behind my burning eyes. Matthias. *Oh, God, do I have to leave him? Will I see him again? Please, please don't take him away.* Weeping—the very act of it—the violent sobs wracking my body, hurled me back into consciousness.

I opened my eyes. Through a veil of tears I saw white. A dotted ceiling. Dull, man-made light. Not like the even beauty of the sun from the vibrant paradise I'd just left.

Paradise. How long had I been there with him? I didn't know. Hours? Seconds? Time wasn't measured there like it was here. But then I hadn't had enough time to even ask Matthias that question.

Another wave of sorrow rose in my heart, crashing with bitter violence through my limbs. I closed my eyes, tears gushing out. *Please let me dissolve. Cease to exist. I can't go on with this hurt eating my heart.* My weeping continued. A very human baptism back into life. I was here. Alive. Mortal. I wanted Matthias with me. He was my guardian—sent to protect me.

Weren't we meant to be together? He'd lived his life, almost a hundred years before me. He was living another life now, without me. Reality sunk me into deep despair. A layer so thick, impenetrable and overwhelming I couldn't face the thought of my life without him for one more second of consciousness.

I blacked out.

Soft, urgent pressure on my arm. A hand. Mom. I knew her touch as if she'd said my name in a crowd of thousands and I opened my eyes. She stood over me.

Mom. *It's so good to see you.* Joy burst in my heart. Mom. *My* mom. I tried to smile. I guess I did, because she smiled back, and gently squeezed my arm. Above her head, white ceiling with black dots. I was still in the hospital. The aches in my body confirmed I hadn't gone anywhere.

"She's awake." Dad's voice. He came next to Mom, peered over her shoulder with a smile. Tears. Joy spilled from his countenance like a waterfall of love spreading over me. I was so pleased they were happy. Happy that I was back. Home.

Alive.

I closed my eyes. *Matthias.*

"Don't talk if you're too weak," Mom's voice reached through my longing for him. I opened my eyes, looked at her. *Focus on Mom. Then you won't think about him.* But that didn't work. My heart yearned for what it couldn't have.

"Hey." My voice. The sound wasn't clear and crisp as it had been in Paradise. The tone carried the rough edge of mortality. Mom and Dad didn't seem to notice the difference. Both smiled bigger at the sound. Tears streamed from Mom's blue eyes.

"Oh, honey." She leaned over. Her faded perfume, mixed with the very mortal smell of flesh and bone, trickled into my waking senses. She pressed herself lightly against me in a hug, as if she was embracing a fragile glass sculpture of me instead of my body.

"I love you so much."

"You too," I said.

She stood upright, turned and wept in Dad's embrace. Their love was so pure. They loved each other first, above anyone or anything else. I always knew that, was never jealous of that because commitment was supposed to be that way. That's how love survived.

Love. The ache in my heart I was striving to ignore grew stronger, pounding through the impossible spheres of two different lifetimes that would never join. A love separated by a power stronger than either of us could influence. I closed my eyes against a fresh onslaught of falling tears.

"Where does it hurt, Zoe?"

It's more than hurt. I wanted to dissolve. Die. *Please take me away from here. Can't I go back? Please.* Behind my closed eyes I searched for the whirling vortex of my life to play out again. I sought the light.

The continuous beep of the monitor pierced my semi-conscious state. Death, a step I'd once feared like most human beings, wasn't coming for me.

I wasn't going anywhere.

The beep of the monitor—annoying as it was—woke me again. I opened my eyes. Same white room, dull light and black dotted ceiling. I was breathing. My heart was pumping blood through my system, and the pain had gone from a furious roar to a low, recurring moan in and out of my body.

"You're awake." Mom's voice. I turned my head, found her coming to my side, reaching out to me. She'd changed from the black shirt she'd had on last time I saw her, into a white shirt. Her smile radiated. She wrapped her hand around mine. "Oh, honey. It's a miracle. They weren't sure you'd come back. Oh, honey." She gently squeezed my left hand with both of hers.

"Where is everybody?" My voice sounded more like my own. *I must be getting better.* A sharp pang of sorrow shot to my heart. I should be glad. Healing meant I could get out of this depressing place. See everybody. Go home.

"Dad had to stop at the office. Abria's at school and so is Luke."

"How long have I been here?"

"Two weeks."

"Two weeks?!" I was stunned. The passing time had felt like minutes at best.

"They weren't sure you were going to make it, Zoe." Again, she squeezed my hand. Desperate. Afraid, like she couldn't believe I was there. "I'm so glad you're awake."

"I'm awake," I murmured. I'd tried to go back to Paradise and had failed. I swept the room for Matthias. Bunches of colorful flowers filled every free surface. The bright colors didn't cheer me. Dear God, where is he? I closed my eyes. "I'm going to be fine, Mom."

"Yes..." But she didn't sound convinced.

"I'm here, aren't I?" I snapped, eyes flashing. I'd journeyed from death back to life. I may never see Matthias again.

Mom's worried expression flashed to surprise.

"Sorry," I muttered and turned my head away. I kept my eyes closed. Being awake was like falling back to sleep, back into a bad dream, one that kept repeating itself. One I couldn't escape.

"You need to get your strength." Mom's voice was soft. She gave me one last squeeze and then the pressure on my hand was gone.

I lay there in a restless state of helplessness. Before I took another breath, I wanted some answers. Where was Matthias? Why wouldn't he come to me now? Was it because I wasn't in any danger? *Please let that be the reason he's not here.* A sense of dread latched onto my bones with a deep grip. I couldn't dismiss the feeling. *Why was I allowed to be with him in Paradise, allowed to hold him, kiss him, led to believe that we were at last going to be together, only to be cruelly torn apart?*

5

Surely, God wasn't that callous. Had I done something wrong? Had Matthias broken a heavenly rule? My mind, still weak and fairly listless, tired swimming with such thoughts.

"You really should rest." Mom again.

"Haven't I been? For the last two weeks." Frustration still lingered, even in my weakened tone.

"I understand you must feel discouraged." Mom looked like she was trying to figure out why her eighteen year old daughter who'd almost been killed in a car accident, sounded like she wasn't happy to be alive.

She had no idea that a few months ago I'd fallen in love with an angel. Not just any angel, my little sister Abria's guardian angel. Mom would never believe that he'd become my guardian angel, too. Never, in her wildest dreams, would she believe that I'd died and spent the most treasured moments of my life with Matthias—in death.

"Are you in pain?"

"Not as bad, no."

"That's good. You were talking a lot," Mom said. "While you were unconscious."

I jerked my head in her direction and my eyes flashed. "What did I say?"

"Well, a lot of it wasn't understandable, but you kept repeating, Matthias."

I squeaked out a gasp.

"Who is Matthias?" she asked. "The young man from the zoo?"

I couldn't believe Mom remembered seeing Matthias at the zoo. We'd taken Abria there one Saturday for a "nice family day" at Dad's insistence and Abria had done what she commonly does when we're out in public—run away. Thankfully, Matthias had been there, found her, and carried her back to us in his heaven-sent arms.

Mom must have been impressed by Matthias' powerful, calming countenance because she remembered his name. "Why would I remember a zoo worker?" I asked.

"That's what confused me. But you've never mentioned any friends named Matthias, so…"

"I'm sure it was just my subconscious doing dumb things, Mom." Now wasn't the time to admit the truth: that the guy she'd been impressed with at the zoo, the one with the halo of toffee hair and eyes the color of two o'clock sky hadn't been a zoo worker at all. He was her daughters' guardian.

The man I loved.

The man I'd never have because I was alive and he was dead.

"Two weeks," I mumbled, wanting to change the subject. I blew out a breath. "Two weeks. It didn't seem like that long."

Mom's hand on my arm again, warm love. "It did for us."

Her eyes glistened. Seeing the raw pain on her face, my heart ached. I covered her hand with mine. Her eyes widened. "Zoe! You moved your arm!"

"Yeah." I lifted my bandaged limb. "What happened, anyway?" If she'd been that thrilled to see me move my arm, I wondered what condition the accident had left the rest of me in.

Mom's expression grew grim and surge of panic welled up inside of me. Had I been disfigured? I wiggled my toes. I felt all the way down, that was a relief. Each finger was in place; wearily I held them in front of my face. But my arms were wrapped like a mummy, with IV tubes vanishing somewhere beneath the gauze.

I tried to sit up, and sharp pain shot across my chest. Mom snapped her hand out to my shoulder to stop me. "You have some broken ribs. Your right lung was punctured, and you had a concussion. They spent four hours extracting shards from your body. It was a miracle none of the glass or metal went deep. One nearly…" she paused, swallowed, reached out and petted my head. "One nearly sheared off your right breast."

"What?" Heart pounding, I lifted my hand to feel but felt only thick wrapping beneath the thin hospital gown.

"They were able to save it, Zoe. The plastic surgeon did a wonderful—"

"Mom, I want to see it. Let me see." My pulse thrummed. *Plastic surgeon?* Sweat sprung from every pore. I tried to throw back the sheets covering me, but the effort was exhausting.

"Zoe, you're alive, that's what matters."

"I want to see!" What did it look like? Did I look like a freak? I closed my eyes, weighing visions of purple gashes across my white flesh, distorted appendages hanging lopsidedly from my body, and other grotesque sights.

Mom raised the bed with the push of a button until I was sitting upright. My racing heart still hadn't slowed. In fact, as the moment drew closer, a wave of nausea rose in my throat. "I'm going to be sick," I whispered.

"Let's do this another time."

"No, no! I want to see it now. Mom, please."

Mom's face was white, and my panic plunged. Gingerly, she helped me sit forward. Aches pounded like a base drum through every muscle in my body. As much as I wanted to see what my breast looked like, the movement of sitting up drained me. I'd never felt so weak. I fell back against the raised mattress, breathing like I'd just run a marathon.

The door whooshed open and a dark-skinned, black haired man dressed in a white physician's coat waltzed in. His teeth gleamed off the brilliance of his jacket. "Zoe!"

Tucked under his arm was a clipboard, which he tossed casually on the table next to the bed. "I am Dr. Semolitis. You are awake. How are you feeling?"

"Like I was hit by a semi truck," I grumbled, on the last of a pant.

He chuckled. "Lucky to be alive, you are." He leaned over, whipped out a mini flashlight, flicked it on and the tiny beam shot first in my right eye, then in my left. "Looking much better, I must say. You were in bad shape when you came in. Your mother is glad today, is she not?" He shot Mom a glittering grin. She smiled.

"Much happier today, yes, thank you."

"You are a miracle girl, you know that?" He lifted my wrist, paused and felt my pulse. My heart finally slowed down some. Was this the doctor who'd sewn me up? Handled my breast? I shuddered at the thought.

"You are nervous?" His black eyes locked on mine deciphering. He let go of my wrist, gently placing my hand back to my side.

"A little."

"I just told her about her breast," Mom said. "She wanted to know."

"Of course she wanted to know. She's a teenager, right?" He grinned. "Zoe, when you came in here, you were covered in glass. It took us four hours just to extricate all the pieces. You have one hundred and sixty-five stitches. Most are little and won't be seen when they heal. Most were on your arms, because you must have thrown your arms up to protect your face. Your clothes were quite shredded. You are a very lucky girl."

He neglected to elaborate about my breast. Maybe I was jumping to conclusions, panicking for nothing. It probably looked fine.

"One of the larger shards was embedded in your chest, and your right breast was compromised. But I was able to make an incision directly underneath and reattach the tissue, much like I do in breast augmentation. You have a laceration, like a T across the right side where the glass went in, but we stitched that and it should heal into white scar tissue."

"I want to see it."

"Of course." Dr. Semolitis helped me sit forward, and eased the blue and white hospital gown away from my back, and around my shoulders, exposing my right side. A large bandage was wrapped around my midsection. "This wrap is to give you support for the ribs. It doesn't have anything to do with your breast. Mrs. Dodd, could you help Zoe hold up her arms?"

Yeck. I felt vulnerable, arms raised, a strange man close, unwrapping thick, white gauze, his eyes—his face—inches from my breasts. As each layer unpeeled, I grew colder and more fearful. Soon, my boobs would hang out like a stripper. Ridiculous, I know, but I suddenly wanted to retract my wish to see myself.

Mom held my hands, which felt even weirder. But my arms trembled and started to fall back to my sides. "Almost done, Zoe."

When the air hit my chest, I looked down. Dr. Semolitis had produced a large mirror from somewhere, and he held it angled so I could see. My heart stopped.

"Of course, there is still some swelling. The eggplant color will take about a month to completely go away. But you can see," he reached out with his physician's finger and traced the right side, "here is where I made the incision. You won't see it in a bra or bathing suit." His words muddled and stuck in my head. My once perfectly-shaped round now resembled a blueberry pancake, shaped like a coffee bean with a slit down the side.

Nausea raced up my throat and I heaved spitty liquid all over the mirror.

He whisked the mirror out of sight and Mom's expression grew anxious, her hands jittery. I fell back against the mattress, eyes closed, my shaking hands reaching blindly for the sheets to cover myself. I'd never look normal again. What would I do? I looked like a teenaged breast cancer victim.

"I have every confidence your breast will heal and look good," Dr. Semolitis said. "Any white scarring should not change the natural shape."

Words meant to console didn't cut through the image of the purple black blob from my mind

Dr. Semolitis was talking to Mom, but I didn't listen to what he was saying. I didn't want to open my eyes, fighting as I was to hold tears back. It didn't work. They streamed down my cheeks.

I felt the whoosh of the door open, heard the padding of feet and then hands were everywhere, holding me upright. I opened my eyes. Two nurses. My arms went over my lolling head. Sharp pains in my ribs caused me to wince. I felt a wrapping session begin, round and round. When I was all bandaged up, the room emptied and all I heard was Mom whispering to the doctor, their hushed voices sneaking underneath the incessant beep of the heart monitor.

Overwhelmed with the accident, with not knowing where Matthias was, at seeing the purple, black and green bruises devouring what was now my breast, I wanted to fall into sleep and wake up to find everything—even meeting Matthias, getting to know him, falling hopelessly in love with him— had only been a very long and detailed dream.

But that was impossible. Every breath I took, each moment that passed, hour that I lived, meant I was that much closer to getting old, dying and seeing Matthias again.

TWO

After Dr. Semolitis left, Mom came over, pulled the one chair in the room to the side of the bed, and sat. Her lips quavered up in a smile. I'd seen that look before—I can't believe this is happening to someone I love. But I'd seen her look that way mostly at Abria.

"It's going to heal and look fine, Zoe. I'm sure of it. Dr. Semolitis assured me."

I closed my eyes, nodded. "Yeah." But inside, I couldn't envision anything but slashes and warped shapes where my breast was.

Mom, in her effort to cheer me up, rattled on about how Britt called every day, asking how I was. So had Chase and the school. Everyone had heard about the accident, the incident had made the local paper, and my teachers were willing to help any way they could with missing assignments or whatever. Even though I was a senior, and the school year was halfway done, school was the last thing on my mind. Still, the allowance of extra time or whatever my teachers would grant me, was a relief.

"Who is Chase, anyway? A friend of Matthias'?"

I cracked a smile. "Sort of. He's in newspaper with me."

"Well, he's come by the house and the hospital half-a-dozen times. Nice looking boy. Very well mannered." She lifted her right brow over a teasing smile.

"Mom, we're just friends."

"Oh, I can tell he sees you as 'just a friend.' He was very concerned. I told him I'd call him when you were up to having visitors."

"I want to see that mirror again," I said. Before anyone I knew set one foot inside this depressing hospital room, I was going to shower and wash my hair.

Mom stood, searched for the mirror, found it on the shelf in the small closet, then brought it over. She held it in front of my face.

My skin was a mottled mess, an extension of the bruises coloring my breast and the rest of my body, only dotted with tiny strips of white suture tape. "I look hideous."

"You were in a car accident, what do you expect?"

"I need to wash my hair. Look at it. It reeks." Strands stuck together in teenaged oiliness, hanging like dead brown vines around my face.

Mom chuckled and the sound made me laugh, too, and it felt wonderful to laugh. We shared a long, lazy smile. I couldn't complain. My face was still intact. It really was a miracle I was alive, even if my heart was somewhere else.

I handed her the mirror and rested my head against the pillow. "So, what happened to the driver?" Did Luke know that the guy was someone from the log house?

"He had minor injuries—of course." Her tone was clipped. "But he's in jail on a DUI. Serves him right. What kind of person is irresponsible like that?"

"At least he's in jail."

"Sweating bullets, I hope. If you hadn't made it, he'd have had a manslaughter charge to look forward to."

I didn't mention Luke's connection to the driver. I would ask Luke when I saw him. Oddly, I didn't feel any animosity toward the driver of the wasp truck. Maybe I was too worn down. Exhaustion took its toll like a ravaging fever. I'd been awake, what, fifteen minutes? I closed my eyes and sleep took over.

Dad came by later that evening, with Abria and Luke. Seeing their faces was like coming up for air after being held under water—to the point of nearly passing out from oxygen deprivation—I couldn't suck in enough of them. For a few moments, I experienced real joy and release from the pain still residing in my body and troubling thoughts of Matthias' whereabouts.

Luke's grin was cheery, the happiness in his eyes at seeing me sincere. I relished the connection as if every past argument and ugly word was wiped away. Dad wept against my shoulder when he took me against him in the gentlest embrace. He didn't say anything, just held me long enough that I knew he needed to feel me, alive and breathing.

Dad finally eased away, smiling through tears as his gaze stayed with mine. "I got us all here as soon as Mom told me you were awake. I'm glad you're feeling better. You look so much better. How do you feel?"

"Tired and sore but other than that, pretty good."

"Everybody's asked about you," Luke said.

"Yeah?"

"I get stopped at least ten times a day. It doesn't matter where I am, at school, at the Purple Turtle—the gas station. Man, you know a lot of people."

I smiled. "Yeah. And they all know you, bud."

"Uh-oh." He laughed. His smile wrapped warm and tender around my heart.

"A lot of teachers have asked me how you're doing, too," Luke added.

"Like I said, they're all willing to work with you, honey." Mom's tone reassured me. "Nobody wants you to stress about assignments or anything."

"Don't think about that now." Dad patted my hand.

I heard Abria's sing-song voice and strained to look for her. Mom grabbed her, lifted her up and brought her to the bedside. "Look, Abria. Zoe is back. Zoe is awake."

"Hey baby," I reached out for her. Abria stuck her fingers in her mouth, looked at me for a moment then leaned the opposite direction toward the curtained window with a grunt. Mom eased her down so her feet hit the floor.

It was so good to see Abria. I smiled. But as instantaneously as joy went through me, that joy was ushered out when my thoughts shifted to Matthias.

⋙ ✣ ⋘

14

My throat tightened. A surge of tears rushed behind my eyes and I blinked, fast, to keep them back.

"You okay?" Dad eyed me.

I nodded. "It's just good to see everybody."

"Yeah, it is," Luke murmured.

"Abria, no-no." Mom's tone wasn't sharp, just a little louder. She crossed to where Abria stood, peering up at the floor-to-ceiling window, and stayed by Abria's side.

"I had to nail the windows in her bedroom closed," Dad said.

"Did she try to get out?" I asked. Had Matthias been there? Or had this happened while he had been with me?

"Luke caught her standing in the window one day," Dad said.

"She was just standing there." Luke's eyes met mine in a secret indication of the day he and I had seen Abria doing the same thing. "She was looking out like it was nothing."

"Oh my gosh," I murmured. "Did you have to nail all the windows in the house shut?"

Mom shook her head. "Thankfully, no. I told Dad to nail hers closed. I was too worried about what was going on with you to figure out some other solution. And you know how it is with Abria—the stress that keeps on giving."

"Yeah." Had Matthias been there? Not knowing the time frame, I had no idea if Abria had been protected by him or if she had been kept safe by Luke's coincidental moment of brilliance.

By the window, Abria now tried to climb up into the large frame.

"Thank heavens these windows don't open," Mom observed. "NO climbing in the window, young lady." Every time Abria lifted her leg and gripped the sill, Mom scooped her and set her on the floor.

"This could go on all night," Mom sighed.

Dad crossed to the window and picked Abria up. "I'll hold her for a while. Maybe she'll lose interest."

"Like that will happen," I joked.

"Seriously," added Luke.

15

"We thought we'd eat dinner here—with you—if that's okay," Mom said. "The doctor said you can have solids, if you start out with something simple. I think he's ordered you soup or something."

I wasn't hungry, no doubt thanks to the clear fluid running into my veins from the IV. I hated tubes and needles. "You guys go ahead."

"Cool." Luke grinned and stuck out his palm to Dad. Everyone chuckled.

"Where do you think you're going?" Dad asked.

"For food."

"Not without me." Dad flashed his wagging brows at Mom and me and he, Abria and Luke went out the door. The air was light, the mood fun, making being alive easier to focus on even with questions about Matthias still looming in my head.

"I haven't seen Luke that happy in months," Mom murmured. A tensionless smile sighed from her.

"He looks sober," I said. "How did he do with all of this?" Had he gotten high? Left home and hung out with his buddies? Or had he been there for Mom and Dad and supported them? I almost didn't want to know, afraid of ruining the good mood.

"The first few days he didn't come out of his room at all. His eyes…I could tell he cried. Of course he put on a casual face, but that didn't hide anything. We were all very afraid, Zoe. I had everyone I knew praying for you. Even Pastor Perrigan sent out a plea for prayer."

Sobering news. While I'd been savoring a carefree existence with Matthias in Paradise, everyone I knew and many I did not were praying for my recovery. I sighed, closed my eyes.

Mom laid her hand on my arm. "It's a miracle. That's what it is."

The door opened, shifting the pressure in the room like a giant whisper. A nurse in dotted pink scrubs that looked more like pjs than a uniform swept in. Her red hair was pulled back into a ponytail, her freckled face bloomed into a smile.

She carried a tray, plates covered with silver food warmers. "Zoe. How are you feeling?" She pulled a raised bed table over, set the tray down. The scent of chicken filled my nose.

"Feeling pretty good."

"Dr. Semolitis ordered you some broth and Jell-O. Yum, huh?" She laughed. But first I'm going to take your vitals."

In an efficient bluster of pumped blood pressure, ear-poked thermometer and a thorough game of peek-a-boo with my various bandages, I was deemed okay enough to eat.

The nurse slid the bed table over my lap, then yanked off the silver warmers and smiled. "Viola."

A bowl of golden liquid, a bowl of red jiggly Jell-O.

"You want some help?" the nurse asked.

"No. I can do it." She adjusted the bed so I was sitting up straighter. "Take it easy at first. It's easy to think you're not full when you haven't had solid food, but a little goes a long way."

"Okay."

She blew out of the room and I stared at the golden, steaming bowl of broth. "I'm really not hungry."

"But you should eat, honey. You need strength."

I had strength. Fresh, pulsing, peeled-free strength just a little while ago in Paradise. My body had never felt so rejuvenated.

My appetite danced on the precipice of nausea. I closed my eyes again. *Please, wherever you are, hear me. Speak to me. Please tell me you're all right.*

Silence.

"Honey?"

I opened my eyes. Mom's brows were knit in concern. I forced myself to pick up the spoon, my hand trembling. I would eat so she wouldn't worry. One spoonful. Warm, rich flavor slipped down my throat. Two. Three. My hand wouldn't stop shaking.

I set the spoon down, let out a breath. "Maybe some Jello-O."

Mom nodded, watching my every move with motherly love. "Want some help?"

I shook my head. I picked up the bowl, spooned a jiggly spoonful into my mouth. Cold, red, jellied cherry. That was enough.

After putting down the bowl and spoon, I laid my head back, let out a weary breath. "No more."

Mom stood and wheeled the rolling food tray into a far corner. "It'll take some time." Her voice was quiet as she crossed back to the side of the bed.

I wanted to weep. Alone.

"Mom." My voice cracked, like a dam unable to hold back water after an earthquake. I wanted to tell her everything in hopes that between her shoulders and mine, I could carry both my world and Matthias'.

She sat on the edge of the bed and reached for my hand, taking it in loving support. "It's okay."

Tears burst and gushed down my cheeks. My shoulders buckled under the pressure. My world. His. Too big. Too far.

Impossible.

Lost in consuming grief, I barely felt Mom pet my head. The whoosh of the door didn't penetrate my engulfing sorrow. Dad, Luke, Abria and pizza. Silence. Whispers. Abria's footsteps. Mom's sharp voice.

The door opened again. Closed.

Mom's hand on my back. Dad's—patting me. My muffled sobs filled the empty spaces between us.

Please leave me alone. I can't be here for you right now. I'm lost, even though I'm home.

I need to find myself.

I floated through the next few days. Part of me wanted to be alive and was glad to see my family. My body: sliced flesh healing, bruised skin pinking, aching muscles softening—my body was happy to have my soul pumping life into it. Another part faced each morning with my heart broken.

As each day progressed, minutes ticking into hours, hours passing into evening without sight of Matthias, morning's arrival tore my already broken heart into hopeless shreds.

Mom, Dad and Luke—their enthusiasm grew with each visit. Abria remained consistently Abria—distracted window fiend endlessly chattering nonsensical words. There was no chance I'd run into Matthias here at the hospital. Too many safety procedures in place. If I was going to see him, I'd either have to jump out a window, fall down an elevator shaft or heist some narcotics. None of those options thrilled me. I was alive for a reason. I should be happy. And I was, I just wanted to know where he was. If I was going to manipulate my safety to see him again, I would have to wait until I was home.

The desperate idea gave me the tiniest drop of hope in my desert-dead soul. I took to healing with new intent. Even if my appetite was nowhere in sight, I forced food down. When the nurses offered sleeping pills, I took them—the more rest the better. I willingly accepted my doctor's recommended three walks around the fifth floor every day.

It was on one of my rounds of the floor that I saw a spirit. At first I thought the transparent image was a figment of my loosely drugged, tired body. My second clue was that the woman was not a fabrication. Her feet didn't touch the floor. She hovered a foot or two in the air, peering into a room. I shuffled closer to the woman, dragging my IV at my side. My heart raced. She was older, her silver hair in a roll at the back of her head. She wore a long robe of some sort, tied at the waist. Fluffy white slippers adorned her feet.

As I drew closer, I saw that she was not like Matthias. He had a body. She had the shadow of a body, a transparent yet completely detailed form in every way except that I could see every angle and side of her in three dimensions.

I stopped five feet away, staring, wondering if she would notice me. She stood at the open door, gazing into another of the private rooms on the floor. I heard mumbling from within the room, someone weeping.

The woman tilted her head at the sound, her pleasant face peaceful and calm, not unlike the look Matthias carried.

"Hello," I said.

She looked at me. Her eyes widened for a moment. "You can see me?"

I nodded, stepped closer. She smiled. "That's wonderful. I'd heard about mortals seeing spirits, but I didn't think it would happen to me my first time out."

I glanced at the open door. "Is this someone you know?"

Her gaze moved to the room, she nodded. "My husband." She clasped her hands at her bosom, and a light sprung behind her face, then radiated out in all directions. Fascinated, I moved around her in a slow circle, her light reflecting on my skin in a soft ivory glow.

"I've been waiting for him for ten years," she murmured, gaze locked on the man in the room. I followed her gaze. I caught a glimpse of him when I passed the door. The bald, skeletal figure lay tangled in white sheets and clear tubes. A nurse stood on one side of the bed, a younger woman on the other. The younger woman was weeping.

"I'm sorry he's..." Dying? I couldn't say that, because I'd tasted the joy that death could bring. Obviously, this lady was anxious to see her husband again.

"Oh, don't be sorry," she said. "It's time. Only, he's not cooperating. Look at him, stubborn old stinker."

I stood by her side, and looked at her husband, lying in the bed, a plethora of life-saving wires and tubes encasing him like rollercoaster tracks. A low, gentle current radiated from the woman next to me. My heart banged for Matthias. "Do you know Matthias?"

Her gaze stayed on her husband. "Matthias? No."

"He's like you." Words stumbled from my lips, hope, urgency, need pushing them out.

She looked at me. "Like me?"

"He's dead."

"Well, there are a lot of folks like me, honey." She returned her concentration on her husband. "He doesn't want to let go. He's afraid of leaving Cissy. That's our daughter. She looks marvelous, doesn't she?"

I nodded, dumbfounded.

"Come now, Frank. Get a move on. I'm here."

The low current surrounding her shifted, like a car changing gears, ramping up speed. The sound grew stronger, reaching out and into the room like an invisible hand. Then, the man's spirit—renewed and whole, just like his body, but in the same spiritual makeup as the woman's—rose up and into the air above him. A shrilling beep from the heart monitor filled the air.

The older woman held out her arms. "Frankie!"

He moved toward her, smiling, relief and joy on his face and in his translucent countenance. "I heard your voice, Martha. It's really you." They embraced—their spirits dissolving into each other, and then, in a flash of brilliant, blinding light, they were gone.

I stood breathless, clinging to my IV stand. Around me, the hall buzzed with uninterrupted hospital normalcy. Awed, I couldn't move. I was so happy for them. They were together, what greater end could there be than that?

Soft weeping drew my attention back to the young woman in the room. She'd fallen over the body of the man, and now she lay grieving. I wanted to tell her everything would be okay, that her dad was okay and that he was with her mom. But she'd think I was crazy.

I let out a sigh, turned and headed back to my room. The sighting infused me with hope. I hadn't lost my sensitivity to see spirits, that was the best news I'd heard since I had come back. I had real hope that I would see Matthias again—somehow.

Finally, I was able to wash my hair with Mom and the nurse's help. I stood at the sink, bent over and Mom scrubbed my head. I'd had a few cuts on my scalp, but no stitches.

Mom brought an extension cord and I sat in the room chair while she blew dry my hair. When I looked in the mirror, my shiny dark hair was so fluffy I laughed. "I look like an eighties pop star."

"You look beautiful," Mom's voice was soft.

Dr. Semolitis breezed in with a smile. "Zoe, look at you! You look very nice today."

"Thanks."

"Something is different."

"I washed my hair."

"Yes! That will do it every time, will it not? I have good news. You are free to go home."

"I am?" My heart buzzed.

"You are. I will instruct your mother on your care, and discharge you back to your busy, teenage life. Sound fair?"

I was already back to my teenaged life. *Fair* had been left behind the moment I was taken out of Paradise. "I guess so."

He tilted his head. "What? You want to stay here in the hospital? I could put you to work, if you like."

"No. No, thanks."

"Your boyfriend will be happy, yes?"

"I don't have a boyfriend."

"A pretty girl like you?" He crossed to Mom and together they looked at the clipboard he had brought in with him.

Home. I rested against the raised bed, still tired, but with enough excitement pulsing through me that I was ready for the next step of healing: out of the protected safety of the hospital and into the world where my questions, which had been restless for the last few weeks, would finally waken and demand answers. Would I get those answers?

I said goodbye to the nurses I'd become familiar with over the last few days, gave Dr. Semolitis a hug—at his insistence—and was wheeled, in a wheelchair packed with my belongings, down to the hospital discharge doors. Another wheelchair held dozens of pots and vases of flowers, cards and stuffed animals.

Mom pulled the car up and I got in. My celebratory gifts were loaded into the back seat.

Done. Over.

Life.

Starting again.

THREE

My eyes ached with the sunlight pressing upon them. I kept them closed during the drive. Mom prattled on about neighborhood news and work and the information drizzled into my brain, did an about face and was gone. I couldn't remember what she'd said, only the upbeat tone of her voice, when we finally pulled into the driveway.

Home was glorious. The sight moved me through a rush of memories and I wept, quickly wiping away tears before anyone could see them. Inside, familiar scents wrapped around me. Vanilla candles. Mom's faded perfume. Laundry detergent.

Dad came out and helped Mom and I carry everything inside. Luke appeared in the entry and took my hospital bag upstairs to my bedroom. Mom ushered me to the family room where she promptly sent Dad for some sheets and blankets, and she made up a resting place on the couch for me.

The short walk in tired me, and I eased onto the couch with a heavy sigh. Abria was running back and forth in front of me, giggling. I guess she was happy to have me home. I smiled at her. "Hey pretty girl."

She stopped, flapped, and promptly and gleefully climbed on the coffee table.

"I brought your pillows." Dad arrived, his arms laden with my fluffy pillows. He propped them around me.

"Thanks, Dad. Smells good in here."

He lifted Abria into his arms. "No climbing young lady." Abria squirmed.

Mom was in the kitchen, opening the oven. "Dad stopped and got Chinese take out. Sound good to you?"

My appetite still hadn't returned, but I didn't want to hurt her feelings. "Sounds great." Everything looked so clean and colorful compared to the antiseptic blandness of the hospital. The drapes were open so I could see the aspens and pines in our backyard, the towering mountains. How beautiful everything about my life was.

Luke came down the stairs. Hands stuffed in his front pockets, he crossed to where I was on the couch. I patted a spot next to me. He hemmed a moment, then sat.

I caught Mom glancing over. She smiled, then called for Dad to help her set the table. He carried Abria to a seat and plopped her into the chair.

"I can help," Luke piped.

"That's okay." Mom gleamed, seeing the two of us together.

In typical clueless-father fashion, Dad searched every cabinet before finding where the tablecloths were kept. He found the dishes faster.

"So, you on Lortabs or anything?" Luke asked.

"No way, those things make me sick." I eyed him. Surely he wasn't being friendly so he could score my prescription.

He nodded, looked around. "You want me to turn on the TV?"

"Sure, okay."

He grabbed the remote and flicked on the TV. An old episode of *Dr. Quinn: Medicine Woman* was on. "Oh, not this," he groaned.

"No, leave it on. Remember when we used to watch this, you and me?" I laughed. "We were obsessed. Me with Jane Seymour and her long hair, you with Sully in his fringed leather outfits."

"Yeah." A faint smile lifted his lips. "Outfit, singular."

"That's right, he only wore one."

We both laughed.

"You guys used to dress up and play Dr. Quinn all the time," Dad called, setting plates on the tablecloth, his gaze flicking to Abria as she now stood on her chair, flapping.

"Remember that fake suede costume I made for Luke?" Mom chuckled. Luke flushed. "Don't remind me."

"I seem to remember buying a wig for you, Zoe," Mom added with a wink. She stood over a bowl of salad, tossing greens.

"Yep, a lovely acrylic nightmare."

"I was glad when Luke got over wanting to scalp people." Dad gave an obvious shudder as he set glasses at each place setting. Hearing my family laugh together was soothing music to my soul.

A sweet silence filled the air afterwards, and I looked around for Abria. "Where's Abria?"

Everything came to a stop. "Let me go look for her," I struggled to stand.

"No, you stay put." Dad set down the last fork. "Abria? Abria?"

"No, Dad, let me. I need the exercise."

"You're still weak," Dad said.

"Dad's right, Zoe," Mom said. "Don't overdo."

If there was any chance I would see Matthias, I'd take it—no matter the cost. I inched to the staircase. "I'm okay. I'll do it." Dad stopped, glanced at Mom. I felt their eyes on me, but didn't care. My heart raced. *Matthias. Please, please be here.*

"Abria?" I climbed the stairs, my muscles quivering halfway up. I should have stayed on the couch. Determined, I gripped the banister and pulled myself along, ignoring the sweat bursting at my hairline and along my back.

Finally at the landing, I gasped for breath. I couldn't believe how tiring a flight of steps was. Heart pounding, I crossed to Abria's room. The door was closed. "Abria?" I gripped the knob, turned it, and went in. My heart sunk. Abria sat alone on the floor, spinning the top.

Tears rushed up my throat, nearly choking me. "Found her." I called, steadying my voice so no one would suspect how devastated I was that Matthias wasn't with her. I should be happy she was fine, that she didn't need a guardian at that moment.

I went into her room and closed the door, resting my back against it. I closed my eyes. *Where are you? What's happened?* Swarmed with longing, the tears I'd fought to hold back broke through my lashes and streamed down my cheeks. The ache I'd felt in the hospital when I'd awakened and found myself without him was back, more powerful, deeper and tearing more profoundly through me. I wanted to sob.

Abria looked up at me for a moment, then went back to spinning her top, oblivious to my anguish. I crossed to the bed and fell onto it, overcome with weariness and grief. Tears continued to run out my eyes, and my body shook, a combination of exhaustion and sorrow wracking my limbs.

"Ah, Zippy, don't cry."

The tart voice broke through my sadness. I opened my eyes. Standing at the foot of the bed was an older woman with blonde hair. She reminded me of a gypsy. She wore a dress in bright pink, kind of like the one I'd worn briefly while I'd been in Paradise, but hers had a lavishly embroidered vest over it. Her blue eyes were just like Mom's, twinkling and pretty. I recognized her from dozens of photos.

I sat up. "Aunt Janis?"

She nodded. "You look miserable."

"I—you're here. What—I thought you were in intake?"

"I was, until I was needed back here."

"Do you know Matthias?"

"I sure do. Super young man."

My heart spun. I felt like I was going to burst right then and there. "Do you know where he is?"

She came closer. "I haven't seen him, Zippy. But I know he's met with some temporary... obstacles."

"Obstacles. What happened? You have to tell me, please."

"Oh, honey." She tilted her head, a look of understanding on her face. "Don't think about this now. You've got to get well."

"I don't want to get well, I want to die so I can be with Matthias."

"Now you're talking craziness." She peered at Abria, spinning the top. "My she's grown, hasn't she?"

"Please, if you know anything at all, please tell me. I've been worried about him. Why isn't he here? Did he do something wrong? Was it me? Something I did?"

Seeing that Abria was occupied, Aunt Janis sat next to me on the bed. "The truth is, I don't know where Matthias is. I was just asked to step back in and watch Abria for the time being."

My heart sunk. "You don't know anything?"

"I'm sorry." She reached out to pat my hand and stopped, withdrawing, both of her hands crossing on her lap. "Some things are confidential."

"So, you aren't my guardian, either?"

She shook her head. "Don't you worry. Everything will work itself out."

"I hate that saying. Mom says that to me all the time and it drives me nuts. How can something work itself out? *We* have to make it work out, that's how it gets worked out."

"The main thing, Zippy, is that you go forward."

"Why do you keep calling me Zippy?"

"Isn't that your name?"

"It's Zoe."

"Ohhh. Much better. I thought your mother had one hen loose in the barn there for a minute. How is she, anyway? Tell me. I want a full report. Did she ever sell the Bryman house?"

I was still adjusting to the news that no one knew anything about Matthias. Was I meant to live out the rest of my life without ever knowing what became of him? I closed my eyes, fighting back a wave of depression.

"Maybe now's not a good time. You're still recuperating. What was I thinking? Besides, Abria's fine. We can catch up later."

"No. I'm good, really." I opened my eyes. "Just disappointed."

She cocked her head. "Haven't you learned anything from all of this?"

"What do you mean?"

"You've had experiences that not too many mortals get to have and you're complaining? You must take after Joe, because your mother's side of the family was never so short sighted."

"Dad's not short sighted at all."

"All right, forgive me. I didn't know your father very well. I think your parents had been married one year when I passed."

"Dad's perfect," I said.

She smiled. "Is he? Well, sounds like I missed something wonderful. Tell me about him. Oh, I've missed your mother so much. She deserved the best, I always told her so, too."

"She talks about you all the time. And she keeps that picture of you and Uncle Jerry right at the kitchen sink."

She clasped her hands at her breasts. "How precious. I'll have to tell Jerry, he'll be tickled pink. Debbie was the happiest little girl. A delight to be around. Always had a smile on her face, and a smile that could melt an iceberg."

"She did?" I'd seen Mom burdened for so long, I'd almost buried the image of her happy. But she had been happy when Luke and I were kids.

"She's not happy?"

"You've been Abria's guardian. Haven't you seen her?"

"When I'm here for Abria, everything else is tuned out."

"Is that the way it is with all guardians?" Maybe Matthias was in trouble. He most definitely had not tuned me out when he'd been here for Abria. "Is that the way it's supposed to be?"

"I don't know of any other guardians who intermingle like your Matthias does."

I swallowed a knot.

"Don't go worrying about this. There's nothing you can do, anyway. It is what it is, now that it is." Her face tweaked a second, then she clasped her hands and let out a laugh. "Back to your mother. What's happened to you guys? Are you all wimping out?"

My mouth opened but nothing came.

"You need to toughen up."

"You think it's easy to have Abria around?"

"It's better than the alternative, isn't it?"

I was arguing with an angel. This didn't make sense. "Of course it's better."

"Besides, she's precious. Look at her."

My body moaned when I leaned a few inches so I could see Abria: lying asleep on the floor, the spinning top in her hands. "Well of course, she's asleep," I muttered. "You guys have a way of doing that to her."

Aunt Janis's brow arched over a teasing smile. "I'll admit, she becomes… very *relaxed* when I'm here."

"I'll say," I snorted. "Could you spread a little of that sleeping dust around to the rest of us? Or maybe leave a bit of it in a jar somewhere for emergencies?"

She laughed, a sing-song tone that bordered sounding like an ecstatic bird. "You have your mother's sense of humor. Wonderful. I was hoping she'd pass that down."

Suddenly the door opened. Mom stood, staring at me. "Zoe?"

I jerked around, then winced from the pain the fast movement caused. Mom crossed to the bed. "Are you all right? You need to take it easy."

My muscles ached like I'd just fallen down a flight of stairs. I nodded. "Yeah. Fine."

"Who are you talking to?"

I shot a glance at Aunt Janis who stood eyeing Mom from head to toe, the smile on her lips gigantic. "Um. Abria."

Mom peered over the bed. "Abria's asleep."

"She wasn't a few minutes ago." I hated lying. I struggled to my feet. Mom reached out her arm for support. "Thanks. I don't think I can get her into bed."

"I wouldn't expect you to. You certainly have a way with her. Look, she's zonked."

"Ah, Deborah darling. It's so good to see you." Aunt Janis gleamed. "That's all right, you let her think you have the magic touch, Zoe."

29

"Thanks, I will." I froze.

"You will what?" Mom asked. "Can you make it downstairs?"

"Yeah, of course." I crossed to the open door. The scent of Chinese food taunted my empty stomach. Aunt Janis stayed in the room, intently watching Mom, now pulling back the covers on Abria's bed.

"Deborah looks like she's lost weight. Tell her to eat more. Does she ever make my Sunset Rolls?"

I shook my head, making sure to stop when Mom moved to the side of the bed and picked Abria up in her arms.

"She used to love those rolls," Aunt Janis continued, "ate a whole batch by herself once when she stayed with me and Jerry. Made herself sick, funny little thing."

I put my finger to my lips to indicate that she needed to stop talking before I blew it and accidentally answered her.

Aunt Janis waved a hand, dismissing me. "You tell her to take better care of herself. Her family needs her." She crossed to Mom and shadowed her, close enough I held my breath, sure Mom would sense Aunt Janis's presence. But Mom merely continued tucking Abria in bed, lovingly stroking her hair, staring at my sister's peaceful face.

"I love her so much," Mom murmured.

"I know you do."

Mom lifted her gaze to mine. "How is my other sweet girl feeling?" She crossed to me, and my heart soared. Time might make children into adults, but there was nothing time could do about changing a child's love for mother. Right then, I wanted to be tucked into bed, just like Abria. Reassured that everything would work out with the ease of a simple but worn out phrase.

"Tired," I sighed.

Mom threaded her arm through mine and we walked out the door. I snuck a look over my shoulder at Aunt Janis who stood by Abria's bedside, watching us, her hands clasped at her bosom. Her smile lit the room.

FOUR

I lay in bed unable to sleep, even though Mom had tucked me in and I'd enjoyed the step back to childhood with the gesture. Still, home was where I had most often seen Matthias and knowing I might not see him again was a sad thought that stayed in the forefront of my mind regardless of sleeping pills and familial comfort.

Every sound I heard left me jerking to see if he was there, watching me. As the long night drew out, I was forced to accept the very real fact that he was no longer my guardian and that I wouldn't see him again, or else why wasn't he with me now? Sure, I was home and safe. But, I could suddenly have a heart attack, right? A blood clot or something.

Anything?

I laid in bed the next morning wasted, listening to the familiar sounds of Dad's shower, Mom getting Abria ready for the bus and a handful of sentences from Luke's bass voice. A morning symphony. I managed to smile.

My bedroom door opened and Dad, dressed in sleek gray pants and a white shirt, popped his head in. He was knotting his tie. "You feeling okay?"

"Pretty good, thanks."

"It's good to see you in your own bed."

"Aw, thanks."

He drew the door closed, but Abria burst past him and ran into my room. She was giggling hysterically, and had a column of Oreos in her hand.

And she was naked.

"Grab her! She got the Oreos!" Mom's voice called from the hall. Dad left his tie undone and leapt after Abria, but she wriggled free like a greased piglet. I laughed.

"Losing your touch Dad?"

"She just got out of the bath." Mom hurried in. "She must have had the Oreos stashed in her bedroom." Watching the two of them corner her was like watching an old black and white comedy movie. Finally, they caught up with her in my closet. Through dozens of thumps I heard Abria squeal. Mom hoisted her out, kissing her neck. Dad followed, his face flushed red from exertion. Behind them a trail of crushed chocolate and white cookies dirtied my bedroom floor. Dad went back to knotting his tie as he walked out the door.

"How'd you sleep, honey?" Mom stopped at the foot of my bed, wet, writhing Abria in her arms.

"Pretty good." I pulled back my covers, every aching part of me moving in slow motion, and extended my feet to the floor. "Yikes I'm sore."

"You going to be okay here by yourself today?" Mom backed out of the room, Abria wriggling and grunting in her grip.

"Sure. I'll probably sleep."

"Don't be surprised if you have visitors. I've had calls since you got home last night."

"Seriously?"

Then Mom was gone, hefting Abria like a sack of potatoes over her shoulder, out the door and down the hall.

I stood, wobbled and took a deep breath. I still couldn't immerse myself in water, so I went into my bathroom and used a washcloth, which took me about a half hour to gingerly dab the moist cloth around the bandages.

By the time I was done, everyone was gone and the house was quiet. It took me a few minutes to creep down the stairs. My stomach growled. For the first time since the accident, I was hungry.

I fixed myself a bowl of cereal, some toast and sat down at the kitchen table, out of breath, astounded at the fatigue seeping into my bones. I finished the cereal and didn't have the strength to put the bowl in the sink. I crossed to the couch and fell onto it in a breathless heap.

The phone rang. I looked at it… *miles* away on the kitchen counter.

Where is my cell phone? I wished I'd asked Mom. Weird how I hadn't thought of it until now, its importance a zero on my list of priorities.

Matthias was number one.

The ringing finally stopped and I closed my eyes, imagining Matthias in the kitchen, his ethereal lightness filling the room with comfort and love. Deep down, I ached. Longed. Needed. Wanted.

Missed.

I hadn't missed anyone this intensely since I was little and Mom and Dad had gone on a trip, leaving Luke and me behind. It was the first time I'd missed anyone since then, and the severing had cut straight through my heart.

I must have dozed, because I heard the doorbell and opened my eyes. I rose and took the long trek to the front door, peering out the sidelights to see who it was. Britt. I opened the door. Her smile bloomed, then faltered as she got a longer look at me. She held out her arms. "Honey?"

We hugged.

"Wow, you look…"

"I know, right?"

I moved back so she could come in and she did, her eyes never leaving my face as I shut the door.

"Do I look that terrible?" I hadn't even thought about checking my appearance before coming downstairs. I didn't care.

"Not terrible, just worn out. But still. It's so good to see you." She wrapped gently around me again, her berry splash scent filling my nose. "I didn't know what to think, Zoe. Everyone was so scared for you. Your mom." She eased back, kept her hands on my shoulders. "She was a wreck."

I nodded. "Yeah, I know." Feeling weakness pull me into the floor, I started for the family room couch. Britt followed me.

"So, how are you?" she asked.

Britt and I plopped onto the couch.

"Sore. Tired."

"You've lost weight."

"Yeah? Well, that's always a good thing, right?"

"Like you needed to, Zoe." Britt tried a laugh, but it came out fake. "You're so pale."

"I haven't seen much sun the last three weeks, Britt."

"Yeah. So…" Britt, never at a loss for words, seemed to search for what to say. "At least the guy is in jail. What a loser."

"Yeah."

"Are you mad at him?"

"I survived, right?" And because of him, I'd had the most wonderful moments of my existence. With Matthias. How could I be angry? Except that, because of him, I no longer knew where Matthias was, either. Matthias would still be in my life if the accident had never happened.

"What is it?" Britt inquired.

"Nothing. What's been going on? I feel so out of it. Are you and Weston still it?"

She curled her legs underneath herself and stared off for a moment. "Weston…"

A surge of panic wracked me. "What?" Had he hurt her? Matthias had assured me that neither Weston nor Brady would repeat their attempted assault after his intervention, putting my concerns to rest.

She picked at a loose string on the sofa fabric. "He's not the same."

"You mean he's scarred? Last you told me, he looked pretty bad."

"Not that. Those zitty things finally went away. But it took weeks. And he's still got some red spots. But most are faded now."

"That should make him happy."

"That's just it. He's totally changed."

"What do you mean?"

"He's different. Reclusive. And he won't talk to me."

"Why not?"

Her shoulders lifted. "I don't know."

"What does Brady say about all of this?"

"He doesn't say much. Neither one of them talk about what happened. I guess it's pretty humiliating, everybody finding out about their boils and stuff."

"So, you went ahead with your plan and spread the word? Did you get over to Weston's and take his picture? That might explain why he doesn't want to talk to you."

"I didn't do that," she snapped. "Do you really think I'd do that?"

"You said that's what you were going to do. You were pretty mad at him the last time I saw you."

"Yeah, well, I wouldn't do that, no matter how mad I was. I love him."

She swung hot and cold like a faucet. "Okay. So, how did everybody actually find out what happened?" A sliver of fear dug into me. Did anyone tie me to the party and Brady and Weston's weird outbreak?

"Nobody knows anything except that Brady and Weston both came down with boils at the same time."

"So, Weston never took out revenge, like he said he was going to?"

She shook her head, looking sad. "That's what I don't understand. He could have, I deserved it. He's too sweet. I guess he just couldn't bring himself to do it. I hate that he won't talk to me anymore. It doesn't make sense."

Weston sweet? I shuddered, thinking about his and Brady's plot to rape me. If Matthias hadn't stepped in and saved me…I shuddered again.

"You cold?" Britt asked.

"No." Disgusted, was more like it. Both boys had gotten what they deserved when they'd come down with the most heinously raw case of acne I'd ever seen. I still wasn't sure that was courtesy of Matthias, but when Matthias had soberly told me he'd taken care of them, I got the feeling the pustules were his creation.

Talking about Weston and Brady drained me. I leaned against the back of the couch, wrapping my arms around one of the decorative throw pillows and holding it against my chest. I closed my eyes, tears welling up behind them. *Matthias, I miss you.*

"So, what should I do?" Britt asked.

Keeping my eyes closed, I took a deep breath. "He's not worth it, Britt. He's scum. A perv. A loser. Find someone else." I looked at her.

Her mouth hung open and her eyes fired. "Easy for you to say. You've never had anyone like him, Zoe."

She was so out of it, I didn't bother defending my explanation. Britt wouldn't know real love if it wrapped its arms around her. "Fine. Then pester him until he gives in."

"Why are you being such a beotch about this?"

"Gee, I don't know," I snapped. "Maybe because I'm still recuperating from being hit by an oncoming car at fifty miles an hour and spending three weeks in the hospital."

The air between us sizzled. Britt tensed, glared, then blew out a breath. "Yeah. That's probably it."

I could have rolled my eyes, but didn't. I was too tired. "I'm really wasted."

"Oh, yeah. You want me to put on something? We could see if there are any *Lifetime* movies on, do a girls day, call for a pizza."

Did she see that I looked like recovering road kill? "What about school?"

"Nah. I don't have to go. Besides, I'll just see Weston and that will be unbearable." She noticed that I squeezed at throw pillow to my chest and plucked one for herself, holding it tight. "I love him so much, Zoe. These last few weeks have been freaking torture!"

So this was how it was going to be: me enduring her and her enduring Weston. "I know."

"I have to get through to him."

"Yeah."

"I have to make him see that I'm still the one for him."

"The one for what? Britt, you haven't even graduated from high school."

"But we will in a few months. He's the one, Zoe. I know it. I've never felt this way about anyone else before. Never. This has to be it." Her eyes locked on mine. "I can't expect you to understand what I feel. It's love, Zoe. *Love.*"

The word speared my heart. My arms tightened around the pillow against my chest. I was a hypocrite. I knew what love was, I loved Matthias. Still, Britt and Weston and Matthias and I... the comparison was like comparing sand to rock. One was solid, something you could hold on to, build upon, something that would last forever. The other blew with the whim of a breeze and washed away. Still, if I had a chance to see Matthias again, I knew what I would do. "Then you have to go after him."

FIVE

Britt stayed and we watched Danielle Steele's *Jewels,* an old mini series we remained glued to for its entire six hours. Bad choice for Britt, because she bawled most of the show. I dozed on and off, awakened by her occasional sobs. Even when my parents came home, made dinner, and we ate, Britt didn't leave her spot on the couch, the used, discarded tissues piling up around her like a shredded wedding dress.

Luke cruised by on his way to the kitchen for a helping of dinner and shot Britt a tweaked glance. Dad tiptoed past. Mom kept offering to bring her something to eat, but Britt declined, her weepy gaze never leaving the screen.

Finally, the show was over and she hugged me at the door. "Thanks for letting me stay. I needed that."

I was so exhausted, I could barely keep my eyes open. "No problem."

"Will you be at school tomorrow?"

She really was blind. "Not for a few days, probably."

"Okay, well, call me. K?"

I nodded. She waved and walked to her car just as another car—one I recognized but couldn't place—pulled up onto the street. Chase got out of the beige Ford Taurus. My eyes opened wide. *Crap.* I shut the door.

I dashed—as fast as an injured person could—to the closest mirror in the half-bath, to see myself. I was so pale, I looked like a vampire with blue under-eye circles and hollowed cheeks. I needed a tanning booth. And a change of clothes.

"Mom, somebody's at the door for me. I need to change."

"Okay, I'll have them wait in the living room." Mom's voice came from the kitchen.

I dragged myself upstairs. "Thanks," I panted out at the top. *Why am I killing myself? It's just Chase.* I turned around and went back downstairs, meeting Mom at the door. She eyed me.

"You sure you don't want me to tell him you're not taking visitors?"

"Mom, that makes me sound like a diva."

"It makes you sound like a girl recuperating, Zoe. I can't believe Brittany stayed as long as she did, quite frankly."

"Yeah, well, I can."

Mom touched my cheek and smiled. When the knock came at the door, she paused. "You sure?"

I nodded. Besides, it would be good to see Chase. He, of all people, could care less what I looked like.

Mom opened the door. Chase's brown eyes latched on mine and grew to the size of quarters behind his gold-rimmed glasses. He wore khakis, a pink pin-striped oxford and penny loafers. "Zoe. Wow. You're back."

"Hey."

His face turned a soft shade of blush, like the stripes in his shirt. He stuck his hand out to Mom. "Chase."

"Zoe's Mom." They shook.

"Nice to meet you, Zoe's mom."

Mom moved back so Chase could enter. After he did, she shut the door and headed to the kitchen where I heard the drone of the TV mix with Abria's monotone ramblings. I gestured toward the living room and Chase and I went into the clean, orderly place Mom had done in antiques, soothing summer pastels and scenic paintings.

"You should sit down," Chase insisted.

I collapsed onto the couch. "Yeah, I'm pretty wasted."

"Maybe now isn't a good time for me to be here."

"No, no, sit." I patted the couch. Chase slowly sat. His eyes never left me.

I squirmed under his intense gaze as it slid around my slippers, up the legs of my flannel pjs, to my chest—had he heard about my breast and was checking it out for himself—with a fast jump to my face.

"So, how are you?" he asked. He sat like a ruler propped on the couch. I smiled, and it felt good to squelch the chuckle in my throat.

"I'm doing better," I said, putting him at ease.

"I've been wanting to talk to you. I can't believe what happened. I mean, it was so unreal. One second you were with me at Starbucks and the next... I was really... it was... it was bad."

I hadn't thought about what kind of an impact the evening had had on him. He paled just recalling the events of the night. I reached out and patted his knee, drawing his gaze to my hand.

"It's okay."

His gaze flicked from my hand, to my eyes. He swallowed. "I'm glad you're—okay."

Withdrawing my hand, I sat back, sighed. "It's been weird."

Chase glanced around before leaning close. "What happened? Matthias was with you."

"He didn't know there was going to be an accident."

"He didn't?"

I shook my head. "He only knew that I'd need him. Then it happened."

Chase's eyes widened. "Sounds like he had a premonition to me."

"My understanding is that he knows something might happen, but details aren't any clearer to him than to anyone else."

"That can't be right, Zoe. How could guardians be there in an instant and step in like they do?"

"Because all they have to do is think and be somewhere, remember?"

"Well, the point is, he intervened. He saved your life."

But, I'd died. That left me wondering what had happened, exactly. "Yeah."

"So, is this hard to talk about?"

"Not at all." I felt peppier having Chase there to talk to, in fact. "I like talking to you about it."

His cheeks turned cherry red. He dipped his eyes before looking at me again. "That's cool." His hands fidgeted. "Everyone in newspaper class asked me about you. I guess they thought I'd know."

"And?"

He shrugged. "That doesn't bug you?"

"Of course not. Why should it?" Then I realized what he was saying. People in newspaper thought we were an item. His cheeks kept turning pink, like a Vegas strip sign. The bashful look was cute. I didn't have the heart to remind him my heart belonged to Matthias. But then, he'd been the one to tell me I was in love with Matthias. Somehow quiet, introspective, intelligent Chase had seen the truth. More shocking than seeing, he'd made me face up to my feelings.

He stared at me for a long moment. For some reason, the dark, unreadable quality in his gaze unnerved me. Not in a bad way. I just wasn't sure what he was thinking.

"You look good." His voice was hoarse.

"I do?" I laughed. "For a girl who was hit by a truck you mean?"

He shook his head. "You look pretty. Even with bruises."

A taut silence sparked between us. "Well, thanks, I guess." At some point I wanted to tell him all that had happened, but I wasn't sure I had the energy for the questions I knew the tale would bring.

"Weston and Brady came back to school," he said.

"That's what I heard."

"From Brittany? Is she still dating him?"

"Are you after gossip or is this off the record?"

The right side of his lip lifted. "Off the record."

"They're not dating anymore. Not that anyone cares. Nobody should care, I mean. It's so stupid to follow who's dating who in high school."

"For you maybe," Chase said. "But there are a lot of guys who want to

41

know if Brittany is available."

I half-rolled my eyes. "Of course."

"Not to mention the girls who are after Weston. But, he's different. I don't know, maybe it was the whole plague-like thing that hit him and Brady, but the guy isn't the same anymore."

"That's what Britt said. Like how is he different?"

"You know how he walks down the halls surrounded by tons of people? Not any more. He sticks to himself. I haven't seen him this way since the football team lost by thirteen points to Lone Peak last season. And even then, he threw a killer pass, the interception wasn't his fault."

"You have a good memory."

Chase nodded and slid his glasses up his nose. "And I never see him stick around school for lunch. Only losers do that. But, lately I've seen him wandering the halls. Alone."

"Man," I let out a breath. "That's weird."

"And Brady's always been kind of... a bully. Now, he's really being obnoxious."

"What do you mean?"

"He's in my Calc class, and the guy has just become one mean sucker."

"That doesn't surprise me." I'd seen that streak firsthand. Both boys were losers as far as I was concerned.

"It's in his eyes. Something bad. Weston did stop me one day and ask if I knew anything about you." He shrugged, blushed. "Maybe he thinks you and I are, you know."

"So what did you tell him?"

"Just what I knew at the time—that you were still in the hospital in intensive care. I still can't believe all of this happened. You almost died, Zoe."

I took a deep breath. Paused. "I *did* die, Chase."

His mouth fell open. "I knew it! I knew it!" He leaned close. "I had a feeling that happened. No one would say anything, but when I went by the hospital to see you and saw that you were in the ICU, I had a feeling it was bad. Do you remember anything?"

I closed my eyes. Could I get through telling him without crying? Time wasn't easing pain or buffering the longing I still had for Matthias as much as I needed it to.

"Yes, I remember." I could barely hear my own voice, so soft and distant sounding. I kept my gaze on my twisting fingers, held in my lap, as I shared with Chase everything from the crash to the moment I woke up in the hospital.

He blinked, his brown eyes wide behind his glasses. When I was finished, a heavy silence lay between us. "Wow. Zoe, that's intense."

I nodded, holding my quaking emotions in check. "Yeah."

"And you haven't seen Matthias since?"

"No. I've wondered why. Did I do something wrong? Did *he* do something wrong? It felt so right—both of us together—I didn't have any dark, bad feelings at all when it was happening."

"One minute he's your guardian, then next, you're back here and he's nowhere in sight."

A pit opened in my stomach. "Yeah."

"Who can know the answer to something like that? Other guardians, maybe. But, how would you get the chance to ask them about it?"

"I did see my aunt yesterday."

"What?! Wow. Zoe, you're scoring more hits than Babe Ruth at a playoff game. What happened? Can you tell me?"

I glanced around, making sure we were still alone. We were, so I continued. "I went upstairs to check on Abria. She'd been quiet for a while and I thought—maybe Matthias would show up—but my aunt was there instead." When I explained to Chase that Aunt Janis had no idea where Matthias was, only that he was gone for a while, a look of puzzlement fixed on his face. He blew out a breath.

"You can see why I'm a little confused," I said.

"I can, but Zoe, your aunt… you're still seeing spirits. You're incredibly lucky. Wow. This just… this is a mind blower to beat all mind blowers." He stood, paced. "Think of what you've seen, what you've done. You've gone places no one else has ever gone, Zoe. Well, they've gone, but few have come back to tell about it. It's amazing."

"I'm sure more people than me have gone to Paradise and lived, Chase." The last thing I wanted to do was think I was better than somebody else for the experience. "But that kind of experience is pretty personal. How many people go out and broadcast it? Not many, I would think."

"I've read just about everything out there about life after death, but I've never heard anyone go as far as you've gone."

"Like I said, there have to be others. They just don't talk about it." A thread of panic dangled inside of me. "You aren't going to tell anyone about this, either. Promise?"

His brown eyes locked on mine. "You're going to keep it to yourself?"

With effort, I struggled to my feet so I could make my point clear. "This is my experience, Chase, not yours. Understand? And, no, I'm not going to tell anyone. Not even my parents know what happened. You're the only one."

"I am?" His eyes widened. "Wow."

"So I need to trust you on this. Promise?"

"Yeah, sure. Promise. I'm honored you'd tell me."

"Who else would understand?" Weary, I lowered back to the couch. Chase sat beside me.

"You okay?"

"Tired."

"Maybe I should go now."

"Sorry, I don't mean to be a deadhead."

"You should go to bed. Can I tell everyone who asks me that you're okay?"

I nodded, smiled. "Yeah, that'd be fine. Thanks for asking."

"Want me to help you up the stairs?"

"Um. Thanks, but I can make it myself." I rose unsteadily to my feet and Chase followed suit, hands itchy at his sides.

"You sure? It wouldn't be a problem." His eyes shot out the living room door and in the direction of the front stairs. "I carried my mom around the house when she broke her ankle."

I laughed. "You want to carry me?" He looked wounded that I'd laughed and I quickly wiped the smile off my face. "That sounds really sweet, Chase. Maybe next time. But, with my parents here and all, they might wonder what we're doing."

"Oh. Oh, right. Yeah."

We walked to the front door and I opened it. He paused under the threshold and looked me over. "Can I hug you?"

"Uh. Sure."

Tentatively, Chase wrapped around me as if embracing a glass figurine. He felt amazingly strong for an office-type. And he smelled like Zest. His head dipped close to the curve of my neck for a second, and the ticklish sensation sent warmth throughout my body.

Then he drew back, his lips in an awkward grin. His cheeks glowed pink. "Thanks, Zoe."

Thanks? I playfully tapped his arm. "No problem. Thanks for coming by."

He went out the door. I watched him stride down the walkway, posture erect. He turned, waving at me once, twice. Then he tripped, corrected himself and didn't turn around again.

SIX

I slept a lot those first few days at home. Like a traveler back from a long journey, seduced by the feel of my mattress under flannel sheets, the scent and scrunch of my soft pillow beneath my head. And, as each day passed, waking got easier. Hours dragged, even with net surfing, reading and the occasional Lifetime mini series re-run Britt ditched school to join me for.

Luke brought home some of my assignments and notes from my teachers, most of whom were still of the 'take it easy' mindset. Evenings, Mom and Dad tried to be with me as much as possible after sharing Abria duties. Even Luke offered to tuck Abria in bed for Mom two nights in a row.

Days recycled.

But always, my first thought upon rising was Matthias, as was the last thought I held onto before falling asleep each night.

After another week of convalescing, I was ready to go back to school. A combination of added strength, boredom and curiosity fueled my decision. As I dressed for the return day, I stood looking in the mirror and realized I'd changed. Not physically, though I had lost a few pounds that still hadn't come back and my skin was so pale, the blue veins beneath looked like fine roadmaps. Even in recoup-mode, I looked light. Happy. My soul had traveled a journey that now shone in my countenance.

I hadn't really looked at myself for a long time and in spite of the fact that beneath my long-sleeved red tee shirt there was a scarred breast, I was more pleased with the way that I looked than I ever had been.

I wore my dark, somewhat-thinned hair down and straight. The stress had taken a toll on my locks, that was for sure. My jeans were a little baggy for my liking, but they were all I had. Because snow was forecast, I wore padded suede boots that looked like Eskimo slippers.

I found Luke in his Samurai, the engine coughing and sputtering to a start. I went around to the passenger side door, opened it and shut it with a tinny clank. "Man, I miss my car."

"Hey, this baby's not so bad." He pulled onto the street, car reeling and halting like an eighty-year-old man dying of lung cancer. "Have Mom and Dad said anything about getting you another?"

"We haven't talked about it." I hadn't even thought about it.

"You know... I know the guy who hit you." Luke held my gaze for a second.

"The guy from the log cabin, right?"

He nodded. "He's off the street. The house is closed down."

That was a good thing. "Have you stayed clean?"

Luke's gaze shifted to the road. He shrugged. "Here and there. Just because the house is down doesn't mean I can't get stuff. I've been trying to stay clean, but, I gotta admit, right after the accident, I blew about fifty bowls in three days."

"Luke, that's insane."

"Yeah, well..."

I stared out the window at the houses we passed. Luke's drug addiction hadn't beset me since the accident. Into my back and over my shoulders, pressing into my heart, the heavy concern I had carried for him before I'd died was there again. I closed my eyes, let out a silent sigh. This is life. Caring for people, loving them so much you willingly take on their pains and sorrows in hopes that by sharing the burden, theirs lighten. Before I'd met Matthias and seen his genuine love for Abria, for me and my family—not to exclude humanity in general—I would have said I could shrug off worries with a 'whatever.' But that didn't work now. 'Whatever' was a flimsy lie I could see

⇒ ✦ ⇐

47

myself through.

"Is there anything I can do to help you?" I asked.

Luke's right hand tightened on the steering wheel. I'd caught him off guard with the question; he seemed to have a hard time figuring out what to say. "I'm good."

I hoped so. "How's school, bud?"

"Doin' okay. I'm getting assignments done. Not acing anything, but, you gotta start somewhere, right?"

"Yeah. That's good you're going."

"It's hard. I see people there, you know? People I've used with. People I've bought stuff from."

"They actually attend class?" I teased. He let out a snort. "Well, I'm back now, so you can hang with me if you want."

"Maybe."

We'd never hung together at school, not since elementary days when shy little Luke followed me and my friends around, his white-blond hair framing his face like a halo over his round, blue eyes. He'd always been the fifth (and male) wheel, but nobody minded. My friends thought he was sweet, cute and cuddly, a fact he seemed to enjoy when we were younger.

I'd go out of my way to include him, and I'd make sure to be there for him, no matter what. I was sent back for a reason. Life was mine again, and I wouldn't waste a second doing something useless when I could do something to help somebody.

Luke drove into the busy parking lot and wove in and out of bodies herding through lanes, toward the buildings. Everybody we passed did double takes when they saw me.

"Sheesh. Feel like I'm with a celebrity," Luke mumbled, searching for a spot.

I'd never had the feeling he was jealous of my popularity. Was he? I cringed inwardly. Popularity was so fragile and fleeting.

He parked and we got out. Students walking nearby slowed and stared. Had they all heard about my breast and were checking my form? I carried my backpack pressed against my chest.

Luke and I merged with the other students. Heat flushed my face, feeling eyes scan me from head to toe.

"Zoe, good to have you back." I heard a male voice from my right and turned. A guy from one of my classes waved.

I nodded, smiled. "Thanks. It's good to be back." At my side, Luke seemed tense under the spotlight.

"Hey Zoe."

"Zoe, how goes it?"

"Zoe, welcome back."

I waved, smiled and greeted everyone who spoke to me, embarrassed, pleased and puzzled. So many people I didn't know knew me.

"Sheesh," Luke said and wandered the opposite direction when we got to the fork in the hall.

I dug out my cell phone and texted him. **meet 4 lunch?** I stopped, watching his blond head in the crowd. He reached into his pocket, pulled out his cell phone—read—and shoved it back.

Heavy-hearted, I continued to class. Luke wasn't off base. Everywhere I went people stared like I was a celebrity. Or a freak. I had no idea what people had heard. Mom hadn't told anyone about my breast injury, she said that was my news to share and mine alone. Had Luke? In one of his baked moments, had he let on that his sister was disfigured now?

I hadn't even told Britt.

Britt found me in history and gushed, her attention like a heavy rain storm, with pelleting water drenching me to the skin. Always with Britt, as attention was showered, she made sure she stood inside the downpour ensuring that she got drenched too. Her voice grew louder, her movements more exaggerated and her awareness became as obvious as a circus clown.

Had I ever acted like that? I was so mortified by her performance, my responses were standoffish, shocked, as if I was a child watching that clown at the circus.

Our teacher, Mr. Brinkerhoff respectfully allowed me a few minutes to acclimate, asked me how I was feeling and endured fifteen minutes of Britt's performance cutting into his class time, but he finally told Britt it was time for class to start.

Britt texted me throughout, at first whining about how boring the lecture was, but that didn't last long. Weston soon became her subject of focus.

lets find him at lunch

im gonna eat with luke

what!?!? fine, he can find Weston with us

lol doubt that

no, serious

i have 2 find him please????

And I have to make sure my little brother is okay at lunch.

later,k? i gotta catch up.

K but ill plan on it

After class, Britt went onto her next class only after I promised to meet her for lunch. Thinking about spending fifty minutes with Britt, the live firecracker, on her chase for Weston, left me exhausted. Nope. Not happening. I texted Luke:

lunch?

I waited for his response. Nothing. In the hallway, brushed by harried students on their way to class, I slowed, each muscle drained from the morning's exertion. I stood at my locker panting. Sweating. Maybe coming for a full day was a bad idea. I twirled the dial, opened the door and closed my eyes, sticking my head inside far enough that no one could see my exhausted face.

"Zoe."

I jerked around. Krissy. She had on her usual blue jumper—the kind pregnant or polygamist women wear— over a long sleeved white tee shirt. But, the smile she wore outshone the fashion faux pas. I didn't care what she wore anyway. What I cared about was that she was still here, alive and smiling after I'd seen her grandfather—her guardian—when she was intent on hurting herself for reasons I still was unclear about.

⋙ ✤ ⋘

"Hey, Krissy. How are you?"

"Good. I heard what happened. Are you okay?"

Tired, I leaned against the open door of my locker. "I'm good, thanks. Sorry I haven't been around to hang out and stuff."

She looked taken aback. "You were in a car accident. I didn't expect anything from you."

"I know. But... are things okay with you?"

She lifted a shoulder, looked around. Her eyes latched on something and I followed her gaze down the hall to the next block of lockers. Weston. He stood staring at us, his stance stony, face pale. His dark eyes wide, unreadable from that distance. The bell shrilled, startling both Krissy and me, but she didn't tear her gaze away from Weston.

Finally, she turned and faced me. "Anyway, I'm glad you're okay."

"Thanks."

Slowly, she stepped back, her eyes flicking from me to Weston as the hall emptied of bodies. Did she know about what had happened at the party? I looked from her, to Weston, who stood like a statue by his locker, gaze shooting across the expanse of hall, aimed at me.

"Can I call you?" I asked Krissy.

She stopped, blinked, as if surprised, then nodded. "Sure."

Then she went on her way, every now and then tossing glances over her shoulder at Weston, who didn't notice. He was staring at me.

A shudder wracked my body. The last time I'd seen Weston, he'd had his arms around me at his house—during the raucous party he'd hosted. He and Brady had put something in my Diet Coke because I'd sworn off drinking and they'd planned to get back at Britt by raping me. The two of them had laughed, told me I needed to loosen up, all of this while evil black spirits crawled like ravenous rats over their bodies.

Remembering the frightening sight caused my blood to ice over. I shivered. I didn't see any black spirits now, and that was a good thing. The eerily translucent creatures creeped me out.

I lifted my chin at Weston determined to send him the message that he

⇒ ✤ ⇐

51

wasn't going to get to me or Britt or any other girl as long as I was alive. Sure my cold brush off would intimidate him into cowering away, I was shocked he didn't move a muscle. *Psycho.* I turned and reached for the books I needed from my locker. My hands shook.

Get your books and get out of here.

I shut my locker and jumped. Weston. His stony face and marble posture next to me. Fear had my throat in a fist. I opened my mouth but nothing came.

His brown eyes were unreadable, his body language indecipherable. Closer to him, I saw faint red spots where pustules had been. Now, the red shadows mostly looked like a blotchy blush.

We were alone in the hall; everyone else had gone to class. I wanted to run but my legs wouldn't move.

He didn't say anything, just stared. His eyes flashed with something— fear? But why would he be afraid of me? Time ticked. My throat loosened with the passing minutes and my pounding heart slowed.

"What do you want?" I asked making sure my tone was strong. My voice broke the odd spell between us; he took a breath, blinked.

He said nothing.

Okay. I don't need to stand here and take this kind of pseudo-psycho emotional manipulation. I turned and walked away. But my back felt like a thousand hot knives were embedded in my skin.

I looked over my shoulder. Weston hadn't moved.

I couldn't stop thinking about how weird Weston had acted. No wonder people thought he was off his rocker. Maybe Matthias had crimped the social globe in his brain when he'd inflicted him with the zit disease. I smirked. *Would serve you right, perv, for what you almost did.*

Every time I pictured myself unconscious and helpless to protect myself from Weston and Brady's assault I shuddered. How close I had come.

Matthias, thank you. Where are you?

My cell phone vibrated. Covertly, I slid it out of my purse and onto my desk.

so lunch k?

I still hadn't heard from Luke. I couldn't force him to spend time with me, but I hoped he wanted to. I was throwing him a line in the stormy sea he chose to swim in.

K c u at ur car

no car – weston stays here now

Could I be her accomplice and track down Weston after his hall weirdness? What would I tell Britt? On the other hand, maybe if she saw for herself how bizarre he acted around me, she'd see him for the loser he was and move on.

My stomach was a gnawing mess by the time lunch came. I couldn't tell if I was pushing it staying at school or if my weak knees and trembling arms were a result of anticipating seeing Weston again.

Britt bubbled like shaken club soda. "It's so strange that he stays here for lunch. At first, I thought it was because he didn't want to be seen with his red zits. But he still hangs here alone. Even without the zits. Go figure."

"I don't know what to say to that." She dragged me down one hall after another, her eyes scanning every door cranny and locker cubby for him. I had a hard time believing he'd go to such lengths to hide.

"I wish he'd at least talk to me. If he did, I wouldn't be slinking around like some *Carrie*-reject on the prowl for a date. I hate that he's making me do this."

"You're choosing to do this, Britt. You don't have to and you shouldn't. He's not worth it." I stopped when we came to the large set of stairs that would take us to the second floor of school. They looked as overpowering as Chichen Itza. "I can't go up. I'm bushed."

Britt pulled me along each step. "He might be up here. We have to check and see. What should I say when I see him? Maybe he won't ignore me with you here. Maybe he'll see you and want to know how you're doing, after the accident and all. So, will you talk to him? Please?"

⤜ ✦ ⤛

53

At the landing I paused, panting. "Britt, I saw him already." I gulped in lunch-scented air sneaking out from the nearby cafeteria. Her eyes widened at the news. I nodded. "In the hall between classes."

"What happened?"

"Nothing."

"Nothing at all?"

"He came over to me, but he didn't say anything. Britt, he's a weirdo. Forget him."

Britt hooked her arm in mine and pulled me up the next flight of stairs. "You don't understand. I love him. I can't forget him. It's impossible."

"It's not impossible."

"Yes, it is."

"Slow down."

"You have something against him, that's all. What is it, anyway?"

Five steps. Three. One. At last we were upstairs. I let go of Britt and grabbed for the railing. She stepped into the hall and looked right, then left. She froze. My heart sped up, matching the pace of my frantic breathing.

"He's here," she whispered.

"Go for it," I breathed out, then turned to head back down the stairs. I really didn't want to see Weston and his cold statue attitude again.

Britt doubled after me, pulling me backward. "He's here," she hissed.

"So go talk to him," I hissed back. "I need to rest." I plunked down on the top stair and refused to budge.

"Please come with me. He thought you were nice. He'll want to say hi, I know it."

Thought I was nice? Yeah. "He saw me already, remember? He didn't say a word. It's you he hooked up with."

"You're right." She smoothed her clothing, eyes locked somewhere down the hall I didn't care to see. "We hooked up. We were freaking hot together. He should want me back. If he doesn't, I'll make him want me." Then she was gone.

What an exercise. Weary, I pulled out my cell phone hoping Luke had texted me. He hadn't. I texted him anyway:

u here at school? wanna do lunch?

A second later, my phone vibrated in my hand.

already ate thx

ok

why u need a ride somewhere?

Lol no c u after school

k

I was relieved to hear from him. I stood, started down the stairs and felt a presence behind me that froze me in my tracks. I turned. Weston. Britt. Why did he keep showing up like some Alfred Hitchcock creep? Britt stood a couple of I've-been-rejected feet behind him. Weston was inches away, staring down at me as I stood on the first stair from the second floor. Britt's face was twisted like a wrung out towel, fresh tears beading down her cheeks.

"What do you want?" I asked.

He didn't say anything. Britt moved to his side, her sniffles annoying and pathetic. Weston didn't take his gaze from mine. "I want to talk to you. Alone."

"But, Wes—"Britt plead.

"Alone." His sharp tone silenced Britt. Her whimpering ceased. She flicked her teary gaze from Weston to me, then back to Weston, before she tiptoed past me.

"You're leaving?" I asked her. What was she, his puppet?

She seemed as frightened of Weston as she was obsessed with him. She paused, waiting for any glimmer of encouragement from Weston, but nothing came. The moment was as if Weston and I were the only two people in the school.

I didn't want to talk to him. Whatever he thought he'd say to me, I didn't want to hear. Confronting my almost-attacker was not part of my healing agenda. Screw that.

Britt's footsteps finally vanished, leaving only the muffled sound of far off chatter, the occasional laugh, and slam of a locker.

I swallowed a knot. Physically, the day had taken a toll on me. I held onto the railing so my knees wouldn't shake but it didn't help.

"What do you want?" I bit out.

Weston Larson, playboy, hottie, football playing woman-eater, looked at me with abstemious brown eyes. He'd looked at me before with the kind of quick glance that decides interest: yes or no. The kind of glance the male species passes out with cavalier masculinity. Now, his countenance held none of that hyped-up testosterone macho crap.

This Weston was... different.

"I heard about the accident."

"And?"

"Are you okay?"

"I'm standing here, aren't I?"

He looked away, then locked on me again. He had a Christian Bale intensity about him. "I wanted to know if you..." He lowered his head. "Can I...I need to talk to you..."

"That's what you're doing."

He struggled, writhing as if inside of him lay a monster trying to work itself out of his skin. I was uncomfortable for him, and fearful the accident made me unable to see dark spirits anymore. Were they riding his back at this very moment?

"This is hard for me."

"You think it's easy for me?"

"I've been waiting for you," he said.

A scratch scraped my spine. I almost turned and ran down the stairs, who cared if I broke my neck. My hand tightened around the rail. "What for? To finish what you and Brady didn't get to the night of the party?"

Weston's eyes widened. His skin paled, and the shadowed red blotches bloomed like zillions of invisible stains come to life. He swallowed, shoved his hands into the depths of his front pockets. "How did you know about that?"

My blood, which had flowed in an even, easy stream since the accident, began its familiar simmering when I got frustrated or angry. I leaned close.

"Did you think I wouldn't know?"

"I—"

"Did you think you could try to rape a girl and get away with it?" His eyes grew huge, like I'd just slapped him. "You two are scum. Pervs. LOSERS." Adrenalin surged through my weak muscles. I turned and took the stairs slowly, hoping he would leave me alone and never talk to me again.

I walked to the end of the hall and Britt grabbed my sleeve and pulled me aside, her face smeared with tears. "What did he say?"

"Nothing." I continued on to class. I needed to sit, close my eyes and nap.

Britt followed me. "I heard your voices. Come on, Zoe."

"Nothing, Britt. He fumbled. Big time. Why don't you forget him?"

"Why did he want to talk to you alone?"

"Like I said," I sighed. "I don't know."

"Maybe he likes you." Britt slowed at my side. My heart pounded at the ridiculous suggestion. I kept walking. Couldn't look at Britt. Soon, she was back next to me. Silent.

"What do you say to that?" she asked, pointedly.

I glared at her. "I say that's the stupidest suggestion I've ever heard you make. Like you said, I'm too intense for him. You know what? I'm ending this conversation. I'm exhausted. Not that you'd notice. You're only interested in you and Weston." I shouldn't have said that, and hated myself the second the words left my mouth. "I'm sorry. I didn't mean—"

"Is it too much to ask for a little support? You know how I feel about him. I've been waiting to talk to him for weeks."

I sighed. "I know you love him. Sorry if it seems like his feelings have changed. Honestly? I don't know why they would. Like you said, you two had a lot going for you. Maybe he's had a change of heart since the...the...zit thing." Though I doubted Weston had been reborn, I hoped the idea would at least salve Britt's heart.

Her slow pace quickened. "Yeah. Yeah, maybe that's it. That's probably it, Zoe."

We stopped outside of journalism. She hugged me. "Are you okay? You look pale."

I'd just said I was tired. "I'll be okay."

"I shouldn't have talked your ear off. Sorry. You want to hang later tonight? I can come over."

And we'd spend the evening talking about Weston. "Not tonight. I'm going home and crashing."

"Okay. I can't wait till you're all better. I need to do some serious partying! Bye hon." With another squeeze she was gone, disappearing in the crowded hall.

The bell rang. I stole a moment to lean against the wall of lockers outside Mr. Brewer's classroom. I closed my eyes, steadied my breath. When I opened my eyes, I caught a light-haired man dressed in head to toe black standing at the end of the hall. His hands were hidden in the front pockets of his suit slacks, his gaze pinned on me.

I glanced around, thinking he must be looking at someone else, but the hall had emptied. When I faced his direction again, he was gone.

What the?

I must be seriously tired. I pressed my hands to my face, the cool flesh of my cheeks, the vision of the stranger causing me to shiver out a cold sweat. Must be a new, lost teacher.

Production stopped when I walked into journalism. Like bees to the hive, my classmates buzzed around me with questions, hugs and handshakes. Even Mr. Brewer came over to offer a greeting.

Chase hung back, his blue and white polo shirt and khakis stark in the sea of faded jeans and loose tee shirts surrounding him. He smiled, waved, and I crossed to my desk, decorated with papers and notes. I took in a deep breath of paper-scented air, mixing with the smell of different colognes and body splashes and read the 'get well soon' letters my friends had left for me over the weeks of my absence. Then I got to work.

Mr. Brewer wanted me to address driving under the influence; a victim's first hand account. He kept telling me I didn't have to write the article, if the subject matter was hard for me. But I saw writing as an opportunity to close a chapter.

I took the assignment.

"A true professional." Chase's deep voice at my ear sent an unexpected tingle down my neck. He had one hand on the back of my chair, the other poised on my desk. "Great op for you to give the spoiled, the clueless, the narcissistic population at Pleasant Grove High School a peek at a tough reality we all live with."

"I'm not sure any of the above mentioned would even care."

"That is the travesty." He leaned close. "As your editor-in-chief, I want you to know that I think you should take this op to share your gift of seeing guardians and spirits in the article."

"There is no way I'm writing about that."

"Yeah, they're not prepared for that kind of spiritual information. All they care about is what's happening this weekend."

"Do I sense a little bitterness, Chase?" I lifted a brow at him.

He shifted, stood upright. "I'm man enough to admit I've been jealous." He yanked a chair over and sat, his posture tense. "Who wouldn't spend their school years wanting to be a part of what looks like the greatest show on earth? You've got all these beautiful people doing everything and anything they want and you sit home with a chess board. It stinks. Just once, I'd like to go to one of those Weston Larson parties, to see what it's all about. Then I could write about it."

"You sure all you want to do is write about it?" I kept my brow cocked.

He flushed. "They're not all they're cracked up to be. Look what happened to me—" I stopped. No one knew about Weston and Brady and the close call I'd had with them after Weston's party, except Matthias and Luke. My parents didn't even know.

Chase's editor-antenna went up. "What? Something happened. What was it? You never did tell me the specifics."

"And I'm not going to. Do yourself a favor and drop your fascination with the party circus." I faced my computer, indicating I was ready to get to work.

"That's easy for you to say. You've been part of it for years. I've never gotten to go to the circus."

"But it's just a circus, Chase. All show and no substance."

"So? Whatever happened to going for a good time?"

"People go and get drunk," I snapped in his face. "They lose control. Do things they wouldn't normally do, things they'd never do in broad daylight. Sometimes, they don't even *remember* what they do! Some of those people then get in a car and drive. Putting people—like me, like you—at risk. In my opinion, the hard party circus should shut down. Permanently. It's not worth it."

"Great analogy." Chase nodded, enthusiastic. Had he ingested a kernel of what I'd said? "You should use that in your article. I'll let you get to work." He left.

Was he so seduced by flashing colors, pretty faces and what appeared to be a free-for-all of fun, that he couldn't see beyond the common sense-blinding tent with its colorful people coming in and out of the party?

I put my fingers on the computer keys, stared at the blank doc on the screen and my mind went dead. I closed my eyes. All I pictured was Weston in the hall, the way he'd stared at me, like I was the monster instead of him. A shiver of fear trembled down my spine.

I started typing:

`Imagine your body lying somewhere. Somewhere you didn't put yourself. Somewhere you would never want to be. But there you are. Helpless. Unable to defend yourself. Vulnerable.`

`Victim.`

I swallowed a hard knot. My hands shook.

`You take a drink from someone you think is a friend and minutes later, your body is not your own. You feel control drain away like sand falling from your fingertips. You can't hold onto it. It's` gone. And so are you.

While you're gone, you have no idea what's being done to you. No idea. Imagine the worst. Think of it. Being naked. Opened. Touched. Tasted. Beaten. Scarred. Used. Whatever your most frightening thought is, think it. Atrocities inflicted and you're there. But you're not.

It's wrong.

Abusing someone is wrong.

And abusers should be punished.

Pay the price.

Again I closed my eyes. What had Matthias seen? I'd still had my clothes on when I'd awakened in that moldy, dark motel room. My shirt had been ripped. Had that been the moment, the instant when Matthias had had enough? The point of impact? Exactly how had he stopped Brady and Weston? Had they seen him? Had Matthias made the room quake?

When I'd asked, Matthias had only said he'd taken care of it.

Matthias? Where are you?

I stared at my experience on the screen. Black and white. Admittance. Revelation.

I pressed the backspace button.

SEVEN

Maybe it was the complete exhaustion from school, Britt, Weston, or reliving the memory of Weston's party while writing it down, but when my body hit my bed later that afternoon, I didn't wake up until the next morning.

I lay in my comforting sheets and blankets, glad it was a Saturday. No school. I couldn't face the curious faces, the smiles of—pity? Curiosity? I was certain some of the less popular population of Pleasant Grove High School had passed me in the halls with a one-of-the-partiers-finally-got-what-was-coming-to-them look. As if I brought that wasp-colored truck with its drug-induced driver on myself.

I most definitely didn't want to see Weston again.

I wrapped my arms around my pillow and hugged. Five weeks and one day had passed since I'd seen Matthias. Five weeks, one day and eight hours. I closed my eyes.

The faint scent of pancakes—and the very human need to eat—had me rising. *I've got to move on. Be happy. Live.*

I smirked. The notion was pretty funny, actually. I stood looking at my reflection in the mirror and laughed. I'd gone back to Dr. Semolitis, had all of the remaining bandages removed and could shower now. Full immersion in water was underrated when it came to bathing, I decided. The purple lines in my breast still caused my stomach to crimp, so I avoided looking at them and dressed in flannel plaid pants and a soft, oversized sweatshirt. I stuck my hair up in a claw, and headed downstairs for some of Mom's wheat pancakes.

One of my favorite breakfasts.

I smiled. She was making them just for me.

*   *   *

Saturday home alone. I didn't know what to do with myself. My nap went well, reviving me a little. No dreams of Matthias. Now semi-addicted to *Lifetime's* cheesy movies, I planted myself on the couch with a bag of Doritos and settled in for another drama, this one about crazy people stuck on an island sanctuary.

I surprised Mom and made a batch of Aunt Janis's Sunset Rolls. The cinnamon and vanilla scented the house like a bakery. I couldn't wait for Mom to see them. Aunt Janis, you'd be proud, I thought, smiling at my golden-brown, white-iced effort.

Mom, Dad, Luke and Abria had been gone for a couple of hours. I used to enjoy the aloneness when everyone was gone. Even when I'd been assigned to baby-sit Abria while Mom held an open house, it was as good as being alone. I'd plunk Abria down in front of one of her favorite DVDs and do my own thing. I cringed now, thinking about how neglectful, thoughtless and selfish I'd been.

I couldn't lie to myself and say I'd spend every waking hour doing something constructive with Abria now, if given the chance. That was impossible. Being that "on" would be like performing on Broadway twenty-four-seven, the energy needed to engage her enormous.

But I could pay more attention to her. Be less impatient. Love her better.

I thought about how wonderful her life was: a safe, content existence surrounded by people who loved her and took care of her.

Perfect.

The movie was in full swing but I hadn't a clue about the storyline, distracted as I was.

Then the doorbell rang.

I hadn't heard from Britt, but she was probably still asleep at one o'clock in the afternoon. I set aside my Doritos and walked to the front door. I peered through the sidelight window.

Weston. Behind him, the sky was gray, evergreens speared into Heaven, brilliant green in contrast to the stormy skies.

My heart banged violently against my ribs. No way was I opening the door. But he saw me. No pretending I wasn't home.

Hand shaking, I reached for the knob, then fear grabbed my knees so bad that I didn't dare open the door. I moved into his view and his eyes locked on mine through the panes of glass.

His brown eyes were wide. Beneath his jeans and blue long sleeved tee-shirt, his posture anxious. I stared, not able to move.

He stuffed his hands in the front pockets of his jeans. "Zoe. Can we talk?" His voice was muffled through the glass.

"Why?"

He shifted. "Because I need to talk to you."

"We talked at school."

"I—no, we didn't. Please?"

Contrition crimped his brown eyes. He reached out and I jerked back, but he only rested his hand on the wood of the sidelight, his piercing gaze fastened on me in a desperation I was sure would lead to him break through the door if I didn't open it.

"Zoe, please let me in."

"No."

"Well, how about you come out here and we can talk then?"

"I'm recuperating, for your information."

His gaze skimmed me from head to toe in a thoughtful, painful look. Then he bowed his head a moment, the winter wind stirring the long chestnut waves against his face. He shifted feet again, then met my gaze. "I know you don't trust me. But I'm not going to do anything but talk. I promise."

Man he was good. His eyes were so big and round and his face had a little boy quality—the kind that erases suspicion with one look. If I didn't know him better, I'd think he was sincere.

"Your promises aren't worth much, Weston."

He bit his lower lip. For a minute, I thought I'd shut him up and this absurd and frightening moment would be over. He'd get the message that I was never going to talk to him again.

But you are talking to him, dork.

The pleading in his eyes mystified me. Like he really had something important to tell me. What if he could tell me something about that night, about how Matthias had stopped him and Brady from assaulting me? Maybe I'd finally understand why Matthias wasn't here anymore.

My pulse tripped. I had my cell phone on my body—like I always did. I grabbed it, held it in my hand with my finger on the preset 911 button.

I opened the door. We stood staring at each other.

A brusque wind rippled through tree branches and bushes in a harried rush, the sound covering my frantic breath. At Weston's feet, fallen pine needles and aspen leaves skittered in a frenzied dance.

"The door's for me, Dad," I called over my shoulder, even though I was home alone. "Say what you have to say and then stop harassing me." The outside air was cold, and I shivered. No way could I stand in the threshold too long, I didn't want to risk getting sick on top of everything else.

"You're cold." He was chilled, too, his hands dug deeper into the depths of his jeans, and he scrunched his broad shoulders.

I should invite him inside, but I was reticent. Alone. With Weston. Was that stupid or what? Like a cat lured across a freeway for a pretty bird.

"I'll invite you inside but Dad's upstairs. I have my phone set for nine-one-one in case you're an ass." I stood back so he could come in. He hesitated, then stepped inside and I shut the door.

"Smells good in here," he said with a look around.

"Um… yeah." I never realized how tall Weston was. Maybe because whenever I saw him, I was with Britt and we were dressed up and I had shoes on. Barefoot, I felt too small, vulnerable and frighteningly uncomfortable in his presence.

I couldn't stop shivering. *Get a hold of yourself, you can't show fear.*

"Thanks," he said, hands still in the depths of his pockets.

My fingers remained poised on the buttons of my cell phone. "Don't thank me. I'm freezing. And I need to sit. I'm going into the living room."

Weston nodded, and his dark eyes scanned the upper hall of our home, then followed me as I walked into the living room and sat on the couch. He stayed in the entry.

"Zoe, I... man, this is hard."

Silence.

Let him squirm. I hope his veins are burning with guilt. But even as these thoughts spewed, guilt overcame me. *He's trying to say something. You're safe, or Aunt Janis would be here.* But Aunt Janis wasn't my guardian—she was Abria's.

I wanted him to say what he had to say and just get out.

I crossed my arms. "What?"

A look of torment drew his features taut. He closed his eyes. A flood of pain rolled through my body. Why? What?

At last, he opened his eyes, leveling me with a firm gaze. "I'm sorry." He held my attention, waiting, searching, aching in it. "I came here because I... wanted to say that."

"Are you talking about the accident?"

He shook his head. "About the... that night. The party." He lowered his head again, toeing the floor with his foot. "It was wrong. All of it."

A knot surfaced in my throat that I couldn't swallow. No thoughts came into my head. No words came into my mouth.

"I'm sorry."

I bit my lips together. Was I supposed to forgive him? Be done with it? Obviously, he was bothered by what he'd done. But still. Attempted rape. The only thing standing between him and a jail cell was me.

"I understand that you think you're sorry," I began. "But you could go to jail for attempted rape, you know."

All color drained from his face. He nodded. "I know. And I'm willing to

> ✥ ≼

do that, if you file a report. But, Zoe, how did you know?"

My blood started to simmer. "What's this really about, Weston? Clearing your conscience or keeping your butt out of jail?"

He held up both hands. "I just said I was willing to go if you file a report, didn't I?" He stepped into the living room. "But, I... I'm sorry. Please. You have to believe me."

"I can see that you *think* you're sorry."

"I don't *think* I'm sorry, Zoe. I *am* sorry."

I rose to my feet. "Why? Because you got caught? You two plotted the whole disgusting scheme."

"No, that's not true. Brady wan—"

"Oh, of course you're going to blame Brady. What a retard! I've heard enough of your stupid apology, Weston. You invited me to the party so—"

"Please!" His agonizing plea silenced me. His face was torn up in an unbearable expression, like some unseen force had his feet, another had his arms, and yet another reached into his chest and twisted out his heart. "Let me explain myself. Please." Sweat beaded on his face. I lowered back down to the couch, spellbound.

"I was angry at Britt for sleeping with Brady. I admit that. I admit that I wanted to get back at her."

"And you told her you would," I piped.

He nodded. "But I would never have thought of anything like... like..."

"Rape?" I snapped. "Say the word, Weston. Taste it on your tongue. Say it!"

He closed his eyes, swallowed. A tear escaped his eye, trailed down his cheek. "Rape," he whispered.

Shocked, I blinked, making sure I wasn't imagining the show of emotion. My heart squeezed. I couldn't look at him; it was like watching someone being tortured.

"I would never rape anyone," he continued, his voice raw. "I have a mother. I would never do that. That was not my intention that night. Yes, I thought it would be... I don't know; cool, to get you drunk. But the idea of going to the motel was Brady's."

"But you went along?"

"Yes." He bowed his head.

"Ever heard of guilty by association? What did you think would happen? That you'd watch Brady rape me? Huh? You're sick."

His distraught eyes lifted to mine. "I was drunk, too. I wasn't thinking straight."

"But you two thought straight enough that you both carried me to the car, stuffed me into the backseat, or was it the trunk? Which was it? Or were there more boys in on it?"

His eyes flashed with something dark. "You're asking me?" His raised voice scraped the edge of curiosity. "I thought you knew what happened, Zoe? You have some sort of sixth sense that enables you to know what happened so why are you asking me? Or do you like seeing me suffer?"

I jumped to my feet. Then swerved, my head swimming. Weston leapt toward me, reaching out to steady me. Heart pounding, I batted him back. "Don't touch me!"

He swallowed and stepped away. The air crackled between us.

"*You* suffering?" I hissed.

"We didn't rape you."

"You were going to."

"But we didn't! No crime was committed, Zoe!"

"So that makes it okay?"

He paused, eyeing me. "No." The rough edges around his countenance softened. "Look." His voice was quiet, penitent. "I came here to ask you to forgive me. I don't know if that's possible. I can see that you're really upset and I don't blame you. Maybe I shouldn't have come. It was probably a bad idea."

"What else happened that night?"

"What do you mean?"

"I mean, let's hear this from the beginning."

"I really don't want to go over it again."

"I really want you to."

He stared at me long, hard, then took a deep breath. "I've done what I came to do."

"Except you haven't gotten my forgiveness."

Another silence crackled between us.

He waited, holding my gaze for a long, tense moment then turned and headed for the door. He put his hand on the knob, stared at it, then looked over. "I really am sorry." Then he opened the door.

"Wait a minute." I crossed to him. "You aren't going anywhere until I hear what happened that night." Could he tell me something about Matthias? He searched my eyes, his desperate.

"How did you know?" he whispered.

It was clear he wanted answers, just like me. I took a deep breath. Even though I hadn't been coherent during the attempted assault—he was right, no assault had actually taken place—but I couldn't get beyond the fact that the two of them would have committed a terrible, irreversible crime that night if Matthias had not stepped in.

"A friend told me," I said.

Confusion flashed in his eyes. "No one knew. Did... was it Brady?"

"Are you kidding? That slime? No, your buddy in crime is as guilty as you are."

He crammed a hand through his hair and shut the door, facing me. "He's not my buddy. We're not friends anymore."

"And this news is supposed to placate me? You really do live in another world, Weston. The Weston world of everything-revolves-around-me, I-get-everything-I-want—including absolution! Well, you're not getting it from me."

"If it makes you feel better holding onto anger, then go ahead." His jaw drew tight. "I can't expect you to forgive me, I can only ask."

"You can spend the rest of your life on your knees. I won't forgive you and I will never forget." I reached past him, elbowing him aside, and yanked the door open. "All I wanted you to do was tell me what happened that night—in your own words—and you can't bring yourself to do that? I don't know, sounds like a lame apology to me."

His dark eyes narrowed. He reached up, took the edge of the door in one of his large palms and slammed it shut. "Fine."

My body trembled, fear skittering like mice loose inside me. I lifted my chin. "Okay. So?"

"You passed out. I carried you into our guest room and put you on the bed. Brady wanted to go at you right there, but I told him forget it. From the start, I didn't like the idea. I mean... it's so... it's wrong." He paced, his hands shoved in his hair, as though his head ached. "Brady wouldn't leave it alone. He kept bugging me about it. I told him we should get back to the party, that you'd come to with a hangover and we could play with your head, you know, tell you we'd gotten on you and stuff, but we wouldn't actually do it. I was afraid to leave him in there with you, he was so... he wanted to mess you up." He stopped, dragged his fingers down his face. "Do you have a bathroom?"

His face paled. I'd seen that look, and I pointed to the bathroom door. He ran. I heard him vomiting violently and covered my mouth, my body going into spasms in response to his sounds.

Finally, he came out, the back of his hand at his lips. "Sorry."

I didn't say anything, just crossed my arms over my chest. "And?"

"And... I told him not in my house. His uncle manages this motel downtown. I refused to go. He said he'd take you there himself, but he was drunk, so—"

"You thought two drunks are better than one?" This story got more horrifying by the minute. "We could have all died in a car crash."

"Yeah, I know."

"Then what?" My nerves shivered with anticipation.

"We drove to the motel. I can't believe we drove there and made it. But we did. Brady went in the office while I stayed in the car. I carried you into the room and... put you on the bed." His body drew tight. "The minute I laid you down, Brady went for it. But he... he literally touched you once and... you're not going to believe me."

My stomach bunched. "Try me."

"He flew back. I'm not kidding. He flew in the air and hit the wall.

I've never seen anything like it. Freaked me out. Brady wet himself, he was so scared. He said you were possessed. And he ran out.

"The air in that room... it was charged with something I've never felt before. Like a lightning storm. The hair on my body stood straight up. I swear. My heart raced so fast, I thought it was going to explode. I thought I was going to die. Be struck dead or something. So, I ran."

Weston looked relieved having told me. I let out a long, slow breath. They'd felt Matthias' wrath, even if they hadn't seen him. *Thank you, Matthias.* I closed my eyes.

"Why are you smiling?" Weston's voice was curious and tentative.

My eyes flashed. I was smiling. I didn't completely dissolve it, any reaction in response to Matthias was worth holding onto and savoring. Even if it made Weston uncomfortable. Or curious. "I was thinking about someone."

"The guy who told you?"

"How—what makes you think it was a guy?"

"Because none of your close friends were at the party. Britt wasn't there."

I reached for the front door and opened it.

"I'm sorry, Zoe," he said again. "I'm sorry we left you there. That was... stupid. Irresponsible."

"It was."

"How..."

"How did I get home?" He nodded. "A friend," I said.

He studied me. "Sounds like a good friend."

"The best."

I heard commotion from outside. Mom's minivan pulled into the driveway.

A few seconds later, a car door opened, then Abria sailed past me and Weston without looking at either of us. Behind her, Luke ambled. He did a double take at Weston, then shot him a glare. As he passed, he whispered, "Loser," under his breath.

Weston's body ticked as if itchy.

Mom came next. Dad followed. Weston shot me an I-thought-your-dad-was-home look. Dad stopped on the stoop and visually assessed the sight of his recuperating daughter talking to a stranger.

"Joe Dodd." He held out a hand to Weston, who returned the greeting with a genial shake.

"Weston Larson."

"Debbie," Mom introduced herself to Weston, then lifted her brows at me as she passed us on her way inside to track down Abria.

Dad continued inside, leaving Weston and me alone.

"I'll go now," he said. He held my gaze. I gave him credit for good eye contact, especially in light of the circumstances. At least he wasn't a coward. Finally, he turned and strode down the walkway to his silver truck.

I shut the door, leaned my back against it and let out a sigh.

Mom's head peered from around the corner. "Wasn't that Britt's boyfriend?"

I nodded. And headed into the kitchen. Mom stopped at the counter, and gazed at the Sunset Rolls. "Are those Sunset Rolls?" Her face gleamed.

I lifted a shoulder and enjoyed the pride surging through me. "Yeah."

"I love those!" She embraced me. "What a great surprise! Want one?"

My appetite was gone after Weston's visit. I shook my head and sat on a barstool at the counter. "No thanks. You enjoy them."

Mom eagerly cut into the doughy rolls. "Are Britt and Weston back together?"

"No." My head was in a jumble. Weston's attempt to make amends wouldn't leave me. He'd seemed so desperate to clear himself, but did he really think words alone would do the job?

Mom pulled out a fork and cut into the rolls. "These look perfect. I can't believe you made them. They're my favorite." She took a bite. "Oh! Paradise!"

I snickered. "Um. Yeah."

"Weston's a nice looking boy." Mom chewed. "Britt's always had handsome boyfriends, hasn't she?"

"Yeah, she has."

"Well, hopefully the two of them can work things out. Britt was so upset the other night. Does he know how she feels?"

"I don't know." I drew invisible circles on the countertop. "Britt's in love with him."

"Oh, again?" Mom chuckled, her fork once again digging into the gooey roll.

"No, seriously." My sharp tone had Mom looking at me. "No joke. She's in love with him."

She stopped chewing, her gaze questioning. She swallowed. "Does she know he was here just now?" I shook my head. "Sounds like something's up."

"Yeah." Deep down inside, I worried what it might be.

EIGHT

Sunday was snowy, with watery flakes falling in slushy tears coating the ground, as if Heaven sobbed. With the start of each new day I tried to be positive, but the weepy winter weather threw a shroud over my heart. Because everyone at church had been concerned about my recovery, Dad urged me to join the congregation, so I did. I wanted to be there, anyway. Somehow, I hoped I'd be closer to Matthias. Friends were pleased to see me, and flocked around me with questions, hugs and well wishes.

With energy slowly coming back, aches nearly all gone, I opted to keep watch on Abria out in the foyer, where she had some freedom to run and climb without disrupting services.

Overall, my spirit lifted being there, even without seeing Matthias. And as our family traipsed through the messy snow to our cars, I was glad to have taken the outing.

I drove home with Luke in his Samurai. The tinny monster chewed through snow like a toy plow. Luke seemed happier since I'd been home. I hadn't seen that glazed, heavy-lidded look in his eyes for so long, I started to think maybe he'd decided to go clean for good.

Talking about his drug addiction usually soured the mood, so I didn't bring it up. I held what joy I had inside and hoped his change was permanent. But I also knew most addicts lived on a rollercoaster and dragged their loved ones along for the ride.

"Man, it's bad out here." Luke held the wheel with both hands, navigating the long road that led uphill to our house. I looked over my shoulder at Mom and Dad and Abria driving behind us in the minivan.

"Do you freak out being on this road now?" Luke asked.

"Because of the accident?"

He nodded. "Do you remember anything?" His blue eyes met mine for a minute.

"I remember it all."

"Man."

I felt moved to tell him about the experience. Maybe, in his sober state, he'd ponder what I said and, with hope, broaden his narrow view on life a bit. But there was always the chance that he'd think I'd hit my head too hard during the accident and suffered the side effects of insanity.

"Let's drive a bit."

He shot me a tweaked look. "In this weather?"

"Just a little." I pulled out my cell and texted Mom. "I'll tell them we'll be home soon."

"Oh, man, I'm starving."

"I'll treat you to a burger. Anywhere."

"Really? Cool. Okay." He pulled the car around and we headed back down the snowy road. Mom and Dad waved to us when we passed. In the backseat of the minivan, Abria stared out the window, a blank look on her face.

"I want to tell you something," I said.

Luke looked over, seeming to sense something important in the air. "What?"

"The night of the accident, something happened. I saw someone in the car with me."

His eyes grew round, like they had when he'd been little and I'd told him a story in the dark coziness of our shared bedroom, when the climax was coming and I'd amp the energy in my voice so he'd feel the excitement. "I know it sounds funky, but... I saw a being in the car right before the impact."

"Like an alien?"

I half smiled. "No. A real being. From Heaven. As real as you and me. He looked like you and me. Hair, skin, bones. Flesh and blood, Luke. He told me not to be afraid."

"He spoke to you?"

I nodded. Shocked, Luke scrubbed his chin and drove one-handed. "You sure? You told Mom and Dad you hadn't been drinking, but, Z, that sounds like a hallucination to me."

"Luke, it was real. I saw him. He sat in the passenger seat of my car."

"What the—you're sure this didn't happen after you were hit? The result of brain trauma or something?"

"Positive."

"Wow." Down below our neighborhood, closer to town, the roads were less caked with snow and slush, the increased car travel cutting pathways through the muck. Luke drove cautiously along State Street.

"I know it sounds out there, but it really happened. He talked to me."

"He knew you were going to be hit?"

"He just said not to be afraid. I looked out the window, saw that black and yellow truck, and then it happened."

"Wow. Do you think he was, like, a guardian angel or something?" For all of Luke's immersion in the world of drugs and low lifes, he was still amazingly innocent and quick to believe some things. Like a little boy, he was willing to hear me out. I loved that about him. Of course, that same willingness was probably what opened the doors which led him to the practice of using.

"He was a guardian."

"He told you that?"

I nodded, watching the slightest changes in his face for belief to shift to disbelief, but the light of pure belief remained. "That's so cool. Hey, but why did the accident happen then? If he was a guardian? Shouldn't he have stopped it or something?"

"I don't know. I'm not sure *he* knows." I swallowed a knot, not sure how much I should share. I yearned for the childhood closeness we'd once had, the innocent, streaming faith we had once exchanged. "Luke, something else happened."

He pulled the car into the parking lot of McDonalds. "What?" He stopped the car in a parking slot and the engine idled.

"The guardian... the one who was in the car with me... I'd seen him before."

Silence.

Luke stared at me, trying to decipher if I was still being honest or if I'd just dumped the biggest load of b.s. in his lap yet. "Before?"

"I saw him with Abria."

"Is this why you were talking to yourself in her bedroom that once?" I nodded. Behind his blue eyes, he was processing information. "You're not playing me, are you?"

"No."

More silence.

"I first saw him at the park a few months ago, when I lost Abria. When I found her, he was with her."

"Is this the guy in the parking lot at church? When you asked me if I knew a Matthias?"

"You remember?"

"Yeah, I remember."

"Sorry, I never knew when you were... high or not."

"I wasn't always high." He snickered. "Just most of the time."

"Past tense?"

He lifted a shoulder. "You're not messing with me, you really have seen somebody?"

"I really have. Luke, I've talked to him. It's been the most significant thing that's ever happened to me."

"You're sure you've seen someone and you're not... dreaming, or in hangover mode?"

"I'm sure. I've touched him." Luke's eyes popped. "After the accident, I died. I went to a place where he was. I know it sounds completely wild, and I don't blame you for doubting, but—"

"Do Mom and Dad know?"

"No."

"You told me, before telling them?"

"I'm not sure I'm going to tell them."

"Why did you decide to tell me?"

I took a deep breath. "I thought you'd believe."

Luke's blue eyes penetrated mine, then he looked out the front window, and time passed in measured thought. I held my breath. I'd taken a risk, telling him. He could tell Mom, Dad—any of his druggie pals, and I could have the reputation of being in the loony bin.

"I believe you."

Relief cupped my heart. I reached out and laid my hand on his shoulder. "Good. Because it's true."

"It makes sense."

"What do you mean?"

"Makes sense that people besides us exist. This universe is huge. What a waste it would be if we were the only ones in it."

"Matthias told me God doesn't waste anything."

Luke held onto the steering wheel with both hands. He stared straight ahead, but at nothing in particular, smiled and shook his head. "Wow. This blows me away."

"Pretty trippy, right?"

He laughed. "So, is this dude here?" He looked around. "Right now?"

"No. I haven't seen him since the accident."

"Why not?"

"I wish I knew. Before the accident, he was Abria's and my guardian. Since then... I don't know what happened to him."

"Maybe he's just... busy."

"No, I saw Aunt Janis. She's Abria's guardian now."

"Wait a second. Aunt Janis, Mom's aunt?"

"Yup."

"Holy. You're joking."

"Nope." I smiled. "She's really cool. You'd like her."

"This is wild!"

"Yeah." I leaned back, sighed. Snow fell heavily from the afternoon sky and Luke's Samurai now looked like the inside of a snow globe, blue covered in white. "All I know is guardians are close to the family. Matthias told me that."

Luke looked over. "That makes sense. Who else would they be? So, how does Matthias fit in? Is he some cousin or something?"

"He never said exactly. Just that he and I were..." connected. *He loves me. I love him.* My heart zinged with a warm flash. I looked out the window to hide the heat racing underneath my skin.

"You and he were what?"

I turned my face further away, but heard Luke's old seat creak as he leaned over.

"What, Z? Are you guys, like, an item?"

I laughed. "How can we be an item? He's dead. Well, not dead. But he lives there, and I live here." My heart hurt. I stared at my hands, tightly clasped in my lap, and sighed.

"Yeah, I guess you're right. But you make it sound like it's something."

Love had never felt more real. Or more impossible. "It's not."

"Man, I'm still getting used to all this. I want to see one of these guys. How do I do that?"

"It's not something you can just do. I don't know how I've seen them. I just see them."

"So, have you seen my guardian?" Luke looked around the inside of the tiny car.

My heart sunk. I wasn't sure what to tell him. What would he think of not having a guardian? Would he feel abandoned? Unloved? Insignificant? Matthias had said that guardians come to those in need singularly or severally, as required depending on whether the charge chooses angelic assistance. My question was: who wouldn't want heavenly help?

"Not all people have them, Luke. My understanding is that only people who are open to help, get it. Or, like in Abria's case, are innocent."

"That makes sense. I don't think I'd want somebody running my life."

"A guardian doesn't run your life. They're there to warn or offer comfort."

"A lot of good it did you. You almost died." He spoke matter-of-factly, without sarcasm.

"But I didn't." My voice trailed off. I stared out the window. "And having Matthias there... helped."

"Are you sorry you're alive?"

I lifted a shoulder. "My life's changed so much since Matthias came into it. He's different than anyone I've ever known. Whenever he's around, it's like I'm immersed in completeness. He's seriously the calmest, most controlled, peaceful person I know."

"Uh, yeah. He's an angel. What else would he be?"

I looked at him, amazed that he'd actually pondered these topics at some point or he wouldn't have anything to say. "So you believe in life after death."

"'Course. It'd suck not to."

I laughed. "Yeah."

Silence.

He grinned. "Think I'm ready for that burger now."

It was too cold to eat in the car, so we parked in the half-full lot of McDonalds and trudged through layered curtains of falling snow, inside. Luke held the door open for me. He looked older, more mature in his grey slacks, blue shirt and tie. Not at all the wandering soul he usually appeared.

"You look nice, by the way." I passed him with a teasing smile. His cheeks rounded into sun-kissed apples.

We walked through the lobby and were assaulted with the greasy scent of sizzling fries and grilled meat. We joined the small crowd standing in line at the counter. "What do you want?" I asked.

"Two cheeseburger meal. You're gonna eat, right?"

The familiar scent of McDonalds' food tempted my stomach into a growl, like a lion tamer teasing a beast. "Yeah, I could eat."

In front of us stood a tall jock-type I didn't take much notice of until he took his tray and turned. Brady. He froze. His eyes grew huge, his mouth opened.

My throat clutched.

Once his initial shock evaporated, his eyes slit. The tray in his hands shook for a second before going still. "I heard you were up and around."

His tone was meant to cut skin, but I ignored it. "Yup."

Brady slid a nod at Luke, who glared back. Luke's arms twitched. Then Brady's dark stare locked back on me. He scanned me from head to toe, eliciting a shudder of revulsion from my body.

I pushed past him to the counter where a server stood waiting for us to order. My insides trembled. Weston yesterday, Brady today? It stunk living in a small community.

I ordered, sensing Brady's foreboding presence behind us, but did my best to ignore him. What did he want? To gloat? His can't-touch-me attitude disgusted me. Luke kept sneering over his shoulder.

After our food was on our tray, we turned. Brady was gone, but I knew I'd see him in the eating area.

"You wanna eat in the car?" Luke whispered. "I hate that guy."

"He's not going to get to me. We'll eat here." I'd faced Weston and shown him I wasn't going to be intimidated. I could do the same with snaky Brady. In fact, my nerves drummed anticipating the chance.

We walked into the eating area. Brady sat alone at a bench. His burger was at his mouth and he lowered it just enough to show me a sleazy grin. I tilted my head and cocked an eyebrow at him. I led Luke to a table one table away and sat facing Brady. Luke sat across from me.

Brady seemed amused by our choice of seats. He flashed his Cheshire cat grin, reaching for a golden fry.

I picked up my Filet-o-Fish, bit into my sandwich and chewed, holding his cocky gaze, relishing that I'd surprised him by staying and eating in.

Brady took another fry, leaned his head back, opened his mouth and very slowly inserted the fry. Luke turned a wide-eyed glance at me.

I rolled my eyes. My stomach followed, but I held back the nauseating wave. I felt stupid, engaging in an elementary school silent battle with the peon. On the other hand, now that I'd sat down, if I was to get up and leave, Brady would think he'd intimidated me.

I concentrated on my food and Luke. Luke savored when he ate, every bite a morsel of culinary perfection whether it was fast food or cuisine. He'd savored food since the highchair. Not much of a conversationalist at meals.

My stomach remained fisted. Trying to shove food into it wasn't a good idea but there was no way I was going to let Brady think he could get the upper hand.

We sat, the three of us firing silent bullets. Fortunately, Brady was not only a perv, but a fast eater. Maybe he was a fast eater because he was a perv, I don't know. But soon he crunched his orange and yellow wrappers between his meaty palms, grinned and stood. He left his trash on the table and walked over. He towered over me, and stared into my eyes. Ten seconds. Twenty. My heart whammed against my ribs.

"Move on, dude," Luke warned.

Brady snickered and sauntered out.

Like a deflated tire, I sank against the seat, my roaring heart slowing. I reached for my drink and gulped down the Diet Coke.

"Can you believe that guy?" Luke's hand trembled as he reached for a bunch of fries. "I should have stuffed my fist in his face. I'm really pissed."

"I can see that."

He pushed fries into his mouth. "Man," he blew out. "What's his problem, anyway?"

"He's a loser and he can't live with himself."

"Kevin's way more chill than Brady."

My cell phone vibrated and I dug it out. A number I wasn't familiar with.

u r syco

Panic broke loose inside my chest. I did a search in my phone for the number.

who is this

brady

well ur a perv rapist

i didn't rape anybody and i'd never touch u

U kissed me at westons you jerk

That silenced him. What a loser. I couldn't unload the fear inside of me, though. What was the vindictive attitude I sensed from Brady? Where did he get off? My lunch gurgled in my stomach, ready to come up my throat and spew. I took a deep breath. "I need to hit the bathroom."

"I'm almost done," Luke said. But he still had another burger and half of his fries. I patted his shoulder, got up and went into the restroom, locking the steel door at my back.

NINE

In tune with the gray sky, falling slush and bone-biting temperature days came and went without significant change in the unforgiving winter. Time passing did not ease my desire to see Matthias. I still loved him. I craved knowing what had happened to him.

Not seeing Aunt Janis regularly didn't help. I guess we were getting too good at taking care of Abria ourselves, because days went by without her—at least, *I* hadn't seen her. I started wondering if I'd lost my gift.

I wouldn't put it to the test, even though I was curious. Only an ingrate wouldn't have respect for powers I didn't fully comprehend—and had absolutely no control of.

Three things bothered me: the never ending question I had about Matthias' whereabouts, Brady taunting me and Weston. I'd only know about Matthias by the grace of God, and as the weeks dragged on, my iron will didn't hold up very well, vacillating from anger to submission then back to frustration. Mortality meant that I could control what was in my life—and I had—but not what was going on in the life yet to come.

Every time I saw Brady in the hall at school, or driving—wherever—he locked on me like a bear on a rabbit. The worst part was the rumors he started about me being possessed. Britt did her best to squelch those, hammering anybody she came across spreading malicious stories. Even Chase told me he'd threatened a couple of freshmen he'd overheard gossiping. But Brady's influence wasn't something to be easily disregarded. He hadn't played first string football and friend to Weston without garnering some fame and position for himself.

Weston lurked like a mystery. Every time I turned around at school he was there, watching me with that piercing stare of mixed messages. What did he want? Britt was sure he was watching her, but I felt his gaze penetrate beneath my skin and knew where his eyes really were—on my soul. I didn't have the heart to tell Britt. Each encounter with Weston left her more and more excited that he was coming back to her.

In journalism, I struggled with writing the article. I had two days until deadline and I broke out in a sweat every time I sat facing the computer. Chase stood over my shoulder, and his presence didn't help.

"Having a hard time?" he finally asked.

"I thought this would be easy to write, but it's not."

"Ask yourself, if you opened the paper and saw the headline: Words from a victim. Or, a victim speaks out. Or, I survived. Or whatever, what would your curious mind demand?"

I glared at him. He shrugged, taking a step back. "Just suggesting. You're cutting it close to deadline, Zoe."

"I know, I know."

I put my fingers on the keyboard. I could take a vindictive stance, but how many articles like that had already been written? And I didn't have any spite for the driver. People get what's coming to them eventually.

I started typing.

Dear driver,

A few weeks ago, you hit me with your car. Do you remember? Has sitting in an austere jail cell cleared your head and enabled you to think about what happened that night? I hope it has — for your sake. And for the sake of other drivers you could endanger by being on the road, driving under the influence.

I don't know whether or not you think about me, but

I made it through. I'm sure you are relieved. Now, you won't have a manslaughter charge on your hands.

I'm not angry. I don't know if that matters to you. What I hope is that you think about what happened — even if only from a self-centered point of view - so you don't drive under the influence ever again.

That night, I saw bright lights, heard your brakes scream with mine, and felt shards slice my skin. That night, even though I saw you coming at me and knew there was going to be an accident, I wasn't afraid. I was calm, because I was clean. I was going about my life, doing what I was supposed to do. If my life had ended as a result of that accident, I wouldn't have worried or felt fear.

What did you feel?

I've come to realize that our actions bring us peace or fear. I was minding my own, law-abiding business so I felt no fear. You, on the other hand, got in your car and drove when your head wasn't screwed on right.

Maybe you didn't feel anything that night. Maybe fear came after, as sobriety sunk in and reality clamped chains around your soul. Maybe you still haven't felt fear or sorrow for your decision to drive under the influence.

I don't know and doubt I ever will.

It doesn't matter. I forgive you either way. Peace is more important to me than vengeance.

I stared at my words.

I saved the doc and sent it to Chase via email. My stomach fluttered, waiting. I peered at him out the corner of my eye. He leaned close to the screen, played with the mouse, then looked over at me. I nodded. His gaze went back to the screen and he read.

Finally, he looked over and gave me two enthusiastic thumbs up.

Relief sighed through me. I sent a copy to Mr. Brewer and pulled out my cell phone.

Britt.

lets go clubbing 2nite i need a man

When I thought about hunting in dark, music-throbbing hangouts reeking of beer and bodies, I shuddered. My mind reverted back to Weston's house; to the black spirits I'd seen crawling all over everybody like rats scavenging corpses.

lets talk later

k

"Zoe?" I jerked my gaze up and to my right. Chase stared at me from behind his glasses.

I snapped my phone shut. How long had he been standing there? Did he read my message from Britt? "Yeah?"

He shifted. Looked like crickets were in his boxers. "Uh. Would you...if you don't have plans tonight, do you want to go bowling?"

Bowling? "I'm not much of a bowler, Chase." I'd never been and didn't care to stand in some warehouse, throwing eighty-pound balls around.

"Oh. It's fun. You should try it." He licked his lips, pushed his glasses up his nose.

He looked so little boyish, I couldn't say no. Besides, Chase would be a safe social activity. No black spirits. "Sure."

Shock whitened his cheeks and his mouth fell open for a minute before he let out a big breath. "Good. Great. Okay." He backed to his desk. "I'll call you about the time and stuff."

I nodded, squelching a chuckle beneath my breath. My choice to spend the evening with Chase wouldn't go over with Britt, but I knew what she'd be doing in my absence. Stalking Weston. I wasn't going to spend the night sitting outside his house in her car, staring at his bedroom window.

After journalism, I texted Britt as I walked to my locker, telling her

I had a change of plans. Then I waited for her to wail. In the meantime, I exchanged books, then headed outside, and searched the parking lot for Luke's blue Samurai. That morning, he'd parked in his usual near-the-football-field spot, but his car was nowhere in sight now. Had he and a load of his drug buddies taken off? It wouldn't surprise me if he'd forgotten me, though I'd be disappointed. I thought we'd connected on a deeper level since the accident, and I had the fragile hope that he'd stopped using.

I texted him, asking where he was.

My phone vibrated: Britt.

i really wanna hang 2nite

chase asked me out

WTF? Who?

Chase from newspaper

Chase Dallin?

Ya

have you lost it?

he's cool

A long pause. I scanned the parking lot again. No Luke. Where was he?

i really need u 2nite pleazzzz

I hated it when Britt begged. *it's set.*

Another long pause.

can I come?

I raised my brows. Britt as a sidekick? Was she trying to make the front page of the school paper a *pity paper*? Or a *pathetic paper*? If she was trying to manipulate the school's editor-in-chief, she'd sunk to a new low.

Maybe she didn't have ulterior motives. Maybe she was just looking for a good time. But she wanted to go clubbing. Being with a desk-type like Chase and doing the wild thing at a club were on opposite ends of the party spectrum.

Still, I was sure Chase would get a buzz out of hanging with Britt. I smirked. I should ask him, before giving Britt the OK, but the scenes of Britt and Chase floating in my head were too hilarious for me to resist.

that'll prolly b ok.

cool

we'll come get you

K

I laughed. Why I was entertaining visions of Boa-Britt all over clumsy Chase, I couldn't fathom, but I got a kick out of the idea.

I let out a sigh. Where was Luke?

I texted him again.

Nothing.

I looked up, scanned the parking lot and my gaze stopped. The dude in the black suit I'd seen days earlier in the hallway was strolling my direction. He glided like a dancer, his smile glittering. His dark blonde hair shimmered. If he was a new teacher, I hadn't heard that any hotties had recently come on board Pleasant Grove High School's faculty.

I shot a glance around me, just to make sure his celebrity smile wasn't aimed at somebody else. I was alone.

"Well, hello there." His milky voice had a familiar cadence and poured into me without hesitation.

"Um, hi." Not only was his voice familiar, but his blue eyes had a magnetic quality I hadn't seen since I'd laid eyes on Matthias. Though his hair was blonde, nearing gray, he didn't look like a senior citizen, and his black suit was totally mod, tapered at his slim hips. His dove gray shirt reflected in the color of his penetrating eyes.

"Do I know you?"

"Just as beautiful as Matthias said you were."

"Matthias?" My heart fluttered. "You know him?"

He threw back his head and laughed. Yes, he knew Matthias, I recognized the way he laughed—just like Matthias. And I'd seen those blue eyes before—in Matthias' memory. My heart started to race.

"I know Matthias very well. I'm his father. Albert."

Matthias' father? Questions jumped for attention in my head. Matthias had said very little about his father. Yet here the man stood. Well, not the man, but the deceased guardian man. I grinned. "Wow. Yeah, I saw you the other day in the hall."

"Yes, that was me."

"It's so cool to finally meet you. Matthias has told me so much about you."

"Has he now?" Albert's gaze shifted from me out into nothing for a few moments. He seemed to ponder my words. Then his eyes latched on mine again. "He's a sentimental boy, isn't he?"

Was that sarcasm or tender musing in his tone? I couldn't decipher.

"Matthias was right. He couldn't find the words to describe your delicate beauty."

I warmed from head to toe. "Really?" Matthias thought I was delicate? Nice.

Albert nodded and clasped his hands behind his back. The resemblance between them was in the striking blue eye color and the sharp dramatic angles of their faces. An air of confidence bounced like invisible energy in the air around them both. *He must be my new guardian, that makes sense.*

"So Matthias sent you?"

"I'm a poor substitute. You'll have to forgive me."

He shared Matthias' humility. Cool. I searched for the feelings of comfort and serenity I had felt under Matthias' protection but couldn't find them. Of course, Albert had to touch me first. "Where is he? Can you—are you allowed to tell me where he is? Aunt Janis couldn't say much."

He tilted his head. "I don't know anymore than Aunt Janis, I'm afraid." Disappointment tried to needle my heart, but I ignored it. His father was here, and that was a gift.

"You miss him, I can see that. I'll make sure he knows."

"Thank you. So, are you my new guardian?" The dark suit was kind of cool, definitely more chic than the ethereal pale clothes Matthias wore.

He nodded, smiled, the familiarity of his face filling the empty recesses of my longing. "If that's all right with you, lovely Zoe. Will you allow me to step in?"

Something in his question sent a thread of unease through me. "Sure. Yeah, most definitely." Why I didn't feel relieved to have another guardian—Matthias' father nonetheless—puzzled me. In fact, the silence that followed crackled with edginess.

A beaten brown LeSabre pulled up the drag where students parked. I peered at the driver and let out a breath of relief. Krissy.

She smiled and stopped.

"You need a ride?" she asked through the lowering passenger-side window.

I nodded, then looked at Albert whose gray-blue eyes fastened on Krissy in an intensity that surprised me. *He probably knows her guardian, understands her back story and stuff.* The fact that I hadn't seen Krissy's guardian in a while made me feel better. The last time I'd seen him, she'd been on a mission to hurt herself. I was pleased that she seemed more content.

I'd look like a whack job talking to Albert—to air—so I tilted my head in Krissy's direction, indicating to him that I couldn't talk anymore. He jerked out a nod of acknowledgement, flashing another winning smile. "No worries, Zoe. I'll see you again."

"Okay," I said without thinking. I opened the car door, got in.

Krissy didn't seem to notice my glitch, saying goodbye to Albert. I shut the door so the warmth inside wouldn't seep out. "Thanks, Krissy. My brother's being a retard."

"Oh, Luke. That's right, he's your brother."

"You know him?"

She slowly drove out of the parking lot. "We've had classes together."

"So, are you a sophomore?"

She nodded. As she drove, she glanced over enough that I got nervous about how little she watched the road. I locked in my seatbelt, turned and looked out the window, my thumbnail between my teeth. Matthias had sent his father in his place. I should be ecstatic. For some reason, I wasn't. *How ungrateful, Zoe.* I vowed to be appreciative for any part of Matthias I could have. Albert was his father after all, as close as it came to Matthias' flesh and

⋙ ✦ ⋘

91

blood.

Outside, snow coated every rooftop, tree and pathway, but the white edges were shrinking back, melting away in endless drips.

"How are you, anyway?" Krissy asked.

"Much better these days."

"When I heard about the accident, I was so shocked. It must have… was it… scary?"

"It happened so fast. Honestly, I didn't have time to think about what was going on"

"You're lucky to be alive."

I swallowed a lump. "Yeah."

"I'm sorry," she sputtered. "I shouldn't talk about it."

I opened my eyes. "No, it's okay."

"No, I shouldn't. I'm stupid, that's all."

I looked at her. "No, you're not. Don't worry about it." I had to move on and stop thinking about him. Forget that he told me he loved me. Somehow, dismiss my own declaration of love for him from my head and from my heart. Painful as it was I had to delete him from my memory.

"What have you been up to lately?" I asked.

She looked surprised I'd asked. "Oh, not much. Studying. And… stuff." she hemmed. "So, are you friends with Weston Larson?"

I let out a snort. "No. Why?"

"Just… I don't know."

I remembered the way she stared at him in the hall at school. "Do you… like him?"

She shook her head, eyes wide. "Oh, no. No. Not at all."

"It's cool if you like someone, Krissy. Though I highly suggest you look around. There are a lot nicer guys than Weston. He's… a jerk."

"Really?" She stared straight ahead out the window.

"Take the next right," I told her, almost forgetting she had no idea where I lived. She nodded.

"He's seems kinda nice," she offered.

I tweaked my face, then saw the unfazed, love-struck look on hers. There was no way I could stand by and let prairie-girl Krissy think playboy Weston was her type. He'd crush her lollipop. "Krissy, what do you know about Weston?"

She drove with her right hand. Her left, snagged a string of hair hanging aside her face and began twisting it. Her shoulder lifted. "Not very much. I mean, I've watched him play football. I've seen him hang around your friend, Britt. But I heard they broke up."

"Yeah, they did." Not because Britt had a moment of genius, either. What was it about Weston that blinded females? I couldn't see it.

"So," Krissy proceeded daintily, like eggshells were under her feet. "They are broken up, right?"

"Yup."

"I just think he's cute. And nice."

"Yeah, Weston's hot. But trust me, you're looking at a beautifully wrapped package. Inside, the box is… empty. I can tell you're a deep girl." She looked over, her eyes wide. "You think about things. You're serious about life and—"

"But I don't want to be that anymore. I'm not having any fun. I'm not getting anywhere."

I tweaked my face again. "Krissy, you're probably going to graduate first in your class, get a scholarship and fly off to Princeton."

"Yeah, I will do all that, but I'll do it without ever having a boyfriend. It sucks! I don't want to be smart anymore. I'm sick of it."

I leaned back and let out a laugh. She stared at me, her eyes rounded. "I'm sorry." She had no idea how lucky and safe she was. "Krissy, I know the grass looks greener, but there are noxious weeds and nasty bugs and snakes on this side, just like there are on your side. It's no different. Except that you're smarter than everyone else so you have the advantage."

Her mouth opened, hung for a second. Her cheeks pinked. "That's easy for you to say. You've had boyfriends, you go to parties. When you and Brittany show up at the football games, every head in the bleachers turns.

How would you know how it feels to be ignored?"

My smile flattened. The air in the car was heavy. "I'm sorry. No one should feel ignored."

She blinked fast, a vain effort to hide tears cresting her lashes. "I'm so lonely," she sputtered.

I reached out and laid a hand on her arm. Like I'd turned on a faucet she sobbed, tears flushing down her cheeks. She pulled the car over, jerked to a stop, crossed her arms over the steering wheel and sunk her head against her forearms. Her shoulders trembled.

I patted her arm. "Krissy…"

"It's true," she blubbered. "No one knows. No one knows."

No one knows? "We've all felt this way. I promise. You know, these last few weeks, people have been spreading rumors about me being possessed and stuff. I know how it—"

"A couple of weeks?" She bolted upright, her face red. "I've lived with anonymity my whole life! A few weeks is nothing!"

"Okay, maybe you're right. My point is every person on the planet goes through this. It's what happens at our age—one of our passages as teenagers. It's not fun for any of us."

"You expect me to believe my invisibility is as hard as yours? When were you not popular? I remember you from elementary school. You were always the center of the circle."

I swallowed a knot. She'd been at my elementary school?

"In junior high school, you always had girls around you. I ate my lunch in the bathroom! Sitting on the toilet!"

I couldn't say anything to comfort her. She'd had it worse than me, that was obvious. I averted my gaze for a moment, giving her a second to control her splattered emotions.

When I met her gaze again, she hadn't moved, was still staring at me like I'd grown horns from the top of my head. "I'm your friend," I said softly.

The fury hardening her face melted into soft disbelief. She turned her gaze to her crossed forearms. "Thanks. I've never had a popular friend before."

"Popularity is a temporary high. Like getting drunk. It feels freeing while you're doing it, but the hangover leaves you sick at yourself and empty."

"I'd still like to try it." She looked over her shoulder at the road, then let out a sigh, turned on her blinker and when traffic cleared, she pulled out. "I got drunk once. I wanted to see what all the hoopla was. My mom keeps cooking alcohol in the house, and one night when she was gone I drank a bottle."

"Of cooking alcohol?"

She shuddered. "It was sick."

I laughed. "Uh, yeah."

"Do I keep going on Canyon Road?" she asked.

"Yeah. Turn right on Twelve Hundred North. Head up the hill."

She nodded. "What do you drink when you party?"

"I don't drink anymore. And I don't party either."

"You're lying." Her eyes widened, staring at me.

"I don't drink or party anymore, Krissy."

She let out a loud sigh. "Then how am I going to get into one of those parties?"

"What is it with everybody wanting to party?" Chase had just told me the same thing in class. "Like I said, there are better things to do."

"Like what? I've studied and read my brains out."

I blew out a breath. Thankfully, we were almost home. As we passed the spot where the accident happened, my heart tripped. In my head I saw Matthias in the car, just like I'd seen him that night, his body and face alight with the glowing essence of his serenity, sitting next to me, his back against the door, his blue eyes clear as diamonds and latched on mine in a comforting hold that wouldn't let me go.

Matthias…

"Do I turn?" Krissy's voice forced me to open my eyes. We were past the point of impact. I nodded. She took a left and was on our street.

She pulled into the driveway and stopped. "Thanks for the ride," I said.

"Sure. Any time."

"I might take you up on that." I opened the door, got out, then leaned into the opening. "If Luke flakes."

"Okay, Zoe."

I shut the door and watched her drive down the wet road. Luke's car wasn't anywhere, which meant I'd be home alone until Abria's bus came and dropped her off.

I unlocked the front door, went in and the door closed at my back. I pressed my spine against the hard wood and closed my eyes. I'd gone, what, ten minutes, without thinking of Matthias until that point of impact when his image had beamed into my consciousness. So alive. So real.

Where are you? I miss you.

The ache in my heart caused my knees to tremble. I turned, faced the door and tried to hide the tears sneaking from my closed eyes. No one was there to see them, but I wanted to shrink from my own inability to leave him in my past and face my future.

I longed for his serenity. Feeling forsaken, I wept openly, crumbling to my knees in sobs. How long I cried, I don't know, but the purge left me feeling some relief, even if that relief was temporary.

I wiped my eyes, looked around at the wood and iron staircase, the brass chandelier overhead, at the pastoral paintings on the walls and was grateful for home. If I couldn't be with Matthias in Heaven, home with my family was the next best place for my wounded heart to heal. Even if healing took a lifetime.

Look at you, bawling like a baby on the floor. Matthias would not dig this. Get up and get your act together.

I stood and took a deep breath.

I went into the kitchen, hucked my backpack on the counter and crossed to the refrigerator. *Eat something. Eating anesthetizes.* But nothing looked appetizing. I shut the door.

Scuffling at the front door drew my attention in the direction of the entry hall. The alarm beeped, signaling that the front door was open. Then I heard running. Abria zoomed past me. The door slammed. Heavy footsteps.

Luke appeared, teetering. His dazed eyes moved in slow motion from Abria, who was running in circles around the family room couch, to me.

"The school called. The bus broke down." His tongue sounded as thick as a snake caught in his mouth. He crossed to the loveseat and flopped.

"You picked her up and you were high?" My veins bubbled with shock. He'd been clean. Why had he relapsed? I wanted to take his scruffy mop of blond hair in my fists and shake him.

"They called me, what was I supposed to do?"

"Have them call me or Mom or Dad."

"They tried that." His bloodshot, hooded eyes avoided mine. "No one picked up the phone."

I dug my phone out of my pocket. No missed calls. I couldn't believe they'd let her go with him. Hadn't they seen that he was loaded? But then not everyone saw the signs. To a novice, Luke could simply appear tired. Still, I couldn't believe he'd driven her home. "You should have called me. I would have—"

"Have what?" he shouted. "Your car is totaled, Zoe. Remember?" He pushed off of the couch and stomped out of the room. "It's not like I wanted to drive like this. You think I'm stupid?"

"I'm sorry, you're right."

Abria laughed like a hyena. The louder arguments got, the higher the pitch of her laugh. "Stop it!" I clutched my fists. Closed my eyes. *Oh no, please don't let this happen all over again: the fighting, the anger, the ugliness.*

"Zoe."

My heart stopped. Silence.

I kept my eyes squeezed closed. If I'd imagined the beautiful voice, I wouldn't do anything to keep myself from hearing it again, even if only in my imagination.

"Zoe."

My eyes opened. I whirled around.

TEN

Matthias stood under the arch that led to the entry. His hands hung at his sides slightly extended as if he wanted to reach out to me, but was holding himself in check. His crystal blue eyes glistened under a tentative expression of joy and something I couldn't pinpoint, but stirred my heart into a frightened pound.

You're here. You're finally here. My insides filled with joy, ready to burst. Still, I didn't move. If I did, would he vanish? The idea crushed me. I wouldn't take my eyes off him ever again.

He dipped his head, stuffed his hands into his front pockets and then met my gaze. *Where have you been? I've been sick thinking about you, wondering. Please, tell me where you've been.* "Are you okay?" I asked.

He nodded. "I'm fine." His soothing voice oozed into me and I closed my eyes, savoring it.

Thank you, God.

Gratitude filled my eyes with tears, and they slipped down my cheeks. Joy surged from each cell, overflowing like a tide out of control until my limbs shook. I wanted to laugh and weep. I opened my eyes. As if an invisible force pulled me his direction, I slowly crossed the room to him.

"I thought I'd never see you again. Albert—"

"Albert?" His expression grew stony. "He was here?"

I nodded, stepping closer. "At school. He told me you sent him to—"

"I didn't send him, Zoe." Matthias drove his hands through his hair, his grave expression freezing my pulse. "What happened?"

"Is something wrong?"

"I didn't send him to you. Whatever he told you was not truth." Matthias's hands slid down his face and fell in knotted fists at his sides. "Tell me what happened."

"He... he's been hanging at school."

"Hanging?"

"I thought—he said he was sent to take your place."

Matthias' eyes closed and his head tilted back. The air around us drew crisp. "What?" I whispered.

His gaze met mine again. "My father is not a guardian, Zoe. He's..." His cheeks flushed a deep scarlet. "He's very dangerous. You must not speak to him again. Understand?"

I nodded. I didn't want to waste precious time arguing about Albert. I wanted to know where he'd been, what was going on. I wanted to touch him.

His blue eyes drew sharp. I continued toward him, but confusion jumped in time with my beating heart. I didn't stop until the toes of my shoes nearly touched his. Until I took a deep breath and his unique scent so clean and completely filling, caused me to close my eyes in bliss I dared to enjoy. I lifted my hands, every nerve in me straining to feel him again.

He stepped back.

My heart crashed to a halt in my chest. *No.*

Anguish crossed his features. He lowered his head, as if gathering the strength and courage to tell me something grave. I couldn't move, stunned that he was refusing my touch.

What did this mean? That we were back to the beginning? *What? What? Tell me!*

After a long, heavy quiet, he raised his eyes to mine. "I can't be your guardian. Not for a time, anyway."

"Why?"

"You have your life to live." His tone was gentle and penetrating, but the comforting assurance of truth he offered skipped like stones across the surface of my soul. "I can't stop that. No matter how much I love you."

His words sunk like heavy led weights down, down, down, taking my heart to the abyss of hopelessness. "You... love me..."

"Yes. And that will never change. But I broke a law when I saved you that night."

"You saved me. I thought that was what you did."

He nodded. "Yes. But I inflicted them with—"

"—You stopped them from raping me. You did what you had to do. You—"

"I broke a law. I imposed my will. And for a time, I am unable to be assigned to you. I'm sorry." His blue eyes flashed with regret and warning: I shouldn't question him further. But I was wound tight like the blades of a helicopter ready to crash. I took a step. He jerked back.

My heart squeezed. The silence between us was unbearable. My dream of seeing him and being with him again was turning into a hellish nightmare.

"Forgive me."

"Why are you asking me to forgive you?" I whispered, still unable to believe what he was telling me.

"Because I changed the course of your life by loving you."

I closed my eyes, unable to stare into the honest and pure truth of his any longer. More tears swept down my cheeks. From the family room, Abria's light mutterings reminded me that she was home. I'd totally forgotten about her.

In a feeble attempt to distract myself, I turned to see where she was. My body trembled. Breath skipped in shallow dips. Though I looked at her standing on the kitchen table, grinning, I was so aware of Matthias standing behind me, I was hardly conscious of being. Abria had a bag of unopened Fritos in her hands.

Open the bag. Go, Zoe. I strode to her, my cheeks, wet with tears, cooling against the air. I wiped at them. Then I snatched the bag from Abria's hands and ripped into it, causing chips to scatter to the tabletop. She laughed, squatted down and started pushing handfuls into her mouth.

I gripped the table to steady my shaking body. *How can you do this to me? Come here and break my heart like this?*

I shook my head, covered my mouth with the back of my hand, biting flesh until I tasted blood. *This can't be right. He's playing some mean joke. This can't be real.* Desperate thoughts reached for rationalization, but truth overpowered flimsy excuses. *Stop. Stop this. It's not his fault.*

"Zoe." His warmth pulsed into my back. He'd come closer. The nearness of his voice stole into my soul and wrapped around me in an embrace he could not give.

Hold me. I don't care if it's wrong. Please.

A sob choked my throat. I whirled around and glared at him. "Why did you come here? To torment me with something I can't have? How could you hold me in Paradise like that and then come here and tell me it's over?"

He held my gaze without a blink until my knees shook from his powerful, penetrating presence. My question was out of line. Disrespectful. But I was frustrated and angry. My soul lay at his feet.

"Forgive me."

"So..." My voice was tattered. I tried to navigate my way through rocky anger, but lost my prideful footing with his request. Tears raced behind my eyes and I blinked them back, refusing to show him how deeply hurt I was. "How long?"

"I don't know."

"How can you not know? I thought you knew everything. Shouldn't that be part of it? Knowing everything?"

"I don't know everything, I've told you that before. My station, like yours, has limits. But even this is not the end so I don't question, I obey."

I hate that word.

Long moments of aching silence passed, punctuated only by Abria's crunching somewhere behind me. Tears streamed down my cheeks in spite of my vain efforts to hold them back.

His gaze traced the tears, pain drawing his chiseled features taut. He stepped closer, then stopped himself and the spear he'd thrust in my heart with his declaration went deeper.

My heart had already forgiven him. When I closed my eyes and saw his smile and searched my memory for the moments we'd shared in Paradise, serenity enveloped me. But the moment I laid eyes on his physical body and looked into the purity of his eyes, my head couldn't forgive him for what I would now be denied.

I swallowed a rock that had lodged in my throat. "You're still Abria's guardian?" The finest thread of hope unwound inside of me. At least I could see him.

He nodded. "Yes. Though Aunt Janis was kind enough to step in for me during my absence."

Relief. I nodded. "It was cool seeing her." *But I missed you.* "I guess that's better than nothing."

He didn't say anything, just held me with his eyes.

I tore my gaze away and looked at Abria, now sitting with her legs spread on the tabletop, Fritos everywhere like yellow chunks of confetti. Like a wind-up doll she scooped handfuls of the crispy chips into her mouth, over and over.

"You're going to be sick eating all those." I crossed to her and gathered her into my arms. She moaned and reached for the table and spilled Fritos so I set her on her feet. Mostly because I needed something to do with my hands, to quell the desire I had to touch Matthias. Out the corner of my eye his soft white glowing form remained. My heart ached. *He's here. Zoe, enjoy this moment and every moment you have with him.*

Now that he wasn't my guardian, I could think what I wanted, and he couldn't hear me, right?

I can still hear your thoughts, Zoe. Once a connection like ours is made, it's always in place.

"Oh… well… that's…."

He nodded and stepped closer. "That's mercy, isn't it?" he asked.

I nodded. Whatever scrap of intimacy he could share with me, I'd take.

"That's …good. I'm glad," I murmured, unable to take my gaze from his. How long did we have? I'd spend every second looking at him, locked in a destiny of look but don't touch and forever want.

"If you would like me to have Aunt Janis come back, I —"

"No. Seeing you… with Abria… is better than not seeing you at all. Are we being punished?"

"We aren't being punished." He inched closer. "This universe runs harmoniously because there are laws. When those laws are broken, there are consequences."

My throat thickened. "I hate that law. It sucks."

He wasn't amused, didn't approve of my dissing subjects he regarded with respect, but I wasn't going to make excuses for myself. "Why didn't I just stay with you in Paradise to begin with?" I bit out.

"It wasn't your time to pass through yet."

"Did you know that? That night in the car, before the accident, did you know I was going to be in an accident?"

"I told you, I am sent as a protector and comforter. Specifics are not made known to me."

"So… in Paradise… your feelings… the things you said to me…"

My feelings haven't changed, Zoe. He reached out his hand, held it in the space between us, his eyes earnest, his body and aura suddenly swamping me with a warm, complete rush of love so encompassing, I tingled and sparked from toe to head. An involuntary breath rushed through my lungs, cleansing and pure, infusing me with him.

I looked at his extended hand and slowly reached for it, my own hand trembling with longing. *I won't touch you,* I thought, wanting to reassure him. Our fingertips hovered parallel, two fragile butterflies eager to join in oneness.

My eyes lifted to his. Undeviatingly, he looked into my heart. *Whatever life holds for you, you will have the feelings of my heart in yours.*

My vision blurred through a sudden rush of tears. I nodded. *I know. But how can I live with you out of my reach? I don't think I can do it. I don't want to.*

⇒ ✦ ⇐

103

"You can." The heat of his hand surged upward into my palm, then spread out like silky fingers of reassurance. "The heart is not limited to just one love."

"Mine is." Emotion tore my voice.

He smiled. "You feel that way now, but there will be many chaps who will come into your life and—"

"No." I snapped my hand back to my side. "Don't say that. You don't know that. You can't know. There'll never be anyone like you. How can you think I would settle for some lame substitute after knowing you?"

His grin softened. He slipped his hands into the depths of his front pockets. "I'm flattered. But you're mortal, Zoe."

"So that makes me some weak-hearted female? Is that what you're saying?"

"I'm saying you could have many years of life to live here on Earth. You don't see yourself living them alone, do you?"

"But I'd have you."

"I'm Abria's guardian. Not your deceased romantic interest, floating around in your closet."

A grin broke the taut tension in my face. He smiled, too, and a pretty shade of tulip pink colored his cheeks. "You wouldn't have to stay in my closet."

"There's my bearcat." He reached out again, and his fingers came so close to skimming my arm, I shuddered. He retracted his hand.

"How long will it take before I don't want to touch you?" I whispered.

He let out a sigh as if the question caused him pain. "As long as it will take me to stop wanting you."

That will never happen—his thought melted into mine.

"You're talking to one, right now." Luke's low voice broke the invisible, tight chords between Matthias and me. I whipped around.

He stood near the table, but he wasn't looking at Abria, who now lay prostrate in the remaining Fritos, waggling her arms and legs as if she was in the snow making a snow angel. His eyes fastened on Matthias.

I looked from Matthias to Luke to Matthias, then back to Luke again. Luke's eyes were alert and round. "I see him." His pointing finger trembled. "He's standing right there."

"I'm not sure what you're seeing," I said, not sure what to think, say or do at this point. Luke was high. How could he possibly see something divine under the influence? Didn't that defy Divinity?

Matthias remained calm, his posture erect, sure, powerful. Around us, the air charged with a strength I'd only felt from him a few times before: when he'd scared the life out of Paul Bunyan—that wasn't really his name, his name was Hank, but he looked like Paul Bunyan. In reality, he was a drug dealer and owner of the log cabin where troops of druggies, including Luke, hung out. Another time I'd felt Matthias' powerful aura had been when I'd first touched him.

"What do you see?" I asked Luke.

"It's him, isn't it? That Matthias dude you were telling me about."

Matthias nodded at me, signaling that it was okay to tell Luke.

"Yes, that's him."

Luke's eyes shot wider, then rolled back in his head. His skin paled and he crumpled to the floor in a heap. I darted over. "Luke?"

"Poor fellow." Matthias stood to my right. He'd moved across the room without a sound. I grinned up at him. His teeth gleamed.

Abria belched. Handfuls of yellow crumbs fluttered through the air, falling all over Luke's face and in my hair.

"Zoe, I have to go now." Matthias knelt down next to me. "Remember what I told you about my father. Under no uncertain terms are you to speak to him. If you see him again, get home as soon as you can and make sure Abria is with you. Understand?"

Abria? "Okay."

"Promise me."

"I promise."

Matthias glanced at Abria. "Abria is safely in your care now. And so is Luke." He nodded with a gentle smile at Luke, still unconscious on the floor at my knees.

"Please don't go."

The corners of his lips lifted. "I'd like that very much. But I have other work to do."

"Something more important than being with me twenty-four-seven?"

His soothing chuckle eased my worries. I'd see him again, that was a given. I'd have to accept the times in between, no matter how long the stretches might be. His laugh died. "Strong, sassy and utterly capable, Zoe Dodd. You're going to be just fine."

"That sounds too final. Don't say that."

"A compliment, nothing more." He stood, hands thrust into his front pockets, his gaze shifting to Luke.

I followed his gaze to my brother's peaceful, cherubic face. "What will I tell him when he wakes up? That he imagined seeing you? Results of being high or something?"

"Trust what's in your heart."

I don't want you to go. Please. My fragile human nature thought that I could keep him there with wishes, but the focused gaze he returned told me these wishes couldn't be granted.

Though our gazes locked, a bright flash of light engulfed him in one powerful burst, and then he was gone. The room fell oddly still. I stared at the spot where he'd just stood. A vast emptiness traveled through me, but I didn't have time to wallow in pity. Luke stirred.

On the table behind us, Abria lay on her stomach, swimming in crumbs like she was at the pool, flicking a yellowy mess through the air.

"Abria, stop please."

She laughed, and scrambled to her feet, jumping up and down. I leapt up, retrieved her and set her down on the floor. "Go clean up." As if that would happen.

She continued creating Frito angels in the crumbs she'd flicked to the floor. I sighed. Luke let out a groan and I stood over him. His blue eyes opened with the labor of a garage door on its last ounce of life. His hands scraped his face. "Man. What happened?" He eased up to his elbows, then shook out his head. Suddenly, his heavy-lidded eyes popped wide. He jerked a look around the room. "That guy. Where is he?"

"Matthias?"

His alert eyes met mine. He stood. "I knew I wasn't hallucinating. I heard you talking to him, came down and saw him. I saw him for myself!"

I nodded, not sure if I was annoyed or happy that Luke had seen Matthias and no longer had reason to doubt. I guarded Matthias with my life, and was not about to have his existence traded around like a used joint.

"Yeah, you saw him. He'll strike you down if you tell anybody, too."

Luke's eyes grew huge and I had to pinch my lips so I wouldn't laugh.

"Holy sh—"

"Swearing's against the laws of Heaven," I quipped, enjoying momentary power. "You can't be foul around heavenly beings."

Luke looked around. "Yeah, but he's not here right now."

I gathered Abria up and surveyed the crunchy mess under our feet and across the tabletop. She let out another belch. Her breath reeked of corn chips.

"Man-oh-man. You'd better keep those Fritos down, young lady." I carried her to the kitchen sink so I could wash her hands. Luke trailed me.

"What was he doing here? The Heaven guy?"

"Protecting Abria from your baked driving." I turned on the water faucet and held her two squirming hands under the running water. She loved water, and went still instantly.

"He was in the car with me? Wonder why I didn't see him." Luke peered over my shoulder, watching. "How many times have you seen him? You two were, like, carrying on this intense convo."

My heart pounded. I didn't look him in the eye, my cheeks were hot and I was afraid they'd give my deep feelings away. "I told you, I've known him for a while." Abria's hands were greaseless now, so I set her on the floor and reached for the broom.

"You two were more than connected, Z. I saw it." He stayed at my side. "I felt it."

I stopped, looked at him. Silence. I couldn't deny what was between Matthias and me. That would be like going outside and denying the existence of the sun. Why did I feel defensive? "We're friends." I crossed to the mess on the floor and started sweeping.

"Friends?!" Luke let out a snort. "Friends hang out. Friends share their bowls."

"Your friends maybe."

"Whatever. You and this Matthias guy were practically hooking up right here in the—"

"Don't talk about him like that! Never, never talk about him like that again. He's not like you and me. He's immortal. Perfect. He's the most perfect person I've ever met. And I'm—"

Luke stood statue still, staring at me. When I didn't say the words: in love with him, I had the sharp realization that Luke easily filled in the blanks. He shifted. "Okay," his voice was quiet. "I get it."

Truth. Truth. Truth. *Trust in the truth, Zoe.* Still, truth could remain private. "Good. Then we're straight."

Luke nodded.

"Don't go blabbing about him to your reefer buddies, okay?"

"What kind of an idiot do you take me for?" he bit out. "Jeez, Zoe. Like I'd do something so stupid." He glared at me, then stormed out of the kitchen. I continued sweeping, but seconds later, I heard the front door slam and the far off rumble of his engine starting up.

I sighed, glancing for Abria. She was squatting down, licking Frito crumbs off the tile floor.

ELEVEN

Chase's Old Spice swamped me the moment I opened the front door. He looked adorably nerdy in his khakis and hunter green crew neck sweater, a hint of plaid button down shirt at his throat, his hair so neat I wanted to scruff it up a bit with my fingers. He stood on the porch, peering at me through the open door like I was Venus, come to seduce him.

"You look… great," his voice cracked.

All I had on was nice jeans and a white sweater. Blush. Mascara. No perfume.

"Thanks." I shot over my shoulder, "Mom, I'm leaving!" I heard Abria's high-pitched laugh, looked down the hall and saw her run past wearing one of Mom's cinnamon red, lacy nightgowns.

"Okay honey, have fun. Abria, come back here right this minute you're going to—"

Trip. Sure enough, Abria's tiny legs became entangled in the long, silky red fabric and down she went onto the hard wood. I gasped. It usually took a few seconds for any pain to register in Abria's head. She looked up, blinked, then stood. Mom appeared at a full run, and swooped her into her arms, then Abria let out a cry.

"Is she okay?" I asked.

Mom checked my sister's head and nodded, coming to the door with wailing, inconsolable Abria in her arms. Abria hated being held when she was in pain—a reaction none of us ever got used to—like human touch merely added to her agony. We hated that she suffered alone.

Mom eyed Chase curiously, in spite of Abria's brief fall. "Chase, right?" Mom yelled over Abria's screams.

"Yes. Hi, Mrs. Dodd." Chase extended his hand. Abria slithered free, ran out of sight, her wailing rising like a fierce wind tearing through the house.

Mom backed away. "Sorry, have to go. Nice to see you again." Mom darted off.

"Will your sister be okay?" Chase's dark brows stitched together.

"Yeah." I shut the door and we headed to his taupe non-descript, four-door sedan. If anything serious was going to happen to Abria, Matthias would have been there. I let out a silent sigh.

Chase opened the passenger door for me and I got in, the scent of his woodsy cologne filling my nostrils with the impact of a thick fog bank.

"You're dressed up for bowling," I said, once he was in and had shut the door.

"Oh. Yeah." The edges of his ears turned crimson. He started the engine.

"Hey, I hope it's okay if Britt comes along."

The car jerked to a stop in the middle of our street. His fingers tightened around the wheel and he looked over, eyes huge behind his glasses. "Brittany? Is coming with us? Tonight?" He gulped.

I rolled my lips under to avoid smiling. "Is that okay?"

"Uh. Yeah. I guess so."

"She wanted to hang out tonight, but I told her I was going with you, and, she kinda invited herself." Sweat popped like tiny clear pimples all over his skin. I started to worry he would pee his pants. "I can tell her to bail if you'd rather."

"No. No." The car started moving, so I guessed he was relaxing a bit. His Adam's apple kept rolling up his throat. "Wow. I guess I'm just a little surprised. She's never said a word to me. Ever. Are—are you sure she knows I'm coming along?"

"Chase, she's the one coming along, not you. You and I are hanging. Remember that." I patted his arm. His bicep was rock hard. He glanced at where we made contact, then returned his surprised gaze to the road.

"Are we picking her up?" he asked.

I nodded, took out my cell phone and texted her that we were on our way. Then I gave Chase directions to her house. The vibe in the car jumped and skipped like a train ready to swerve off track.

"Wow." He pushed his glasses up the bridge of his nose. "This is one house I never thought I'd find myself at." He stared with awe at Britt's red brick house. He parked on the street, centering the car where the bricked pathway began that led to the door. "Early American Colonial design. I bet the house is about three thousand, twenty-five square feet with custom moldings and hardwood throughout."

I covered a snort. "You can tell all that from just looking at the outside?"

He nodded. "I've studied architecture."

"Why am I not surprised?" I raised a brow at him. He smiled. I reached for the door handle, but Chase's hand wrapped around my left arm. I was surprised at the steel in his grip, and it was my turn to stare at where he came into contact with me.

"Can I?" he asked.

"Why not."

He was out of the car and straightening his clothes before giving me a response. With my gaze, I followed his perky stride up the brick pathway to the door. He knocked, looked back at me, then faced the door again. The porch lanterns shed a soft golden glow over him.

The door burst open in splashy Britt fashion. She'd been ready to leap out and hug me, I could tell from the effervescent smile on her face. Her smile stuttered when she saw Chase instead, but not an obvious wilt. I rolled down the window so I could hear them.

She wore black from spiked heels to black jeans and soft sweater. "Hey. Chase, right?" She shut the door and pressed her back against it, like Marilyn

Monroe coming out of her dressing room, greeting a fan.

Chase didn't move. He didn't even respond to her question. *Poor guy.*

Britt slowly leaned so she could see me, and she gave me a look, then focused on Chase again. "Thanks for letting me crash the party." She gingerly stepped around him. He followed her moves like a panting pup after a biscuit.

"Sure," he said. "But we're not going to a party. We're going bowling."

Britt waved at me. "Hey baby."

"Hey."

Chase outran her to the back door of the car, and eagerly swung it wide open for her. "Thanks," she said before dipping into the backseat.

He shut the door.

"Eager, isn't he?" she whispered, then giggled.

"Be nice," I told her.

She cocked her head. "Aren't I always?"

Chase got into the car, bringing a fresh waft of his cologne along with him. He shut the door, grinned first at me, then at Britt, then back at me. His expression was priceless. Like he'd just scored.

"Now this is what I call a date."

"You like these odds, do ya?" I teased.

Britt's brows tweaked in an obvious display of, 'as if' I hoped Chase didn't catch. He started the engine and drove with the carefully meted caution of a senior citizen. I waited for Britt to make some snide comment. Her tolerance level for anyone less than socially savvy was minus zero.

I reached over to the CD player. "Can I?"

Chase's brown eyes widened. "This is my Mom's car," he said. "I don't know what's in there. I'm just warning you. And you, Brittany." He peered at her through the rear view mirror.

"Oh, no problem," she lied. Irritation shriveled the upturned corners of her fake smile.

Barry Manilow?

Chase flicked the song off. "Mom loves the guy." He shrugged.

"Most Moms do," Britt muttered. "Don't you have your iPod Zoe?"

"Sorry. I don't."

"I was just wondering." Britt's eyes bulged at me. "Hey, Chase, would you mind taking a detour on the way to the movie?"

"We're going *bowling*." Chase swallowed. As if he had to clear his plans with Britt. My blood started to boil.

"We're not going by Weston's house, Britt," I said.

"Chase doesn't mind, do you, Chase?" Her tone was sweet, like saccharin.

"Uh." Chase looked at me. I shook my head. Then he looked in the mirror at Britt. "Sure. We're not scheduled for our lane for another fifteen minutes."

Britt flashed her teeth at me. I rolled my eyes.

Britt gave him directions to Weston's house and we wound around the streets of Pleasant Grove in silence. I couldn't believe Britt was using him. But then what had I expected? Britt's obsession with Weston was without precedence. I whipped out my cell phone and texted her.

i cant believe u r making him drive by westons

he doesn't care

Chase glanced over but didn't say anything. I put my cell phone away, because I didn't want to be rude.

"It's nice of you to go by Weston's," Britt piped from the back, her voice oozy and sweet like marshmallow crème—the voice she used to seduce unsuspecting, innocent guys like Chase. I bristled, regretting I'd allowed her to come along.

"No problem." Chase sat up straighter. "You two still together?"

"Sort of." Britt shot me a glare of warning. She said '*sort of*' for two reasons: she wanted it to be true and wanted to insulate herself from Chase thinking she was available.

"She's checking up on him," I said. "Girls do that."

"He's mine," Britt's tone had a defensive edge. "I'll kill any other girl that comes near him."

The air in the car popped. Chase looked ready to jump out of his skin.

113

A shudder rammed my spine for some reason I couldn't explain. I didn't care what Britt said. But the flash of intensity I'd seen in Weston's eyes when he'd come to my house was branded into my brain.

"You... wow." Chase's voice trembled. "You feel passionately about this."

"You don't have to do drive by his house," I told him.

"No, it's okay. I don't mind." He kept glancing back at Britt for her approval.

Chase turned onto Weston's street. Britt looked like she was ready to jump from the car and land right at his front door. Lights were on at the porch, the garage and along the front walkway. I shrunk. Stalking always presented a risk of being seen. Britt was in the backseat, behind darkened windows and I was exposed up front. With Chase. I looked like a psycho.

Chase, inexperienced at the obsessive habit of stalking, drove right to the curb and parked, bringing a laugh from Britt. I slipped further down the seat. "Perfect. Thanks, Chase."

"So this is where he lives?"

"This is heaven," Britt murmured like a love-sick weirdo.

No, this is not Heaven. Nothing remotely associated with Weston Larson could ever be considered heavenly. Not the Heaven I'd seen. A pair of bright headlights shined at our faces.

"It's Wes!" Britt bounced in the back seat. I sunk below the dash, my heart pounding.

Chase's gaze darted around. "Am I supposed to sit here? Should I drive on? What?"

"Let me see him," Britt panted.

"GO! GO!" I hissed. Chase was under Britt's invisible spell and wasn't listening to me. "You know how this looks?" I whispered to Britt.

"I don't care. I love him. He needs to know I won't leave him without a fight."

I heard the engine of the truck outside stop. The reflected beams of the truck's headlights went out, returning Chase's cab interior to near darkness.

I couldn't believe Chase sat there like a spectator at a movie. And I couldn't believe Britt finagled her way with Chase and now we all looked like psychos.

"He's coming!" Britt wiggled.

"Are you serious?" I whispered a shriek. My heart banged against my ribs. "Chase, drive!"

"I—I can't. He's... right..." Chase rolled down his window. I closed my eyes, covered my face and tried to vanish underneath the dashboard, but hiding was impossible.

"Can I help you?" Weston's coffee and cream voice flowed into the car. My pulse swirled with embarrassment. I didn't dare open my eyes. I could pretend I was sick, right? Vomiting? I felt nauseated.

"Wes." I heard Britt scramble out of the car. *How desperate can you be?*

I peered through my fingers. Weston had his hands on the edge of the open window and his stark brown gaze on me. "Zoe?"

I squirmed back into the seat and let out a sigh. My skin flushed with heat.

"Wes, can we talk?" Britt butted her body into Weston's shoulder. He ignored her.

"What are you doing here?" Weston asked the question clearly aimed at me.

Chase looked at me, then at Weston, then back at me. Britt had a look of stunned annoyance on her face. "Britt wanted to come by," I snapped.

Weston shifted. Underneath his snug, long sleeved tee shirt, the muscles in his arms roped and drew tight as he gripped Chase's door. He slid a look of condemnation at Britt who shrunk back a step. Then his dark eyes fastened on me again.

Chase cleared his throat. "We're going bowling."

"Is that right?" Weston's jaw twitched. "Sounds cool. Mind if I come along?"

My eyes gaped wider.

Britt crossed her arms over her chest. "You? Bowling?" she snickered, following his taut connection to me.

He looked at her. "Not as ridiculous as you bowling."

"Zoe's my best friend. What's your excuse?" she demanded.

Weston moved his intense gaze to me again. Why was he staring? "It's Chase, right?" He nodded at Chase.

"Yeah. Yes, it is. If it's okay with the girls, you can come. I've reserved lane fifteen at Jack and Jill's. Ever been there?"

Weston nodded. He shouldered Britt aside, opened the back door and filled the backseat, bringing with him a tense energy that splintered like a whip. My heart trembled. Not so much from fear, but from the unknown.

Britt let out a sigh and stood outside, peering in at him. "I want to know why you're going. You haven't spoken to me in weeks. Now, I show up on your doorstep with Zoe and some guy you've never met and you're all ripped to go bowling?"

"I'm not going because of you."

Britt let out a gasp. "If you think I'm going to let you go bowling with her, then you're brain damaged."

Weston reached over, grabbed the handle and brought the door closed with a slam. "Drive."

Wide-eyed, Chase looked at me. Britt stomped outside the car like a toddler throwing a tantrum. "You pig!" Her fists hit the back window. She yanked at the handle, but Weston locked the door and faced forward.

Britt came to the front window, wagging her fist at me. "Get out of the car, Zoe! He's mine!"

"I'm with Chase, you retard!"

Chase started to sweat. "What should I do?"

"Drive," Weston repeated.

"But… I can't leave her here."

"She's got a cell phone and a stable of guys, man. Drive."

"She's going to break the window," Chase whispered at me.

"She's out of control," I said. Part of me wondered if I'd be better off joining her. The other part was irritated that she'd used Chase and I, was acting like a spoiled brat, and now the tables had turned on us all.

Suddenly, the car lurched forward and we were driving. Weston ran his hands down his face.

I didn't know what to say—to either boy. How weird was this night? I faced forward, trying to deal with the fact that Britt was gone and Weston now sat in her place. My cell phone vibrated. I pulled it out. Britt.

if u go with him i'll never speak 2 u again

whatever. he barged in after u insisted we go to his house!

come back and get me!

no way u 2 will kill each other

he's dead anyway!

I heard Weston's finger tapping furiously on his cell phone. Then he snapped it closed and looked at me. "That ought to shut her up."

"You two need to fight your battles in private," I spat.

"I've tried. She doesn't take no for an answer."

Britt was overboard when it came to Weston. Still, that he sat in the car with Chase and I while she stood back at his house burned me for a reason I couldn't identify except to say I was pissed.

I flipped around in the seat and glared at him. "You're really going to go through with this?"

Weston lifted his shoulders. "Yeah."

"It's cool," Chase piped. He seemed unable to sense the jagged vibes in the air. "We don't mind, do we, Zoe?"

We? *We?* Like we're and item? *Grrrr.* "It's just that, if Britt came, we'd have enough for doubles. Right? There is such a thing as doubles in bowling, isn't there?"

"Not technically," Chase said matter-of-factly. "Though, Britt—"

"And none of us *are* couples," Weston said, his expression serious. "That's the beauty of it."

*   *   *

We bowled. Chase was enthusiastic about the sport and effervescent that he was with two of Pleasant Grove High School's elite. The genial host to both Weston and me, he showed us his favorite spots at the alley, offering us Pepsi's—on him.

Weston was surprisingly nice to Chase. But then Weston knew the game—and I don't mean bowling. Weston was adept in the art of social pins, how to set them up, how to avoid getting knocked over and, if necessary, how to strike and annihilate. Though, as the evening wore on I realized Weston was not going to annihilate mild mannered Chase. Chase bowled 220. Weston 185. The two of them at a dead heat near the end of our last game. I slid by on a 70 to which Chase simply pushed up his glasses, grinned and said, "You did great for a beginner."

Weston tossed a deep red ball from one strong palm to another, slowly coming toward me. "You don't know how to throw, Zoe." He came to a dead stop when the cold marble ball was between our chests. My heart pattered. "Let me show you."

He swept around me, wrapped one solid-as-steel arm around my left, the other whipped the marble ball to breast level as if it were nothing more than a fluffy pom-pom. His face was so close to mine, I jerked my head to the side, sure his jaw would come into contact with my cheek.

In front of us, blocking my swing, Chase stood, a befuddled expression causing him to cross his arms and bite his lower lip. "No, that's not the best way," he joined us, standing next to me, making it clear to Weston that he was the better bowler, he should be demonstrating the moves.

Weston's warm body hovered over mine like a panther ready to mate. Whatever cologne he wore nullified common sense, wafted into secret places in my brain and body, luring and taunting to life female desires.

I locked my knees, tried to block the flutterings coming to life in my system. *This is Weston, you retard. Britt's ex.* Weston's skilled fingers wrapped gingerly around my hands as he showed me how to hold the ball. I swallowed a knot.

"You cradle it like this." His low voice snuck into my ear and tried to caress my eardrum.

"Thanks, I got it." I wiggled free, took a few steps to the lane and readied to roll the ball.

My hands shook.

I felt him behind me again. "Now, bring your arm back nice and strong in a full—"

"I can do it." I moved back and landed on his instep. He grunted. I shot a smirk over my shoulder and took the swing. The ball rolled off into the gutter and sped down the lane and out of sight without hitting anything but the slatted curtain hanging behind the standing pins. Oh well, I sucked at bowling. At least I got Weston off my back.

"Great try," Chase cheered behind me. I turned and bumped into Weston, his dark eyes holding me still. My heart bounced in my chest.

"You just need a little work on that arm," he said.

I needed to get away from him. "I'm going to leave the next game to you guys and sit this one out." I crossed to the red Formica bench and sat.

"You sure?" Weston followed me.

"Yeah, come on, Zoe. My right arm's getting tired, I'm sure I'll bowl a lousy game."

I grinned. "Not you, Chase. You're a machine. I've never seen anyone like you."

Weston shifted, looking rather miffed by my comment. I enjoyed pinching his ego. Maybe it was because he'd been muscling me with his manliness and now I was getting back at him with my tongue.

Suddenly, I noticed how quiet it was in the place. I looked down the lanes. The rest of the patrons had left. I checked the large clock on the wall. Five minutes to eleven. We'd been playing for two hours. The place was about to close.

Commotion drew my attention to the door where three guys had just entered the bowling alley. My heart dropped. Black spirits crawled all over their bodies like writhing serpents, hands caressing, teeth gnashing, bodies whipping in a frenzy of evil that reached out across the building to where we lingered at the lanes.

TWELVE

I jumped to my feet, grabbed Weston's shirt, and Chase's sleeve. "We need to leave. Now."

Both followed my gaze to the check-in desk where the gang was headed. "What is it?" Chase whispered.

"We need to get out of here." I didn't need to drag them, they put down their bowling balls, we all slipped off our shoes and Weston took the lead.

"Stay behind me," he commanded.

His face drew tight. Did he see the black spirits? Chase and I followed him to the desk where we set down our shoes. Weston kept his gaze on the three guys. When their darting eyes met his, he gave them a casual nod. Only one nodded back, a tall guy with a bandana wrapped around his head. All three looked around the place again.

Their baggy clothes were draped with chains. Tattoos decorated what skin they bared. One had a cap on backwards. They didn't look like your typical bowlers, and the young guy and girl working behind the desk became jittery.

I tried to tear my eyes from the crawling creatures, but they were so hideous, their evil so menacing, I was caught in the snare of fear. I'd never seen black spirits seep from eye sockets. Every time one of the guys opened their mouths, a creature slipped out in fanged frenzy, then joined the others already infesting the men, wrapping, writhing and taunting in a wicked silence that felt like a magnetic field, trying to suck us closer.

The creatures were male and female, and, like when I'd seen them before, were oblivious to anything but arousing their hosts. Each guy had two perched on his shoulders, their mouths whispering into the men's ears while the talons on their hands stroked effortlessly over the men's bodies. I shuddered. What could they be saying?

I wanted to get out of there as soon as possible and noticed that I'd moved closer to Weston. He took my hand, pulled me into his side and looked at Chase. With a jerk of his head, he indicated the exit. Weston on my right, Chase on my left, we headed for the door. My heart raced. I didn't dare look back, too afraid the three men would sense something was up—we were onto them or something—even though I had no idea what they were going to do if anything at all. For all I knew, they could be three guys trying to get in one last game before closing. Three guys who happened to be infected with the worst case of black spirits I'd ever seen.

The further we got from them, the less pull I felt from the magnetic evil they carried.

I dug out my cell phone once we were out the door. I dialed nine-one-one. "That was bad in there," Chase said. "Did you see those guys?"

"Keep going." Weston didn't break the protective hold he had on me, ushering me to Chase's car. He glanced over his shoulder, then saw that I had my phone out. "What are you doing?"

"Calling nine-one-one."

"You think something's going to happen?" Chase pressed the button on his key remote and the car beeped. Weston opened the back door and gestured for me to get in. I did.

When the dispatcher came on the line, I swallowed. "Um, we just left Jack and Jill's bowling and three suspicious guys went into the place."

"Can you describe them?"

"They had on bandanas and chains and they had tats and stuff. Maybe like gang members? But it was more than the way they were dressed. It was like they were checking the place out."

"Can I have your name please?"

"Zoe Dodd." She took my cell phone number and thanked me for reporting the suspicious behavior.

I hoped the police would show.

"Let's get out of here," I said.

Weston slid in beside me. Chase jumped into the front and started the engine. We drove in silence for a minute, and I stared out the window into the dark neighborhoods we passed. I hoped the employees at Jack and Jill's were safe. I hoped they had guardians. I hadn't seen any. Maybe nothing bad was going to happen—that's why I hadn't seen any. The thought didn't case my fear. I closed my eyes, not comfortable with the black night surrounding me. Why did bad things happen when it got dark? To more easily camouflage wickedness? Did darkness bring out the worst in a mind already turned in that direction?

"You okay?" Weston. I looked over, found him studying me. His hand was close to mine as it lay on the backseat—fingertips nearly touching. His brown-black eyes sparkled in the occasional reflected light we passed.

No dark spirits here.

"Yeah. That was just… bad back there, you know? I felt it."

He nodded. "I felt it, too."

"Me three," Chase piped. He kept glancing at us through the rear view mirror. "Anybody want a Starbucks?"

"I just want to get home," I said.

"Yeah, man. Thanks for the offer, though." Weston patted the back of Chase's seat. "This was cool tonight."

"Yeah, it was," Chase nodded. "I wonder if we'll hear anything in the news tomorrow about Jack and Jill's."

"For their sake, I hope not," I said.

"I'm just glad we got out of there when we did." Weston kept his gaze on me. Unnerving, because I was still deciphering who he was and what he was after.

"Britt would have freaked," I said, watching his reaction to the mention

123

of her name.

Weariness washed over his face. He looked out the window for a moment, then slid his gaze back to me again. "She probably wouldn't have noticed."

"I don't know about that," Chase put in. "She seems pretty intuitive."

Weston shook his head. "Intuitive? She hasn't gotten many of my clues. I'm done with her."

"You make her sound conveniently disposable," I said, disgusted.

"That's not what I meant. Look, I know you find this hard to believe, but she's not my type anymore."

"And when did that change? Just a few months ago you were very happy deep sea diving in her mouth."

Weston's eyes widened. He swallowed, glanced at Chase. "We're done now. I thought you knew that."

"Your love life isn't something I keep up with."

"How about I put on some music?" Chase suggested, clearly trying to lighten the tension. Barry Manilow serenaded us about being ready to take a chance again.

Weston's eyes were fierce and hurt, his body tense.

I rolled my lips under. *Shut up, Zoe. You're attacking this guy and he's been civil all night.*

"Maybe I should drop you off first, Weston," Chase said.

"Drop Zoe off, first."

Weston and I stared each other down, my heart pounding in trepidation. What was this all about?

Soon we were in front of my house. Chase put the car in park and jumped out. So did Weston. Both strode to my door. Weston opened it. I got out. Weston slipped into position at my side, lightly pressing his hand at the small of my back, claiming the job of walking me to the door.

To make sure he knew I wasn't giving him an inch, I moved away and hugged Chase. "Thanks. This was fun."

Chase returned the hug. He faced Weston, and shot him a victorious grin.

I started for the walkway. Weston stayed at my left side, Chase at my right, the two of them in a stare down with me in the middle. When we reached my front door, Weston stepped between me and Chase. "I need to talk to Zoe, dude. I'll walk home from here."

Chase's mouth fell open. Weston turned, faced me, indicating to Chase that he was done with the topic of a ride home and the evening, as far as Chase was concerned, was over. "You and I need to talk."

"It's eleven-thirty."

"I know. But…" He reached up and pressed a hand to the brick wall of the porch, as if frustrated. "We need to talk."

"I'm not sure Zoe wants you to stay," Chase sputtered, blinking behind his glasses.

"Dude, she's fine."

"Zoe?"

"Um." I swallowed. "It's okay, Chase. Thanks again for the fun night."

Chase hesitated, blew out a loud, annoyed breath, then leaned close, his hand gripping my elbow, and he kissed my cheek. He sent Weston another glare and left, the sound of him starting the car followed by the soft rumble of his engine fading into the cold, winter night. A light breeze rustled the trees. Bushes trembled. I did too. Weston kept his hand anchored on the wall and stared into my eyes. Just to be safe, I unlocked the door and pushed it open.

"What happened tonight?"

"What do you mean?"

"I mean, something happened when you saw those guys at Jack and Jill's. I saw it on your face. You saw more than just three homies ready to rip off the place."

A knot formed in my throat. I tried to swallow it down but it wouldn't go.

His hand slid from the wall. He moved closer, bringing himself nearly flush with my chest. "You're different, Zoe. Special. I knew it that night when… when…" Pain scored his face. He looked away. "When Brady and

125

I…" He closed his eyes. "Something happened that night." He opened his eyes and searched mine for the answers he sought. "What happened?" he asked.

"I… don't know what to say."

"Are you clairvoyant?"

"No."

"Then how did you know those guys at the bowling alley were bad?"

"Apart from their clothes and attitude you mean? I don't. They could have been—"

"What? There to play?" he snickered. "I don't think that and neither do you. Come on."

"There's nothing to tell you. I looked at them and got a bad feeling, just like you, just like Chase."

He shook his head, stuffed his hands into his front pockets. "I don't believe that's all it was."

"You're going to have to." No way would I ever tell Weston about anything spiritual.

"You're not a liar, Zoe."

The air crisped with truth. At that moment I realized there was the real possibility that Weston Larson had changed. I'd changed, couldn't he?

He seemed to sense that I was debating truly believing him. Relief spread from his intense gaze, loosening the taut corners of his jaw into a hopeful smile.

"Okay, so I'm not a liar."

"At least we agree on that. I wish you'd agree that I'm not the same."

I tilted my head. "What changed you?"

He scrubbed his hair with both hands, blew out a sigh, his skin flushing soft pink. "You."

My eyes widened. He nodded.

"That night. There was something in the air around you. This invisible strength. This vibe. I can't explain it except that I felt it build the moment I held you in my arms. Like I was holding someone…"

"What?" I urged, curious.

"Like I was holding someone important. I don't know." He paced, his hands roving his hair, then down his face in an expression of exasperation and intrigue. "Brady was going on and on about hooking up with you—but I knew, to my core—I shouldn't do that. That if I did, I'd be... that I'd... I'd be in deep trouble."

I took a deep breath, trying to assimilate his experience.

"There was so much happening inside of me, I couldn't deny the feelings." His hands dropped to his sides. He stepped close. "Using you like that was wrong. But it was more. Way more. I felt it. Like some unseen force was shielding you."

A shiver rippled down my spine. "Maybe your conscience was getting the best of you."

He shook his head. "More than that. Like I said, there was power in it. A force."

"I think you've seen one too many Star Wars movies, Weston." I reached out for the doorknob.

His fingers wrapped around my wrist. "Zoe."

I worked to control my knocking knees. Questions still haunted his eyes, deeply probing mine. A few quiet moments ticked by as if he was taking one last stab at hoping I'd tell him something. He released my wrist. "Never mind."

I went inside to the safety of home, turning to look at him one last time before I shut the door.

Weston Larson. On my doorstep. Could things be any weirder?

*   *   *

I shut the door and pressed my back against it. Closed my eyes. Let out a sigh. The house was asleep, without light except for the soft glow of the nightlight in the long hall from the entry and the kitchen, family room area.

What a bizarre evening.

I started up the stairs. My cell phone vibrated in my pocket and I dug for it. The screen glowed electric blue in the black hall. Britt.

where is he?

at home i guess

i'm at his house, he's not here!!!

I forgot that Weston was walking home. He lived a good four miles away. It was freezing outside. I slammed my forehead with my palm. He probably called one of his friends to pick him up. The clock on my phone said midnight. Guys like Weston had plenty of buds they could ask for a ride. Guilt gnawed at me. What if he hadn't called anyone?

I stared at Britt's text. I could tell her to find him. She'd blow apart if I told her that he was walking home from my house.

Crap. I made my way down the stairs, feeling for each step in the near-darkness, and once I was in the night light of the main hall, I booked it to the key rack in the kitchen where Mom and Dad hung their keys. I grabbed Dad's and went out through the garage door.

"You must be out of your mind going after Weston," I mumbled. The garage door moaned open. I'd wake the whole house with the charitable escapade.

I got in Dad's Jeep and started the engine, then closed the garage door—better to be safe than sorry, Mom always said—even with the groaning door. And after having just seen those creeps at Jack and Jill's I didn't want to invite any theft to the house with an open garage.

I drove slow, keeping my eyes out for Weston. My breath plumed out in front of my face and I cranked up the heater. Roads were empty and lit only by the occasional street light. My cell phone kept vibrating. Britt, obsessive Britt. *Get a life. Go to bed.*

Finally, I saw him, shoulders hunched, stride long and quick. He glanced at the car and moved off the road to the side. I slowed, rolled down the passenger window.

His eyes grew wide when he recognized me. "Zoe?"

"Need a ride?"

He smiled and jogged over, opened the door and brought an icy blast of air in with him. He was white, blue and shivering.

I pulled back onto the road. "Why didn't you say something?"

"I figured I'd said enough," he sputtered, hunching.

"Britt's looking for you."

"Yeah. I've got seventy-five messages from her." He reached over and flicked the heater dial to high. "Man, I'm glad you came."

"I almost sent Britt after you," I joked.

His dark eyes sparkled at me across the car. "Nah, you couldn't do that."

"Not that you don't deserve it."

"Hey, I've tried to tell her—nicely, I might add—about fifty times, that we're over. She just won't accept it." He rubbed his hands back and forth then cupped his mouth and blew. The smooth skin spreading over his taut cheeks rounded for a minute. He had strong looking hands. Hands that had caught and passed the Pleasant Grove High School football zillions of times in zillions of games as quarterback. Hands that had carried me when I'd been unconscious. A shiver trickled through my belly. He caught my appraisal and slowly, his hands eased from his face.

I cleared my throat and faced the road. His gaze stayed on me, unnerving as it was. "What are you looking at?"

"What were *you* looking at?" he asked.

I didn't care what he thought of me, so it didn't matter what I said. "I was looking at your jaw and hands." Such honesty had not been a part of Weston's female relationships that was obvious. His eyes dilated, giving his surprise away. "What were *you* looking at?"

"Your lips."

Pow. My heart thudded.

"You have the poutiest lips I've ever seen."

"Pouty?" I snorted. "Like I look bratty?"

"Like you look kissable."

Bang. Knot in the throat again. "Thankfully, we're almost at your house."

"Why's that, Zoe? Can't take the truth?"

"Can't take the b.s. is more accurate." I turned left onto his street.

He let out a low laugh. "No b.s—ing here. I've always thought you were gorgeous."

"Okay, stop. My friend—my best friend—is in love with you. Or at least she thinks she is. I'm just getting used to the idea that you're not the same woman-banger you used to be. This, whatever it is you're doing, is starting to take my opinion of you backwards."

He let out a sigh and leaned against the door. "Sorry. Sometimes the obnoxious woman-banger tries to resurface. I hate that guy. Honest."

I tried to read him. The darkness didn't allow me to see anything more than stark shadows. Was he telling the truth? We drove in silence, snapping and sizzling with his charisma, like beads of water on a hot skillet.

I pulled into the circular driveway, smiling when I remembered the night I'd boldly pulled my VW onto his grass and parked. The engine of Dad's car idled.

"I would have frozen to death if you hadn't come and gotten me," he said.

"Let's not exaggerate."

He reached out and tentatively took my right hand from the steering wheel. His gaze didn't leave mine and it didn't seem like either one of us was breathing. "I'm going to keep saying this until I know you've forgiven me. I'm sorry."

His fingers were warm now, and they lightly caressed mine. I tried to pull my hand free, uncomfortable with the tangled feelings inside of my body. But he held on. His gaze dropped to my lips.

His face, half shadowed the other half intense and exposed, stirred desire. No wonder Britt was in love with him. He was gorgeous, and the passionate remorse I saw in his eyes made him appear vulnerable and very touchable.

Any signal that I was cool with him, and he'd be all over me. But thinking about allowing the nascent desire inside of me for him full-on growth felt wrong. I still had a hard time completely believing he was changed. I also felt guilt. I loved Matthias. He wholly occupied my heart. No one would ever take his place.

I gently drew my hand from Weston's and gripped the wheel again. "It's late."

He nodded. His eyes stayed on mine as he opened the door. "Thanks, Zoe."

He got out and the cozy warmth that had been in the car was sucked away. A blast of chilly air snuck in. I shivered. He shut the door.

He started up the path to his house. Britt sat perched on his porch. She stood, her marshmallow winter coat popping out in the dark night like a light bulb. She wobbled toward him.

Uh-oh. I didn't bother sticking around. I backed the car down the driveway, but caught Weston checking me out over his shoulder. I actually felt sorry for him. But then, I was certain to face Britt's wrath myself.

At home, I tried to relax, but kept thinking about how weird the night had been. I undressed, took a hot bath and kept checking my phone, waiting for Britt's chastisement. Not that I would take crap from her. I may not be interested in Weston, but she needed to get a life and leave him to his.

I dried, put on my flannel pjs and my phone rang. Britt.

I plopped on my bed. "Hey."

"Skank."

"Excuse me?"

I heard her gulping. She was no doubt downing a bottle of vodka. "You left me and stol' him from me. I'll ne're forgive you."

"I didn't do anything."

"You wen' bowling wif him!"

"And Chase, who you have conveniently forgotten. Chase and I were on a date—that you invited yourself along on, remember? Then somehow Weston was involved. I didn't do anything to him."

"You bowled him o're with yer innocence."

"Me? Innocent?" I snorted.

"That's wha I tol him," she mumbled. "Tha you were a ho. But he didn believe me."

My stomach rolled. "I'm not going to listen to this."

"You better lisen! I hate you for taking him away from me, an I'm gonna to make you pay, Zoeeee. I yam."

I clicked off my cell phone. It rang again. Britt. I snapped it up. "Don't threaten me you drunk loser. He told me he's not into you anymore. Get over it."

"Why? So you can get it on wi' him? Never! You... you ..." I heard a sob, then the phone crashed and her heavy wailing pushed through the air waves.

I disconnected. My stomach was so upset, I knew I'd never relax enough to fall asleep now.

My phone vibrated. Weston. *Great.*

"Hello?"

"Zoe, are you okay?"

"Yes, of course. Why?"

He let out a sigh. "Britt left and was threatening you. She's not there, is she?"

"No. She just called me from her house."

"How do you know she's at her house?"

"Because she was getting wasted. She keeps a stash there. But then, you might already know that."

"Yeah. She freaking lost it, man. I'm telling you, that chick is out of control."

"I told you, she loves you."

"She doesn't love me. She's, like, obsessed. But it's not about me anymore. Her ego's bruised and she's playing some sicko game."

"She's not playing with me. I won't take her crap."

"If she says anything, does anything at all to you, you tell me. Understand?"

Now I had another guardian angel? I fought a grin. "Weston, I can take care of myself. But thanks."

"No, I'm serious. She's a whack job."

"A whack job you were into not too long ago."

Silence. I should let dead dogs lie. I banged my forehead with the palm of my hand. "Sorry. That wasn't cool."

"It's okay."

My phone ticked. Another call. "I bet that's Britt. I better see if she's okay. Don't want her doing something drastic."

"Promise me you'll call me if she gets crazier."

Weston. Coming to my rescue. What a thought. Weirder things had happened.

When I clicked on the line for Britt, she'd already disconnected.

THIRTEEN

The next morning I could barely see my way through the forest of clothes in my closet to put on jeans and a royal blue PGHS Vikings hoodie. My hair went back in a claw and I brushed on some blush. That was it. Who cared if I looked dead tired? I felt pretty close.

I went downstairs for breakfast. I hadn't gotten enough sleep—five hours didn't cut it, not after the mixed up night I'd had.

Mom always watched the morning news and had the TV on in the background since she never had time to read the paper. A lion-sized yawn cracked my face and I glanced over at the screen on my way to the kitchen.

A young reporter stood outside of Jack and Jill's, the yellow tape behind him flickering in the soft winter breeze. Black uniformed police officers scurried like ants in and out of the building.

"Two employees were on the premises when the robbery occurred. Both were found bound in the office. Three men are in custody, thanks to a phone tip. Officers arrived just as the suspects were leaving the scene with over seven hundred dollars in cash."

The blood in my head sunk to my feet.

Mom was talking to me, her voice wound around in my head, but I didn't hear the words.

"Zoe?" Mom's gaze met mine across the room. "Are you feeling okay?"

"Y—yeah." A knob of shock lodged in my throat.

Mom left Abria at the table and crossed to me. "Honey?"

"Is Luke around?" My voice scratched.

She gently stroked my cheek. "Are you sure you're okay?"

I nodded. "Hungry." Avoiding her deciphering, I went into the kitchen, pretending to look for something to eat. I grabbed a Yoplait lemon yogurt. She'd freak if she knew I'd been at the bowling alley last night, that close to another life-threatening experience, even I had been home by my midnight curfew. It was better if she didn't know.

"I saw him a few minutes ago. Better try to catch him if you're looking for a ride to school." She went back to Abria, playing in her cream of rice cereal.

"K." I pulled out my phone and texted him, asking for a ride.

im out in the car, hurry

"Bye Mom!" I jogged to the back door, went out and found Luke's blue car idling at the curb.

I got in the car but couldn't think to say anything more than a grumbled, "*hey.*" My mind flashed with the faces of the two employees bound in an office. How close we had all come to something dangerous. Did Matthias know what had happened? I was disappointed he hadn't shown up. I shouldn't be. He wasn't my guardian anymore. That boy and girl hadn't had guardians. But then, Weston and Chase and I had been there.

*   *   *

I was in the middle of class when my cell vibrated. I slipped my hand into my bag and brought it up for a peek.

Weston.

Butterflies fluttered in my stomach.

His eyes came into my mind. I reminded myself that Britt loved him, an emotion I would never feel for him and, even if she and I were on the outs right now, I had to respect her over-the-top desire to win him back.

hey.

hey.

r u ok?

yeah. U? did u hear?

yeah.

weird, huh? wanna do lunch?

Uh-oh. I stared at the words on my phone screen. I figured there was no harm in lunch, since Britt wanted to kill us both at this point. I hadn't seen her at school today; she was probably at home with a huge hangover.

sure

c u then. meet me at my truck.

K

My stomach was filled with butterflies the rest of the morning. I was so distracted by what had happened last night and Weston's invite to lunch I didn't notice Krissy until she tapped my arm in the hall. I was at my locker, unloading books, the scent of cafeteria tacos seeping out in the halls.

"Krissy. Hey."

She smiled. She had on her usual blue jumper and long sleeved white tee shirt and ankle boots. "Hi. How are you?"

"Good, you?" I shut my locker door. Around us, the hall buzzed with moving bodies and buzzing voices.

"Okay. I wondered if you wanted to go get some lunch."

"Oh. Jeez. I'd love to, but I already have plans." Her hopeful expression wilted.

"How about tomorrow?"

"Oh. I guess that'll work."

"I'm sorry, but I've gotta run. Wait. Why don't you come with me? I'm going to lunch with Weston." This was the perfect way to be with Weston without him getting the idea that anything more than friendship was going to develop between us.

Krissy's face bloomed like a daisy under the rising sun. "Seriously?"

"Come on." She followed me through the pack of students and we went out of the building.

"Gosh, I'm nervous. Are you sure he won't mind?"

"He's pretty cool about crashing. He does it himself."

"Really? I would have thought he had dates booked months in advance and he didn't need to crash."

"He's just a guy like any other."

"No, he's not."

Whatever. Girls' fantasies blinded them.

Weston leaned against his silver truck. When he saw me, he stood upright. He stuffed his hands into his front pockets, the corners of his jaw shifting. His gaze flicked from me to Krissy then back, his smile faltering a little.

"Hey," he said.

"Weston, do you know Krissy?"

He gave a sharp nod. Krissy jittered at my side. "She coming?" he asked.

"I knew you wouldn't mind." I flashed a grin, wondered if Krissy caught the slight tilt of his head, the annoyance in his eyes or if she was too buzzed just looking at him to notice. Like any other kid who'd had their share of social experience, Weston smoothed over his annoyance with a sleek smile. He opened the back door and gestured to it. "Zoe, why don't you sit in the back? Krissy, you can sit up front with me."

I cocked a brow at him over a teasing smile. After Krissy got in and he shut the door, I started around the back of the car, but he blocked me with his body. He stared into my eyes. His lips curve up in a smirk. "You afraid to be alone with me?"

My heart pattered out of control. "No."

Weston lowered his voice. "I wanted to talk to you about what happened last night. Alone."

"Sorry."

"How do you feel about it?"

"Close call, you know?"

He gave a nod. "Yeah."

I got in and he shut the door. My jumping pulse began to settle a little.

"This is exciting," Krissy whispered. "People are staring."

I hadn't noticed until now. I swallowed. *Britt will get wind of this, but having Krissy in the picture will throw her off balance.*

Weston's masculinity filled the car: faded cologne, laundry detergent and testosterone. My head swam. Krissy, glowing in the front seat, didn't take her eyes off him.

He started up the engine. "Where would you like to eat?" he asked Krissy.

"Anywhere," Krissy swooned.

Weston's smile shined back at me. "How about you, Zoe?"

"The Purple Turtle." The hangout where rumors were born; I couldn't resist suggesting the place. Was Weston brave enough to go?

He cranked up something pop on his CD player and we drove in the direction of the hamburger place. Apparently he wasn't concerned about being seen with either me or Krissy.

He parked the truck, got out and opened Krissy's door. She jumped out like popcorn popping. "Thanks," she blushed.

"No problem." He eyed me through the glass, his gaze staying with me as he rounded the car, opened my door. "Zoe."

I got out. He held the door open, but once I stood, blocked the pizza-slice sized opening with his body. His dark hair tousled on a french-fry breeze. Then he stepped back and I took a deep breath.

I crossed to Krissy who stood watching us in wide-eyed fascination. My bouncing heart leapt to my throat and caused my voice to tremble. "I'm starving? You?"

*   *   *

We ate at a window table, one Weston chose, in a blatant move to challenge my choice of eating there, I guessed. Krissy ordered a chicken and chips basket. I ordered a chocolate shake and fries. Weston chose a triple cheeseburger, fries and a Pepsi. He paid for the meal, which impressed Krissy and didn't surprise me.

"I went to your games," Krissy admitted. "All of them. Just to watch you."

"Oh yeah?" Weston's practiced bravado was admirable. Only because I'd hung around Britt did I actually see past the performance to where reality fought with pretense. "You like football?"

Krissy nibbled a fry. "I like watching."

Um…yeah. I reached over and stole Weston's Pepsi to hide the smile blooming on my lips. His brown eyes locked on my mouth, wrapping around the straw.

Krissy followed every move of Weston's like a cat watching a bird. "How well do you two know each other?"

"We're friends," I blurted at the same time Weston said, "Really well."

Weston reached over, his warm fingers covered my hand on his cup, and he gently eased the Pepsi away, promptly bringing the red straw to his lips. "Zoe's the first real girl I've known." His mouth went around the straw.

A warm trickle dripped through me.

Krissy's focused gaze shifted from Weston, to me, back to Weston. She didn't say anything for a few seconds. "Are you going to have another party soon?"

Weston looked antsy for a minute. "Not likely. Why?"

"I'd like to go to one. They sound fun."

Weston sat forward, crossing his arms on the table. He plucked a fry and twisted the long, golden string potato, his brown eyes looking into mine. "Parties are overrated, Krissy." He ate the fry, his jaw slowly knotting and unknotting.

"Well," Krissy's tone was defensive. "I'd still like to go. I've never been to one. You think you'll have one, Zoe?"

"Me? No way. My house is not a party house."

"How come?"

"My sister has autism. My family doesn't go *anywhere* or *do* anything unless they have to with her."

"I could have one," Krissy piped.

Weston and I stole glances at each other. Weston swallowed another fry. "At your house?"

"My parents are never home."

"Krissy, people do things at parties," Weston's tone was both instructive and disgusted at the same time. "Drink. Get high. Hook up. Steal things. Annihilate things."

"Sounds like an adventure." Krissy squeezed her shoulders together and beamed.

She reached for Weston's Pepsi, smiled when his eyes widened, and brought the red straw to her lips.

* * *

Weston escorted Krissy and me out to the parking lot. I felt curious eyes follow our movements and thought: don't you guys have anything better to do but speculate? Krissy beamed in the temporary spotlight of popularity, soaking up the moments of being watched and scrutinized.

Outside in the cool winter air, Krissy was first to the truck, making sure she secured the front bench for the ride back to school by standing at the passenger side door. Weston's boy-charming face hid amusement at her eagerness. He didn't even send me an *uh-okay* grin. Kudos to him.

He opened Krissy's door and she got inside. Then he came around to the driver's side where I stood at the back. With a press of a remote button he unlocked my door.

"Scoring with possessed chicks now? Bro, that's brave." Brady, surrounded by a small pack of other jocks, came up behind us. He slapped Weston on the back and snickered.

Weston shrugged off Brady's palm. "Screw off."

"Careful." Brady leaned close, and a black spirit rose from his back. The female straddled his shoulders, her talons stimulating his scalp, down his neck and further down his chest. Her gaping mouth gnashed in silent laughter. "I heard her head spins when you get on her."

Weston's right snapped out, hooking Brady's nose, sending Brady stumbling back into his buddies. Brady's face twisted in fury. The black creature on his shoulders jumped up and down like a crazed monkey.

Brady lunged.

Weston's fists wrapped around the front Brady's shirt and he yanked him close, their noses nearly touching. Then he shoved Brady back. Brady lost his footing and fell like a domino into his pals.

Weston turned, opened my door. "Get in."

I did. Behind him, Brady and his friends stood like a pack of restless wolves. Brady swiped blood into smears underneath his nose. Weston ignored them, opened the driver's door, got in, shut it and started the ignition.

Brady strode to the hood and banged his fists down, shaking the front of the truck. His furious gaze locked on Weston. "This isn't over!"

Weston accelerated enough to send Brady leaping back, then the truck screeched out of the parking lot.

We drove to the school in silence the short mile it took to get there. In the front seat, Krissy's face paled. She kept her gaze on her hands, twisted in her lap.

After Weston parked, he got out and opened my door first, his expression apologetic over sparkling brown eyes. Then he jogged over to Krissy's side where she patiently waited.

My gaze caught Luke's blue Samurai parked a few aisles over, a handful of his friends jumping out of it. "I've gotta go," I called to Weston and Krissy, and started in Luke's direction.

"Bye Zoe," Krissy's voice shook—no doubt from shock. Weston's eyes were huge with you're-going-to-leave-me-alone-here? I almost broke out in a laugh.

One of Luke's mop-headed buddies saw me and elbowed Luke who whipped up his blond head. His friends conveniently scattered. "Hey," I said.

"Hey."

"You okay?"

"I'm good."

He started up the drag toward the buildings and I stayed by his side. He smelled of cigarette smoke, but he had his backpack, which meant he at least intended to go to class.

"I wanted to make sure you were okay. You came in late last night."

His blue eyes met mine. "You were up? No lights were on."

"It was a crazy night. I went to Jack and Jill's."

"Wasn't there a burglary there last night?"

"Yeah. My friends and I just missed it."

"Serious?"

I nodded.

"Man, you have bad luck." He opened the glass door to the main building and we paraded in with other students.

"It's not bad luck. I went there on a date."

"Did you see anything?"

"Kind of. The place was closing. Then these three dudes came in, just as we were walking out."

He whistled. "Man."

"Yeah. Creepy to say the least. My point is I couldn't sleep. That's why I heard you come in."

"So, is this you checking up on me?"

"No. Well, maybe. This is me saying I'm sorry for being a retard yesterday."

He looked at me, as if he had to see for himself that I was truly apologetic. He didn't say anything for a few minutes.

I followed him to his class. I had no idea what it was and I was sure I'd be late for mine, but I felt the need to talk to him. "Why have you relapsed?"

He glanced around to see if anyone was listening. Of course, no one was. It bugged me no one cared enough to. "It happens, now get off my back about it."

I grabbed his sleeve and he slowed. "You saw Matthias. Doesn't that mean anything to you?"

"Like what? I'm supposed to fall to my knees and praise God?" He pulled free and glared at me.

"That's harsh."

He leaned close. "It freaked me out, okay?" he whispered. "That's all I'm going to say about it."

The bell shrilled. He was ten feet from his classroom door and he turned.

"I'm sorry," I said again. He paused at the open door but didn't look at me, before he went inside. I had to jog across campus to my class, through empty halls echoing with my tardy footsteps.

*   *   *

I found Chase in newspaper class. He sat at his desk until I came in, then he jumped to his feet and came right to me. "Zoe, can you believe what happened?"

I tossed my backpack on my desk. "Freaky, huh?"

"It's a good thing you called."

"Yeah."

A shudder wove through me. I made myself sit, suddenly weak-kneed. Chase leaned close. "You okay? You look pale."

I nodded. "I didn't get a chance to tell you last night because Weston was there," I began. "But those guys had the worst case of black spirits I'd ever seen."

Chase lowered himself into a chair next to me. "Really?"

"Like maggots on a dead body. They were everywhere. Coming out of their eyes, mouths. Disgusting." I shuddered.

"Wow. I wish I'd seen them."

"No you don't."

"Zoe, yes I do. I want to see all spirits, both the good and the bad."

"Why? I was so creeped I couldn't sleep last night."

143

"Because it'd be the coolest thing to see them, that's why. Did you see guardians with the employees?"

"No."

"That's odd."

"We were there. We were the guardians," I said.

Chase stood, seeing that Mr. Brewer was starting to give out instructions. He crossed back to his desk.

After class, Chase was tied up talking to Mr. Brewer. I wanted to ask him for a ride home, since I'd texted Luke and gotten no answer. He was no doubt pissed at me.

I exchanged books at my locker, the familiar streaming noises of laughter, talk and slamming metal oddly comforting. Chase, Weston and I had done our part in preventing something last night. A warm confirmation spread through my soul, brought a smile to my face and I shut my locker door. The hall had emptied to a handful of kids who were about the business of getting out of the school as fast as was humanly possible.

Albert stood ten feet away.

FOURTEEN

How had I not noticed him? A shudder of the unknown rammed through my system. Matthias' warning flashed in my head: *Do not speak with him.*

Today, he was sharply dressed in a sleek pair of black slacks, the same dove grey shirt, blood red tie and fitted black suit jacket that tapered over his narrow hips. His dark blond hair was neatly slicked back. He smiled and started my direction.

The hall was empty now, echoing my heart pounding in my chest. He wore shiny black shoes. His smooth gait seemed to hover above the tiles without any sound. His gaze held me in a taut intensity that sent ice down my spine.

"Afternoon, Zoe." He stopped inches from me.

He reminded me so much of Matthias—his pretty blue eyes, angular face and expressive mouth. Matthias' words of warning muddled in my head. "Um, hi."

His glance swept the hall. "Schools certainly have changed since I was at university."

"Well, this isn't a university, it's a high school."

"Yes. I know. I attended Brighton Beach College. Charming place, if not administratively challenged. I don't believe it's still in existence."

"I...I don't know."

145

Albert clasped his hands behind his back. He started walking toward the exit, tilting his head that direction, his white teeth gleaming in friendly invitation. "Shall we?"

I didn't want to be rude. He was charming, magnetic and charismatic like Matthias, the resemblance to his son an attractive lure that wiped away any misgivings I carried. "Oh, sure." I walked with him.

When we arrived at the glass doors, he waited for me to open them. He chuckled when I figured out that in order for us both to go out, I would have to. I opened the door and we went into the bitter winter air.

I started toward the parking lot and brought out my phone. "I need to find a ride. My brother, Luke, is being a retard."

"Mm yes. Family can be like that."

Albert eyed my cell phone and texting with interest. "You've never seen a cell phone?" I asked him.

His slicked back hair shined under the hazy winter sun. He shook his head. "I've heard they're wonderful transmitters. Imagine being able to broadcast anything your heart desires to anyone in the world with the push of a button."

Something in his voice sent a thread of unease through me. Matthias' warnings had never been wrong. *I shouldn't ignore this feeling for a second longer.* "Um, I need to go." I turned and started toward the half-circle section of the parking lot where students were dropped off in front of the high school. I prayed for somebody—anybody, to grab a ride home with.

I dialed Weston.

"Hey, Zoe."

"You still here?"

"Yeah, you need a ride? Where are you?"

"At the marquee."

"Be right there."

I snapped my phone closed and tried to quell the unease spreading inside of me. I tried not to be obvious, but Albert's heavy presence remained pressing behind my back. I was afraid to confirm that he was following with me with a glance.

I walked to the Pleasant Grove High School marquee and sat on the white-stone base with built-in bench. A few students stood idly waiting for rides. Albert sat next to me, stretching out like a rich man on a lounge chair, watching the teenagers go by.

Why didn't he leave me alone?

Albert's blue eyes had an eerie quality that sent a fresh trickle of fear through my blood. The same intensity Matthias had when he looked at me, but different—piercing the soul, hungering for it. Hungering with a drive that threatened devouring.

"Perhaps I could give you a lift home." His voice was smooth, dangerous, like black tar.

"You… drive?"

He threw his head back in a laugh. He reminded me so much of Matthias, my nerves settled for a second. "No, I don't drive anymore. I have another way of transporting you. Hasn't Matthias taught you how to close your eyes and use your thoughts to get you anywhere your heart desires?" He *tskd*, shook his head slowly, his icy blue eyes sending a whisper of freezing fear along my skin.

Unnerved, I looked away, my heart speeding like a rocket.

"Look at me, Zoe."

I couldn't *not* look; his aura surrounded me in a sudden burst of energy, snapping like the tentacles of an octopus after prey. I couldn't keep my attention away from him. His lips lifted, baring white, gleaming teeth. "Yes, like that. Your eyes are so lovely. So expressive. This will be easy, you'll see."

That same wet dread I felt whenever I saw black spirits sunk into every recess of my body, filling me up, closing in around my heart, stopping my lungs from taking another breath.

"Zoe. You're not afraid of me, are you?"

I opened my mouth. Nothing came. *Run. Flee. GO!* My body wouldn't move. I felt cemented to the stone on which I sat. Drowning in fear. Albert leaned close. My heart punched, a frightened fist, through my ribs. *Move! Run!*

"Do you know what I am?" he whispered.

Every hair on my body sprung up. I still couldn't make my voice work. "You're not welcome here."

Matthias' voice cut through the air like a blade in full swing. I jerked my head left. He stood with his hand outstretched, fingers extended as if at any moment he'd strike his father with an invisible force from his fingertips.

Fear paralyzed me. I didn't breathe. Didn't blink. My body felt as though the aura encompassing Albert would leech every last bit of energy and oxygen I had left into obscurity. Matthias was surrounded by light and an invisible current that bounced and snapped, angry and forceful, a whispering lyric of angelic power.

Albert slowly rose to his feet. Around him wound a dark energy, one that started at his shiny black shoes in deep black smoke and inched around and around him in a voracious tornado.

I sat between the two energies. Both fought for me, reaching out in swirling power. Albert's gripped me with fiery teeth, tearing me in half. Matthias' was an all over pull.

"I knew you'd come." Albert's voice slithered through me.

As each one spoke, their words traveled straight through me. Had they torn me open? My body screamed. I didn't feel in control of myself. I was only aware of their conversation, of the whooshing pass of words traveling in my system I was helpless to exorcise.

"You're not welcome here," Matthias repeated.

Albert laughed. "You can't stop me from taking her. You can't touch her. She's mine."

"Leave."

"Try to stop me, Matthias. Try. I'd savor the experience."

A violent jolt ripped me from head to groin, and I gasped. I looked at Matthias, his face taut and stony as he reached a hand out for me.

"Yes." Albert's voice was in my ear, swirling down my neck, a hot, greedy snake that raced through my body, just under my skin, rippling my limbs into convulsions. "Come and get her."

Matthias' eyes colored with bright flames—as if he might burst into a brush fire at that very moment and consume everything in his path. His gaze was locked on me, following the trail of the serpent that had invaded my body. Breathing stopped. I couldn't move, but I felt the unearthly movement of something else inside of me swirl around bones, curl around my lungs and pass over my pounding heart.

As if throwing an invisible ball, the fingers on Matthias' right hand reached my direction, formed a claw and he drew back his arm. At the same time, I felt the creature sucked out of my frame, a whirlwind of screaming so high pitched and frenzied, I covered my ears with my hands and grimaced as Matthias removed Albert from me and discarded him with a powerful thrust into the sky. A screeching wail filled the air, so unnerving, my knees buckled.

I let out a scream. Matthias' tight face turned to me and softened. "Zoe."

The moment he spoke my name, invisible arms of comfort and security surrounded me and pulled me to my feet. Should I touch him? He'd told me we couldn't touch. Seconds ticked by. *I can't*—

Without any contact, his outstretched hand drew me closer to him, out of the realm of the ravenous tornado still whirling in black grief where Albert had once stood and into the warm safety of Matthias' protective power. I wanted to feel his warm, alive flesh—I'd missed the feel of him, and yearned for it. My desire was my undoing. I collapsed. Everything around me went black.

FIFTEEN

"Zoe?" A familiar voice. "Zoe?"

Warm fingers touched my cheeks. Matthias. My eyes flew open, my fuzzy gaze sharpened, bringing Weston into focus. His brows were knit over concerned brown eyes.

He held me against him, on his lap. Behind him stood four random students I'd never seen before.

"Where's Matthias?" I slurred.

"Are you okay?" Weston had one arm around me, cradling me against his chest, his other stroked my face. "You fainted just as I was pulling into the parking lot. You hit your head."

I reached around and felt a small egg on the back of my skull. "Ow."

"Ow, yeah." He sat me upright. Aware that we were under scrutiny by those still waiting for rides home, I slid off his lap and stretched out my legs so I could stand.

He jumped up and helped me to my feet, his hands steadying on my arms. "You sure you want to stand?"

I nodded.

Weston inched closer, reaching out as if to embrace me, then he seemed afraid to, like I was too fragile, and he was unsure of what might happen next. I looked around for Matthias. For Albert. Neither was anywhere in sight and the vibes, and the battle both of them had brought had also gone.

150

"What happened?" Weston whispered.

"I… blacked out." My quick scan of the nosy pairs of eyes watching us sent the loitering students on their way. I rubbed the back of my head.

Weston's palms rubbed my upper arms. His gaze raked my face, his eyes dark with worry. He pulled me against his chest and wrapped around me. "Scared me," he whispered against my hair.

Residual fear caused me to shake. I was mortified, clinging to him like he was my savior, but too scared to let go. Feeling someone, having strength to hold onto—even someone else's strength— comforted me. I allowed myself the moment to hold and be held even if I might regret the decision later.

With his arm wrapped around me, he carefully walked me to his truck, idling at the curb, his driver's side door wide open, like he'd jumped from the automobile. He opened my door and helped me into the seat as though I was fragile crystal.

We drove in silence. No music. My breath static, his heavy and male. I rested my aching skull against the headrest, aware of his frequent glances.

"Are you—you think you fainted because of what happened to you in the car accident?"

"No." I shook my head. "No." I saw Albert' empty eyes, his slick smile and a deep shudder wracked my body. I heard his declaration *she's mine*, and wanted to dissolve into the seat, so afraid just the echo of his words in my head would enslave me to a force that mere mortality wasn't strong enough to fight off.

"Are you cold?" Weston leaned forward and turned on the heater.

"No. Yes." I wrapped myself in my own embrace. Matthias. He'd been there. His heavenly presence had only been with me for a minute, maybe less—my accounting of time distorted in the fear surrounding the moment—but I'd seen him.

He'd saved me.

Please, please, I hope his intervention didn't further condemn us somehow. I closed my eyes, a tear escaping down my cheek.

Weston's finger touched the tear, and I looked at him. Concern wracked his features. "You sure nothing happened? Did one of those losers back there touch you?"

"No."

"You're still trembling. What happened, Zoe? You can tell me."

I turned my face toward the window. Black and gray clouds billowed in the afternoon sky, thick and dense, sealing Heaven away from me. Is this how it's going to be, Matthias? Me only able to see you when my soul is at stake? I'd never felt such profound evil as I'd felt from Albert. *Albert.* Matthias' father. The way his piercing eyes had looked into mine, the memory prickled every nerve in my body and threw me into a fit of shivering that rattled my teeth. Whatever he was, he was bigger than anything I could measure with my mortal capacity. Whatever was going on between the two of them was fierce. Deadly.

And I'd stepped into the middle of it.

Albert was dead. And yet he looked as alive and real as Matthias. I was weighed down with confusion and questions. Why had Albert come to me? How had he been able to get inside of me like that? Recalling his possession of my body threw me into a fit of nausea. I covered my mouth and held back the urge to vomit.

Weston pulled the truck over, shoved the gears in park and reached his arm around my shoulder. His fingers pressed into my skin. "Zoe."

Tears crested my eyes. My swollen emotions were on the verge of erupting. I longed to talk to someone. Share my confusion. Get some answers. He searched my face, his brows tight, fingers digging into me, urging me closer to him. "What? Tell me."

"I can't talk about it."

"Something happened back there at the marquee, what was it?" His fingertips pressed harder into my shoulder. "Who? Tell me. I'll kill them."

"Nobody did anything, Weston. It wasn't that."

"Britt? Did she threaten you?"

"No. I really can't elaborate."

"Why?" Our gazes held. Seconds dragged. "Because of… you still don't trust me, do you?"

"That's not it. What happened was very... personal."

Confusion shadowed his eyes. "I'll try to understand if you try and trust me."

"I can't share this with anyone. I'm sorry." My agony was my own cross to bear. Only one person could answer my questions and calm the rampant fears about the evil abyss I'd just stood close enough to that if I'd moved an inch, I would have fallen and been lost forever.

I shuddered again, convulsing with dread. Albert's face embedded in my brain and every time his empty eyes came into mind my body wracked with terror.

Weston slid closer, his arms wrapping tight around me. His strong palm cupped my cheek and pressed my head against his chest.

It wasn't weakness that enabled me to slip my arms around him and hold tight. Need. Fear. Convenience. Weston was there and I needed someone. His body was warm, strong and the comfort I sought slowly seeped into my tense, terrified body. I uncoiled in his embrace, tears filling my eyes. His heartbeat thudded against my face, burrowed in his chest. Steady, relaxing. I closed my eyes and sobbed. The next thing I knew, I opened my eyes and the car was surrounded by darkness.

I jerked upright, my face and body cooling when severed from the warmth of Weston. His dark lashes fluttered open. He was leaning against the door, as if he'd cradled me for hours and for all I knew, he could have been. I glanced at the dashboard for a clock, but the engine had been off for a while, the chill in the car gave away the length of time we must have been sleeping together.

He ran his hands down his face, gripped the steering wheel and sat up. "Man. Must have dozed."

"What time is it?" My veins pulsed with urgency to know the hour.

He turned his wrist and looked at his watch. "Six."

"Phew." I sat back, let out a sigh. At least I could explain the three hour lapse to my parents. Somehow.

"Want to grab some dinner?"

"Uh. Maybe another time. Thanks. I think I'd better get home."

Across the dark cab of his truck, his sparkling eyes held mine. I'd fallen asleep in his arms. He'd been there for me when I'd needed Matthias and thought no one else would do. "Thanks for... everything."

"No problem." He started the engine.

Mom and Dad were watching a basketball game when I walked through the front door and both jumped up from their spots on the family room couches. Traces of fear—no doubt memories of the accident—scored their features into pale ghosts, waiting for bad news.

"Zoe." Mom's voice was fragile.

"Sorry I'm late."

"And you didn't call," Dad put in as they drew closer, needing to check me out for themselves. They hovered as I walked into the kitchen, my stomach growling. Weston had offered to take me to dinner, but I needed to end this bizarre day as soon as possible, and end it in the comfort and safety of home.

I hugged Mom, then Dad, for them as much as for myself, very much a little girl home from a difficult day and in need of security. Mom, seeing that I was in one piece, sighed with relief. Dad remained jittery at her side.

"I was with Weston. We started talking and time got away from us."

"Britt's boyfriend?" Mom's brow shot up.

I nodded and went to the stove top, lifted a lid on a steaming pot. "What was for dinner?"

Mom followed me. "Clam chowder. There's still some left. Luke didn't come home either, so you know the kind of night we've had."

I glanced at Mom, then Dad standing at the fringes of the kitchen, his mind caught up in what to do about the way I'd chosen to handle the evening. "I should have called." I hoped to ease their worries. They had to be wondering how long it would take before I got the message to check in like they'd asked.

"I'm sorry." I ladled the creamy white soup into a heavy bowl, and crossed to the kitchen table, enjoying the mundane act of eating dinner after the horrendous experience of being in the presence of an evil spirit like Albert.

"I tried to get Luke at school and never got a hold of him." I pulled out a chair and sat. "Have you heard from him?"

Mom shook her head.

"It was lucky for me Weston happened to come by."

I sat at the kitchen table, and Mom brought me a spoon, napkin and some Oyster crackers. Dinner smelled wonderful. I dipped my spoon in and blew off the steam before eating. My hand shook. I blinked, staring at it. My whole arm shook. So as to not draw more attention to myself, I rested my elbows on the table, a faux pas Mom despised, but in light of my trembling, I chose to break the good-manners rule.

"Where's Abria?" I asked. The house was so quiet. Dad watched me with hawk-like eyes.

"Around somewhere." Mom crossed to the sink and started rinsing dishes. "I'm trying not to be so obsessive about watching her. She has to have some freedom, and so do I. The house is as child-proof as I can make it. I'm trying to have faith that she'll be okay."

"Mom, that's great. You're right. And you'll see, she *will* be okay. I know it."

"I wish I had your faith."

I sipped another spoonful of soup. "You do."

She smiled, but didn't say anything more. Dad came toward me and my stomach clamped around the soup sloshing in my gut. His steady gaze was sharp. "You're eighteen, Zoe. I can't swing you over my lap for a spanking or ground you and I shouldn't have to—"

"I know, Dad. I'm sorry. If it happens again, I'll willingly put myself on house arrest for as long as you think I need it, ok? That's how sorry I am."

"I'm sure that won't be necessary," he sighed. "But I appreciate the offer. A phone call at least. Easy." He waited until I nodded in agreement before crossing to the couch and sitting down, immersing himself in the basketball game.

I ate, cleaned up after myself then, feeling exhausted, went upstairs for a bath. I stopped by Abria's bedroom and found her writing on the walls with permanent black marker.

Too tired to scream at her, I rolled my eyes, sighed, took the pen and left her with a stuffed animal in her hand. She'd look at the elephant for about five seconds then toss it and go in search of more ink pens, I was sure of that. I didn't have the heart to tell Mom about the graffiti, she'd see it for herself when she put Abria to bed.

I went into my bedroom, closed the door and stripped for my bath. In the moist air of the bathroom, hot bubbles of freesia filled the air, so intoxicating and relaxing, I had to work to keep my eyes open while I soaked.

Muscles heavy, mind burdened with questions still waiting for answers, I dried, dressed in pajamas and grabbed my phone, checking for messages before I crashed.

Weston. The smallest burst of excitement sparkled through me.

just making sure u r ok?

i am. thx again for being there.

my pleasure zoe

Krissy had also left me some texts.

party at my house this sat?

zoe?

Can you text me?

Helllllooo?

party. sat. what time u think?

will you tell everyone u kno?

TEXT ME!

Oh brother. I texted her back.

sorry was busy. u sure u wanna party?

ya where were u?

busy

what were u doing?

Sheesh. Was she going to be nosy and clingy and everything girls detest in a friend? I had a flash of her being a little loony. The image wasn't helped by the fact that I'd seen her deceased relative as her guardian, trying to protect her from herself.

talking 2 someone

O help spread the word, k?

K

it'll b fun

yeah c u 2morrow

The thought of Krissy, mousy, timid Krissy having a party where jocks and partiers would hang like pirates pillaging an innocent town, sent me into an inundated sigh. No way was this dream party of hers ever going to happen. No one knew who she was, for one thing. For another, I couldn't see her putting out booze and opening her absentee-parents' house for kids eager to score a line or a bowl or two. Or tear into the family sheets hooking up.

She had no idea what she was getting into.

I fell back into the fluffy softness of my pillows and fell asleep. My eyes flew open some time later and I was under the covers, the lights off. But something had awakened me, and I lay still, listening. A far off thump. Luke finally dragging himself in? Abria?

My body moaned with fatigue when I got out of the warm toastiness of bed. I pulled on my slippers and quietly crept down the dark hall toward Abria's room. Yep, light gleamed from under the door.

Mom's bedroom door squeaked. I motioned to her that I'd take care of Abria. She yawned, nodded and vanished, shutting the door behind her.

My heart quickened. Maybe Matthias was here.

I opened Abria's door and found her standing on the headboard of her wrought-iron bed, trying to reach the ceiling with yet another black permanent marker. Matthias stood, ready to catch her.

SIXTEEN

Every bit of heaviness in my body vanished, and in its place, thrill pulsed. A smile spilled onto my lips. I shut the door behind me. He turned. His eyes met mine. The corner of his jaw drew into a square and his undeviating gaze didn't blink once.

"Zoe, we need to talk about what happened today."

His calm assurance enveloped me and I understood everything would be fine, but this discussion had to take place and no matter how dreadful it was for me to relive the encounter with Albert, Matthias was there to offer me comfort.

He swung Abria into his arms and she instantly rested her head in the crook of his neck, melding against his chest like a rag doll. Jealousy lit my nerves. I imagined myself in her cradled position.

"I tried not to talk to him. I was stranded. I didn't have a ride. I'm so sorry."

Matthias' hold on Abria tightened. "I'm sorry that he frightened you."

"I've never been more afraid." My voice warbled, the feelings of fear I'd felt in Albert' presence as fresh as if the man stood outside Abria's closed bedroom door, waiting to come in. "What does he want with me?"

A long pause followed. "Me. He wants to destroy me."

I stopped breathing. Anguish tore across Mattias' features. He carried Abria to her bed, laid her down and, with both hands, lightly traced his fingers over her eyes, closing them. He leaned, pressed a gentle kiss on her face, and when he stood up, she was peacefully asleep.

Stunned, I stared at her serene expression reminded of his heavenly powers. Matthias took a deep breath and faced me, the air around us suddenly thick.

He closed his eyes. A rush of his emotions whirled through me like I stood in the midst of a tornado. I tried to grab at them—confusion, hurt, disappointment stayed foremost in my consciousness. His serene face relaxed and his eyes opened again.

"I felt that. I don't feel any anger coming from you at all. None."

He nodded. "We weren't close, my father and I. I wanted us to be, of course. Children always do."

His clear blue eyes draw me into his memories, which open and display like a giant movie screen that I suddenly step into.

I look up into Albert' smiling eyes. I—Matthias—am younger, smaller. A vulnerable child, longing for something, the longing pressing from my insides out so corporeal, the need nearly burst through my skin. Words race through my head: don't leave, please stay here, where are you going? Can I come along? I'm afraid. I don't like being alone.

"I'll only be a little while." Albert and I are in a small room, paneled, dark, one small window up high at street level, iron-grated and locked, and so dirty you can't see out. A desk, cluttered with paper. In the corner, an imposing vault with a door that opens only if you know the combination and place your hands on the massive, steel wheel. A single light bulb dangles from the crumbling ceiling.

"I want you to wait here for me. Stephano, Julius and Martin are working the place but you're not to disturb them. You have your book. Read it. Understand?"

I nod. Sweet perfume fills the air. I turn, see a buttercup yellow dress with flowers, fringe, a veiled floating dream. A dark haired woman leans her face toward me. Her cheeks are pink, her lips red. Pearls swing from her neck. She smiles, grips my chin gently in her fingers and says, "What a sweetie pie."

I gaze at the back of my father's ice-gray suit. He slips his arm around the waist of the buttercup dress and I wonder if the fabric is as soft as it looks. He gets to feel it. I want to. Without a backward glance, he shuts the heavy wood door with a quiet thunk. I stare at it. Beyond the closed door comes the faint sound of laughter, lively music mixed with the occasional shout or woman's hysterical scream. Through the grate-covered alley window at the ceiling of the room, I hear automobiles pass. Honk. A siren.

My fingers wrap tight around the black Bible in my hands.

Lonliness stretched through every part of my body, living Matthias' memory. In my life I'd never been neglected, left with only longing and unanswered questions as company for inordinate amounts of time I couldn't measure because children aren't capable of reasoning neglect. Abuse doesn't have place in a guileless mind. And, though I'd only seen that one memory, it had brought with it the understanding that neglect was a sibling Matthias had lived with.

A veil of sadness fluttered behind Matthias' eyes but the sadness didn't stay long. His chest rose in a deep breath and the corners of his lips lifted slightly.

"I'm sorry," I whispered, his past mourning still throbbing inside of me.

"Zoe, don't think about those things."

"But he hurt you." *And that hurts me.*

Your compassion is one of the qualities I love about you. "Those days are long gone. I don't dwell on the way it was."

My chin lifted. "I'm glad justice was served."

A flash of dark light sparkled in his eyes. He stepped close. "Relishing the consequences of those who make poor choices is wrong, Zoe."

"I'm only saying," I swallowed a lump, "that justice was served. Right?"

"He's still my father. And, hard as it has been for me to see him choose the evil path, I…" He pressed his hand over his heart, eyes glistening. "I hope for more."

Wonder for him swelled in my chest. I couldn't believe he wasn't angry, dwelling on the injustices he experienced in his life. Why did he still care,

➤✤⊰
160

when his father was so far gone—indeed the man, in my opinion anyhow, appeared hopelessly wicked. Lost.

He shook his head. "No one is lost forever. Not while the battle is still going."

"What do you mean? Matthias, the guy reeked of evil. I mean, I wondered when I was with him, why I didn't *feel* like I feel when I'm with you." I took a deep breath. "I'm sorry. It just burns me to think your own father wants to destroy you."

He nodded. "That's the intent of all evil, to make others miserable like they are."

"Misery loves company," I muttered.

"Their pursuit is relentless." He stepped closer, his countenance sober, sending a flash of panic through me. "And my father is one of Satan's leaders."

My body shook. Matthias, seeing the quake rambling through my limbs, instinctively reached out to ease me, but his hands stopped inches from my shoulders. He slowly rescinded, and clasped his hands behind his back. "He's determined get me, and he's going to use you to do that."

"But you're refined." My voice trembled. "If you're refined, how can he still get to you?"

"I still make choices. I chose to inflict my will on those boys, didn't I? My love for you clouded my ability to follow through the way I should have. A choice I now must pay for."

"So, I'm your weakness? Your father…. he's… targeting your weakness?" Shock squeezed my bones.

Matthias nodded. "Know this, Zoe, I'll do everything in my power to protect you. But you are still human."

"And what does that mean? Do you think I'd actually be a ditz and consciously choose to do something wrong?"

"Most mortals don't start out that way, and, no, I don't think you would purposefully choose to follow evil, but you can never underestimate the power of dark spirits. That, Zoe, is a mortal's first mistake."

A cold chill snapped through the comfort which usually engulfed me in Matthias' presence. He was telling me the truth, I couldn't deny it, and understood the gravity to my core.

"I will never follow him, Matthias, please believe me." I'd never felt more sure of anything. Again he reached out as if to take hold of my hands and offer me a comforting caress. Yearning to touch him, I met him halfway, our hands in mid-air between our bodies frozen in unattainable craving.

He brought himself as close to me as he dared, his clothes nearly brushing mine, the scent of his skin reaching out to me in an invisible, cruel lure I couldn't grab hold of to satisfy my escalating desire to touch him with the exception of taking a deep breath.

"Zoe." His gaze brushed my face where his fingers could not, traveling over my cheeks, lips and finally fastening with yearning to my eyes. "I couldn't bear him bringing you down."

"He won't," I whispered. *I'd die before I let him destroy you. I'll guard your soul with all the power inside of me.*

"Even though we can't touch?"

His eyes closed, he nodded.

That will be harder for me to resist than anything your father could throw my way.

For me, too. He opened his eyes and his crystal blue gaze bore into mine. We needed a subject change. "What's the difference between your father and the black spirits I've seen?"

"My father takes on the appearance of having a physical body because he lived. Dark spirits never have, and never will have, a mortal body, a position which leaves them driven to control and influence those who do."

"What do you mean—appearance? Albert looked pretty real to me."

"An illusion."

The air around us pierced with invisible long, greedy fingers jabbing an evil vibe, trying to break the cocoon of serene safety Matthias carried with him.

"Is that… them?" My heart spun in my chest.

"I told you, even talking about evil invites it."

162

"You're scaring me."

"I'm preparing you. This is not some bad dream you're going to wake from. Evil is everywhere and whether you like it or not, you're a part of it. You've always been a part of it. Stealing the souls of men has been Satan's design since Earth's inception." His gaze wandered over to Abria, where it lingered for a moment, then came back to me in sharp focus. "Now that my father has targeted you, you'll have to be even more discerning of every person you meet."

I swallowed a knot. "Forever?"

His hands lifted to my cheeks as if to cup my face. "As long as you're mortal. I'm sorry." Tears rimmed his blue eyes. He turned, and walked to the window, looked out.

I stayed with him. "This isn't your fault."

"If I hadn't come into your life, you wouldn't be facing this."

"You just told me I've always been a part of good and evil, Matthias. Haven't we all?"

"Yes, but I should have kept my heart out of this." He closed his eyes and a tear streaked his cheek. I reached up, instinct, love and need pressing me to comfort him. His eyes shot open and locked on my extended hand. I froze. "I shouldn't have fallen in love with you."

I'm glad you did. Don't regret that, ever. Please.

His lips flickered into a wary smile. "Are you ready to be brave, Zoe?"

For you I can be anything.

"Not for me," his voice was a raw whisper, "for you."

*   *   *

I woke the next morning with a start. My sheets and blankets were in tangles around me, like I'd struggled through sleep one hour at a time. Had I dreamt seeing Matthias the night before? I didn't remember getting in bed. My last memory was of standing in Abria's bedroom, Abria fast asleep, Matthias explaining to me the very real fact that his father was targeting me to destroy him.

163

I let out a moan, shivered and covered myself in downy blankets to combat the chill scraping my bones.

Would I ever *not* be afraid?

Gloomy gray light peered through the shutters of my bedroom. Once again, the sun and its warm beams hid behind a thick wall of winter clouds. Thursday. Two more days of school.

Would Albert be there?

Another icy shudder shook me. I may not have Matthias as my guardian, but he told me he'd be close by because he was watching his father's moves carefully. Maybe I'd see more of him—the one positive I could count on.

My cell phone jumped, the alarm set to wake me at six. I reached over and retrieved it from my night stand and turned it off. Through the night, I'd gotten six texts from Krissy. The girl was obsessed with the party. *I'll read those later.*

I threw back the covers, got up and readied for school. Britt's absence from my life left a social hole I had a hard time adjusting to. Usually, she called or the two of us texted upon waking. She was more than angry at me.

I showered, mulling over whether or not I should tell Chase about Matthias' visit. My nerves prickled. Who could I trust? Who was my friend? Who was my enemy?

This sucked. It wouldn't be so bad if Matthias was my guardian—then I'd know for sure when I was in danger. The way he explained it, I was on my own, for the time being, having to figure out everything for myself.

I dressed in jeans and a gray hoodie, brushed some blush on my cheeks, put on a little shadow and mascara and went out my bedroom door. The house smelled like pancakes.

Luke bumped into me in the hall. He had on his usual baggy jeans and baggier tan hoodie. His eyes weren't bloodshot—a good sight to see.

"Hey bud." I patted him on the back.

He seemed taken aback by the gesture, but allowed me to take the stairs down first, following me.

"Pancakes?" he asked as we both entered the brightly-lit kitchen. Mom smiled over the pan, and flipped four golden cakes. "It's not Saturday," Luke said.

Mom laughed. "So I can only make pancakes on Saturday? Sit down, honey."

Luke seemed thrown off with the weekend-luxury breakfast coming at him on a weekday, but he plopped at the table, ready to eat.

"Sleep okay last night?" Mom slid pancakes on a plate and handed it to Luke, but she was eyeing me.

"Sort of." I'd tried to hide the circles under my eyes with some concealer, but I guess it didn't work. I went to the fridge, opened it and stared.

"How about some pancakes?"

"Yeah, okay."

Mom beamed when she took care of her family, a quality I'd once been embarrassed about until I was old enough to find out from my friends that most of their moms weren't around to do anything more than toss a cup of Ramen at them.

My stomach was in a jumbled mess. Contemplating last night, what to expect today… I wasn't sure I wanted to eat, much less could get anything I shoved down to stay. Mom kept her 'eagle-eye mother's stare' pinned on me, which didn't help.

Luke, oblivious as usual, shoveled in two plates of stacked cakes while I dug at my tower of three like a picky toddler. To appease Mom, I ate half.

A few minutes later Luke stood, took his clean plate to the sink, set it down and belched. He grinned. Then he crossed to Mom, stirring a bowl of cereal for Abria, and he kissed her cheek. Luke looked at me and jerked his mop of blonde hair in the direction of the front door indicating it was time to go.

He swung his backpack over his shoulder and disappeared down the hall.

Mom's mouth fell open sometime after Luke kissed her cheek, and now her hand was poised at the spot in shock. I smiled, rose and took my plate to the counter. Then I kissed her other cheek.

"The pancakes were great." I savored the joy on her face, waved goodbye to Abria, standing on her chair at the table, and went out the door with my backpack.

"Nice one," I said getting in Luke's car. I shut the door and buckled up.

"Nice what?" He was predictably clueless as he pulled onto the street.

"Kissing Mom? You made her week."

His cherub cheeks reddened. "She made me pancakes."

Something brash screamed from the CD player. I wanted to turn it off, my nerves already raw like they'd been scraped through a grater. I leaned over to flick the switch but Luke stopped me.

"Hey, I like this song."

Arguing over a song for the three minute drive to school was stupid, so I sucked it up and shut up, allowing him his enjoyment.

At school, he parked and we headed up the drag toward the buildings, streaming with other students girding up their psyches for another day of education. My stomach bunched. Would Albert show up?

"You left me yesterday."

"Oh. Yeah. Sorry. Business."

I snorted. "Business? Don't think I want to know how you make your money."

He and I herded through the door, my nose filled with the mixed smells of freshly showered skin, shampoo and cologne. We shared a smile before he went his way and I went mine. My gaze swept the halls for Albert but I didn't see him.

SEVENTEEN

I saw Britt in history. She sat next to me, but since she'd been absent for a day, I hadn't felt the discomfort I now felt seeing her. Facing her. I lifted my chin and returned the brick exterior I felt coming from her. I hadn't done anything wrong, didn't deserve her attitude and wasn't going to take it.

Class started and my phone vibrated. Britt. I glanced over. She had her phone under the desk and her thumb was busily tapping the keyboard.

u r just going 2 ignore me?

u r ignoring me

u stole weston i think i have a rite

i didn't steal anyone

whatever

She kept tapping her nails on her phone, but I didn't get anymore texts so I put my phone away and listened to the lecture. So this was how it was going to be?

Tired from being up late the night before and feeling the weight of living on the edge of a black, bottomless canyon, I laid my head down on my desk, closed my eyes and everything in my mind vanished into a swirling memory of Matthias.' His neglected past.

The bell shrilled, chairs screeched and I jerked upright, startled. Had I slept? The hour was gone, so was Britt and most of my classmates. I stood, hoping the teacher hadn't noticed me dozing in class. His back was turned as he wrote on the blackboard, so I scurried out.

Krissy was next to my locker, waiting for me. Today, she had her hair down. I'd never seen it in anything other than a ponytail. I was surprised that it went past her shoulders, was thick and had a nice sheen. The style changed flattered her. She wore a sheepish expression on her usually eager face as she watched other talking, chatting teens pass by without notice. My heart stung for her. The party she wanted to have was in one day. Who would go?

For her sake, I hoped no one. Sweet, naive Krissy shouldn't be within five states of a party, not unless it was a birthday party with clowns, balloons and pizza. Her gaze found mine and she grinned, squeezing her books tight to her chest.

"Hey." I whirled the dial on my locker. "I like your hair down. Looks nice."

"Thanks. I'm so excited about Saturday night. Have you told anyone about it?"

"Um. Not yet. You?"

"A few people. I actually made little invitations, wanna see them?" Her fingers trembled as she pulled out a hand decorated Post-It with Please Come to the Party! in hot pink and bright yellow. Daisies lined the paper. Her address and name were scrolled on the bottom. I gulped.

"Wow," I said.

"You want some to give out?" She produced a giant stack of the ready-made Post-It invites just for me.

"No, I'm good thanks. I prefer word of mouth. In fact, that's kinda the way these things are spread."

Her jubilant expression faltered. "Oh. So I shouldn't hand them out?"

"How many have you given away?" What kind of damage control needed to be done? I exchanged books and shut my locker.

She followed me through the packed hall. I felt the curious stares of passers by and wondered how long it would take for word to spread that I was hanging with Krissy ...I-didn't-even-know-her-last-name. I wasn't worried about my reputation; I'd handled worse in junior high (labeled loser) and even here at Pleasant Grove High School being known as everything from slut to popular. There was the real possibility Krissy would be judged as okay simply by being seen with me.

Krissy noticed the stares, too, because she glowed like she had at the Purple Turtle the day she'd gone to lunch with Weston and me.

"I've given out about… ten." Her eyes rounded innocently, as if she was waiting for me to laugh at her social blunder.

"Oh. Okay, well, no need to hand out any more, I think. They're cute and all, but let's stick to word of mouth, 'kay?"

She nodded, accepting my instructions as if they were commandments. Then her eyes lit and held across the hall. I followed her drooling stare to Weston at the door of a classroom. He stood with Brady.

Please tell me the two of them aren't pals again. I smiled genially at Weston, ignored Brady, then faced Krissy. "I've got to get to class."

Without tearing her gaze from Weston she nodded. My cell phone buzzed in my hand. Weston.

hey u ok?

Yeah

im not hanging with brady if u r wondering

not wondering

What he did with Brady was his business, right? But if I heard the two of them were buds again, I'd keep far away from them both, and I'd make sure neither went to Krissy's party.

I looked up. Krissy was gone. She'd crossed the hall and now stood at the door of the classroom with Weston and Brady. If she was inviting them to her party, she was gutsier than I gave her credit for.

I headed to my next class, and my phone vibrated. Weston. I grinned.

krissy + party = WTF?

lol I know

she's really doing it?

guess so.

u going?

≫ ✢ ≪

yeah u?

if u r, yeah

"You're texting him now?" Britt's voice cut through my concentration. I dropped the smile on my face.

"You're reading my texts over my shoulder *now*?" I held my phone so she couldn't see the screen and I kept walking. She hung by my side. From all appearances, we were friends again. I had to admit, the comfort of familiarity swamped me: her perfume, the easy way she walked in stride next to me, all things I'd grown used to over the years we'd been friends.

"I am when my best friend sabotages my boyfriend."

I stopped. She did too. Bodies filed around us, quieting, staring as they slowly passed.

Britt was hammered: circles under her eyes, skin sallow, hair messy. What was with the torn jeans and shabby shirt? Britt never left the house unless she looked perfect.

"I didn't do anything purposefully, Britt," I tried the compassion I felt it in my heart for her.

"What's this party you two are having?"

"We're not having it. Krissy—a girl in one of my classes—is throwing it."

"The chick with the jumper and boots?"

I nodded, hoping she would laugh, hug me and put all this nonsense behind us where it belonged. She gazed down the hall to the classroom where Weston had stood with Brady and Krissy—all of whom were gone now.

"She likes him, doesn't she?"

I blew out a sigh. "Yeah. But she's—"

"She's a dog," Britt snapped, her bloodshot eyes locking on mine again. She scrubbed a hand down her face. Her white-tipped nails chipped and neglected, like everything else in her life I guessed.

"She's not you," I said. "Britt, why do you worry about girls like her? She's really shy and definitely not Weston's type."

Her glazed eyes sharpened. "It's you he wants." The tardy bell's high pitch sheered my ears. We both stood staring at each other.

"I'm not after Weston," I said through teeth. "I've told you a thousand times. Now, I've said it a thousand and one times." I took off for class, infuriated she was beheading me for something I wasn't guilty of.

"I'm going to that party." Her threat echoed through the hall. "I'm going!"

* * *

In newspaper class, I stared at my computer screen like a zombie, the white page with writing in front of me annihilating my brain with boredom. I was supposed to edit this article on the brand new football field that had just gone in this past summer. YAWN.

Who cared that the painted royal blue grass had actually lasted through the season? What did that prove but an über paint job? Either that or our team didn't do much tearing up and winning. I couldn't remember how the Vikings had scored this season.

I couldn't do this. "Chase!"

Chase was glued to his computer but jumped to his feet when I called, and strode over.

He put one hand on the back of my chair, the other on the desk, boxing me in. Spicy sweet cologne swirled in my head. "Yeah?"

"I can't do this. I told you, sports and me… that's like drinking a Rockstar while trying to sleep. Can't be done."

Chase's discerning gaze traveled over me. He pulled a metal chair next to me and plunked down. "You're not happy today. What happened?"

"Are my moods that obvious?"

"Circles under your eyes, a listless, bored expression on your face. Signs, Zoe."

"Could it be this yawnsville copy you assigned me to edit?"

He reached over and clicked on the mouse, minimizing the offending article. Then his brown eyes fastened to mine in a piercing gaze that rivaled

Matthias'. "You want to talk about it?"

"Oh. Sure. So the paint stayed on the Astroturf through all ten home games. WOW." I faked a yawn and grinned.

The right corner of his lip lifted. "So the article's a parochial approach to reporting. We're dealing with beginning, inexperienced writers on staff. What's really bugging you?"

"I'm just tired." I leaned close to him, indicating I had something private to share and he mirrored me. "The freakiest thing happened," I whispered. I told him about Albert. About how I'd assumed he was my new guardian, sent by Matthias—and what had happened out at the marquee. Through the unfolding story, Chase's face paled.

He swallowed. "That's... I don't know what to say."

"Yeah, well, it was about the scariest thing I've ever had happen to me. The worst part, was how convinced I was—for a while—that Albert was... a good guy. I mean, he looks so much like Matthias. It's... Chase, the whole thing was worse than a nightmare. I wasn't in control of my soul. Albert... he..." I shuddered.

Chase laid his hand on my arm. "Don't talk about it. You might invite the dude back."

As if chilled to the bone, my body continued to convulse. Chase set both of his hands on my arms and, finally, the torrent of shudders left me. I blew out a breath.

Chase's hands slipped away. "Zoe, this is huge. This Albert dude is... he takes this to a whole other level."

"Do you mind? I'm trying to calm down here."

"Oh. Yeah. Right. Is that all that's bothering you?"

"And I'm a little worried about Krissy's party."

"Krissy. Oh, yeah. She gave me one of these." He pulled a Post-It invite Krissy had decorated from the front pocket of his khakis and held it up. "She told me you said I should have one. Did you really say that?"

"In a roundabout way. You should go, Chase. I'm worried no one will show up."

"I had to admit, when she told me the two of you were throwing a party, and that Weston was going, I thought she was joking. I didn't even know you two were friends."

"I'm not throwing the party, Krissy is. And I saw her guardian. So, I kind of feel responsible for her."

"Now I get it. Yeah, I'll go to her party."

"I figured you would." I laid my hand on his knee for a second. His Adams apple bobbed and I slid my hand back to my lap. "I don't know what she's got planned. I mean, the parties I've gone to are pretty raw. I'm not sure she knows what she's getting into."

"You, me and Weston can make sure everything stays above board."

Why was I discussing this with Chase? Like he knew about parties. But he radiated excitement. "Yeah, we can. Hey, you're such a nice guy, maybe you can, you know, hang with her a little before Saturday."

A deep crease formed between his brows. "Like... how?"

"I know you don't like her like *that*, but, you can be friendly, right? So that when you show up Saturday, she knows more than just me and Weston."

His face relaxed. "Oh, sure. Okay. Do you think I should tell people about the party?"

Chase's friends were harmless. "Definitely." There was a slim chance Krissy's party wouldn't be a disaster after all.

Chase looked at the screen of my computer. He reached over, his arm brushing mine, clicked on the mouse and the article popped up again. He stood. "You gonna be okay?"

I nodded. "Thanks."

"Then get back to work." He wagged his brows at me. I swear there was a cocky spring in his walk when he strolled back to his desk.

My cell phone vibrated. I pulled it out, anything to avoid the inevitable of facing the editing job. Weston.

can i give u a ride home?

A flock of birds let loose in my stomach. I tapped the phone with my fingernail, gnawing on my bottom lip. I needed a ride, Luke wasn't one-hundred percent reliable, and Britt was off Weston's to-do list, so… why not?

sure

k cya

I took a deep breath. The flock of birds spread from my stomach through my arms, legs, to my toes, and circled around my heart. I checked the clock on my phone: thirty minutes to finish editing. Thirty minutes until I saw Weston. I shouldn't be this excited about a ride home.

EIGHTEEN

Weston stood by his truck, arms tucked across his chest, legs casually crossed at the ankles as he leaned his tight frame against the door. He was alone. His gaze locked on me across the parking lot. Wow. He must have 20/20 vision with that hawk-stare.

I swallowed a nervous clutch in my throat and continued toward him, keeping a distracted eye out for cars backing out of parking places and other students making their way to waiting autos.

Where were his guy friends? The packs of girls usually loitering in his aura trying to catch his eye, his scent, desperate for his attention? Where was Britt? With that thought, I glanced around the thinning parking lot but didn't see her white Mustang.

I continued toward Weston, my palms sweatier with each step, my heart fluttering.

He smiled and came away from the truck, his arms falling to his side. "Hey."

"Hey."

Awkward silence. Horns peeping, voices calling out. Random CD tunes blaring.

Weston stuffed his hands in his front pockets. "So…"

"Yeah…"

Weston laughed. His smile spread across his strong cheeks in a contagious expression of awkwardness that I caught and savored with a smile of my own. "Okay." He shrugged his shoulders and his right foot toed the asphalt.

"Okay," I teased. "You're not nervous are you?"

His brown eyes sparkled. "Not at all." But his hands remained anchored in his pockets and his toe kept digging at the ground. *Cute.*

He stepped close towering over me with his broad shoulders, faded cologne and maleness. My heart pattered against my ribs. Weston held me in a hot stare both curious and exciting. If he wanted to play, I could play. In fact, it had been a while since I'd played with a guy and pleasure dripped through my body, catching in a refractive pool low in my stomach.

Finally, his dark eyes narrowed.

I tilted my head. "You ready to drive me home?"

"Yeah, I'm ready." He grinned. Suddenly, his warm hands slipped around my waist and his body skimmed mine. His fingers gripped me, and my heart pummeled in all directions. Then he turned me around, his hand at the small of my back as he escorted me around the bed of his truck and to the passenger door.

He opened the door. I didn't dare look him in the eye. I was sure my skin was flushed with red heat from face to knees. I climbed in and he paused.

Then he shut the door.

I blew out a breath.

Weston got in and the truck rocked with his presence: muscles, scent and heat. I swallowed. Low in my body a whirring desire I recognized swam with the frenzy of sharks readying to be fed.

I bit my lower lip.

We drove in silence. I was so overcome with Weston's flesh and bone, the very humanness of him in the cab, reminding me of how I'd fallen asleep in his arms, that I was sure I'd have tripped on my thickening tongue if he tried to carry on a conversation. I was embarrassed by my reaction.

Whispering through my mind were frenzied memories of kisses, heat, touching.

Weston drove with one hand on the wheel. Did he sense ripe desire in the air? He kept glancing over, the sparkle in his eyes growing more intense, joining the rhythm of my heart. *Don't drive me home. Pull over. Stop the car and let me kiss you.*

But Weston couldn't read my thoughts. Thankfully.

He wasn't Matthias.

The thought of Matthias poked a hole in my building desire for Weston. I turned and forced my gaze out the window. When I thought of Matthias, my body flooded with so much love, the pure nature of that love suffocated lust.

Could I want Matthias with the raw desire I had for Weston?

Ab-so-lute-ly. I grinned. One of Matthias' words.

But would I if I could? I had such respect for Matthias, such admiration, and the love in my soul was founded on his spirit, not on flesh.

Could I love Weston the way I loved Matthias?

It was too early to tell. I was still walking the thin ice of trust. But on a purely physical level, there was no doubt that Weston made my flesh sing.

Weston's gentle finger touched the vein on my neck. I shivered. "You okay?"

I closed my eyes. *I'm hungry. Starved. I want companionship.* "Yeah," I rasped. So what if Weston knew I wanted him. That's what he wanted, wasn't it? And there was nothing wrong with one human wanting another.

The sharpness in his eyes confirmed my suspicion. He yanked the car to the curb. My heart danced. He slid over, his hand reaching behind my neck, his body moved to mine, unable to deny the magnetic draw we had to each other.

His gaze devoured my face for two, five, seven seconds. Then he kissed me. Gentle. Tentative. Then more urgent. I wrapped my arms around his neck, melting from the feel of his chest fused to mine.

He leaned me gently against the door, his right palm cradling my head, his fingers in my hair. Kneading. *Needing.* To be wanted. To have and be had. Exhilaration soared through my body, zinging every nerve and fiber into a lively dance celebrating the fusion of male and female.

I needed a breath, to slow down. I turned my head, gasping. He pressed his forehead to my cheek, panting, his hot breath tickling my neck.

"Zoe," his voice shook.

I swallowed. Could he feel my heart leaping his direction?

"Yeah?"

"You're…" His warm mouth grazed my ear, down my jaw, leaving hot tracks. "I've wanted to do that…"

The next kiss was tender. Soft. Like he was kissing a petal. Then he eased back, his face in a fist of desire unable to fully let go. "Are you okay?"

I nodded, glad we stopped.

"I…" He sat upright, and fell against the back of his seat, thrusting his hands into his hair. "I shouldn't have done that." His palm hit the steering wheel with a thud.

"What? You're sorry?"

"Did I screw things up?" Fear colored his eyes. "Did I? Tell me the truth. You hate me now, right? I'm such an idiot." He scrubbed his hands down his face, groaned. "I'm sorry."

I grabbed his hands in mine, locking us together. "Don't. I…wanted you to."

His chest lifted, fell, lifted in rapid succession. He looked at our joined hands. Then his sober gaze met mine. "Are you sure? Because I'd never want you to hate me. I couldn't take it."

"I don't hate you."

He sighed, seemingly relieved, and closed his eyes. "Impulsiveness is one of my weaknesses."

"It can also be a strength." I tried to lighten the mood. "I mean, impulsiveness is what drives you to pass the ball when you've only got a split second to decide, right? That's a good thing."

He grinned. "You've watched me play?"

"I've gone to my share of games."

"But not for the game, for the guys, right?"

178

I lifted a shoulder. "I'll admit I like a guy in a football uniform."

"It's cool that you're honest. I'm sick of girls who say what they think I want to hear. They have no idea how boring that is. And most of the time, I don't want to hear it. It's all a game, anyway."

"Yeah, well, we've all been guilty of playing."

He looked at our joined hands and ran his thumbs over my knuckles. "See? I could never have this conversation with Britt. Or anyone else for that matter."

"I haven't always been this honest."

Weston's fingers pushed back a stray strand of hair hanging aside my face. "I hope you know that you can trust me."

I was still making sure of that. But how can you ever be ab-so-lute-ly positive? Again, Matthias' face flashed into my mind. I withdrew my hands from Weston's, his eyes shading with disappointment when I did. Somehow, I felt untrue to Matthias. I couldn't deny the feeling of infidelity. *That's ridiculous, Zoe. You can't be unfaithful to someone you don't belong to.* True as that reality was, my heart belonged to him, bonded by experiences more profound and long lasting than an evaporating kiss.

"Something's wrong," Weston whispered, his examination of me growing more concentrated.

I shook my head.

"I see it in your face. I turned you off, didn't I?"

"No." I took one of his hands again. "No, you didn't. I'm thinking about something else, that's all."

"What? Whenever I get close to you, I see this...I can't describe it. You get this look on your face. Like looking at me reminds you of that night."

"That's not it, Weston. I've put that behind me. Seriously." I tugged his hand, hoped he saw that I was telling him the truth. I was amazed that he saw subtle changes in me.

"Then what is it?" He inched closer, as if need pressed from his insides out. "Every time I get close to you, it happens."

I sighed. "I can't share that with you, I'm sorry. Just know that it has

179

nothing to do with you and what happened that night. It's someone else."

A flash of male suspicion passed over his face. *Uh-oh.*

My cell phone vibrated, and in an effort to divert the focus of the moment from me and the mystery surrounding my changing emotions, I plucked it out of my pocket. Luke.

where r u? im waiting

Oops. **got a ride bud sorry i didn't let you know thx**

I met Weston's now-cool gaze. "My brother. He was supposed to give me a ride home."

Weston didn't react, he just studied me. I slipped my phone back in my pocket and met his scrutinizing straight on. What did he expect? We weren't a couple. We'd kissed, and the kiss had been one of the hottest of my life. I'd be honest with him, but details about Matthias were something I wouldn't share unless I knew with surety that Weston was trustworthy and believed.

The air in the car bubbled with a mix of curiosity, jealousy, suspicion and my refusal to say anything more on the subject.

Finally, Weston shifted, started the car and we drove in silence the remaining two blocks to my house. When we arrived, he parked next to the curb, stared out the front window and didn't look at me.

Oh brother. I reached for the door handle. Suddenly, I heard a rustle of fabric, felt the truck rock and his nearness stopped me.

"Hey." His voice was low, troubled and once again anguish crimped his face. "If you can be honest, I can be, right?"

I paused, wondering what he was going to say next, then nodded.

"I don't know where you go…in your head…when you think about whoever it is you're thinking about. I'm going to try not to let it bug me. But you're in my head now, Zoe. You're where I go."

A lump in my throat blocked me from replying. His declaration didn't scare me, in fact thrill pushed its way through the last scraps of doubt I still carried.

"Can I take you to the party Saturday?" he asked.

* * *

My parents weren't happy I was going to the party. Dad was especially reticent because I'd fallen down, not telling them my whereabouts. But I understood their concerns about their children better now. Love, not control, drove them to want to know where we were and what we were doing.

I reassured them that Krissy was a nice girl and that if the party even started looking like it was going over the top, I'd leave. I think they were a little relieved when I told them Weston was going with me.

I was relieved Weston was going with me. Since Krissy had boldly announced that she was throwing a party, a lead ball of uncertainty had lodged in my gut. She said she was taking care of everything. Did she know what that meant? The kind of party she wanted to have versus the kind of party I figured was going to take place were polar opposites.

Chase texted me ten times, his enthusiasm for the event like a kid readying for his first trip to Disneyland. He even asked me what to wear. I told him to wear what he usually wore but to ditch the cable knit sweater.

With the Weston and Chase at the party, at least Krissy would have a small showing. Weston's attendance alone meant a social score, even if no one else was there to see it.

Saturday, I searched my closet for something comfortable but hot. Normally, I wore jeans and a tight shirt, maybe a jacket or hoodie to top off the outfit. Weston being there changed that. I wanted to wear something nicer.

I chose a flirty skirt in red and black flowers, a black slim hoodie and red flats. I wore my hair up in a fluffy knot at the back of my head and brushed on enough blush so I wouldn't look too pale in the dark.

My phone vibrated on my dresser and I retrieved it.

im out front

Weston. My palms began to sweat. I heard the far off ding of our doorbell, Abria laughing and running and Mom chasing after her. I envisioned

Abria racing to the door—she liked to peer out the sidelights at whoever was outside.

The timbre of Weston's voice downstairs amped the sweat drenching my palms. One spray of perfume and I went to greet him.

He radiated hotness in the royal blue Vikings hoodie, white tee shirt and jeans. Weston didn't wear his jeans baggy and I liked that. I appreciated a guy who knew how to wear clothes that hinted. His smile gleamed against his smooth skin.

Mom hoisted Abria on her hip and stood very mother-like at the door, waiting for me to join them.

"Hey," Weston said.

"Hey." I took Abria's baby doll hand in mine and squeezed her fleshy palm goodbye. "Bye Abria. Say bye Zoe."

Abria wiggled and squirmed for freedom. Mom's grip tightened. "Abria, say goodbye to Zoe." Mom's tone held the usual authority needed to get Abria to do something.

Abria's gaze passed over me for a half second and she grunted, arching her back in hopes of diving to freedom. Mom laughed.

"Weston, nice to meet you. I'm going to take this little monkey and put her in the bath."

Weston gave Mom a gracious nod, patted Abria on the arm and we watched Mom carry Abria upstairs.

Taco seasoning filled the air. Chatter from CNN drifted in from the family room where Dad watched TV. My gaze locked on Weston, to find he was already staring at me.

"You look amazing," he murmured.

"Thanks."

He opened the front door and when I passed him, I was submerged in his exotic cologne—a tangled scent of sensuality and sweetness. I felt the gentle pressure of his hand at my back all the way to his idling truck.

The cab was warm inside, filled with a lulling rock beat that poured from surrounding speakers and pulsed into my body. *Uh-oh*. I'd been seduced before, I recognized the velvet carpet when it was unrolled at my feet—lush and soft.

Weston shut the door, his brown eyes on mine. Seconds oozed into minutes. He was incredibly hot looking, the royal blue of his hoodie, his sable hair, white teeth and eager eyes. He sat with one wrist poised on the steering wheel, his other hand between us on the seat. I had the sudden urge to touch him and see what my touch did. Would he kiss me?

How long was he going to shoot that poster-boy look at me? I'd be a melted mess before we got to the party. "Better drive, or..." I stopped myself from saying 'kiss me.' But I sent him a teasing grin.

"Or?"

"Why are you staring at me?"

"I still can't believe I'm with you."

"Yeah, it goes both ways."

"No." He shook his head. "There's a difference." He slowly leaned toward me, and placed a tentative kiss on my lips, as if kissing me would prove that the moment was real.

My heart spun. This was real, all right. I almost suggested we ditch Krissy's party, find a dead end street somewhere and fog the windows. The grin spreading his lips wide made me wonder if he'd read my thoughts.

He put the car in gear and drove. "Have you ever been to Krissy's?"

"Never have."

He handed me his cell phone, screen lit up with a text from Krissy with her address. "Read me her address when we get closer, will you? I'm terrible with remembering numbers and stuff."

"Sure."

When we pulled up to Krissy's round, wood house, Weston stopped the car with a jerk. We stared at the igloo-shaped building. "This is Krissy's place?" Weston muttered.

Everyone in town knew about the 'round house.' I just never knew the odd-shaped place belonged to Krissy.

"It kind of fits, don't you think?" I said. "She's a different girl, after all."

"Yeah, but…I heard some hermit-dude built it thirty years ago and never came out."

I snorted. "And I heard it belonged to the guy who invented the wearable dog house. Come on, it can't be that bad."

Weston looked around at the empty street. "Yeah it can. No one's here."

"Crap." My gaze swept the street. Unless this had turned into a surprise party, Weston was right. "Should we call some people?" I whipped out my cell phone.

Weston did the same. "Man. I hate doing this." His brown eyes lifted from the keypad and met mine. A long pause drew our concerns for Krissy—and the party—out into the air.

"I know," I finally said. "What should we do? I mean, she wants this, but we can't force anyone to show up. Did you tell anybody about it?"

He took a deep breath and averted his gaze in an adorable gesture of denial. "I didn't know what to say. I don't hang with my old friends anymore."

I smiled. Suddenly, a handful of cars came zipping up the street. Weston sat up.

"Chase. Thankfully."

"Are those friends of his?" Weston craned his neck.

"I don't know."

Chase pulled his car nose-to-nose with Weston's truck and parked. He waved enthusiastically from the front seat. His engine clicked off, he checked his reflection in the rearview mirror and jumped out. Over his shoulder, he waved at the four cars that had followed, parked and whose owners now hopped—with the same enthusiasm as Chase—from their cars.

"I know those guys," Weston murmured. "I've seen them around school."

I had too. Chase ambled over, his grin huge. Weston and I got out of the car and met him at the front of Weston's truck.

"Hey, guys!" Chase bubbled. I kept my grin in check.

Weston nodded. "Hey."

"You guys… came together?" Chase pointed from me to Weston, his

184

grin floundering like a popped birthday balloon.

Weston's shoulder brushed mine. "Yeah. You cool with that?"

Chase's eyes rounded behind his glasses. Weston was clearly making his move for me public. I bit my lower lip. Hard as it was watching Chase's puppy dog face slowly understand and accept what he saw, a breath of relief snuck over me and mixed with the smallest thrill.

Chase's friends slowly made their way over, hesitant because none of us were chummy. Chase shifted, disappointment shadowing his eyes as he looked at me. "Well. Okay, I guess." He cleared his throat and turned toward his friends, all dressed like they were on their way to a church dance. "Guys, this is Weston and... Zoe." A lonely echo sprang off the way he said my name, pinching my heart.

The four clean-cut, starched-shirts and dress pants-dressed guys nodded. One even shook Weston's hand.

"Chase, why don't you guys head inside? We'll be right behind you," Weston suggested.

Chase hemmed a moment, his gaze volleying from me to Weston. Then he jerked his head in the direction of Krissy's round house and the group of them crossed the snow-covered lawn toward the front door.

Weston stared into my eyes. "Was that okay with you?"

"What?" But I knew. We both smiled.

"Come on." He reached up and his finger grazed my chin. My body buzzed.

"You know what I'm talking about, Zoe. You're a smart girl. That's one of the things I like about you."

"It sounded to me like you were telling Chase that we were here together."

"I was. So, you're okay with that?"

"Yeah, I'm okay with that."

A loud bass beat came barreling down the street, the sound pulsing from Britt's white Mustang. Instinctively, I took a step away from Weston.

"*She's* coming?" Weston's question tweaked with disbelief.

185

I swallowed a nervous knot in my throat. Behind her, a stream of cars followed. Weston paced, shoving his hands into his hair. "This sucks."

"Leave it to Britt," I mumbled.

I knew the cars—and their drivers— I'd seen them hundreds of times at hundreds of different parties over the years. Soon, the street was clogged with horn-honking, bass pounding automobiles squirming like worms in the dirt for a parking place. Brady's black compact tore through the street, onto Krissy's front yard.

He jumped out of the car and five guys from the football team poured onto the lawn and into the snow.

My heart pounded. Black spirits clung to Brady and his buddies, riding their backs like soulless phantoms in a silent celebration of impending trouble. A flood of icy shivers raced through my system, freezing me in place.

This changed everything. I had to go in now, warn Chase and Krissy— do something to protect my friends from this onslaught.

Brady stared defiantly at us, and waited for Britt who parked her Mustang behind his car. She strode in her spiked heels, tight jeans and skin-tight sheer blouse with black push-up bra bursting through the fabric in invitation. Two evil figures floated in continuous circles around her, like vapors of pollution ready to smother.

Britt joined the pack of guys and Brady's eyes narrowed at Weston. He slid an arm about Britt and crushed her into his side. Britt played at fighting him off, writhing with practiced moves I'd seen before, moves that looked more like she was teasing Brady into an aroused frenzy than actual hostility.

Around the pack buzzed anxious, jittery black spirits—like banshees at a human sacrifice—their mouths gaping in soundless screams, arms caressing, winding, taunting in a continual stimulation.

Weston let out a snort of disgust and moved closer to me. I tried to feel comforted. Safe. But that was impossible, standing this close to such a malevolent display.

"We shouldn't stay," I said. Weston glanced from me, to Brady, back to me. I swallowed. Unlike Weston's party, where I'd witnessed other guardians outside the house, waiting to help, I saw none tonight. Not even Krissy's. I realized then that Matthias' words were true: when someone chooses to step in dangerous territory, they give up the protection of heavenly hosts.

"I'm not letting Brady think he can get to me."

"It's not about him," I said.

Weston's jaw twitched. "And it's not about Britt."

"She's just trying to make you jealous."

His face contorted, as if looking any longer at Britt would make him heave. He averted his gaze, shame closing his eyes for a long moment. I touched his sleeve. "You okay?" I asked.

His eyes opened and he nodded.

Britt's glare shot like a beam of fire across the yard at me when I touched Weston. She tore free of Brady and stormed over.

Weston moved in front of me, his arms braced protectively behind around my body. My chest pressed into the strong planes of his tense back. I appreciated the shielding gesture, but Britt was not going to get to me, either. I eased out of his backwards embrace and stood at his side. He kept his stance rigid, as if ready to pounce.

Brady snagged Britt and stopped her. Around them, black spirits spun in a frenzy of flapping arms and gnashing teeth. A jag of fear shot through me.

"I'm here to party," Britt spat. "Not watch my loser boyfriend hook up with the biggest slut I know."

My mouth dropped. I lunged, but Weston's arms linked me tight to his immobile frame. "It's not worth it," he whispered into my ear.

He was right. Anger furled from my feet, up my legs, through my cells. The black spirits celebrating on Britt and Brady shot black stares my direction, pinning me, as if at any moment, they would leap through the air and latch themselves on me. I broke free of Weston, straightened my clothes. Britt tossed a chunk of blonde hair over her shoulder, glared, then linked her arm in Brady's and the lot of them went inside.

I blew out steam.

Weston cupped my face and my eyes locked with his. Anger began to subside. "You wanna bail?"

"No. I can't leave Krissy and Chase here with that psycho on the loose." Someone needed to make sure things didn't get out of hand.

That shouldn't be you, Zoe.

I whirled around. Matthias.

NINETEEN

He stood ten feet away, his aura jagged with electric power that snapped and sizzled bolts of energy so powerful, I was sure Weston and I would disintegrate instantly. His body was tense, hands fisted, skin tight across his beautiful face. The blue in his eyes beamed bright.

"Zoe?" Weston asked, seeing my stare into what was, from his point of view, empty air.

"Um, could you go inside and wait for me? I—I need a minute."

"Are you okay? What happened?" Weston's tone held panic. He moved into my line of vision, blocking Matthias. At that moment, a bone-breaking punch jolted the tight energy in the air. I shook from head to toe.

"Zoe?" Weston put his hands on my shoulders.

I tried to focus on him, but the aura from Matthias was so overwhelming, reaching out to me, reaching out *for* me that my body weakened, insignificant and very mortal. I clasped Weston's wrists and held on.

Whatever this energy was coming from Matthias, it was stronger than anything else I'd felt. *What are you doing?*

Don't go in that house, Zoe. Please.

"Weston?" I whispered.

"Yes? What? What? Tell me."

"Can… you… go… inside and wait for me?"

"I don't want to leave you like this. Something's wrong."

189

"No, I'm good. I just need a second alone. Promise."

His dark eyes searched mine. I nodded and he released me, slowly crossing to the house before going inside.

When I faced Matthias again, he was inches from me, his aura submerging. I nearly collapsed. I sucked in air and was filled with calm, soothing light, as if he'd pressed his lips to mine and breathed into my soul. My eyes closed and for a moment I was back in Paradise with Matthias in peaceful serenity.

My father is in there. He will try to destroy you if you go inside.

But my friends, I have to help them.

You're no match for the hosts he has with him. Please do not go inside.

Take me with you, Matthias. I want to be with you. Can't you just take me?

In that instant, my eyes opened. I was in Krissy's front yard. Matthias was still close, and I was sure I really hadn't gone anywhere, just imagined the dream.

"I can't take you from your life." His gentle eyes soothed my disappointment. He reached out to touch me, but withdrew his hand.

"I can do this," I said, determined. *I can't have you, I can't have the life I want with you, so I'm going to live the life in front of me, and right now, that means Weston, and saving my friends here at this party.*

He took a deep breath, his chest rising beneath his downy white shirt.

"Matthias, people face evil every day. And you're not my guardian anymore, so I have to face this and not let it get to me. You told me to be brave, remember?"

He nodded, his face sober. "It's dangerous."

"Yes. I know. But I have Weston."

Sparks lit the air around us, startling me. Matthias' face, though serene, drew taut in what appeared to be displeasure. I was stunned. "Am I safe with Weston?"

He held my gaze without a blink. Seconds ticked by. Neither of us moved. *He can't protect you from evil.*

Are you angry that I'm with him?

The slightest twitch in his jaw was the only change in his demeanor. "Not angry, Zoe."

Then what is this I feel coming from you? It...it's not like anything I've felt from you before.

He dipped his head, closed his eyes, then brought his sparkling blue gaze to mine. *As a companion, you'll be safe with him. But the house is fraught with black spirits. It's not safe for either of you inside.*

I let out a breath. "I understand. But... Krissy. Chase. I have to at least go inside and tell them to come out... or... send everybody home. Something. Chase will listen, he listens to me. He'll believe what I tell him."

Matthias' blue eyes shifted to over my shoulder, and his kind expression squared enough to alert me. Arms slipped around my waist and locked. Warm breath tickled my neck. Weston.

"Hey. You coming in?"

I cleared my throat. "Yeah."

Matthias' aura danced in bright colors, as if his soul had no other way to show his angst-ridden feelings other than the silent, brilliant, unrequited display.

My heart tore. *I'm sorry.*

He shook his head and turned his face, as if seeing me in Weston's arms was excruciatingly painful.

Weston kissed my neck, and another bolt of fiery light sprung from Matthias into the black night sky. I turned, gripped the front of Weston's hoodie and dragged him toward the door. I couldn't put Matthias through this.

Weston chuckled. "Okay, okay, I'm coming. It's not really that bad in there. Krissy's got some decent CDs and somebody bought a ton of booze."

I came to a halt on the porch and looked him in the eye, still gripping the front of his hoodie with both hands. "Promise me you won't drink tonight."

"Not at all?"

"Not one drop. Promise."

Confusion flashed on his face. He shrugged. "Okay."

I glanced at Matthias, standing where I'd left him, his face tattered. Around him, light sparked and bolted in the colors of an angry rainbow. My heart ripped deeper. *I'm sorry*. Matthias shoved his fists in the front pockets of his slacks. I looked at Weston. "And promise me you won't leave me tonight."

He grinned. "Done."

Inside, the house smelled like cinnamon. Krissy had lit dozens of candles, and no other lights burned. A nice if overt touch. Music pounded from somewhere. About two dozen kids roamed, eyes darting in hunt-mode, red plastic cups in their hands. Weston shut the door behind us. The shudder wracking my spine vanished with the pressure from his hand at my back.

I glanced up at him and he grinned.

Britt cackled from somewhere in the house. Weston let out a sigh. "Man."

"Crank up that music, let's rock this place," Britt shouted. The music boomed even louder. I was certain the windows would crack.

Weston's hand wrapped around mine and squeezed. I longed for the complete comfort and feeling of protection Matthias' presence gave me, but that was impossible with Weston. He was mortal. Though he meant well, and offered me support, I felt very human and fallible.

Not everyone in the house had black spirits straddling their bodies. That was a relief. I must have looked like a weirdo as I passed, staring at the creatures salivating for each host's submission.

As Weston and I made our way through the house, joined by our hands, I worked at keeping my focus. I'd find Chase and warn him. Then I'd make up some excuse for Krissy to kick everybody out so she'd be safe. I'd start a fire if I had to.

Chase and his friends stood in a semi-circle around the kitchen table, laden with candy and cookies. *Cookies?* Chase was jumpy as a cricket. So were his buddies. Each had stacks of sugar cookies in their hands. Chase had a red cup. Behind them, one solitary figure stood.

Albert.

I stopped. At my side, Weston halted and peered into my face. "Zoe?"

My throat clutched. Across the room, Albert's eyes fastened onto mine in a stare that stripped me to the bone. My heart banged against my ribs. With the slickness of a shark, Albert slid behind Chase and his friends in a menacing game of eenie-meanie-minie-moe.

"Hey." Chase lifted his cup and grinned. He pressed the red plastic to his lips, chugged and his face contorted. His buddies watched him in wide-eyed fascination. Weston missed the moment, focused as he was on my marble stupor.

I reached out, felt the air until my hand gripped Weston's sleeve. Matthias was right. We shouldn't be here.

Though Albert was alone, the sheer magnitude of his wickedness was as powerful as the comfort Matthias presented. This evil was thick as a smog bank, blinding, choking, tainted with a rabid viciousness. Standing in its path meant certain destruction. There was nothing of the sinewy evil the black spirits carried, the kind that slips in slowly, readying its subject for complete takeover and submission. Albert took. Period.

I didn't dare move an inch. Inside, my voice screamed, *move Chase! Run! Everybody get out of here!*

"Zoe?" Weston's voice sounded so far away. Mouth open, I looked at him. *Take me away. We have to go now!*

"Chase," I scratched out.

Then Chase was next to me, his eyes concerned behind his glasses. The faint scent of beer dressed his breath. "Zoe? Is she okay?"

"I don't know. She's been acting funny since we pulled up."

Chase's eyes widened. *Yes, he gets it. Talk you idiot, tell him!*

"Zoe, look at me." Chase nudged Weston aside and pressed his palms into my shoulders. "Do you… see something?"

Weston's concern shifted to wary curiosity.

Why couldn't I use my voice?

"Cat got your tongue, Zoe?" Albert's voice drove through me like paralyzing venom. Somehow, he'd moved and now stood directly behind Weston and Chase, his lips curled under his piercing gaze. He wore dark colors I couldn't identify, not in the candlelight, but the tie around his neck was made of white rope.

I gaped at the tie, disgusted at the irony. Albert threw his head back in a laugh. "Stylish, don't you think?" He patted it. "I wore it just for you. Look closely, Zoe. Tell me what you see."

My stomach heaved. The rope threads writhed. White souls, stretched taut, were wound together without identifying form of male or female—only faces, hands and legs, linked impossibly in unforgiving twisted hopelessness.

"Powerful, don't you think?" Albert hissed.

Blackness threatened to engulf me. I was sure my pounding heart would break through my ribs and skin. I turned and threw myself into Weston. His arms came around me. His hand stroked my hair.

Albert laughed, the sound slithering into my head. "You think this boy can keep you from me?" He sounded so near, I shook, threw my hands over my ears and burrowed deeper against Weston's chest. I felt Chase touch my back, heard the concern in his voice when he said my name.

"That's it," Weston's deep voice buzzed against my face from his chest. "We're leaving."

"No." I jerked back. I faced Chase. Albert hovered over him, his blue eyes—the same crystal blue of Matthias' but jagged with evil intent rather than goodness—stayed glued to me. "Chase, I need to talk to you. Alone."

"Are you sure?" Weston held onto me, even as I gently pulled free of his embrace.

I nodded. "Don't go anywhere," I told him. His face was anxious but he didn't move.

I dragged Chase away. Albert, in his perfectly tailored suit and disgusting noose tie remained behind. In fact, he inched closer to Weston, eyeing him like a wolf eyes a dog. *Oh no.*

"Zoe, what is it?" Chase asked over the music.

The house had filled with more teenagers who mingled and danced and drank. Black spirits floated in the air like macabre hot air balloons, following. Watching. Searching.

"This place is infested with black spirits," I said, gripping the sleeves of his shirt. "You have to get out of here, now. Matthias' father is here and he's…" I swallowed a lump. Words weren't sufficient to describe how fatal Albert was. "He's targeted you."

Chase's eyes popped. "Me?"

"Take your friends and go. Please."

"Where is he?" Chase's head swerved around. I grabbed his chin and held it firm.

"Don't look for him, you idiot."

I blinked and Albert was there… next to Chase. Smiling. "You see?" Albert said. "Some want us. They actually *invite* us inside."

"No!" I yanked Chase, pulling him in my direction in hopes that physically moving him would keep him away from the impending invasion. Chase stumbled with the move, and bumped into Britt, who had I hadn't noticed.

Albert swirled to Britt and smiled at her, then slid his smile to me. "Ah. Much easier." He dissolved into Britt.

I gasped.

Britt leaned close. "I told you I'd come here. Your little friend Krissy? She's meat."

Britt's breath reeked. She produced a sweaty red cup, tilted her head back and chugged.

Albert. Inside of her. Just like that. Hand gripping Chase's sleeve, I stepped backward, the pounding music, the screams and laughs from the kids mixing with the moment too much for me. I was so far out of my element I couldn't believe I'd actually been naive enough to think my puny efforts would make a difference.

Britt didn't come after Chase and me, but sneered from her spot in the hall like a rejected whore. Then Brady appeared next to her. He followed her angry gaze to me, and sent me a snicker before he started whispering in Britt's ear. Behind them both, Albert lifted into the air, and began a slow circle around the two of their heads, his bright eyes beamed at the two of them. Again, my stomach heaved. "Chase, get out of here now."

"But I can handle this, Zoe. Whoever this Albert guy is, I can handle him."

I glared at him, shocked. But then he hadn't felt the menacing like I had. Matthias was right. I couldn't save anyone. My efforts were pathetic with a force this strong. Like an ant trying to move a boulder, it couldn't be done.

"Look, I'm leaving," I said. "I'm not messing around with this."

"Why can't I see them like you?" Chase groaned, his head craning as the two of us wove through bodies back to the kitchen. Krissy bumped into me. She had braided her long hair and combed it out, and now looked like a flower child, dressed in low riding jeans and a baby doll shirt, baring her slim waist. She gleamed.

Her arms wound around me in a hug. "Zoe!" she squealed. "I wondered where you were. This is fantastic. Don't you think?"

What happened to quiet Krissy in her bland denim jumper? Krissy eased back. "Britt was so nice. She brought me over this outfit. Isn't it cool?"

"Britt?"

Krissy nodded, her hair swinging to the pounding music as she uncoordinatedly rotated her hips. "I would never have thought Brittany Walker would be so generous. She came by earlier and helped me get ready." Krissy leaned. "We smoked too. She said it'd loosen me up and get me ready for the party. It did. Boy, it did. Looove it."

My eyes bulged. *Oh maan.* Next to me, Chase blinked at the new and changed Krissy.

"Are you guys having fun? Need more beer? Britt and Brady brought that by earlier too. Wasn't that coool of them?"

Nifty. I let out a snort and shot a glance over my shoulder at Britt, but she wasn't in the hall any longer. When I faced Krissy again, Albert's image was layered in hers. I blinked hard.

"Me again," he quipped. "Wonderful party. Lots of opportunities." He shimmied, as if trying to fit himself into every curve of Krissy's body. Krissy, obliviously inebriated, closed her eyes, as if listening to the music.

"Chase, you want to dance?" Krissy asked.

I clutched Chase's sleeves and shook my head at him. He glanced from me, to Krissy, then back to me. "But she looks hot tonight," he whispered in my ear.

"Chase, you need to leave."

Krissy's eyes shot wide and latched on mine with an alertness that stopped my breath. "The boy wants me. Get over it, Zoe." But who spoke, Albert or Krissy? With that, Krissy hooked her arm in Chase's and took him to the living room, closer to the music where the thumping beat demanded surrender.

"Hey you," Weston's warm breath tickled my ear. I whirled around and wrapped my arms around him.

Weston's expression grew grave. He hugged me, seeming to sense my desperation. I was torn. Stay, and try to convince my friends they were in danger? Or go and save myself?

But were they really in danger? Sure, they were dancing and some were getting drunk, but black spirits didn't hang around everybody. Partying was partying, right? Everybody had choices. Black spirits couldn't *make* anybody do anything. So I was safe to stay, right?

A chill whooshed around me and I jerked. I couldn't feel Weston through the icy bank of air which pressed at me from every angle. Albert's face. Smiling. His hypnotic eyes. He was trying to cross the threshold into my being. My excuses for the partying—my rationalization—had created a crack, and now he was trying to squeeze the opening apart.

I felt Weston then, his warm, human embrace suddenly returning. "Let's get out of here," I yelled over the music. His right arm stayed around my waist as he navigated the two of us through the thickening crowd to the front door.

My friends could stay if they wanted. I was done, even if guilt had a deep hold on my conscience. How could I leave Krissy and Chase and all of Chase's friends to Albert's whims? Of course, if Albert was after Matthias because of me, there was the possibility that once I was gone, Albert would also leave.

Weston pushed open the front door and we stepped onto the porch. My cell phone vibrated in my pocket. On the off chance the text was from Chase, I retrieved it from my pocket. Britt.

chase is a hottie

he's leaving, loser

fraid ur wrong, he's dancing with me

I looked up into Weston's peering gaze. He'd read the text, too, and now rolled his eyes, letting the front door shut behind him with a thud. A gang of his teammates strode up to the porch, six-packs tucked under their arms.

"Dude, you're leaving?" one asked.

Weston jerked out a nod. "Party's a dud, man. Skip it."

The half-dozen guys stood in disbelief.

One groaned. "Seriously?"

Again, Weston nodded, and firmly blocked the door. I bit my lip. Seeing popularity hierarchy at work in its finest form—Weston telling his team pals to split—gave me a pat of satisfaction after Britt's text. I knew Britt well enough. She wouldn't spend five more minutes at Krissy's without a big enough audience.

"Oh, man," another whined.

Weston shrugged and his hand was at my back. He escorted me down the steps. Passing the bunch, I waited for more queries, but none came. Whispers danced in the air. Weston only stood more erect and brought me more tightly to his side.

"You're really okay with leaving?" I asked.

"Yeah, definitely." I felt his gaze and peered up at him. "As long as I'm with you, that's all I want." Without a break in our stride, he kissed me. I glanced around for Matthias and didn't see him. Of course not. Once I made the choice to go inside the party, I was left to live with the consequences of that choice. So was everybody else.

TWENTY

Weston and I crossed snow to his truck and he pulled keys out of his front pocket, pressed the remote and the doors unlocked. I climbed in with a sigh of relief, glad to be leaving the party.

I gazed at the house. Weston's team pals had turned around and now loitered near the truck. Weston opened his door and got in, then started the engine. Weston rolled down the window to talk to the guys. "Trust me," he shouted. "The party sucked."

Each shot glances at the house, as if still undecided, then the pack of them ambled back to the cars they came in.

Weston drove in silence. My head pounded with images of the party, but overriding those was Albert's sinister presence. Just thinking about him chilled my blood. His eyes…the same piercing blue of Matthias' but with an ominous edge that could only be described as terrifying.

"You okay?"

I nodded. I needed a change of subject. But it was hard to think about my failure at the party. "Do you think I did the right thing, leaving?"

Weston's hand captured mine on the seat between us. "You want to tell me what you saw back there that freaked you out?"

I gulped. "Saw?"

"Chase asked you if you saw something. What was that about?"

"Uh…" I averted my gaze, but he squeezed my hand, tugged, and

200

brought my attention back to his concerned face.

"Zoe." He blew out a breath. "You can trust me."

Matthias said he'd be a safe companion... I could trust Weston, right? Why was it hard to believe? Especially when I trusted Chase, who was now dancing with the devil himself.

"What?" Weston pressed. He pulled the car over on a side street and parked. "You can tell Chase and you can't tell me? What's up with that?"

"Chase and I know things about each other. That's all."

His dark eyes flashed with frustration. Around the steering wheel, his hands tightened until his knuckles went white. "I suppose Britt knows, too."

"No. Britt doesn't know about this stuff."

"How did—why did you—how did Chase get to be the lucky one?"

"There's nothing premeditated going on here, Weston. I told this stuff to Chase before I knew you."

He seemed to consider my words, understand and then accept them. His gaze shifted to the front window. "Will I ever be where Chase is?" His eyes fastened on mine. "The one you tell your secrets to?"

I bit my lower lip.

He closed his eyes and lowered his head. "You really can't forgive me for what happened, can you?"

"That's not it—"

"It has to be. I don't blame you. What I did was inexcusable. I just can't believe..." He turned his gaze to the front window, pain on his face. "I can't believe the one person I want the most is never really going to be mine."

I understood him. Completely. Still, what I carried in my heart about Matthias and seeing guardians and black spirits was deeply personal. The stuff traitors and blackmailers and blood friends and soul mates were made of.

"I'll tell you this much," I said. His gaze jerked to mine, his eyes eager. "There is nothing... *romantic* going on between Chase and me. We both have something in common. That's all."

"You are clairvoyant, aren't you? The both of you are."

"No, that's not it, I promise. But it's something... along those lines."

His gaze intensified on my face, searching deeper. "Why can't you tell me?"

He moved closer, one arm extended behind me on the back of the seat, the other reached out for my hand and he grasped it. "Something... happens to you when you're in certain situations. Something comes over you. What is it?"

"Please don't ask me about this."

A long thick moment pulled between us. Disappointment shadowed his eyes, and he looked at our joined hands. His thumb scrolled across the top of my fingers. He let out a sigh, turned and put both hands on the wheel.

The car didn't move. In my chest, my heart skipped, wondering if he was fed up with me. Would he tell me to screw off and never talk to me again? Part of me was disappointed at that idea. The other part figured if he wasn't able to accept my answer, then tough.

He shifted the engine into drive and the truck rumbled out onto the road, merging with traffic. I let out a breath of relief—for now. Maybe he'd drop me off at home and then tell me to shove my lack of trust.

I liked Weston, no getting around that. He was gorgeous, and I sensed depth beyond the it-boy smile and wave he granted everyone he passed. But could he take me on my terms?

He turned onto my street, just as the far off wail of sirens pierced the night air. He parked in front of the house and his truck idled like a lion. Would he do his customary gesture and get out, open my door and walk me to the door?

Heated seconds ticked by. Apparently not. I reached for the handle, but his body snapped over mine, his hand wrapping around my wrist, his maleness pressing me into the firm seat. His thudding heart rapped against my chest.

His face, torn in confusion, inched closer and his lips covered mine. His tattered emotions seemed to beg my mouth not for the satisfaction of lust, but for words of trust.

His hands slid into place on my cheeks before he broke the connection, resting his cheek against mine, our ragged breaths in unison. "Please trust me."

Need poured like warm water through my limbs, responding to him with a tight embrace meant to comfort. "I'm sorry. I don't mean to make this hard for you."

"I don't care if it's hard." His grip deepened. "As long as I know someday you'll trust me."

He asked the impossible. Of course I could trust him. I just could never betray Matthias' trust, or God's trust for that matter. What if I lost my gift? Nothing was worth that risk.

Weston eased back, but cupped my face. "I love you, Zoe."

Love? I tried to quell the shock surging through my system, but Weston was smarter than that—his brown eyes sharpened as he read my face. His hands remained fixed on my cheeks, his determined expression didn't shift. "I'm sticking my neck out here, but I don't care. It's real—the way I feel. And it's not like what I've felt before. It's real, Zoe."

His honesty silenced me. Oddly, his admittance didn't scare me or turn me off. Rather, the pureness touched me. I covered his hands with mine, hoping to calm any fears he might have in admitting such a deep feeling.

He kissed me again, with sweet respect and gentleness, before letting me go. My cheeks cooled in the absence of his flesh.

He got out of the car and opened my door.

Inside, the warmth of home coddled me. The house was silent. Everyone was in bed, and that was fine. My blood sang. I needed time alone to fantasize about Weston. Smiling, I took the stairs up, glad what had started out as a great night, then morphed into a horrifically frightening party, had now ended wonderfully.

Thoughts of the party, of Chase and Krissy, stole a little of my effervescence. I hoped they were okay. I tugged out my phone and texted Chase.

u still there?

I crept down the hall, passing Abria's darkened room, on the way to my bedroom. I hoped Chase had listened to me and had the brains to see that Krissy, drunk as she'd gotten, was not herself and that he'd left the place.

As I approached my bedroom, I glanced at Luke's. A dull light shone underneath his closed door. At least he was home. That was good. Just as that thought left me, a strong presence came at me from the direction of his bedroom. Heavy, thick and foreboding.

I froze in the dark hall, taken over by an icy shudder. I stared at the door. I should check on him, but fear danced in my pumping blood. Slowly, I crossed the carpet to his door and knocked.

Nothing.

"Luke?" I made sure my whisper was loud enough to go beyond the door but not awaken anyone else.

No answer.

I turned the knob and eased the door open. Here, foreboding submerged me. My grip on the knob tightened. "Luke?"

I stepped into his room, the air dense with the same wet dread I'd felt at the party. My heart started to pound. I closed the door, not wanting to awaken Mom and Dad.

Half of his room was lit by a Tiki lamp hanging next to his bed, the rest remained in darkness, corners appearing deep and black.

Luke sat on the floor, his back propped against the bed, legs crossed, gaze staring straight ahead. Littered around him was an empty Vodka bottle and an open, near-empty bag of weed, along with wisps of white paper, burnt to stubs and some burned fabric softener sheets to mask the scent of marijuana.

"You're smoking in the house now? And drinking?" I hissed, planting myself in front of him. He didn't move, just sat like a half-dead soldier after war.

Another shudder shook my spine. Why did I feel such wretchedness? My eye caught movement in the blackness of one corner.

Albert's shadowed form inched into my vision just enough that his menacing presence stole my breath. I took a step back.

"Did you think I was finished with you, Zoe?" His voice slithered into the air.

An invisible hand seemed to have my voice in its clutches. My mouth opened, but, once again, I wasn't able to produce any words. Albert moved out into the open and soon, he circled me—his feet not touching the floor— like an angry eel ready to sink his fangs into my soul. He wore the same sleek suit I'd seen him in at the party—complete with that disgusting tie—making him look like some kind of macabre jewelry salesman from Las Vegas.

In spite of the fear running rampant in my body, I smirked. His eyebrow lifted just enough that I knew he wondered where I got the nerve at a moment like this to smirk at him. I took a deep breath, searched for bravery and lifted my chin. "Get out of my house."

He stopped beside Luke. The corners of his lips lifted. "I heard you had spunk. I like that. So does my son, apparently."

"I live here," Luke muttered, his tongue sounded thick.

"I'm not talking to you," I snapped. "It's your fault this demon freak is here. You invited him, you moron." My eyes shot wide at my words. What had gotten into me? Anger. I was spouting off like a hot geyser.

Luke lifted his head. I couldn't see his eyes through his shaggy blonde hair but I didn't need to, he was hard-baked. "Want one?"

I kicked at his near-empty bags and burnt rolls. "No, I don't want one, you friggin' loser." Anger roared through my blood, filling every vessel taut with the need to lash out and pound Luke with my fists, gnash at him with words, pummeling his spirit until nothing was left.

Albert smiled. He moved closer to Luke, substance no obstruction for his essence as he slowly circled Luke now. "Again, again."

Evil was so thick, I was breathing it in, making it a part of me. I couldn't let Albert taunt me.

Warmth bore into my back and a glorious, clear light beamed into the darkening room, tearing through the black wickedness encroaching on Luke and me. I turned. Matthias.

His crystal blue eyes fastened on Albert. "Leave."

Albert tossed back his head in a laugh. "Son—"

"Leave." No sound of emotion, no trace of a child's disappointment in a wayward parent. Only a command: pure, simple and profound.

Albert's icy blue eyes—so like Matthias,' yet worlds different—slid to mine. "I'm not here to take Luke in your place, Zoe. I'll take you both."

Matthias stretched out his hand and the room vibrated with a cleansing wash of light and energy. His face, serene, yet intense and sure, drew taut, his eyes pinning his father. In a burst of white fire, Albert was gone.

Luke's head rolled forward. He let out a chainsaw snore.

My breath, which I'd held in my chest, blew out. My body sagged and I collapsed onto the foot of Luke's bed. Matthias moved close. I yearned for him to reach out and touch me, calm me, but his hands hung anxiously at his sides.

Concern flecked his blue eyes. "I'm sorry."

My limbs quaked. "I... I." My voice trembled. I hadn't noticed how afraid I was, but fear seemed a resident in me now. "That was... he... scared me."

Matthias nodded and sat next to me, close enough that his aura swamped me with comfort and my bunched nerves, the jangling in my limbs began to subside. "His efforts will be relentless, Zoe. He will never stop."

I gasped, my breath was just starting to smooth from a rapid tap to a steady drum beat. Meeting Matthias' sober gaze stalled the air in my chest. His countenance grayed.

"What?" I was more afraid of his answer than I had been in Albert's presence. Something was coming, heaviness clouded the tranquil air.

He will come after you and everyone you love... as long as you are important to me.

For a moment, I stared at him, sure my frightened, vivid imagination had created the horrible possibility now playing in my head. But the look of absolute sobriety in Matthias' blue eyes confirmed my worst fears.

I don't care.

I do.

I can handle this.

"Zoe—"

I stood. "You can't leave me." My heart tore. "I don't care what he does to me. You can't go away. I won't be able to live without you being here... I..." Every cell in my body rebelled at the idea, buckling, and my body crumpled back to the bed in a weak, useless heap of threatening sobs.

I rolled onto my side, weighted down with the most overwhelming sorrow I'd ever had take over my soul. Worse than death. I heard nothing but my wracked torment—the anticipation of never seeing him again so enormous, I might as well have been crushed by a mountain and buried alive.

Please, please tell me that is not what you are thinking. Please.

Silence.

I jerked my head left. Matthias hadn't moved, but sat watching me in mirrored anguish. Yet his countenance was not as tormented as mine. He didn't sob, though his blue eyes glistened with compassion. A permanent knot held his firm jaw tight. Closed. No words of consolation. The truth had been delivered in terrible silence to my heart.

"It's the only way," he said softly.

"No." More tears. More sobs. His voice carried the words into the air now, making his declaration real and totally unacceptable to me.

I brought my legs up, curled into the fetal position. *No. No. No. No. Zoe.*

Impossibility dragged time on. I'd thought I had solved this—that Matthias would always be a part of my life somehow. Why was this coming back to tear me apart?

It's the only way.

I bolted upright, swiping my teary face with my hands. "No. I don't care what he does to me. Or to anyone else. I want you here. Abria needs you!"

Matthias let out a sigh and glanced at Luke. Then his gaze met mine again. *None of this would have happened if I'd kept my heart in check.*

I reached out to touch him and his blue eyes fastened on my

207

outstretched hand. My hand stopped. "I wouldn't change any of what's happened. Even Albert. You coming into our lives was the best thing for us all. You know that, right?"

"Had I known my father would come after you, I would never have placed you in such a precarious position."

I know. I believe you. Anguish over the decision pounded his ache through my body. *Please don't feel bad about it, please.*

Still, this does not change what is real. He will continue to pursue you and your family, Zoe.

You can keep him away from us. Did you see how easy it was for you to get rid of him?

His blue eyes lit with a smile. "That's because good has absolute power over evil." When my eyes widened, he nodded. "They're a misled lot, the hosts of Satan. Misled by the great deceiver himself."

"Evil really can't win? Ever?"

"Never. But that won't stop them. They'll take whoever they can get… sadly, there are always misguided souls who lose sight of what's real and good and buy into his lies. Lies are tailor made, Zoe. As precious as a soul is to God, that same soul is just as valuable to the other side, and there's a fierce battle on both sides to win."

"But if they can't win, why do they keep trying?"

"I told you, they've been lied to."

"So that's why Albert leaves when you tell him to?"

He nodded. "He must. It's an eternal law. Evil must bow to Good."

"That must make Albert happy," I snorted.

"He hates it." Matthias grinned. Then his grin dissolved. *My father.* Matthias averted his gaze. The sorrow he carried each and every moment for a man he had loved sent a throb of loss through my body.

"I'm sorry he's… not more like you. What happened to him?"

Matthias held my gaze steadily—with only a trace of pain. Inside, I didn't feel the remorse I'd felt before echo through him.

I wondered why he didn't answer my question and why I couldn't see any more memories.

Matthias' thought came into my head. *I have hope that sometime he will see the error he's committed, but I'm bound to the eternal law to defend Good and those I love.*

He really thinks he will take me?

Matthias nodded. *And your loved ones.*

I glanced at Luke, his head rolled to the side, body slumped in sleep, his soft snores filling the air. "Luke is vulnerable as long as he makes himself weak, isn't he?"

Matthias nodded.

"Why can't Luke see what's happening to him?"

"Like I said, lies come tailor made to entice our weaknesses and make us weaker."

I reached out and petted Luke's head, feeling helpless. "Why can't you protect Luke from all of this?"

"Luke has strengths he has yet to discover, Zoe, and he will, when he digs deep enough."

I let out a sigh. "You sure about that?"

"Very."

"What about… me?" A long moment of love tied our hearts together in silent union. "Why am I forced to not have you in my life?"

"Not forced."

"It feels like that. It'd be so much easier if you were my guardian. Then I could see you—be with you, and Albert would be the one forced to stay away."

Matthias's blue eyes sharpened. "Easier for whom?"

"How about for everyone involved? It sounds to me like the most absolute way of making sure Albert never comes near me again is if you are my guardian."

He stared at me a moment, his expression ponderous. "I told you why I chose not to be your guardian."

Because you care about me—

Love, Zoe.

I swallowed. A sober expression remained fixed on his face. Feelings collided inside of me: comfort, serenity and peace that always accompanied Matthias' presence, but a thread of longing—his—male and strong, twined with my own female longing for him.

Sweet misery. That's what I would face should I step in as your guardian again.

I couldn't ask him to spend his life—his existence, or part of it anyway—watching me frolic through mortality while he stood in the background. Guilt made me avert my gaze from his.

"Frolic?" He chuckled, bringing my eyes to his.

"It's true. I refuse to be selfish. Sorry I mentioned it."

"Zoe." He inched closer on the bed. His nearness sent a flood of yearning through my blood. "If I am your guardian, you'll be protected against Albert. He will continue to have access to those around you, but only if he's invited."

"There's no point in talking about it. No way am I putting you in torture mode. I won't do that to you."

Matthias' lips lifted slightly. "Sassy bearcat."

"This isn't funny." I jumped to my feet, paced. "Life is so freaking *long*." I crossed my arms against my thumping heart. *Why did I survive that accident? We could be together now, not here, worrying about some psychotic devil who wants my soul.*

Warm strength pressed into my back. Matthias stood so close I caught the familiar—and missed—scent of him. I closed my eyes and breathed him in. As much as I wanted him to lay his hands on my shoulders at that moment and make me his, I couldn't knowing he would see me go on about my life and my loves—from a distance.

"I told you before, the heart has a great capacity for love." His calming voice melted into my soul. "You shouldn't—and won't be—denied anything, most especially not love in this life."

But I already have love. You.

The kind of love a man and a woman share, Zoe.

My body tingled. In my head, images flashed of Matthias and I, kissing, touching—engaged in completing mortal love. Fire raced under my skin. Ashamed my human mind had drifted to the fantasy, I stepped away from him and kept my face averted.

More humiliating was the fact that he'd no doubt seen the image in my head. I wanted to dissolve. What could I say? The thought had appeared, just like millions of thoughts in my life, only when I'd had them before they'd been the fruits of a very lost girl who saw sex as a cure-all, not a sacred expression of commitment.

I shook my head. "You should go now."

The desperate silence between us thickened. "All right."

Propped against the bed, Luke let out a blubbering snort and his head rolled to the other side.

I blew out a breath. I put frustration aside and turned to watch Matthias go.

"Goodnight." His blue eyes didn't leave mine, even through the flash of blinding white light that took him.

A sigh eased out of my chest. My cell phone vibrated in my pocket. I dug for it, too pleased to be annoyed that someone would have the audacity to call me at one a.m. Chase.

"Brady's in the hospital."

TWENTY-ONE

"What? What happened?"

"I don't know," Chase panted. "I wasn't there, I mean, I was in the other room. The next thing I know, Brittany comes through the house screaming. She was hysterical. Nobody understood what she was talking about." The sound of shouting voices and commotion scraped through the line. "It's bad, Zoe."

"Oh no."

"She dragged me to this room and Brady was on the floor with a tie around his neck."

"What?!" My heart jumped.

"Yeah. Man, it was awful. He was pasty. He didn't look good, Zoe. I don't know… They were playing that hanging game. The one where you—"

"I know what game it is!" I snapped. I'd heard about it—Britt and I had even talked about how stupid it was for people to take themselves to the edge by hanging. My pulse skipped through my veins. "Where's Britt?"

"I don't know. It's a madhouse. The cops are here, the paramedics—they just took Brady away in an ambulance. I called 911 and everyone ran. Brittany was totally smashed. I mean, she could barely walk. I don't know how she made it out the door much less got away from here."

"I have to call her."

"Yeah. Okay."

"What about Krissy? Where is she? How is she?"

"She's freaked. But I think she's also high, because she was acting all casual one minute, freaked the next. She isn't herself. Man, what a night. It's bad. And because I made the call, I had to answer all the questions. Lucky for me, I passed the alcohol test. The cops are handing out alcohol tickets like candy. My parents are going to be pissed."

"Where are you?"

"Still at Krissy's. Listen, they're taking a bunch of the kids down to the police station."

"They let you use your phone?"

"They haven't taken it yet. I'm being sneaky," he whispered.

"I'm gonna call Britt. Text me later, k?" I disconnected and dialed Britt. Her phone rang and rang. Luke let out a snort and fell to the side, completely out of it. I dialed Britt again, my fingers tapping on the screen as I waited.

"What?" Her voice slogged.

"I heard what happened, are you all right?"

"What do you care?"

"Forget Weston for a second, Britt—what happened with Brady? I heard he's in the hospital."

"Yeah." Her voice trailed off. "I don't know...we were..." she choked out a sob. "We were all hanging, you know? That game..."

"Britt!" I slapped my palm against my forehead. We'd talked about this, why had she done something so asinine? "What happened?"

"I—he—one minute he was laughing and the next... we couldn't... he stopped breathing and turned all white."

A knob formed in my throat. "Jeez."

"Everybody freaked. Somebody called nine-one-one and that's all. That's... all. I don't re... member anymore. I feel sick. I—" I heard her barf. My stomach rolled. On her end, the sound of her convulsing and sobbing wretched on.

"Britt? Britt!"

The phone clattered and her sobs grew distant, so I disconnected. Bit my lower lip. What to do? Go to her? Did Weston know?

I dialed him. He picked up after one ring. "It's me. Did u hear about Brady?"

"I'm at the hospital."

"How is he?"

"Not good."

Oh no. Even though Brady and Weston had had a falling out, they'd been friends for as long as I could remember. He must feel terrible.

"Are you okay?"

"Can we talk later?"

"Yeah. I'm here if you need me."

"Thanks." Click.

Luke still lay collapsed on his side, his mouth open in a snore. At least he was home and not in the hospital—fighting for his life. Gratitude swamped me. I bent down and gently shook him. I shouldn't have gotten upset at him earlier. His scattered brain seemed to coagulate behind his blinking blue eyes. He groaned and sat up. With a look around, he seemed to realize where he was.

"You fell asleep," I said.

"Oh." He rubbed his face with his hands. "Man." He got up and fell onto his bed, rolled to his side and was out again.

"I'm sorry" I muttered. Not that I was looking for his forgiveness, my gratitude was enough for us both. I pulled his comforter up and over his shoulder, turned off the Tiki lamp hanging next to his bed and quietly left the room.

I couldn't sleep, not with what had happened at Krissy's. Was it my fault for leaving them? Should I have dragged Chase away from there? Demanded Krissy listen to me? I stopped in the darkened hallway and closed my eyes.

I'd tried, but Albert...his face, brandished in my mind, sent my body into a convulsion of shakes. I did what I could without putting myself at risk. And I'd come home and found him here, hovering over Luke like a grizzly salivating over his next kill.

≫ ✦ ≪

My cell phone vibrated, the glowing screen lit up the dark hall. Weston. "Weston?"

Silence, long, heavy and horrible. "He didn't make it."

I sunk to the floor. "Oh no."

I heard sniffling, then more deathly silence. "How could this happen?"

"Where are you? Do you want me to come down?"

A cough. In the background, wailing. "I can't believe it," Weston muttered. "I can't believe it."

"Which hospital are you at?" I had to go to him, the need to comfort surging through me.

"American Fork. But I'm leaving now. I'm…I've got to go home."

"What can I do?"

More silence, the wailing growing faint. Time dragged by with each of Weston's sniffs and coughs. "I don't know. I've got to go, Zoe." Click.

Helplessness engulfed me. I closed my phone, stood and went into my bedroom. Staying home in my warm bedroom didn't seem right while Chase was dealing with the police along with Krissy and whoever else was getting busted. Weston suffering with the loss of Brady… a thought occurred to me and I quickly went to Luke's bedroom.

I felt my way to his bedside and clicked on the swinging Tiki lamp. He snored from the bed, in the same position I'd left him in. I gently shook him. He remained dead to the world, so I shook him again.

"What?"

"Brady's dead, Luke."

He labored upright. "What?"

"I just heard from Weston."

Luke scrubbed his face, white streaks staining his shocked pink skin. His hands stayed fixed at his gaping mouth. "What happened?"

I sat on the foot of his mattress. "He was at a party and accidentally hung himself in that choking game."

Luke finally dragged his hands from his mouth. He was white as paper. "Does Kevin know?"

215

"I don't know. Weston didn't say much. He was very upset."

"Man." Luke was alert now, no traces of being bombed anywhere in his eyes or countenance. "You're serious?"

I nodded.

"That sucks."

"Yeah."

Luke whipped out his cell phone and started tapping. "They're probably still at the hospital," I pointed out.

"I gotta tell him I'm sorry about it, though. Man. Man. I can't believe it."

"I know."

Luke brought his legs up and wrapped his arms around them. Behind the shaggy veil of his blond hair, his blue eyes teared. A pang in my heart made me pat his knee. At least it wasn't him. *Thank you, God.*

He stared at the screen of his phone, then started tapping messages. "I've got a million texts."

I nodded, stood. Word spread fast through the texting grapevine. "I just wanted you to know."

He sniffed and swiped under his nose with the sleeve of his hoodie, and he continued to text. "Yeah."

I left heavy hearted. Four hours ago, I'd seen Brady alive and breathing. I wondered what would happen now, to Krissy. I hadn't seen her guardian at her house—had he known about the precarious position she'd been in? Would he think I'd let her down?

It wasn't my fault all of this had happened. Rationally, I understood that. Krissy had wanted to have that party. Both Weston and I had warned her about the odd pitfall that could happen at such a gathering, but this was so far out of that league, I couldn't help but continue to question my involvement and feel hampered with guilt.

I sat in my dark bedroom, staring out the window at the night sky. Gauzy clouds stretched over the bright moon. Matthias was up there somewhere—at peace. Safe. Far from the ugly troubles this life presented. The white light of the moon lifted my soul, and his face came into my mind. I wished I was with him, far away from the upheaval and pain happening in my world.

Yet, even in Matthias' perfect existence, he carried love and concern for his father. In spite of existing in peace, compassion never rested.

Midnight blue sky overhead and its infinite vastness speckled with sparkling stars reminded me that this dark night, Brady's life had ended. Brady was somewhere—where, I didn't know. Did he regret the night? How did he feel right now? What was he thinking?

The heartache his family must be experiencing pained me. My own near death experience flashed in my memory, vibrant and deep as the galaxy I peered up at. I was grateful to be alive—for my family and for whatever else I had been sent back here to do.

My cell phone, clutched in my hand, vibrated.

Weston.

im outside

TWENTY-TWO

I skipped down the stairs and opened the front door. Weston's shoulders hunched underneath his royal blue Viking hoodie against the cold; his hands were deep in his front pockets.

His face was twisted in grief.

I wrapped around him, and his arms surrounded me in a long, silent hug. He wept against my shoulder, his body shaking against mine, ridding itself of sorrow.

After a moment, I eased back, took him by the hand and led him inside, shutting the door. He looked around at the dark interior, and I pointed to Dad's office—a room directly off the entry. With a gentle tug of his hand, I urged him to follow me.

Inside, I shut the glass French doors and flicked on a low-lit lamp. His cheeks were scored with red slashes—finger marks, like he'd rubbed his face over and over. Pink rimmed his brown, glistening eyes.

"Sorry," he said.

"No, I'm glad you came."

"I didn't want to go home yet. Man. I'm...this is so unreal."

I nodded and drew closer so our bodies touched from knees to chest, and kept my hands anchored on his arms.

"We hadn't talked in a while, you know? Since... that day I... hit him. But, I've known the guy since first grade. We... grew up together." He lowered his head, shook it, then covered his face with his hands and a sob broke out.

I hugged him.

"I don't get it," he muttered into the curve of my neck. "Why would he do something like that?"

"I don't know."

His grip grew tighter. "Didn't he know the risk? I mean, why did he do it?" Another sob shook him from head to toe, vibrating his loss into me. With one hard squeeze at my waist, he released me, stepped back and scrubbed his face. He blew out a sigh, his hands hanging uselessly at his sides.

"I'm so sorry," I whispered. "It's terrible."

"Yeah. Kevin's... he's out of his mind angry. His parents..." He closed his eyes. "I've known them all my life." He shook his head and turned around, hiding his face, shoulders buckling in another round of sobs.

I went to him and wrapped my arms around him, pressing my head against his back. I wished I could ease his pain, but I also knew a certain amount of purging took place in the grieving process.

Weston's weeping finally came to an end and he wiped his face with his hands and let out a sigh. He turned and his stormy brown eyes locked with mine. He studied me, without saying anything and the air around us grew heavy. "You knew something bad was going to happen. You saw something— what was it, Zoe?"

My pulse skipped. "Not this again."

"If it has something to do with Brady's death, then, yes this again. What did you see?"

I stepped back, crossing my arms over my chest. "I saw danger."

His face crooked into mocking. "Danger? What? How?" He advanced, and my heart started to race. He gripped my shoulders. "Tell me what you saw and why you didn't tell me about it. If you'd told me, maybe Brady would be alive."

I wrenched free of his grip. "This is not my fault."

"You said you saw something there—at the party—how can part of it not be your fault?"

219

"How about because Brady chose to play the stupid game, Weston? We weren't even there!"

"If I'd known he was in danger, I would have stayed!"

"And put yourself in harm's way? I was the one who told us to get out of there, or have you conveniently forgotten that?"

"I remember you wanting to leave, but, dammit Zoe, I want to know what you saw tonight!"

"Excuse me," Dad's voice boomed from the open door. Weston and I whirled around. Dad and Mom, sleep-mussed, stood with wide eyes in the open doorway.

"I don't know what's going on here, but you've awakened my family, young man."

"I'm sorry, Dad." I stepped around Weston and stood in front of him. "We just got some terrible news."

Mom drew her flowered robe more tightly around her.

"Brady died," I said.

Mom and Dad's faces grew stony. Mom's hand went to her lips. "Oh, no. What happened?"

"He…" I glanced at Weston whose gaze was averted to the floor.

"He accidentally hung himself," Weston finished with a snap. He shoved his hands through his hair and sighed. "It's…unbelievable."

"How does one accidentally hang oneself?" Dad asked.

"How terrible. Oh no," Mom murmured.

"It's… horrible," Dad muttered under a sorrowful sigh.

Weston swallowed. "Yeah."

"How—how did this happen?" Mom asked.

"It's a game," I said, highly aware of Weston beside me. I couldn't believe he was placing some of the blame on my shoulders.

"A game? Hanging is a game now?" Mom's face was etched with a mother's sorrow.

Dad shifted, displeasure mixing with disbelief on his face. "You have got to be—how—did this happen at the party you two were at earlier?"

Weston and I exchanged glances. His shock melted into fear. "Yeah," he admitted.

Dad's hard stare slid to me. "Zoe, you promised us you—"

"I promised I'd be careful, I'd keep to curfew and let you guys know where I was. I did all of that. This happened long after Weston and I left the party, Dad."

"Still," Mom rubbed her face with both hands. "You were so close."

"We left because it wasn't a place we wanted to be," I continued, hoping they'd understand I had done my best.

"She's right," Weston's voice was nearly a whisper. He stared at the floor, his expression dead.

"What happened to Brady wasn't our fault, Weston," I said.

"What had happened to Brady was a horrible accident," Dad stated, as if still trying to convince himself of the reality of Brady's death.

"His family..." Mom's voice petered off. Her eyes closed, she shook her head.

Long moments of wretched silence heated the air. Mom kept her face buried in her hands. Dad's gaze flicked from me to Weston.

Finally, he said, "We'll talk about this in the morning, Zoe."

I nodded. Mom and Dad said goodnight to Weston, turned and headed up the stairs.

As soon as they were out of range, Weston leaned close. "You're lying to me," he hissed, his body coiled with rage. Fear screamed through my nerves. My eyes darted right, then left. Was I in danger?

Weston gripped my shoulders. "What are you looking at?"

"You're making me nervous, that's all. You want my dad to come back down?"

Weston's palms left my shoulders; his head fell back in a deep sigh. Then his head snapped up and his eyes latched on mine. One last penetrating glare and he turned and stormed out, slamming the front door behind him.

What the eff?

I stared out the sidelight, watching Weston stomp to his truck. He got in, turned on the engine and the diesel rumbled away. Whatever. Okay, cool down, Zoe. I had to remind myself that his best friend had just died.

The thought sobered me and I texted him.

i really am sorry

I bit my lower lip.

forgive me, k?

I didn't expect to hear from him, he was driving after all, and we knew not to text and drive, though every teen I knew broke that rule.

Still no texts from Chase. I hoped he wasn't in huge trouble. He hadn't seemed too concerned about being busted but then we had both been caught up in talking about Brady.

I turned off the office light and climbed the stairs to my bedroom. Dad opened the master bedroom door and slipped out. "Everything okay?"

"Yeah."

"It looked like you two were having an argument."

"We were, sort of." I sighed.

Dad shut the door and crossed to me, bringing his dark blue robe tight around his body. "Zoe, this partying has got to stop."

"It has stopped, Dad. Seriously. This wasn't the usual party."

"Obviously."

"No, I mean, Krissy—she's like this molly-girl—had the party. She's not on the circuit or anything. I tried to tell her about how parties can get, but she didn't listen to me."

Dad's stare penetrated. Deciphered. "You seem to live close to the edge these days, Zoe."

"I would never have played that game, Dad. Never. I know better than to take chances with my life."

"Seems to me going to the party to begin with was a chance."

Silence hung in the dark hall. "You're right."

"Thank God you're okay."

Yeah. I turned and continued down the hall to my bedroom. He stayed outside his door, watching.

The next morning, I was so exhausted, my limbs felt like bricks. I let out a groan. The scent of pancakes on the griddle snuck underneath my bedroom door, stirring my empty stomach.

Last night's events dragged in my soggy mind: the party, Albert, Weston, Britt, Brady   *Brady* Please God, make Brady's death just a bad dream—for his family's sake. The picture of Brady hanging by Albert's noose-tie blared into my mind, snapping me to full wakefulness. I sat up and rubbed my face, the scant tears in my eyes vanished, but sorrow clung to my heart.

Sunday. I could use today to leave these dreadful thoughts behind. I threw back the covers and stood, not sure ditching the events of last night was possible. Church would help, and I decided to go.

I grabbed my phone and checked for texts, hoping to hear from Weston.

Four texts from Chase, one phone call from Britt.

I opened Chase's text.

hey im home

man am i busted

remind me why i went to the party

I had the sinking feeling Chase might blame me for his choice to attend Krissy's party.

i hate life right now

Who to talk to first? I called Chase.

"Yeah?" His voice was husky, like I'd awakened him.

"Hey, it's me," I said.

"Zoe? Hey."

"So, are you okay? What happened?"

The sound of fumbling came through the line. "I gotta talk quick. My parents grounded me for a month. Jeez. But, yeah. Anyway, so it was a madhouse. Those of us stupid enough to stick around were hauled down to the police station. They held us in this cell until our parents showed up, all the

>✦<
223

while giving us this big talk about the ills of partying without chaperones and having alcohol etcetera, etcetera, which royally screwed Krissy because she fell into categories A through Z. Anyway, my parents came down and picked me up and I got more railing on the drive home. What happened to Brady? Have you heard anything?"

I swallowed. "He's dead."

Chase gasped, then silence followed. "Man."

"Yeah."

More thick silence.

"That's... sad."

"Yeah, it is."

"How's Weston taking it? You were with him, right? I assume he knows."

"He knows. He's really upset."

"No doubt. Man. This is just... bad."

"Yeah."

"I should have listened to you, Zoe. You... warned me."

"Please don't say that."

"But you did." He sighed. His voice grew tight. "Tell me more about this Albert guy."

He was the last person I wanted to talk about. "Later, 'kay?"

"Oh. Sure. Wow. It's just unbelievable."

"I know. I'm glad you're okay."

"Yeah, my parents aren't speaking to me and probably won't for the next five years, but I'm okay."

"Did you hear anything more about Krissy?"

"No. She was at the station, bawling, when I saw her. She was in bad shape. Her parents are out of town and, man, with what's happened to Brady now, they could be looking at involuntary manslaughter. I don't know. Wow."

"This is your CSI brain talking, Chase."

"Not involuntary manslaughter, but man. If my parents grounded me for a month for just being there, hers'll probably ground her for life."

"I'm going to call her and see if she picks up."

"Oh. Sure. Let me know what she says."

"Okay. See ya."

I disconnected with Chase, my belly filled with butterflies thinking about talking to Britt. I figured Weston was still wrapped up in grief. I was okay with that, I just hoped when he saw clearly at some point he'd forgive me and call.

I dialed Britt, but only got her *'Hey, it's me. Leave me a message.'*

I showered and dressed in a lavender skirt and white blouse, with a cropped black sweater and boots. Out the windows, gray clouds threatened snow and chill. After applying some makeup, I headed downstairs. The rumbling engine timbre of Luke's voice drifted upward, mixing with Abria's giggle and Mom and Dad's chatter. The sounds soothed me.

Dad, dressed in dark slacks, shirt and tie, smiled when he saw me. "You're coming to church?"

I nodded. *I need to be there.* "Sure, why not?" I was surprised to see Luke dressed up, and I lightly tousled his damp mop when I sat next to him at the kitchen table. "You going, bud?"

His shoulders lifted as he bit into a browned sausage. My stomach grumbled.

"Pancakes with your pile of sausages?" I teased him.

He kept his face angled at his plate, and didn't respond. I patted his shoulder. He was no doubt thinking about Kevin.

Talking about such a horrible event was like wondering if I should cross an icy lake—unsure of the thickness of the ice, of falling through. I gave Luke a side hug. "You okay?"

He nodded, but didn't lift his head or try to look at me. I glanced at Mom, then Dad. Mom handed me a plate of pancakes. At the end of the table, Abria stood on her chair, hands flicking the air as if she was trying to swat at unseen bugs.

Dad, plate of cakes and sausages in hand, shot a glance at Luke and sat down across from us. "I can't imagine what Brady's parents are going through."

"It's so horrible," Mom murmured as she sat down with her breakfast.

I took a deep breath. I was trying not to focus on it, but Brady's untimely death was everywhere. It's not like Brady didn't deserve the thought, he was a human being and even though he'd done despicable things, I forgave him and my thoughts weren't directed in any way at retribution. His death was a terrible, unnecessary tragedy.

"Were you at the party, Z?" Luke finally looked at me. I nodded.

Luke mumbled something, then drank from his orange juice glass.

"I've never heard of the game," Dad said.

Luke set his glass down with a thud. "Yeah. People who do it are stupid."

I was happy Luke saw the game as dangerous and hoped that Brady's death, and the inevitable domino effect this would cause was a wake up call for him.

"I'm really surprised he participated." I cut into my pancakes. "I've been to a lot of parties where Brady has been and he never did anything but the usual partying." He'd had black spirits crawling all over him at Krissy's house. Then Albert had swarmed him like a hive of killer bees. Was Albert's influence what had pushed him over the edge?

A shudder wracked my body and I reached for my glass of juice. Dad eyed me.

"You okay?" he asked.

I nodded as cold juice went down my throat. My hand trembled as I set the orange juice down on the table.

"I never met Brady, but I've heard you speak of him." Mom, too, was studying me. "How is Brittany taking it? Or have you talked to her?"

"I haven't yet. We're not exactly on speaking terms." Or we hadn't been, since Weston had professed his feelings for me.

"I imagine not, with Weston showing interest in you." Mom's tone was factual. I appreciated her not grilling me on the subject.

"No one else was injured?" Dad asked.

"Not that I know of. My friend, Chase, said the police hauled a bunch of kids to the station and held them until their parents arrived."

"Sucks for them," Luke snorted.

"Yeah, it does." I was mostly worried about Krissy. My sickened stomach rolled. I took my half-eaten plate of pancakes to the kitchen sink.

"I'm ready when you are," I said, pulling my cell phone out, checking the screen for messages.

Dad's brows lifted. "Zoe... anxious for church?"

"Okay, okay, stop it," I teased back. Still no word from Weston. Or Krissy. Britt's phone call blinked up at me in reminder. I excused myself and walked out the front door, into the bitter winter morning air.

Snow coated the grass but all walkways and the streets were dry. Though icy, the air carried the winter scent of evergreen from pine trees in the yard and on our street. Overhead, the heavens were gloomy and gray. I closed my eyes, took a breath. *I'll take some of your strength now, Matthias.* A smile lifted my lips and my soul responded, feeling lighter and more positive.

I dialed Britt.

"Zoe?"

"Hey."

Her weeping started instantaneously and turned into sobs that twisted my heart for her. She cried for what felt like the longest minutes of my life, but I didn't say anything, I listened and waited.

"Can you believe it?" she sniffed.

"Are you okay?"

"How do you think I am?"

"I'm sorry."

Britt blew out a sigh into the phone. "It shouldn't have happened. We were right there. Right next to him."

I nodded and slowly paced our front walkway. "That game is risky, you know that. He knew that."

"I know, I know." She sobbed into the phone again. "But he's done it before. He knew the timing."

"He has?"

"Yeah. I—I still… I can't believe he's gone. It's so wrong."

"Yeah."

"So… Tyler drove me. I was too upset to get behind the wheel. My parents freaked, of course. I mean, I usually sneak in late if I'm blasted. Dad grounded me until I'm eighteen after he heard about Brady. But, what the hell, that's only two months away. Whatever. He called me a slut, can you believe that? I mean, after everything that happened my own dad called me that!" She wept into the phone again.

"Britt…"

Hysterical, Britt sounded as though she was about to pass out. "This is too much for me. I can't do this anymore."

"This—what?" Britt had always manipulated, and like the boy who cried wolf, I'd learned not to jump too fast at her declarations. Still, she'd taken a tidal wave of life lately—all of which was a result of her choices. "I guess you've got some thinking to do," I said.

Pause. "What's that supposed to mean?"

"We all have to grow up, Britt."

"I am grown up!"

"You are." I worked to keep defenses from prickling. "So facing life won't be a problem, will it?"

More silence. "I've faced life. I'm done talking to you." Click.

Okaaay. My cell phone vibrated after I disconnected with Britt. This whirlwind weekend seemed to only pick up speed. Weston.

"Hey."

"Hey." His voice was soft, beaten down. "Where are you?"

"Outside my house, freezing."

"What are you doing outside?"

"We're going to church."

"Oh." The line between us was tight. Quiet. "That's probably a good place to be today."

"Yeah. How are you? Did you get my text?"

"I want to talk to you. Where do you go to church? I'll meet you there."

Weston? At church? I told him the address and he ended the conversation. My stomach mulched what breakfast I'd eaten into a vomitous pulp. Was he going to rail on me again? Continue to blame me for Brady's death? Every nerve in my body drew into a tightrope.

Wrapping my arms around my shivering self, I once again gazed heavenward. Whatever Weston had to throw at me, I'd face. I was grown up. I could do this.

TWENTY-THREE

Luke, Abria and I slid into the back of Mom's minivan. Mom's Sunday music soothed me today, and I actually appreciated the lofty tunes, their serenity buoying my courage.

Next to me, Abria rattled off sentences in no particular order. "Poddy shrabbit do. Where are you birdie? Iaskthemoon."

"She said a four word sentence!" I exclaimed. Luke grinned. Mom whirled around in her seat, beaming.

"Good job, Abria!" I clapped, snapping her attention to me. She clapped along with Luke and Mom who joined in the applause. In the rearview mirror, Dad's green eyes smiled.

"She's making progress." Mom was so pleased, her eyes glistened.

"It's so cool." Luke took Abria's hand and patted it between both of his. "Good job, Abria."

"We like it when you use your words," I chimed. Abria ripped her hand free of Luke's and flapped like a bird strapped down—buckled in her car seat as she was.

The car filled with joy. A rush of emotion surged through me, and tears crested in my eyes. Luke's gaze met mine. I turned and looked out the window, at the stores and businesses we passed. What was happening to me? I was becoming an emotional lush. It's not that I hated crying. My emotions were strong and often got out of control, so I kept them tucked and hidden.

Luke seeing my eyes tear bothered me until I realized how retarded that
attitude was. Matthias didn't hide his emotions. Neither did Dad. Genetically,
I didn't have any hope of not being easily moved to tears. Dad had pretty
much made sure of that.

At church, Weston stood by his silver truck in a white shirt, tie and
black slacks. I'd never seen him suited up. He looked hot. Mom and Dad
exchanged glances. Luke carried Abria in on his hip while Dad and Mom
walked by my side.

"Were you expecting him?" Dad asked.

I nodded. Weston's expression was unreadable.

Dad leaned close. "You going to be okay?"

"He doesn't look very happy," Mom whispered.

"I'll be right in," I said. They followed Luke into the building along
with the other church members just arriving and I crossed the parking lot to
Weston. His brown eyes were narrowed, a knot held in his jaw.

"Hey." Every nerve in my stomach fluttered with anticipation.

He unfolded his arms and the movement let loose the cologne on his
skin, caught underneath his white shirt. "Hey."

A dozen uncomfortable silent seconds ticked by.

"Cold?" he asked.

"Kind of."

"Want to get into the car?"

"How about inside the church?" I'd take all the help I could get and
being inside church might help. He nodded and we walked inside.

The doors to the chapel closed once it was eleven o'clock, and Weston
and I stood in the quiet, empty foyer alone. "I'm sorry if you somehow think
I'm response—"

"Zoe, no. I don't." His head dipped. "I was upset. I shouldn't have said
that." His pleading eyes lifted to mine and he brought himself close. "Forgive
me?"

I nodded.

"How do you do it so easy?" he asked.

"Do… what?"

"Forgive like that."

I took a deep breath. "I don't know. I guess between the accident and Abria, I've learned not to hold onto bitterness. It's lame."

He nodded, studying me as if he couldn't believe I was telling him the truth. But I'd stopped lying. I hoped that counted for something. Ready to repeat myself, I opened my mouth. Before I could get a word out, he yanked me against him. His arms wrapped around me and locked. His face burrowed into the curve of my neck, sending heat from my head to my toes. I put my arms around him.

"I'm so sorry," he whispered.

"It's okay. We're all in shock."

"I was angry."

I nodded into his shoulder. He eased back, linking hands with mine as if he was reticent to let go of me. "One more stupid thing I've done to you."

"Stop it. That's so over, I've told you that."

An anguished expression still clung to his features. "I guess I can't forgive myself. And then I go and do something like last night—I'm an idiot sometimes."

I rose to my tip toes and kissed his cheek, enjoying his freshly-showered scent, imagining him hurrying and dressing in his finest—to come and settle things with me. "If you continue to dwell on the past, I'll have to burn you at the stake."

He grinned. "Yeah? So you're a witch, is that it?" His arms wrapped around my waist again. "And here all this time I thought you were an angel or something."

I cocked my head back. "An angel? What makes you think that?"

"I don't know." His dark eyes grew soft. "I guess it's the way I feel around you. Like…you're…oh, man, I sound like a freaking nutcase here."

"No, no. What do you feel? Tell me. I want to know."

He looked into my eyes for a long moment before speaking. "You're special, that's all I can say about it. I see it in your eyes. Something…good radiates from you."

I was flattered, pleased and overjoyed to have even the tiniest effect that Matthias had on me, on someone else. "That's sweet." Again, I lifted to my toes and kissed his cheek.

He cupped my face. "I want you, Zoe."

I swallowed.

"We're in a church," I whispered, hoping to lighten the thick mood his request had cocooned around us. His concentration—his desire, didn't break.

"You know what I mean," his voice was hoarse.

Yeah, that's what scares me. I nodded. "I… think this is something we should talk about… outside."

His taut features held one, two seconds more, then a smile lifted his lips. "Man… you drive me crazy, you know that?"

"I don't mean to."

"It's okay." He stepped back, keeping a hold of my hands. Mischief lit his eyes. "You're right. We might get struck by lightning."

I laughed.

He looked at the closed doors. "I've never been to church."

"You want to go inside and listen for a while?"

He swung my right hand, eyed the door again, then nodded at me.

*　*　*

After the service, Weston offered to drive me home. Mom snuck me a grin when Weston was talking to Dad. I grinned back. Dad spent five minutes in parental mode, asking Weston if he enjoyed the service and what he thought about God and church. I cringed. Weston remained cool and respectful. Luke slinked behind like a tomcat, wary of Weston. When Abria let out a yowl that rattled the stained-glass windows, I grabbed the opportunity the distraction offered, said goodbye and tugged Weston out of the building.

"Your parents are nice." Weston started his truck.

"Yeah, they're pretty cool."

The cab warmed up like the desert in July once he turned on the heater. I was already sweating, thinking about Weston's words, *I want you.* I didn't need hot air from the vents blasting in my face.

"I'm burning up, mind?" I reached over and turned it off.

Weston's teeth gleamed in the square set of his jaw. "You're the first girl who's had the guts to touch my controls."

The obvious innuendo in the air kindled the already smoldering sparks between us. "Is that so?"

He nodded. "I don't let just anybody handle her."

"Her? This beast? Way too huge to be female. This buck's all testosterone."

Weston laughed. "Yeah, you've got a point."

"You can gender her anything you want, she's your beast."

He rubbed his jaw. "You floor me, Zoe. The things you say, the way you do what you want. It's hot."

The heat in the cab—even minus the heater—notched up. "I say what I say." I shrugged, trying to stay cool and collected even though my insides buzzed. "If people don't like it, oh well."

"I wish I could be more that way. I don't know maybe it's because I've played team sports all my life and had coaches barking in my face. I'm too conforming."

"You have to conform to be a team player. I never played team sports. I hate people telling me what to do. Don't get me wrong, I don't think I'm right about it. In fact, I'm trying to be more…" I thought of Matthias and grinned. "Obedient."

Weston's gaze shifted from light and jesting to serious and intense. He pulled the truck onto the first random street, yanked it to the curb and jerked to a stop, slamming the truck into park. His right arm stretched out behind me, cupped my neck and with the speed of a reptile's tongue, I was snugged against him, staring up into his round, brown eyes.

My pulse skipped. When his desire spiked, it really spiked. And we were on a neighborhood street—not what I called romantic.

⮞ ✦ ⮜

I pressed my palms against his rapidly rising and falling, brick-hard chest. His mouth came over mine when I opened my lips to suggest we…wait. Thoughts of waiting, even changing locations were lost in the urgency of his mouth. Who needed romance?

I slipped my arms around his neck, the low groan from his throat music to my female yearnings. I'd never felt so consumed—by someone. Except Matthias.

Matthias.

The desire racing rampant through my blood jolted to a halt. Was I being unfaithful? Not this question again. But there it was, like a tap dancer across the stage in my head.

"I… have… to… stop," I panted out.

Weston's eager mouth chased mine. "Zoe, please."

"I… have… to…" My words were swallowed away, Weston now pressing me back into the seat, both of us prostrate. My frame crushed easily under his muscled body.

I wrangled my head to the side for a breath. "You're… smashing… me."

Weston froze, then inched up like a drunk lying on the couch. "Oh. Uh. Sorry." He sat, pulling me up with him. "Did I hurt you?"

"No, just… you weigh… a lot. I couldn't breathe."

"Man, sorry about that."

The dazed look in his eye warned me he was still wound tight. He slid his right arm around my shoulders and brought me against him again but I stiffened. His gaze sharpened. "Something wrong?"

"We're on a street."

He looked around. "Yeah?"

"Well, it's not the ideal place to make out. I mean, passing cars can see us."

The right side of his lip lifted. "Kinda cool, right?"

"What?!"

"Okay, okay, I'm joking. I'll drive us up to the mountains where we won't be disturbed." He put the idling truck in first gear.

235

"How about we wait."

"Wait? Zoe, I thought you were trying to be obedient."

I elbowed him with a laugh. "You'd like that, wouldn't you?"

"Oh, yeah."

"This isn't the best time, I mean, with what's happened to Brady and everything,"

Weston's exuberance vanished.

"I don't want to be your distraction rebound, you know?"

Weston sighed. "Man." He looked over. "But you're right. I shouldn't use you to distract myself. I mean, I wasn't. I don't want you to think—"

"Forget it. Your best friend just died. You have every right to have a lot on your mind."

"The funeral's Wednesday." His tone softened. "His mom wants me to say something."

"Oh, wow."

He nodded, scrubbing his jaw again. "It's weird because she never liked me. Always was kind of rude, you know, whenever I was over there. I was kind of shocked she asked me. And Brady changed. That's why we stopped hanging. The stuff he was into... I couldn't be a part of it."

"Think about the good times you had and you'll find something comforting to say." I patted his arm and the gesture brought his thoughtful gaze to mine.

"I'm glad you're here... during this," he murmured. "Will you come with me? To the funeral."

"Of course."

Weston took me home. He parked his truck by the curb and extinguished the engine. "I don't want you to get out yet."

"You... don't?"

He shook his head. Gripping the steering wheel with both hands, he stared out at the empty street through the front window. Sundays were quiet in Pleasant Grove, with families spending the day at church and engaged in togetherness which left the streets of town pretty empty. A soft wind rattled bare aspens, feathering through the extended branches of elegant evergreens that seemed to beckon wildlife with a protective place to stay for a while.

"You make me feel… safe," he said.

My pulse ribboned in pleasure. I'd never been told that before. "Oh. Cool."

"It's more than cool, Zoe." He looked at me. "I told you I love you and I mean it. All the girls I've been with—they're… they're nothing compared to you. I don't know how else to say this. I'm not very good with words. You write, right? Maybe you can't understand how hard it is to say what's inside, but it's hard."

Touched, I rested my hand on his shoulder. "I can see what you're feeling on your face, and that speaks truer than any words ever could."

He turned, and covered my hand with his. Gratitude sharpened his gaze. "Man." He shook his head, let out a soft laugh. "I went to church today. That's weird."

I chuckled. "I won't tell anyone."

"I don't care if you do. Whatever, you know?"

"Exactly."

"Does this have to be over?"

"My parents like me to be at home on Sunday. I know cheesy, right? But they've been through a lot and I need to be there."

He nodded, lowered his head. "It's cool that you care about them like that. Don't get me wrong, I care about my parents, too. But they're busy."

My heart pinched. "Even today?"

"They're busy all the time. Mom works as much as Dad." He leaned back into the seat, sighed, but he still held my hand, now resting on the seat between us. "I don't know. Sometimes I don't feel like a priority."

"I'm sorry."

He turned his face toward the window, as if hiding and the pinch in my heart deepened. Weston, social, popular *it* boy, was lonely. I squeezed his hand. "You have brothers and sisters, right?"

"A brother, but he's up at the U of Utah." His voice cracked. I could see now that the recent changes in his social frontline had left him without a lot of friends. "Do you want to come inside? Spend the day with us?"

He turned and his expression lightened. "Seriously?"

"Yeah. My parents won't mind."

"Maybe you should ask, first."

"I don't need to. As long as you don't care if Abria stands on the table or climbs up your legs or eats your dinner, you're good to go."

He laughed. "No, that's cool." He studied me a moment, then lifted his hand to my face, his hand touching my cheek. My heart flipped over.

Weston got out, shut the door and came around to open my side for me.

TWENTY-FOUR

Mom and Dad extended themselves to Weston as if he was an old friend. The tight hesitation Weston carried across his shoulders when he walked into our house slowly eased as Sunday unfolded. He was amazed that Mom had prepared a meal of roast, potatoes, carrots and biscuits followed by chocolate cake. That the table was set with a tablecloth and matching plates. "We use paper most of the time," he said. "And take out."

Abria buzzed around Weston like a bee around a daisy. And even though she didn't look right at him, she kept an eye on him in her peripheral vision, flapping, singing and laughing to get his attention. I held my breath. Weston was a little edgy at first, but when I picked her up and carried her to him, told her who he was, he seemed a little more at ease. My experience with introducing Abria to people told me a lot. Those who couldn't handle her, simply ignored her as if she didn't exist. Others tried to continue socializing with uncomfortable glances at her, like she was a loose, lit firecracker that might explode at any minute. Few addressed her, and treated her with kindness and compassion. I guess that's why Matthias stood out.

I glanced around, half thinking I might see him somewhere, but of course I didn't. Abria was safe, so Matthias was somewhere doing good for someone else.

Dad asked Weston about his teams: football, which was over, and basketball which was nearing an end. Weston talked like a player interviewed for sports talk or some other program.

Luke hung in the room in listening-mode, watching Weston with cagey curiosity. At one point during dinner, Luke texted me.

r u and him it?

um maybe

wt?

Luke was still bothered by what had happened between Weston, Brady and I. Wariness remained in his eyes. Bangs couldn't hide his suspicion. Weston seemed itchier around Luke than he did around Abria, and the discomfort started to leak into the air like a putrid smell.

Finally, Luke went upstairs. Mom's disappointed gaze followed him, so did Dad's, and I felt responsible for Luke's sudden absence though I was sure Weston hadn't picked up on the wrinkled moment.

"Your parents aren't home today?" Mom asked Weston as she loaded the dishwasher after our meal. Weston and I cleared the table, occasionally smiling at each other.

"They usually take off on Sundays."

I heard Mom's unspoken words in the silence that followed. *Without their child?* "Oh."

"The meal was great, Mrs. Dodd," Weston said.

"Glad you liked it."

To save Weston from further Mom-style interrogation, I tugged him toward the stairs after we'd finished with the table. He followed me. "We're going upstairs," I said. "And, yes, I'll keep the door open." I shot Mom a grin. She lifted her brow at me and smiled.

Weston. In my house. In my bedroom. My heart swooped in a rollercoaster twist. After we were inside, I turned. His arms wrapped around my waist. He kicked the door closed and pinned me against it in a thud.

"The door—"

His lips pressed into mine, hot, fast and hard. Zing. My knees buckled. He was so deliciously kissable. So… hot. The hard planes of his chest pressed me into the unyielding wooden door.

He panted out a kiss along my jaw, down my throat, his arms gripping me tighter, lifting me off my toes. My head spun. I gripped his face in my hands, urgently nipping at his lips. Roving through my body now was a ferocious hunger I hadn't realized I had.

Weston easily carried me the few feet to my bed, where he gently eased us both onto the fluffy spread, stretching me out underneath him. Our lips broke contact and our eyes locked.

I cared about Weston. He was gorgeous, sweet and so intensely engrossed in me; flattery seduced my feelings for him. In the back of my mind Matthias' image floated in a ray of smiling light, reminding me that a greater portion of my heart yearned with the same intensity—for him. But Matthias wasn't mine. He wasn't here now, craving me. And being craved was delicious.

"Zoe, is this okay?" Weston's voice rasped.

Are you kidding? I nodded, feeling lusciously feminine beneath his masculine body. His lips lowered again to mine, just as the door burst open. We both shot upright.

Heart pounding, breath gone, I was relieved it was only Abria who had burst into the room, giggling. Weston shoved a hand into his hair. "Man."

"Abria." Her timing stunk. I jumped to my feet and scooped her into my arms, both of us twirling in a half-circle. A solid beam of white appeared in my peripheral vision. Matthias. I stopped.

He stood in the corner of the room, hands in his front pockets, body stony as marble. A lump lodged in my throat.

The air suddenly charged with frustrated energy, bouncing off the walls and ceiling like a thousand white doves let loose. I swallowed. Abria slid from my arms to the floor. She saw Matthias and ran to him, then stood at his feet, jumping up and down, chirping like a baby chick. His attention remained riveted on me however, bringing my body into a sweat.

Heat pressed into my back and Matthias' tight gaze shifted to Weston who stood behind me. "She's got great timing," Weston chuckled in my ear.

Matthias' energy popped. He came away from the corner and stepped closer, his aura swarming me with enough force my knees crumbled. Weston slipped his arms around me.

"Whoa, you okay?"

Sizzling jags of light—visible only to me and Abria, for her eyes followed the display like a fireworks show—danced in the air around us.

Is Abria in danger?

Matthias's gaze slid from Weston back to me and I trembled. *Not mortal danger, no.*

Then…

Why am I here?

Yes.

I put my hands on Weston's, still gripping me in a lovelock, and tried to wriggle free. Weston let me go.

"Something wrong?" Weston asked, eyeing me.

"Has the chap no decency?" Matthias' voice was tight as he circled us, his aura heating the swirling air. "There's an innocent in the room."

I swept Abria into my arms. "Is Abria in danger?"

"What?" Weston asked.

I whirled to my right, facing Weston, my mouth open. "Uh."

"She's not in danger," Matthias said. "I thought it best to stop what was going to happen here."

My eyes bulged. I flipped left, staring at Matthias. "Excuse me?"

Weston took a step back. I couldn't take my attention from Matthias. "You… are you allowed to do that?"

Matthias tilted his head. Around him, bolts of light and energy fired in brilliant patterns of lightning so powerful they demanded my respect, reminding me that I was speaking to a *being*. Not a mortal.

"Zoe…" Weston's tone was cautious. "Who… are you talking to?"

I was stunned that Matthias had intervened in my private moment with Weston. Matthias and I stood in a stare down. Abria flapped and sung and giggled. Weston backed further away; his head jerking back and forth as he watched me, then looked in the direction of Matthias.

There was a lot I didn't know about Matthias and his powers. The realization astounded me. "Weston," I tore my gaze from Matthias. Weston's face was paper-white, his brown eyes huge. He stood utterly still. "Can you wait outside the door for a few seconds?"

"Seconds?" Matthias' right brow lifted in a taunt. "The chap's going to need longer than that to cool his engines."

"Weston, take Abria with you, 'kay?"

Weston didn't move.

"Weston?"

His wide eyes shifted from me to Matthias like he was watching a ping-pong match. *Does he see you?* I asked Matthias.

Of course not.

Matthias' right hand lifted mid air; his fingers extended Weston's direction. My heart pounded. *Don't hurt him!*

I would never hurt him, Zoe.

Weston's stiff body seemed to ease a little, like a seam undone. He blinked.

"Sure. Okay." Weston crossed to Abria, scooped her into his arms and, eyes on me, backed out the door, shutting it behind him.

I faced Matthias, whose vibrant display of energy still danced in a frenzy of frustration. He shoved his hands into his front pockets and leveled me with his eyes.

"What did you do to him?"

"Calmed him a little."

"Are you allowed to do that?"

His head tilted, as if to say, silly question, Zoe.

"What gives you the right?"

He slowly crossed to me, bringing himself nearly flush with my body. "*Who* gives me the right? Zoe, come now."

"You stopped Weston from kissing me! That's a major breach of privacy."

"That was more than kissing," Matthias' snorted on a tense laugh. "Abria's entrance was timely, wasn't it?" His piercing gaze shot rays of warmth underneath the surface of my skin.

"You planned that?"

"Ab-so-lute-ly."

He was so beautiful, so magnetic; any anger budding inside of me vanished. "This isn't fair," I whispered. "I wasn't in danger, and you're not my guardian."

"You're right. But I don't have to like you being with Weston."

My heart pounded. "You're… jealous?"

A flush of pink spread to the knotted corners of his jaw. "A characteristic I thought I left behind in mortality and which you have challenged."

My hands covered my mouth. "No. I knew this would happen. I don't want…I can't let…" My heart ached. *You can't fall because of me, I'd never forgive myself.*

Matthias inched closer. "I'm not going to fall." His eyes were endlessly blue, and for a moment I thought I saw the clear beauty of Paradise in their depths.

"I don't want to hurt you," I said.

He reached up as if to trace my cheek with a finger. Even though he didn't touch me, the nearness of his flesh lit sparks of want from my face to my toes. I closed my eyes. "Why can't you be real?"

"I am real."

"Real and here. Now."

"I am here. Now."

The warmth of his breath fanned my face and my eyes opened. He'd stepped closer, so close my breath caught. His hands slowly lifted, and my heart tripped wanting to feel his touch again. Yearning burst my cells open in submissive anticipation. "Prove it."

A deep crease formed between his brows. His hands, drawing achingly near my face, radiated heat into my skin. Gently, he laid his palms against my cheeks. My body nearly burst from light and heat. Tears of joy rushed into my eyes. Happiness, pure, sweet and heaven-sent filled my body as if a reservoir of love had just burst and was caught within the mortal confines of my flesh.

I wrapped my hands around his wrists. So completely comforted and embraced by love I felt adrift on a soothing wave of bliss I never wanted to let go of.

"I love you, Zoe."

His love sunk into my senses with my next breath, feeding my mortal body as well as my longing soul. There was nothing like being in the arms of total love like this, no mortal expression of affection could compete. Gratitude overwhelmed me. At the same time, I understood what his being my guardian again meant for him.

"I don't want to hurt you."

"Dear, dear Zoe." He brushed my cheek with the back of his fingertips. "The decision was mine to make and I made it." He brought my chin up and gazed into my eyes. "Do you have faith in me?"

I nodded and squeezed him tight. "Of course I do."

"Then dismiss this from your mind. Besides, you have other pressing matters. Like that firecracker out in the hallway."

I bit my lower lip. "Weston. Hmm."

"He's goofy for you, you know that, don't you?"

I snickered. "Goofy?"

"Yes, in love. He's in love with you."

Talking about Weston's feelings for me while I was wrapped in Matthias' arms made me itch. I gently drew back and Matthias' comforting embrace loosened until his hands fell away. We stood staring at each other.

"He says that," I spoke around the lump in my throat. "But he can't mean it."

Matthias' expression was hard angles and taut planes. "He means it. I don't blame him. You're easy to love."

I swallowed. "But he's... he's a teenager. His friend just died. He feels a loss right now."

"His feelings are real. You know that in your heart. As real as mine."

"Oh... my." I turned away, weighed down with the truth. "I care

245

about… him." I blew out a breath. I would never hurt Matthias by telling him I liked Weston.

He came up behind me. His nearness heated my neck. "You can't deny yourself life's experiences. I was out of line just now—stepping in the way I did."

"I don't want life experiences."

His chest rumbled in a chuckle. "No choice in the matter I'm afraid."

"Yes, I do have a choice. I don't have to love anyone else."

"Sassy bearcat." His fingers tapped my chin. "You'll steal many hearts in your lifetime, and you won't be able to stop it."

Frustrated, I broke away. "Yes, I can. You know how stubborn I can be."

"And you were doing a fine job of fighting off the chap just moments ago, I have to say." He grinned and rocked back on his heels, trying to lighten the mood. "I'm going to have to get used to seeing you with other gents."

He stepped closer. "Zoe, I acted in haste. Don't hold back because of me. I don't want you to."

"But how can I care for someone else and love you at the same time? I don't think it's possible."

He placed his hands on my shoulders. "You love Abria, don't you? And Luke?"

"I know where you're going with this, and, yes, I can love a lot of people at once, but this is different. You're… there will never be anyone as perfect as you in my life."

"Zoe, I'm… refined, but not perfect. Like you, I still have much to learn and understand as witnessed by my rather impulsive reaction just now. Regardless of my love for you, I understand that you have your life to live." He embraced me again, and comfort swept me from head to toe. I could rest in his serenity indefinitely.

"Zoe?" Weston's voice.

I freed of Matthias' arms and turned. Weston stood wide-eyed and ashen in the open door.

≥✢≤

246

TWENTY-FIVE

My heart tripped. *Are you sure he can't see you?*

Ah-so-lute-ly.

Even from across the room I saw Weston trembling. I quickly crossed to him, took his hand and urged him inside, before shutting the door.

His lips moved, but nothing came out. He stared at me. "Where's Abria?" I asked.

"I—your mom—she—"

"Okay. Good. I just wanted to make sure she was with somebody."

"Poor chap's scared to death," Matthias observed.

"What should I do?" I mumbled.

"You're a smart sheba," Matthias came closer. "You'll think of something."

"Can't you—I don't know, zap him or something? Anything?"

Matthias' chuckled. "When you are capable of helping him, my powers aren't necessary."

"It'd be easier if you just did your thing," I pointed out.

"Zoe…" Weston's voice scraped. "You're…" He swallowed. "Who… are you… are you…. are…"

"Come sit down." I took his hand and gently tugged him toward the bed.

"Perhaps a *chair* would be less distracting for the fellow?" Matthias quipped.

I shot him a grin over my shoulder. "Does he look... revved up to you?"

Weston's head jerked around and he looked in the direction of Matthias. "Who?"

Hands on Weston's shoulders, I pressed him down onto the foot of my bed. He stared up at me, face still white as snow. "I need to talk to you."

His Adam's apple bobbed, his mouth opened. Nothing came out. At my shoulder I felt Matthias' heated presence. "You've left him speechless."

"No thanks to you," I snickered. Weston's eyes grew huge. I had to calm him, poor guy. I sat down beside him. "Don't be afraid."

"I—I'm not, I'm just wondering what's going—on."

"It's kind of hard to explain, and you might never want to speak to me again when I tell you." I glanced up at Matthias. His face calmed me and encouraged me to continue. *What's the worst that could happen? If he thinks I'm nuts and never speaks to me again, that eliminates one guy from my life.*

Matthias tilted his head at me.

I blew out a breath and took Weston's hands in mine. "You know how you said that you sense something—special—about me?" Weston nodded. "Well, there is something about me that is... different. I..." I glanced again at Matthias who nodded. "I can see...." *Man-oh-man this is hard. Am I committing social suicide here? He'll never believe me, never. I might as well tell him I'm hopping on the next flight to Venus.* "I can see spiritual things."

Weston's eyes rounded to the size of quarters. "Like, ghosts?"

I nodded. "Well, they're not ghosts, that's the thing. The person is dead, but their spirit is alive."

"And that's what you see?"

I nodded again, my breath holding in my chest as I waited for him to run out of the room laughing, screaming or both. He studied me, his clammy hands slowly warming in mine.

"So," he cleared his throat, "just a minute ago, when you were—um, talking—you were talking to a spirit?"

I nodded.

His eyes widened again and he glanced around. "There's some here, right now, in this room with us?"

I couldn't tell if Weston believed me or not. His face was still in shock, and he hadn't moved an inch. Only his eyes darted in search of something he couldn't see. "One, yes," I ventured. I'd already dropped the bomb. I had nothing left to lose. "My sister's guardian angel." Relief soothed me as I breathed out the words. *There. Out. In the open.* Weston could either accept or reject what I was telling him. Either way, speaking the truth lightened my shoulders.

Minutes ticked by in a silence building with tension. Weston pulled his hands from mine. He took a deep breath. "You are clairvoyant then. I asked you that before."

"If you think I lied to you, I'm sorry. I wasn't ready to tell you because I wasn't sure you were ready to hear."

Weston's gaze moved around the room. At my side, Matthias remained quiet and listening. *Does he believe me?*

I'm not able to discern his thoughts, Zoe, only yours and Abria's.

I waited while Weston appeared to take in the information in, digesting it. The wide-eyed look on his face slowly vanished, that was a relief. But whether or not he'd open his mind to what I'd told him, I had no idea.

Finally, he met my gaze again. "I should have known you'd say something like this." His voice was soft. My nerves jittered. Was he going to chastise me now? I didn't care, I couldn't deny what had happened, and what I saw. I knew it, and nothing Weston said or did would change the truth.

"You have one, don't you?" he asked, his tone still quiet.

"Yes."

Weston stared at me, his eyes shadowed. He inched back. Looked at me like I'd morphed into a monster. "That's what I felt that night. I knew there was someone there."

The air whirled with shame and fear.

I glanced up at Matthias who eyed Weston with an undeviating stare.

Weston followed my glance and he moved off the bed, stood a few feet away, his body jumpy. "It's here? The—your—guardian is here?"

"He's coming around," Matthias murmured.

"Yes, he's here." I stood and stepped Weston's direction. He jerked back another step, his face white again, eyes huge.

"He? Your guardian is a he?"

"Right-o, chap," Matthias said.

"Yes, he is."

Weston bumped into the chair at my desk, sending the messy contents of books and pens and framed photos toppling and rolling to the floor. He held his hands out to his sides, as if feeling for the next piece of furniture, or his way to the door, unable to take his eyes off me as he inched closer to the exit.

I crossed to the door and blocked it, sending white panic over his face. "Talk to me."

"I—I'm not sure I can, Zoe. This is a lot... of information."

I nodded. Matthias stood at the foot of my bed, unmoved, but still watching and listening. "I know this is a lot. When I first saw him, I thought I was hallucinating, hung over or something. It took me a good three or four interactions with him before I realized what was happening."

He swallowed. "Oh."

"The thing is, since then, I've seen not only him, but others. And I'm not alone. Chase can see them too."

Weston's frame was stiff as iron. "Oh."

"That's the thing we have in common I told you about. He sees them too, or he has, anyway when he was younger."

This news seemed to relax Weston some. He swallowed again. His eyes appeared less fearful and color returned to his cheeks. "Oh."

I nodded. "There's nothing to be afraid of. They're not here to hurt us. They're here to help. They're guardians, Weston, guardian angels." I crossed to him and he didn't back away, which I took as a good sign. I placed my hand on his arm. His eyes darted without aim around the room.

"Should you be touching me?" he asked.

Matthias chuckled.

"Why not?" I asked.

"Zoe," Weston swallowed, "he's here. In the room."

"Yeah, so?"

"Watching? Oh jeez. Was he here when we… when you and I were…"

"As a matter of fact, I was." Matthias came up behind Weston. Would Weston sense his presence? Matthias' aura was so strong and powerful, I was sure Weston would feel something.

Weston stood still. "Where is he?" he croaked.

"Behind you, hooligan."

"He's over there," I lied, pointing at a corner of the bedroom where Weston's gaze shifted and I bulged my eyes at Matthias.

"Are you sure?" Weston sounded like he was out of breath. "Because it's like… like it was that night. It feels like it did that night…in the motel room."

"How did it feel?" I asked.

"Like I was about to be thrown into a furnace." He stepped away from me, out into the middle of the room, jittery as a greyhound at the gate. "This dude doesn't like me, whoever he is."

"He likes everyone." I crossed to him but Weston kept a safe distance between us. "And his name is Matthias."

"Ma—Matthias? You know his name?"

"Of course. We… *know* each other."

Weston drove his hands through his dark hair. "Wow. This… is really… out there."

"You're not going to be thrown into a furnace. In fact, Matthias told me I was safe with you."

Surprise crossed his face. "He did?"

"Yes."

Weston set his anxious hands in his front pockets. "Yeah, well, you are. You can tell him that for me. I'm not going to do anything," he announced to the room in general. I bit back a laugh. "She's safe with me, swear to G—"

"Don't—" I cringed.

Matthias cringed too.

"Oh shi—man," Weston shuddered. "I'm sorry. I probably shouldn't swear—man, am I in trouble?"

I crossed to him and took his hands. Weston tried to relax, but he couldn't stop looking around the room, and his body wouldn't stop trembling. "You sure he's not mad at me?"

"Why would he be mad?"

"For... you know, what happened that night in the motel."

"That's so over, forget it," I said, checking Matthias for a reaction.

Matthias' expression was expectantly neutral, no traces of anything unforgiving in his countenance.

"Still," Weston jittered. "I think maybe I should go."

"I don't mean to scare you." I kept hold of his hands.

"You're not—it's not you. I really do feel something here."

"But you shouldn't feel afraid. He's not here to do anything but spread comfort, I promise."

Weston eyed me, curiosity and awe on his face. "You really believe that, don't you?"

"Of course. I've felt his power. Weston, he's real and he's not here to hurt you."

"Then how come that night, I felt..." He glanced around again. "I felt danger."

I'd seen black spirits crawling all over him that night at the party, stimulating him into a wicked frenzy. No wonder he'd felt danger. Telling him about the evil spirits would probably push him over the edge, he was already brimming with angst. "There's something else."

Weston held his breath, then said, "What?"

"I also see... bad spirits."

His eyes grew wide. He glanced around and I tugged his hands. "Don't worry, there aren't any here right now. Matthias would have dismissed them."

Weston stared at me for what seemed like an endlessly long period of silence. Then he swallowed.

"You have given the chap quite the bucket, Zoe," Matthias murmured from my right.

I hope he believes me and doesn't think I'm a whack job.

Give him some time.

"Bad?" Weston's voice scratched out. "Like... what does bad look like?"

I tightened my grip on his hands. "Imagine the darkest, dirtiest loathsome humanish thing you can picture and..." The skin on Weston's face washed white. Was he getting this or was he ready to turn and run?

"Is that what I felt... that night?" His voice was a terrified whisper.

Probably best if I didn't tell him he'd had his own pack of black spirits that night, not right this second anyway. But Weston pulled on my hands when I tried to ease mine from his. "Zoe, tell me the truth."

A knot formed in my throat. "Yes."

Weston let me go, stepped back and thrust his hands into his hair. More long moments ticked by. I glanced at Matthias who remained intently focused on Weston, as if reading his thoughts.

Not reading his thoughts, but he is making an effort to accept what you're telling him.

Good. Inexplicable relief settled into my soul.

Finally, Weston's brown eyes met mine. "Were these... bad things... around Brady too?"

I nodded.

He released a slow, troubled breath. "I...get it, and...I believe you. But, do you know why they were there?"

"Whatever evil you felt that night was your own doing," I said.

Matthias nodded with approval. "Right-o Zoe."

Weston appeared humbled by the frank comment. "Okay, I agree I was *with* someone who was going to do something bad." Weston scraped his hands down his face. "Sorry, but I get sick when I think about it."

"Good," Matthias murmured, drawing closer to Weston. "Then he'll never repeat anything so heinous again."

"You sure your guardian didn't cast a hex on me or something that night? Because, after that, I came down with the worst case of boils the hospital had ever seen."

I bit my lip. Over Weston's shoulder, Matthias stood, patiently listening. He didn't react to Weston's suggestion other than to shift his gaze to me for a second.

"Yeah, I heard about that," I said. "Nasty."

"More than nasty. There wasn't one centimeter of my body that didn't have a boil on it, not one, if you get my drift."

"Yikes." I shuddered.

"Recompense for the intended deed," Matthias murmured.

"I don't want to mess with ghosts," Weston said. "Good or bad."

Matthias snorted. "Ghosts?"

"Look, I know this is a bucket load," I glanced at Matthias, "for you to understand, but I'll tell you anything you want to know. Promise. Just don't worry about it." I took Weston's hands in mine and the gesture seemed to relax him a little, his gaze stayed with me. But his eyes searched me as if he wasn't sure he could believe me. *I wish I was like you, Matthias, that just being in my presence was enough to convince Weston that what I was saying and who I was, was real and true.*

You underestimate yourself. Matthias' blue eyes twinkled. *Besides, he's not as faithless as you think.*

"You wanted to know, Weston," I said, soberly. "If you think about it, what I'm telling you feels right, doesn't it?"

I waited for his answer. Finally, he nodded. "Yeah, it does."

"Okay then."

Weston blew out another breath and looked around the room again, his gaze missing Matthias entirely. "How come you can see him and I can't? Didn't you say Chase could see him?"

"I'm not sure why some people can see them and some can't. And Chase can only see guardians."

"How did you two start talking about it? It's not the normal conversation you have with just anybody."

"He brought it up one day in newspaper. I guess he thought I'd believe him."

"Did you?"

"I'd already seen Matthias by then, so, yes, I believed him."

"Is Matthias... still here?"

My gaze slid to Matthias, standing a few feet behind Weston's shoulder. "Yes."

"Does this mean he's always around? Wherever you go, he goes kinda thing?"

Matthias leaned forward, as if whispering in Weston's ear. "I might, just to keep an eye on you."

"Not unless there's a reason," I tilted my head at Matthias. "His main purpose is to comfort."

Matthias' blue eyes locked on mine and his aura swept over me in a warm wave of lusciousness. My eyes closed involuntarily. Consumed by the unseen vortex of sensation whirling around me, my hands slipped from Weston's.

"Zoe?" Weston's voice sounded very far away.

I assembled my fluttering thoughts. *If you are trying to make me miss you more, you're doing a great job.*

Matthias's soft chuckle resounded through my being. *Just saying goodbye.* He approached, and my heart leapt. His hands slipped up my arms, my shoulders and fastened to my cheeks. I closed my eyes, waiting. Delicious. Lingering. Anticipation.

Matthias' warm breath ticked my ear. "Goodbye, Zoe." A savory buzz drizzled through every fiber of my body, leaving me with warm contentment.

I opened my eyes. Matthias was gone.

Weston's eyes were huge. "What just happened?"

"Um." Words weren't enough to describe Matthias' parting bestowal. I let out a pleased sigh.

"You... look... happy." Weston swallowed.

"Matthias is gone now."

Weston's mouth opened. "Does that happen every time he leaves?"

"Yes." I wrapped my arms around my body, smiling.

Silence dropped like a cement block between Weston and I, and a cold aloofness fell over him. "Did he… touch you?"

"What? Weston…"

"It's just that you look so satisfied—"

"Not everything satisfying has to do with sex." I turned and walked to the window, hiding the heat flushing my cheeks. I felt Weston come up behind me.

"I'm sorry, I don't know…"

I couldn't blame him for something he didn't understand and was still trying to digest. "So you believe me?" I faced him.

A moment passed, then he nodded. "Something came over you. I saw it. I even felt it in the air."

"What did it feel like?"

He hesitated. "Like… I don't know, Zoe."

"It's okay. I just don't want you to feel in danger or afraid. Do you?"

A few seconds ticked by as he studied me. He shook his head, a smile forming on his lips. "This is way out there, I'll say that. But I feel like you're telling me the truth." He looked around again. "So, he's gone, right?"

I nodded.

Weston's smile grew. He brought himself against me, his arms sliding around my waist. "Cool."

TWENTY-SIX

Mr. Brewer took me aside and asked if I'd write an article about the dangers of the choking game and other hazardous party activities for the newspaper. "Don't mention names," he added. *Like the whole school didn't already know names?* PGHS still had extra counselors available for students dealing with the repercussions of Brady's death.

I figured Mr. Brewer, along with the more astute administration at the school, had probably chatted about Brady's death and the partying scene. No doubt my name came up, and Britt's. Probably Weston's. All of us who'd frequented the party circuit. I heard their rationale in my head: *Let's have Zoe—who almost died a few months ago—write an article to make sure the kids get a double dose reminder to be smart.*

I stared at my computer screen and the empty white Word doc. My other article to the drugged driver had run and I'd gotten great feedback—from both students and teachers alike. But I didn't want to be the moral preacher for the school. Not that I didn't agree that the topic of partying needed to be addressed, it did. But did I have to be the one to address it?

I sighed.

Felt a presence to my right. Chase.

His usual boy-wonder exuberance wasn't in his countenance. His brown eyes had smudges of grey underneath them, like he hadn't slept well for days. "You okay?"

He shrugged and hiked his butt on the ledge of my desk. He wore straight-leg jeans and a pink and white striped, button-down shirt. "Dealing with angry parents stinks."

"Aw, I'm sorry."

"My parents believe in holding onto a good thing. They like being angry. Sucks for us kids."

"Yikes. Sorry."

"When I refused to give up my phone, they forced me to sleep with my little brother—who snores like a B-1 bomber—knowing I wouldn't be able to sleep."

I squelched a laugh. "Awww, mean."

"Yeah, well, it's better than coming to school naked—my other choice."

"Nuh-uh."

"Yuh-huh. '*That naked dream come to life, Chase, you decide,*' they said." He sighed. I couldn't tell if he was being serious or not. "What did your parents say?"

"Weston and I were long gone before that… happened," I said. "Thankfully."

"Wish I'd left when you did. Let me tell you, the dance with Britt wasn't worth it," he snorted. "She was… okay, well, she was smokin' hot, but she was also weird. I've never seen her so obsessed."

Possessed is more like it, I thought but didn't say. Albert had slipped her on faster than a pair of shoes. I shuddered, remembering. "Obsessed about what?" I asked, curious how Britt had behaved in my absence.

"After we danced, she was all over me." Chase leaned close, his cheeks flushing. "I was, you know, flattered at first. Then she bit my ear!"

I giggled. "What?!"

He nodded, his face crimson. "Drew blood. I thought, 'man, this chick's a vampire and nobody knows it.'"

"She's not a vampire, Chase. She was probably super drunk."

"Obviously. I still can't believe Brady's dead. Are you going to the funeral Wednesday?"

258

"Yeah. Weston's speaking."

Chase's brows lifted. "So you and him really are... together?"

"We're seeing each other. I don't know if that qualifies as 'together'"

"Man, Britt sure hates you for that."

A lump lodged in my throat and I tried to swallow. Sometimes I hated Chase's frankness. Of course she dissed me while she was with him. "I'm sure she does, but Weston doesn't feel that way about her anymore. She needs to get over it."

"She told me she doesn't like him."

I tilted my head. "And you believe her?"

Chase's eyes widened behind his glasses. "Are you being sarcastic? Or..."

"Never mind." I faced the empty screen, now dark in sleep mode. Britt wasn't worth talking about and Chase didn't get it, I didn't need to hurt his feelings by telling him she'd only used him the night of the party. In fact, I was sorry I'd snapped at him.

His wide eyes still looked wounded, so I smiled. "Hey, sorry. I'm just frustrated Mr. Brewer asked me to write this article."

He let out a breath and looked at my screen. "Looks like you've got some work to do."

"Um. Yeah. Want to meet at Starbucks tonight? We could bring our laptops and stuff," I suggested.

He stood. "Maybe. Britt... well, she wants to hang out tonight."

"What?! Chase, she's—" Using you. *Zip it, Zoe.* I lowered my voice, "I thought she bit your ear?"

"Yeah, she did. I admit, she's kind of kinky, but... she's Brittany, you know?"

I rolled my eyes and Chase stiffened. He didn't say anything more, he turned and crossed back to his desk proving that guys will do just about anything for a pretty face. Especially guys who'd spent plenty of time in a social holocaust.

The blank screen and newspaper article could wait. I dug for my phone, yanked it out and texted Britt.

⇒✦⇐

we need 2 talk

why?

lunch

busy

whatev! leave your claws off chase

hahaha

im serious

wht r u his mamma?

leave him alone!!

he's fresh meat

I wanted to scream at Britt. I wanted to drag Chase over and shove my phone in his face so there was no doubt that Brittany was a loser, using him. Why I felt so passionately protective of him, I wasn't sure, except that I felt like his sister.

He sat at his desk, obliviously typing away on his computer. He used to look over, see what I was doing, smile. I missed that. Was I jealous Britt had stolen his puppy affection for me? Even though I hadn't returned the feelings, I was his friend and glad to be. I had to admit it was flattering when someone liked me. Like a drug. No wonder Britt acted like she was always high. Most guys at school had crushes on her at one time or another. Imagine—a full-fledged diet of nothing but adoration.

Funny that she'd glommed onto Weston, the one guy who hadn't taken her crap for very long. My cell phone vibrated again. Britt.

im gonna eat him alive

go for it

Silence.

I grinned and snapped my phone shut. Chase was smarter than Britt; he'd see the light eventually. If not, he'd get more than a bite in his ear. Life experiences, as Matthias called them. Unavoidable. Teachable. Life-altering experiences. I put my fingers on the keyboard and started typing out the article.

Weston met me at Starbucks later that night. I was almost finished with my article, *When Partying Bubbles Over the Top*. Maybe it was my sassy bearcat mood, maybe I really was jealous Britt had stolen Chase's innocent crush from me—I wasn't sure—and admitting the truth was a little painful at that moment, but the article was peppered with sarcasm. Too much, and as I read through it again, I cringed. *Oh well, first draft.*

"Let me read it." Weston sat across from me. He set aside his drink and reached for my laptop.

"It's too rough." I didn't want him reading my angry frustration at stupid decisions teenagers make when they're under the influence. I'd had my share of stupid decisions. He had too.

"Zoe," he shot me a playful glare, "let me read it."

Weston reading my work? He and I were definitely stepping into the: you, me and us territory of a relationship. Thrill fluttered in my veins. I'd never edited myself in any friendship or relationship. Was I afraid he might reject me if he saw my mean streak?

But my mean streak had softened over the last few months, I couldn't deny that. I'd dropped a gigantically hard to believe bomb on him when I'd told him about Matthias and my abilities to see spirits. If he wanted out of our blossoming relationship, he could have gone already.

I turned the laptop around to him and he grinned. He set the pink device directly in front of him, rubbed his hands together and wagged his brows. I let out a laugh. "Don't be so excited, it's nothing."

He picked up his drink and sipped. "I'm a lame writer, so I won't be the judge of that, but I will tell you what I think if you want."

"Sure, why not."

His dark eyes shifted to the screen and the icy blue light reflected onto his skin. He was so cute. I took the moment to study him, and as my gaze slowly moved over the smooth skin of his face, down his neck to the tight black tee shirt he wore—sleeves pushed up to the elbows—a low buzz hummed inside of me, like one lone bee searching for a flower. His lips, lightly creased in the center looked even more kissable at that moment.

Maybe it was just his age or the fact that he was mortal, but Weston's masculinity seeped into the air around him wherever he went, a force as prominent as a bull readying for a matador. He challenged me. Intrigued me. I definitely had feelings for Weston, but not like the deep love I had for Matthias. I tried not to linger on the differences, and it wasn't too hard with Weston's testosterone soaking the air like the heady cologne he wore. My skin flushed like I'd swallowed cayenne pepper, the burn spreading throughout my whole body. Over the years, I'd thought Britt's guys were hot, but we kept our tastes separated to avoid what had now happened: in-dating.

Knowing Weston better, I could see why he and Britt weren't well matched, and that, coupled with Britt's spiral into weirdness and Weston's ascent into change, diffused any guilt lingering. It was fair to deduce that Weston was mine now, and that was that.

His brows drew together in a tight line, creating emotion on his face. He finished reading and looked up, his torn emotions like scratches across his features. "That's great, Zoe. Really." He blinked. Were those tears in his eyes? He averted his gaze, gingerly picked up the laptop and handed it back to me. I didn't stare at him, conscious of not making him feel uncomfortable.

"Any suggestions?" I asked, avoiding his eyes so he had time to blink.

He set his elbows on the table and rested his chin in his hands. Seconds ticked by without him replying. "No," he murmured. "You're amazing."

"I am?" Heat skimmed my cheeks. He nodded and leaned over the table, bringing his face to mine. The kiss was soft with admiration.

He broke the moist seal of our lips and sat back, but his heavy-lidded gaze stayed on me, and I melted. "I'm not going to be able to get anymore work done if you keep kissing me."

A grin spread on his face. "Good," he jerked his head toward the door. "Let's go."

I laughed.

"You have *got* to be kidding me," Britt's voice shredded the nice buzz in the air. Weston and I looked up. Britt stood in her white fur-lined coat and tight red jeans, her blond hair like a Maltese caught in a windstorm. Clinging to her neck, a black spirit writhed, mouth gnashing in a silent, frightening display of fury. Icy discomfort launched through my blood. Behind her, Chase kept his head lowered.

"You really are a slut," Britt spit out, loud enough so her voice carried. I couldn't take my eyes off the slithering black form now moving around her head, throat, down her back, between her legs, and up her chest, over and over, onyx fangs bared, spindly hands caressing and curling. My spine bristled. "And you have the nerve to get on me for being with Chase?"

"At least I'm not rebounding," I bit out.

"No, you're stealing," she hissed in my face. I jerked back, afraid the evil creature she harbored would jump on me.

Weston shot to his feet and inched Brittany back with his body.

"Weston!" I reached out for him, afraid he, too, would get too close and the black spirit would leap on him. But the creature stayed with its host, completely engrossed in arousing rage.

Britt's expression faltered, as if the mere sight of Weston weakened her knees. "She didn't steal anything you didn't lose first," Weston said.

Britt's mouth gaped.

I caught Chase's attention and sent him an I-can't-believe-you're-with-her look. I wanted to warn him about the black spirit, but he averted his eyes.

"You can't forgive me, but you can be with her?" Britt whined.

Weston rolled his head, like he was tiring of this back and forth exercise of Britt's begging. "This isn't the place to talk about it."

"You'll never talk about it. You're glad this happened. So you can hook up with her!" Britt sneered. "Have you hooked up? Have you?" Britt grabbed for him. "Tell me!"

Weston's hands snapped on Britt's shoulders and held her back. "You need to leave now."

"I'll leave when I'm ready." Britt scowled at me. Then she leaned close to my face. The creature's black-lucent limbs locked around her neck, piggybacking, its sinewy legs, long feet and talon-like claws digging into her flesh as it threw back its head in soundless laughter. "Watch your back," she hissed.

"Watch your own," I snorted. "You too, Chase. She's a man-eater," I added, though his mere glance told me my warning fell on deaf ears. I couldn't wait for her to leave. She straightened, hooked her arm in Chase's and they found a table and sat. Britt faced us.

Weston's jaw was rock hard. His hands hung in tight fists at his side, the tendons of his forearms bulging. I leaned and tapped his stony flesh, tearing his attention from Britt, to me. His angled expression softened.

"Want to go?" I asked.

To his credit, he didn't waste another second watching at Britt. "Only if you want to. She's not going to get to me. But I don't want her getting to you, either."

"She's got enough problems," I said, glancing over. She sat with Chase, neither of them talking, Britt's fiery gaze on Weston from across the room. The black spirit swarmed her body, its tail whipping her. Sweaty palmed, I closed my laptop. "Maybe it'd be better if we left."

Weston looked surprised. "You want to? She can't bully you, I'll pound her first."

"You can't pound a girl," I teased.

He grinned. He stood and took my hand. I tucked my laptop under my free arm and Weston led me out of the shop. I stared at Britt, holding her angry gaze as we passed her and Chase. The creepy black creature jumped up and down on her back, like a furious monkey.

Man, those things were ugly.

* * *

"You're shaking." At his silver truck, Weston stopped and drew me against him, his arms wrapped warm and safe around me. I snuggled into his firm strength. "She... had a black spirit on her back."

Weston's eyes widened and he craned his neck, his curious gaze over my shoulder searching the place for a look. "Really?"

I shuddered in his arms. "They're so disgusting."

His attention returned to me. "You see them? Randomly like that?"

I nodded. "Kind of a grotesque curse."

"Don't worry about her." His arms tightened around me. "I won't let her anywhere near you."

"I'm not worried about Britt for my sake," I whispered against his chest. "And I've got Matthias, remember? I'm going to be fine."

Weston's silky hold stiffened a little. I eased back and looked into his face. "What?"

"Nothing."

"Yes, something. What?"

He averted his eyes for a minute, but still kept his arms lightly around my waist. "Nothing. I swear." He let go, turned, unlocked my door and opened it. I wasn't buying his act. He was bugged.

I got in and he shut the door. The cold interior brought out goose bumps on my flesh. And, in my mind, I kept seeing the menacing black creature slithering all over Britt.

Weston got in and started the engine. Hard rock blasted into the cab. He drove with one hand on the wheel, the other scrubbing his jaw. I turned the music down. "What's wrong?"

"Nothing. Seriously."

"You were all hot and ready back at Starbucks, Weston. Now, you're like not happy or something. Tell me." He didn't say anything. "Is it Britt?" I hated playing twenty questions with guys.

Weston snorted. "No."

"The black spirits?"

"No."

"Is it because I mentioned Matthias?"

His dark eyes flashed to mine. "Yeah, it is."

Silence.

"Weston, let's chuck the twenty questions and talk. We're capable.

Right?"

He thought a moment, then nodded. "Okay."

"So, tell me."

"I believe you about Matthias, and the whole everything-you-see stuff. That's not what's bugging me. I'm just—I don't know—I think about him—Matthias—always being around and—"

"He's not always around. He isn't here now."

"Yeah, but I never know when he's going to be here and when he isn't. And, like back there, I said I'd take care of you…"

"And you did. You took me out of there."

"Yeah but, I want to… I want to…" He let out a sigh. "This sounds dumb."

I reached out and slid my fingers into the hair at the back of his collar. He seemed lulled into a daze by the action, but his fingers tightened around the steering wheel. When traffic permitted, her pulled the car over and stopped.

"Just talk. Tell me."

"I want to be the one protecting you."

Awww. I moved closer, and turned his face to mine, keeping hold of his chin in my fingertips. "That's sweet." I kissed his parted lips. His arms slipped around me in a tight lock.

Weston never kissed me that I didn't feel his urgency pour into me with flooding need. I was amazed and flattered he chose to share his feelings and himself with me. That vulnerable trust made me realize how much of Weston was a façade of everything he'd grown up thinking he should be. Who he was inside promised to be much kinder, sweeter and more real than the practiced exterior.

"I want you to need me," he whispered against my cheek.

He all but pressed me into the seat with his body, so insistent were his feelings. An echo of panic called out inside of me, challenging me to accept someone so desperate for what I had to offer—whatever that was. Whatever it was, Weston wanted it all, of that I was positive.

"Give me time." I enjoyed kissing the fullness of his upper lip, staring into his eyes. He closed them. One thing I decided right then: I would never hurt him. He deserved honesty and someone who cared about him. I could give him those two things right now.

"At least you're honest. Always be honest, 'kay?" His eyes opened, searching mine for truth. I nodded, and tightened my grip around his neck. "I hate lying." He held me, his hand stroking my back.

"Me too."

"I can deal with anything, as long as I know it's the truth. It's the lies that are hard."

"I know."

"I love you Zoe."

He wanted honesty. I squeezed him tighter and didn't say anything more.

Wednesday morning, voices trudged through my brain, making their way to my consciousness like bodies swimming through mud. Mom. Dad. Shouting. My eyes opened. I lay in bed, utterly still. Foreboding pressed down on me, as if forcing my soul deep into the suffocating confines of my mattress and beyond. The feeling was in my room, in the very air I breathed, and it sunk through my skin.

"I'm tired of waiting!" Mom yelled.

"How can you be tired of waiting? What other option is there? You think something is going to come along and change her? She is who she is."

"If we could afford programs for her, she might improve."

"I'm doing the best I can. What do you want me to do? Get a second job? Take out a second mortgage on the house? We only have so much money we can work with, and I'm trying to save for our retirement."

"Some kind of retirement we're going to have—the three of us," Mom's shout rumbled the walls.

Abria. Mom and Dad rarely argued, but when they did, it was usually about one of us kids. I sat up, rubbed my eyes, threw my legs over the side of the bed and crossed to my door. I opened it a crack so I could listen better.

A cabinet slammed.

I hated hearing they weren't happy, that any of us made them unhappy.

I stepped into the hall. Luke's bedroom door was closed. Didn't he hear them yelling? Feel the dread in the air?

"You're already working more than I like," Dad shouted back. "We can't give more than we have."

"We have to do more than we're doing, that's all I know. We have to! I can't go on living like this." Crash. Bang. Another cabinet door.

I cringed.

"I can't talk about this anymore now," Dad snapped. "When I get home—"

"I'll be bathing Abria," Mom barked. "Chasing after her. So bone tired I won't want to talk about it, let alone live through another moment of it!" Another cabinet slammed.

Dad's heavy sigh rose to the second floor like a dirty cloud of smog. My heart ached. I crept down the stairs so I could see them and stopped. My heart plummeted to my feet. Albert stood in the corner, arms crossed over his chest, his silver-blue eyes waiting for me. Just as horrifying was the sight of the black spirits riding my parents' backs. Crazed, wild, vicious, they leapt, slid, then floated in whirring circles, stirring invisible tentacles of rage that snapped out in my direction, pulling my bones with a gravitational draw so strong, I knew I'd never be able to fight.

I blinked, sure I was seeing things. My heart nearly burst through my ribs, the pounding so fierce.

"Ah, there you are." Albert's voice wove into my head.

"What are you doing?" I rasped.

Mom and Dad turned my way, shocked to see me. Anger still simmered in both of them, their façades like clear teapots filled with boiling water.

"We're having a discussion," Dad steamed.

"Music to my ears, Zoe." Albert's arms unfolded. "Discontent.

Beautiful, isn't it?" He wore the black suit, a burgundy shirt and that ghastly rope tie of souls.

The sight of him stirred my anger enough that I forgot fear for a second. "Still wearing the same hideous suit? Your boss is kinda cheap, isn't he?"

The charged air shocked with an unseen bolt of choking power that wrapped around my throat and stole my breath. Albert didn't say anything, his grin didn't falter, but his slivered eyes burned with amusement.

"What did you say?" Dad's eyes slit.

"Um. I wasn't talking to you, Dad. Sorry."

"Who are you talking to then?" Dad snipped, clearly irritated.

"It's about time you're up," Mom bit out. "You and Luke are getting lazy. I'm sick of it." Her eyes widened after the words plunged from her mouth.

"Mmm," Albert hummed. "Purrrfect."

I wanted my parents to stop. Not to buy into Albert's loathing crap. Couldn't they tell something was wrong? Didn't they feel the creepy creatures playing with them? I glared at Albert. "I'm surprised you brought your low-life friends. I thought you worked alone."

Albert lifted both hands in the air and for a moment, terror shook my knees, not sure what he would do next. He waved his hands and the black spirits whooshed together in a whirling tornado of gnashing wretchedness, up through the ceiling until they finally vanished.

Dad set fists on his hips. "Zoe, who do you think you're talking to?"

"If he only knew," Albert whispered. "And, you're right, Zoe. I work alone. They owed me."

I swallowed a lump. "Sorry, Dad." I looked past him at Albert, grinning from his spot in the corner. "You, get out of here!"

"Excuse me?" Dad said.

"Not you." I breathed out, free to inhale at last. "Leave my family alone, loser!"

"Louder, Zoe, louder." Albert applauded. "Like your mother, with real bite in it."

On shaky knees, I took the rest of the stairs down and Dad didn't move from my path. "You're out of line, Zoe."

Frustrated, exasperated, I could barely breathe, let alone speak. "I wasn't talking to you."

"She was talking to me," Mom hissed. "So that makes it okay, I guess."

"I wasn't talking to you either, Mom," I glared at Albert, realizing the closer I got, the stronger his evil force. Like a giant oven of heat and fire, scorching kindness and decency and love in the path of its frightening open jaws.

"Don't argue you guys, please," I plead.

"It's too late for that," Mom shouted, then slammed another cabinet.

Dad headed for the door. "Now, I'm late!" The door thudded behind him.

Albert stepped away from the corner he'd occupied and into the kitchen, delighted as the Cheshire cat. "Ah. Perfect. The beginning of the end, Zoe." Slowly, he came my direction. "Watch me."

My pores broke open with sweat. "I said leave."

Mom glared at me. "Quit talking to me like that."

Albert's laugh filled the air with frightening horror that slipped into my body, gripped me by the bones and wouldn't let go. I couldn't move. *What am I going to do?* Albert was so much bigger than me. I felt dwarfed in body and soul and completely at his mercy. I heard Abria's giggle upstairs. Albert went silent. His eyes sharpened and he looked her direction. *Oh no!* Matthias, where are you? Would Albert hurt her? "Leave my sister alone," I growled.

"You spend one quarter of the time I do with her, and then you can tell me what I can and can't do with my child!" Mom advanced, wagging her finger. *Mom, stay back! Can't you see him? Feel him?* But no words left my tongue.

Abria's footsteps pattered down the stairs. The minute she entered the area, Albert's face turned stony. I grabbed Abria, scooped her into my arms and held her against my chest, my pulse ready to burst through my veins.

Albert closed his eyes and turned his face from her, as if he couldn't look at her, and then he was gone. I blinked. Blinked again. In an instant, he had vanished, and gone with him was the horrible vice he'd brought into the house.

Disbelief forced me to step where Albert had once stood. I searched empty air for him. Vacant. Negativity evaporated. Relief poured into me like crystal clear water off a rocky ledge.

Mom let out a sigh. "I'm sorry, Zoe. I don't know what came over me." She crossed to me, her eyes glistening. "I didn't mean any of what I said. Really."

"I know. It's okay." My voice was hoarse.

"Are you all right? You're whiter than a sheet." Mom pressed her hand against my forehead and cheeks. Wriggling Abria slipped from my arms to the floor. She scrambled on to the table and stood in the middle, reaching for the chandelier.

"Chan! Chan!"

"I'm fine." I reached for Abria, took her in my arms again. Whatever you did, you got rid of that creep, I thought, squeezing her wiggling body against me. She squealed for freedom.

I set her on her feet and she scurried up a chair and onto the table again.

Mom was hunched over the sink, her shoulders wracked in silent sobs. I crossed to her and put my arms around her, resting my head on her shuddering back. Her sobs intensified for a moment, then went silent. She took a deep breath and let it out. "I'm sorry you heard that."

"It's okay."

"It's not eight o'clock and I already feel like my cup is full, you know?" Her red-rimmed eyes met mine before shifting to Abria. Weariness shadowed her face, dragging her pretty features into a somber surrender.

"Want me to get her ready? I have some time."

"You're not going to school today?"

"Brady's funeral. I imagine lots of kids will miss school—or part of it, anyway."

271

Mom wiped her nose with the hem of her robe. "I guess I shouldn't feel sorry for myself. I could be Brady's mother." She sniffed, forced a smile. I patted her arm. "Maybe that's why I haven't seen Luke yet."

"He's probably going. He's Kevin's friend."

"Kevin is Brady's brother, right?"

I nodded and handed Mom a napkin for her nose. She blew, then crumpled it and tossed it into the trash. Her watery eyes stayed on Abria and she let out a sigh.

"Let me get her ready," I said.

Mom's countenance looked alarmingly fragile. "Okay," she sounded like a little girl too tired to take another moment of the day, and it was only eight o'clock in the morning.

Abria jumped up and down on the table, squealing and flapping. *Matthias, where are you?* For a second, I was pissed he hadn't been there to sweep Abria out of this mess so Mom and Dad didn't have to argue. But then, I was there.

I grabbed Abria, squeezing her tight in a covert way to silence and still her, but she only screeched and writhed like a trapped cat. Her hand reached out and her fingernails scraped across my cheek.

"Ouch!" I screamed. Pulsing stripes burned on my face.

"What'd she do?" Mom ran to us. Her eyes widened. "Oh, no. No, no, Abria. Bad girl for scratching Zoe."

Mom snatched her from my arms and planted a firm swat on Abria's butt. Stunned for only a millisecond, Abria's blue eyes widened.

"Come on." I grabbed her from Mom again.

"That's okay, Zoe, I can—"

"Forget it, Mom. It's no biggie." Mom's efforts at trying to cover up her argument with Dad were admirable, but overshadowed by the reality of life. Abria and the challenges she brought, were never going to end and I knew my parents struggled with the endless possibilities.

I carried a resistant Abria up the stairs. Luke's door swung wide and he stood in the jamb, scruffy hair standing on end, striped boxers riding low on his hips. His blue eyes peeped open. "What's going on?"

I chuckled. "Fireworks show is over, bud." I continued down the hall to the bathroom. He followed me.

"What?" he asked.

I set Abria's bottom on the sink, her feet hanging over the tile countertop as I warmed a washcloth. "Mom and Dad."

"Was that them I heard yelling?" He ran his hands down his face, yawned.

"Yeah."

"What were they fighting about? I'm here," he snorted.

I snickered. "Yeah. Never mind, it's over."

I washed Abria's face and she squirmed. "What happened to you?" Luke nodded at me, his eyes on my cheek.

The scratches still stung, and I looked at myself for the first time in the mirror. Three bright gouges striped the left side of my face. "Man. I look like I'm preparing for war," I cringed. "I just need three more on the right side."

"Abria?" Luke passed Abria and I, went into the toilet room and shut the door.

"Who else?" I glared at Abria, her skin smooth and perfect, while I had three lovely red lines running down my face and a funeral to attend. Brady's funeral. I'd rather have crawled back in bed and hid under the blankets. "You going to the funeral?"

"'Course," Luke's voice came from the other side of the door.

No amount of concealer would cover the scratches. Questions would no doubt arise as to how I got them. "Thanks a lot, Abria," I mumbled, hoisting her on my hip. I carried her into her bedroom.

She wrangled out of my arms and made a beeline for the window. I let her climb up, too frustrated to chase after her. The window was locked anyway, and maybe Matthias would show. I could ask him why he'd been absent when Albert had made a showing, and ask why Albert had vanished the second he'd laid eyes on Abria.

"Because he can't be in the presence of an innocent."

Matthias. Today, he wore robin's egg blue from head to toe—a soft, billowy shirt and slack combination that lit his eyes to sparkling gems. "Hello, Zoe."

I ran and threw myself around him. His comfort enveloped me with safety. "Where were you earlier?" I whispered. "Albert was here."

His body tensed for an instant, then the tension vanished in the strength of his frame. "And?"

"And," I leaned back and looked at him, "I tried not to talk to him, but he launched a full fledged attack on my parents. He scares the hell—excuse me—out of me. He brought along a few of those disgusting black creatures." I shuddered, squeezing Matthias tighter. "Why does evil have to be so... disgusting?"

"Makes you wonder why anyone would choose evil, doesn't it?"

"When there are other, better options, uh—yeah," I quipped. "He totally blanked when he saw Abria," I said. "That was amazing."

"Innocents are protected from his kind."

I looked at Abria, who stood in the window frame, giggling at us. Matthias arms fell away from me and I rubbed myself, highly aware of his absence. He scooped Abria into his arms with a smile. "You're a determined little monkey, aren't you?"

"Little monkey," Abria parroted.

"That's right." Matthias tapped her chin and then kissed her cheek. A flush of warmth filled my body.

"I'm getting better at handling Albert," I said. Matthias tilted his head. "Yeah. I'm not afraid to tell him how tacky his day-old suit is, either." I grinned.

Matthias was not amused. "He's not the sort to be a bearcat to, Zoe."

"I did what I had to do."

"His efforts were directed at your parents. Though that does affect you indirectly, you weren't in mortal danger."

I had to keep reminding myself that I'd agreed to this. If I was going to have Matthias in my life, I'd have to deal with Albert's assaults on my family.

"I guess I'm just not sure where the line is drawn here."

Matthias' expression sobered. "The only thing you have to know with an absolute knowledge is that I will never let my father take your soul."

Heaviness hung in the air, the gravity of his words like a mountain ready to engulf me. "Of course," he gently eased Abria down to her feet, "you may choose for yourself, which side you will give yourself to."

"Why do you say it like that? Like I'm undecided."

"I'm sorry if I sound like I'm implying something." He set his hands on my shoulders and his aura whooshed through me. "I'm not. I only know that life can be long and arduous. But you're right to decide now. Stay firm with your choice. How different my life might have been if I'd been on the level."

He cupped my face. His gaze dropped to the scratches on my cheek and he grazed his fingers over them. "Abria?" he asked.

"Battle scars," I shrugged.

His face neared. My blood hummed through my veins. The heat of his breath fluttered against the skin of my cheek, moist, sweet heat, as he kissed the scratches. My eyes closed. The pause in his kiss caused me to open my eyes and look into his, now lowering to my mouth. "You've got a great kisser, Zoe Dodd." His thumbs brushed my lower lip.

I smiled, tingling from head to toe. *You like my mouth? Show me.*

"Sassy bearcat." His breath shot fireworks from my poised mouth to my fingers and toes. "I'm going to grant your wish."

His lips took mine from sleep to wakefulness. I slipped my arms around his neck and locked him in place, my mind reeling with his clean scent, the love I couldn't contain pouring from my waking kiss into him.

Abria's laughter poked holes in my bliss. Matthias' tender caress slipped from my face to my wrists and he eased me back. My mouth refused to part from his. *Not yet, please.*

His soft chuckle cooled the skin around my mouth. "We have an audience, I'm afraid."

My head jerked left. Luke. His eyes shot wide. He was dressed in a pale gray shirt and black dress slacks. His skin drained of color, leaving him pasty.

Matthias slowly eased back, holding my left hand in his right.

"Luke," I said, not sure what he saw.

Luke's mouth opened. Then his eyes rolled back in his head. His knees gave out underneath him and he crumpled to the floor. I raced over. "Luke!"

Worried Mom might discover him, lying unconscious in the hall; I pulled him by the ankles into the room. "Man, he weighs a ton," I grunted. "Could you help me out here?" I shot a look over my shoulder at Matthias who stood, watching. "Wait, you can't touch him."

"He'll be fine, though he might have a small egg on the back of his head."

"Thanks for the diagnosis, doctor." One last heave-ho and Luke's head cleared the doorjamb. I shut the door and stood, panting. "Phew. He's got some serious muscle mass."

"Impressive, Zoe."

I wiped my hands back and forth. "Thank you."

Abria climbed on top of Luke and tried to stand on his gut, bringing Luke's eyes to a flutter. He grunted, followed by a cough.

Matthias swept Abria into his arms. "Probably best not to climb on big brother at the moment, little one."

Abria settled and stared at Matthias' face.

Luke's eyes opened and he blinked, then found Matthias and his gaze widened. He sat up, his Adam's apple bobbing in his throat.

"Are you okay?" I asked.

Luke appeared too stunned to move, let alone speak. His blue eyes remained fastened on Matthias.

"Greetings, Luke." Matthias' creamy voice smoothed the air into invisible calm. I was positive Luke felt it.

"You're that angel guy," Luke croaked.

Matthias nodded. "My name is Matthias."

"Are you okay?" I asked again.

Luke climbed to his feet, still focused tightly on Matthias. "I... I see you. You're talking to me."

"Right-o." Matthias took Abria's hand in his and waved it. "Abria, can you tell Luke I'm here and I'm real?"

"Real." Abria's monotone voice spoke clear as the song of a bird.

"How is this—how can I see you? I mean, I saw you that once, but I was baked. I wasn't sure I really saw you. This is insane," Luke muttered. He shoved both hands into his mop of blonde hair and held his head as if it might roll off his shoulders from shock.

"You've a believing heart." Matthias' soothing tone delivered his words with indisputable truth and the air around us clarified with understanding.

Luke nodded, and his hands slowly slipped down his face, disbelief vanishing with the gesture. "Wow. Yeah, I do." He looked at me for the first time, like I'd seen him look at me when we were little kids and I'd told him something exciting. His face came alive with childlike enthusiasm. "This is...."

I nodded.

He stepped forward, reached out.

"No!" I jerked between them, causing Luke to jump. "He can't touch anybody he's not guarding."

"Oh." What looked like a glint of disappointment flashed over Luke's face.

"Heavenly law, my friend." Matthias's kind tone was obviously meant to ease any disappointment Luke felt.

Luke's gaze stayed fixed on Matthias as if Matthias was a celebrity. More—Deity. Luke's countenance glowed with awe. I was relieved he *got* Matthias—who he was and what he was really about.

Abria, content in Matthias' arms, reached up and touched her fingers to his lips, eyeing them as if seeing a mouth for the first time. Matthias grinned at her, took her hand in his and kissed her fingertips. "Careful, I like to nibble."

"Wow. I'm seriously... I don't know what to say. Zoe, told me about you and I... I thought you might be real, but this is beyond me."

"Would I lie to you?" I jested. His round eyes met mine, returning the joke. I added, "Recently?"

277

"No. Man." Luke's cell phone vibrated, the soft burring sound the only noise in the room. He pulled it out, flipped it open. "Hey, can I take your picture?"

Matthias threw back his head in a hearty laugh. "Ab-so-lute-ly."

"Really?" I gaped. "He can?"

Matthias drew closer to Luke, eyeing his cell phone. "Goodness, cameras have shrunk since my day."

Luke's cheeks reddened. His twinkling blue eyes met mine, like we were sharing our first trip to Disneyland. "He's real, Z. He's standing right here."

I nodded, a little annoyed I hadn't thought of taking Matthias' picture first. All this time I'd suffered when he was out of my presence, and I could have been salivating over a photo—or fifty—of him stored in my phone.

You can have as many as you'd like, Zoe.

My eyes flashed to Matthias' and my cheeks heated.

Matthias stood erect, held still and even Abria seemed to sense something special was about to happen, for she remained posed in his arms. Luke snorted out a chuckle of amazement, held his phone at eye level and I moved behind him, checking out Matthias' image in the screen. He radiated in all of his Heavenly glory. Abria stared at the lens. Click.

Matthias relaxed and joined us, peering over Luke's shoulder at the camera phone. My eyes widened. Abria appeared to be sitting—mid air— in the middle of a bright beam of blinding light.

Luke gasped. "Check it out!"

"Hmm," Matthias said. "It's been a while since I had my portrait taken."

I shot him a smirk. Then I realized how close he was. His blue eyes blinked slow and heavily into mine, sending my heart twirling helplessly to my feet. "I wish I could have seen your portrait," I murmured.

"So," Luke, engrossed in the dazzling image on his camera, had missed the tightness drawing Matthias and I together. "You can't be photographed, like a vampire?"

Matthias laughed, the hearty sound tickling my ears. "Nothing like a vampire."

"Should I try again, or are you going to like blaze my screen just because you're... you know... an angel."

"Obviously," I said, taking Luke's camera out of his hand and staring at the bright beam, searching for even a ghost of Matthias' image. But it wasn't there. "He's a refined heavenly being. You could use all your memory space taking pics of him and it isn't going to change the fact that God probably doesn't want his angels in pictures."

As if the idea just dawned on him, Luke slowly nodded. "Yeah, of course. Imagine what the tabloids would do if they found out."

I tilted my head at him, shot him a don't-even-THINK-about-it glare. He shrugged. "Hey, I'm not that stupid. You'd have to be a total bake-head to mess with God like that." He snatched back his phone, staring again at the image, his lips lifting in a big grin. "This is cool." His amazed and grateful eyes lifted to Matthias. "Thanks, man."

Matthias nodded. "You're welcome."

"Are you going to the funeral?" Luke's gaze wandered up and down my pajamas and no-doubt disheveled appearance. I hadn't looked at myself since I'd gotten up. Panicked, I grabbed my face.

Oh, no! I can't believe I haven't showered or—

Zoe, you're delightfully girlish in the morning.

I glanced at Matthias, who eased Abria to her feet. His smile brought a warbling sigh of contentment from my chest that almost shamed me, if it hadn't felt so good. *Thank you.* "Yeah, I'm going."

"It's late," Luke said.

"Zoe!" Mom's voice was drawing near somewhere behind the closed bedroom door.

Luke's eyes popped. "Do we need to hide him?"

Matthias rocked back on his heels in a laugh.

"She can't see him," I said.

The door swung open. Mom stood in her suit, dressed for work. We froze. Abria, next to Matthias, seemed so taken by him; she didn't even notice Mom had opened the door. She stared up at him through her big blue eyes.

≥✦≤

279

Suspicion lit Mom's face. "Something going on?" she asked. "I thought you were going to get her ready for me?"

"Luke and I were just talking." I picked up Abria whose gaze stayed yearningly with Matthias.

"Aren't you two going to be late?" Mom asked, eyeing my scruffy appearance.

"Yeah, I gotta book," I said. "Luke."

"Me?" Luke cocked his head.

"Yeah, you," I said. "Throw her into something." I passed Luke and handed Abria off like we were in a relay race. He grumbled, but didn't refuse, not with Mom standing there.

In the hall now, I glanced over my shoulder for Matthias but the hall remained empty. I hadn't even had a chance to say goodbye. Pinched with disappointment, I entered my bedroom and shut the door with a sigh.

Just as well, I needed to get dressed for the funeral.

TWENTY-SEVEN

Gone. The scratches down my cheek from Abria's fingernails were gone. I stared at my rumpled, morning reflection in the large mirror in my bathroom. On my cheek the skin was smooth. How? Matthias had kissed me there. My fingers felt the flesh skin of my cheek. I shouldn't be surprised he was endowed with healing abilities. But once again I was humbled and thrilled at how much I still had to learn about him.

I went to my closet and stared at my wardrobe. What to wear to a funeral? I chose a charcoal sweater and black skirt. To dress it up I wore a distressed silver belt, the round shield-like circles that hung around my waist strung together by a black chain. I slipped on black tights and knee-high leather boots. I didn't bother with more jewelry, not wanting to appear too ostentatious for the occasion.

My cropped black coat with a fur-lined hood went over my gray sweater. Luke waited for me by the front door. "You're gonna freeze, bud. It's supposed to snow." He still had on his nice slacks and shirt, but needed a coat.

He shrugged. "I'm not cold."

What was it about high school guys that made them think they could brave sub zero temps without protection? Probably the same delusion that made them think they didn't need other forms of protection, either.

Mom met us in the entry. Abria, dressed in green sweat pants and a purple turtle neck, sat on her hip. "Nice," I said, eyeing her outfit, then smirking at Luke. "She looks like the Joker."

Luke snorted out a laugh. "I told you I'm no good at that kind of stuff."

"You guys off?" Mom asked.

I nodded, leaned and kissed her cheek. "See ya. Not sure how long this will be."

"What happened to your scratches?" Mom asked, her gaze on my cheek.

I touched the spot. "Great concealer, right?"

"I'll say." Her gaze volleyed to Luke. "Should I call and excuse you two from school?"

"Um, sure." Luke opened the front door and he and I stepped out. He shoved his hands into his pockets and shuddered.

"We're going to be outside," I said in an effort to convince him of his stupidity in not wearing a coat.

"I'm good," he said between chattering teeth.

"Give my condolences to the family," Mom called from the porch as Luke and I walked through falling snow to his car.

After I slipped the fur-lined hood of my coat up over my head, I turned and waved to her. Luke opened the door on the driver's side, got in and I got in on the passenger's side. He shut the door. "Man, I totally spaced. I had a friend call and excuse me today."

I chuckled. Britt had done the same for me more times than I wanted to count. "You're going to have some explaining to do then."

Luke started the engine and the tiny car rumbled to a start.

Memorial Hills Cemetery spread out on the foothills of one of the valley's surrounding mountains. Cocooned by towering evergreens and aspens, the quiet resting place looked more like a park than a graveyard. Any grass was covered in old layers of snow, now receiving a fresh dusting of white flakes. Hundreds of tombstones rose from the white covering in the shapes of stumps to angels sitting forlornly staring into space.

Cars lined the narrow paths criss-crossing the cemetery. In the distance, a green awning was erected over an open grave, a dozen chairs in neat rows beneath it. Already a large crowd was gathered on both sides of the grave.

"Man, I hate cemeteries," Luke muttered.

"Yeah."

He found a spot between the limousine and the hearse and pulled the compact blue Samurai in without any effort. Weston's silver truck was parked a few cars away. I figured he'd probably gotten there early, since Brady's mom had asked him to speak today. I also saw Britt's white Mustang. She was in the crowd, her white coat stuck out like a snowball in a pile of coal. She stood just outside the grieving huddle beneath the tent. Weston stood not three feet away from her, his tall form easy to spot in the middle of the black-clad bodies gathered under the tent.

I got out and headed over. No way was Britt going to play weeping wuss to Weston. Not that he couldn't see her act for what it was. She'd opened his eyes to her performances long before he'd had feelings for me.

I passed her without saying a word, fully aware that she stared at me. Luke trailed at my elbow. The growing crowd was a mix of family and students—most of whom I'd partied with over the last three years. I recognized Kevin, seated in the front row of seats next to his mother. His glazed eyes shot to Luke standing behind me, then settled back on the cherry wood casket poised over the deep, dark open grave. A scratch rambled down my spine.

My quick glance over the group landed briefly on Chase, standing in the back alone. He averted his eyes. Krissy also stood alone, her gaze downward, her face red, streaming with tears. Weston stood behind the family, now all seated along the front row. His pale face showed signs of sorrow: pink-rimmed brown eyes, tears cresting as if he could barely hold his emotions inside. When he saw me, he moved through the crowd and came to the other side of the grave where Luke and I stood with dozens of others. I wrapped around him and he around me.

"I'm so glad you're here," he spoke against my hair and pulled me tighter.

"Me, too."

We held each other for a few sober minutes. More mourners streamed from their cars, across the snow packed earth, reverently treading around headstones and monuments, their gazes sad, some even curious as they read words etched in stone, on their way to join those gathered to remember Brady.

"I hope I can do this," Weston whispered, clinging to me.

"You can."

"If I can have your attention." A gentle voice parted the intense silence hovering around the grave. Weston's arms loosened and I turned, so we stood side-by-side, facing the funeral director in front of us, speaking to Brady's family. Two other carnation-lapelled men flanked his sides. His dark suit and evergreen tie accented his black, pasted hair. Behind silver-rimmed glasses, he had forgettable hazel eyes that looked out over the group in constant, non-specific motion, as if eye contact would ruin his practiced performance or, heaven help him, create a human connection with the mourners. "We will begin the services for Braden Jay Wilcox. The family wishes me to thank you for coming to celebrate the life of their beloved son, and would like us to begin our service with his favorite hymn, 'Nearer My God to Thee.'"

Weston glanced at me, confusion and surprise on his face. I had no idea Brady had gone to church, let alone had a favorite hymn.

Those gathered sung acapella. As the verses progressed, fewer and fewer people sang, their voices drifting into the falling snow at a loss for lyrics. When the last note fell from the air, Brady's mother's sob pierced the hush. She collapsed into her husband's chest, a white handkerchief clutched in her fist against his black lapel. Her other hand remained buried inside a furry muff on her lap. Weston's right arm tightened around my waist.

"Braden's father will now take a moment to share his memories of his son. Mr. Wilcox?" The director extended his hand and moved aside.

Mr. Wilcox stood, his dark suit collecting giant flakes as if he was being buried alive by snow. The bitter cold seemed to pass by him, even though his breath, like everyone else's, plumed into the air in white clouds.

Brady's dad stepped closer to the casket. His dark eyes remained locked on the wooden bed that held his son's body, the carved top bathed in red and white carnations.

Behind him, Brady's mom sobbed uncontrollably.

"I... can't believe I'm standing here at your funeral, Brady. That I'm burying you." His dad's voice shattered into a wrenching moan. Long, painful moments stretched by. I thought of my own parents, and how devastated they would be if they had to bury one of us. How close they'd come to burying me. The strung out line Luke walked on as a drug abuser. Would he stop, seeing how death's jaws could bite into a family and tear them to pieces?

I glanced at him on my right. He stood shivering, eyes on the casket, hands deep in his front pockets.

Mr. Wilcox still hadn't said anything more, he simply stood comfortless, staring hopelessly at the long, narrow wooden box that would, within the hour, lower into the black hole.

"We'll miss you," he finally mumbled. As if at a loss for anything more he could squeeze from his heart, he turned and sat down next to Mrs. Wilcox who now sat eerily still, her gaze on Weston.

Behind her stood Albert. Next to him, Brady. My pulse iced. How long had they been there? Albert's razor-sharp blue eyes stared into mine, shooting across the site like poisonous arrows. Brady's glare was fastened on Weston.

"You're mine," Brady hissed at Weston.

Panic grabbed hold of my throat. I couldn't speak. Couldn't even utter a sound. Albert's menacing aura seeped into the icy air, through the falling snow, filling the area with the horrid foreboding I had felt from him before.

The next thing I knew, Weston gently eased my arm from his, and he stepped closer to the casket. A chill slapped my body.

Weston started talking about Brady, emotion riding his voice, close to bursting.

Brady snickered at Weston's comments. "You always had to be number one!"

I couldn't believe his threats weren't overheard. But my glances around the reverent crowd told me no one heard Brady but me.

Brady's hands slipped to his mother's shoulders—as though he was caressing her with comfort. But the menacing hissing from his restless, angry soul was not meant to bring peace. With his dark gaze latched to Weston, he stirred Mrs. Wilcox's fury into a storm that reddened her skin and caused her eyes to bulge with rage.

A glint flashed from the mink muff on her lap. Clutched in her right hand was a black pistol. I gasped. Weston continued talking, his gaze on the carnation-bathed casket. Mrs. Wilcox's hand trembled as the shiny black weapon slowly emerged from the depths of fur. Albert's lips curled up. Brady's wretched caresses grew more intense and Mrs. Wilcox's furious gaze drew darker, and more savage.

I looked left. Right. Then back at Mrs. Wilcox, her white-knuckled hand inching out of the muff, exposing the entire gun. Time stopped. Mr. Wilcox, seeing the gun in his wife's hand, locked his stunned gaze on the weapon, his mouth open. I opened my mouth to scream, saw Weston's face when his gaze flashed from me to Mrs. Wilcox. Someone laughed. Albert. Brady's hands pressed down into his mother's shoulders—vanishing—as if forcing deeper wrath into her torment. *She's going to shoot Weston.*

I darted in front of Weston.

TWENTY-EIGHT

The shot rang out and Matthias appeared in front of me. Every motion slowed, along with time. He lifted his hand and the flying bullet hit his palm, dissolving on contact. Our gazes connected. Around him, light radiated in such blinding strength and power I was sure everyone present would melt or vanish.

My knees buckled. Weston's arms wrapped around me. Pandemonium broke out, like wild animals loose in a zoo. Matthias' intense gaze shifted to Albert and Brady, still standing behind Mrs. Wilcox. Albert's wrath bled scarlet up his neck and face, his eyes bulging in fury. Brady's eyes widened and his face froze in shocked fear.

Albert's hands shot into the air and dozens of black spirits appeared, swarming around the panicked crowd like raging black birds.

"Zoe?" Weston's frightened voice. Adrenalin draining, I peered up at his white face, inches from mine. His grip tightened. "Zoe?"

Snow seemed to envelope me. *I can't be dying again. I can't. Matthias, what happened?*

"Zoe?" Luke's voice.

I closed my eyes against the onslaught of icy flakes and screams.

*   *   *

I opened my eyes to a protective awning of bodies and peering faces. I lay on one blanket, covered by another. Snow still fell in a blinding curtain from the sky, coating everyone who stood over me. Clattering voices filled the air. Sirens. Rumbling diesel engines. Weston's brown eyes were crimped in anguish. Two paramedics flanked me. One probed my abdomen, the other wrapped a blood pressure band around my arm, and the vise grip slowly grew tight.

"Zoe," Weston choked out.

Luke crouched next to him, his features taut with concern. "Jeez, Zoe." He thrust his hands into his now soaking wet hair. Icy air wracked my body with shudders.

"You're going to be okay," Weston said.

"What happened?" my voice barely scratched out.

"The bullet missed you," Luke said.

I'd seen the bullet traveling in slow motion toward Weston, that's why I'd stepped in front of him. Then Matthias had appeared. "Matthias?" I choked out, trying to sit up.

Luke glanced around. "He's not here."

Weston, too, stole a quick look around the cemetery.

"Please stay still," the EMT taking my blood pressure demanded.

Weston exchanged glances with Luke.

"Zoe?" Chase. How long had he been there? Krissy. Britt. Faces I knew, others I did not suddenly appeared hovering over me.

"Thank God she's okay." Britt held her hands to her chest as if in prayer. Her gaze hopped from me to Weston, whose eyes never left me.

"Would you like to sit up?" The EMT taking my blood pressure released the band around my arm and set it aside.

I nodded. He and Weston drew me upright. The police officer reappeared, broke through the tight circle of bodies and handed the EMT another blanket, which was wrapped around me. The fabric was heavy, but cold as the air, so it didn't do much to warm my trembling limbs.

"You're a lucky girl." The officer remained, and towered over the circle.

Matthias? I looked around for Luke, but he had gone, and I couldn't see him through the bodies mulling.

"I saw the gun and…" Weston reached for my hand and held it between both of his. My spine trembled. "She was going to kill you. I couldn't—"

"I know." Weston's fingers touched my lips. "Zoe, you… saved my life."

"The freak," Britt snapped. "That woman deserves to be in jail." Sitting eerily motionless on Britt's back was a black spirit. "At her own son's funeral! What a loser!"

"Miss, you're free to step aside now." The police officer's bark allowed plenty of room for the annoyance he carried at Britt's cold comment.

"My best friend was just shot by a psychotic loser, I'm not leaving her!" She was not leaving Weston was more accurate.

"I'm so glad you weren't injured," Chase's face was tight with concern. He crouched closer. "They can't find the bullet," he whispered.

"They… can't?" I muttered around a lump in my throat. I really wanted to see where Matthias was. If Albert was gone. If he'd taken Brady with him. "I'm going to stand up now."

"Take it slow and easy," the EMT said, grasping my right arm. Weston took my left and the two of them helped me to my feet. No woozy feeling. My legs were strong. I let out a sigh, grateful.

Standing gave me my first opportunity to get a good look around. Five police cars, an ambulance, and a fire truck. Wow. No one was under the tent, the seats empty.

The casket still sat over the open grave.

A pit opened in my stomach. What a horrible day this had turned into. I gazed up into Weston's face. "Are you okay?"

"You're asking me? You were the one who almost got hit."

"I'm fine. I'm standing, right? She was aiming at you."

He closed his eyes. The officer stepped closer to us. "You two can sit in the back of my car if you'd like some privacy. It's warm in there." He nodded in the direction of an idling black and white police vehicle.

"Thanks, we will." Weston's hand slipped around me and he led me across crunching snow to the car. I stole a glance at Chase, Britt—the stony black spirit still perched on her back— and Krissy who remained solitary, hunched in a long camel coat, watching me.

In the distance, my eye caught Luke's blond hair. He stood talking to Kevin, whose face was red, eyes weepy, shoulders hunched. Luke glanced around, reached into his front pocket and passed something to Kevin. Could he really be giving Kevin drugs with the place buzzing with police? I wanted to storm over there and shake the two of them, but didn't dare draw attention to what I was certain had been an exchange. I'd talk to Luke later.

In another idling cop car sat Mrs. Wilcox, her body crumpled against the closed door. Her husband stood next to the vehicle, jittery, talking with an officer.

I craned my head around the buzzing area for a glimpse of Matthias— but I didn't see him or Albert. Or Brady. I shook, thinking how close I'd just come to being killed. My eyes closed in a silent prayer of gratitude for Matthias.

Weston helped me into the backseat of the warm, idling police car and I tilted my head back, ready to dissolve into the safety of police protection. The door shut, then the other passenger door opened and the car rocked when Weston got inside.

I was so cold. My body wouldn't warm in spite of the blanket around my shoulders.

Weston sat with his elbow propped in the door window, his long fingers at his tense mouth as he gazed out. His right hand sat on the bench, in the empty space between us and I reached out and placed my hand over his. He looked at me.

He was paper white and ice cold. His hair and clothing were wet from melting snow. "Are you okay?" I asked softly.

"I—she planned this. I can't believe it. She asked me to speak and planned on shooting me with the gun. I… I can't believe it."

I squeezed his hand, seeing Brady's image—standing behind his mother—in my head. "I know. It's… unbelievable." I didn't know what else to say. The day, if it was even possible, had gotten worse by the minute.

"Do you think anyone else knew?" I asked. While I'd been out of it, had I missed any facts coming to light?

He shook his head, then leaned back against the seat, eyes closing, his hand turning upright, gripping my palm. "Mr. Wilcox seemed as shocked as everyone else was." He let out a sigh. His eyes met mine. "They didn't find the bullet, Zoe."

I nodded. "Matthias stopped it."

The corner of Weston's jaw shifted. "You *saw* it?"

"It was so amazing, like everything slowed down. I saw the bullet flying… in the air. Then, Matthias appeared, took it in his hand like it was nothing, and the bullet dissolved on contact in his palm."

Weston's eyes widened. "Wow," his tone was full of awe and respect.

Three news vehicles sped to the site and screeched to a stop. Weston sat up. "Oh man."

Soon, cameramen and reporters headed in the direction of the scene. An officer stopped the eager group in their tracks and talked to them, keeping them from further progressing near the gravesite. The reporters immediately threw questions at the deputy.

"What a mess," I mumbled.

Weston's expression was a mix of disbelief and fascination. His hand remained tight around mine, as if grasping every element of peace that he could. Compassion for him had me reaching over with my free hand and touching the hardened corner of his jaw.

His eyes fluttered closed. A single tear escaped from his right eye, and streamed down his cheek. In a flash, he wrapped his arms around me in an agonizing sob. I embraced him.

"What's happening?" he wept against my shoulder. "Why is this happening?"

I shook my head. "I don't know."

"It's so hard."

"I know. I'm sorry."

"Why would she do that?"

Grief? Hate? How much had Albert and Brady's influence pushed her? Should I tell Weston about Brady? He was so distraught, I decided that bit of fact could wait. How awful that Mrs. Wilcox had allowed hate and anger to consume her to the point of revenge. Now she was handcuffed, sitting in a police car, on the eve of her son's burial. The tragedy tore my heart. How compounded the tragedy would have been if her bullet had struck Weston. Or me. Or others.

Weston's weeping subsided and he eased back releasing me. His hands scraped his blotchy face, wiping away tears. "Man." He blew out a sigh. "I'm out of control. Sorry."

I reached out and let my fingers play in the soft hair at the back of his neck. His teary eyes turned to mine, and sharpened with need. "I love you, Zoe." He waited for my reply, but I couldn't say anything. I didn't want to lie to him, and I didn't want to hurt him. My feelings were still taking root.

A knock on the window caused both of us to jump. The sound of the gunshot jackknifed the fresh memory in my head. Chase peered through the glass. Krissy stood, eyes averted, shoulders hunched a few feet behind him in the falling snow.

Chase's hair was wet, as was his face and clothing from the onslaught of icy flakes. Drops of moisture dotted his glasses. He pushed them up his nose and tilted his head in Krissy's direction, as if to tell me she wanted to speak to me. I opened the door.

"Sorry to interrupt," Chase cleared his throat. "Krissy really wants to talk to you. Is that ok?"

"Um. Yeah." I glanced at Weston. "Will you be all right?"

He nodded. I got out, the cold air seeping through my already wet clothing, blanket and chilled skin, and Chase and I joined Krissy. Around us, police continued doing their work and behind me, I heard questions from reporters still interrogating the officer.

"Excuse me?" A tall, suited reporter called to Weston and me. "Can you answer some questions?"

"Nobody's talking to anyone right now." The officer held the reporters back from approaching us. Relieved, I faced Chase and Krissy again. The last thing any of us needed was to be thrown to the pack of press wolves. If my parents heard about what had happened without me calling them first the neglect, on my part, would crush them. I dug out my cell phone, ready to call them after I spoke to Krissy and Chase.

"Hey, Krissy," I said.

She kept her eyes lowered. White flakes of snow dusted her moist hair. She was back to wearing her blue jumper, long sleeved tee shirt and brown ankle boots. "Hey."

"Are you okay?" I asked.

Her eyes stayed fixed on the snowy grass. "Are you?"

"Yeah, thankfully."

"Yeah." Chase seemed to sense Krissy's discomfort, and filled in our conversation when silence caused words to lag.

"You wanted to talk?" I asked.

The cold air seemed colder with a long pause. "I feel bad about what happened."

"We all do," Chase said.

Krissy gripped the handle of her purse. "I can't help but feel that I'm responsible."

"It wasn't your decision to play the game," I said, in hopes of offering some comfort.

Krissy still wouldn't meet my gaze. "I know. But I had the party without my parents' permission. And… and…" Her voice shredded out a sob. Her hands wrung. "I… I bet Brady that he couldn't do it. That… he couldn't hang for that long." Her clutched hands covered her face and her shoulders buckled.

Chase and I exchanged glances. A knot lodged in my throat. I patted her shoulder, but she didn't stop weeping.

I took a deep breath. "It's still not your fault," I said softly.

Krissy sniffed. "My parents weren't going to let me come today. They're sitting in the car over there." She pointed to a burgundy minivan. From where we stood, two shadows were visible inside. "When the gun went off, they came running over."

"Because they love you and were worried about you," I said.

Krissy lifted a shoulder. "It should have been me she pointed the gun at, not Weston." Krissy's voice trembled out, her shoulders rounded in a buckling sob. Chase stared at me behind his silver-framed glasses, his eyes wide with *uh-oh*.

I hugged Krissy. "Nobody deserved that shot, Krissy. Not you or Weston."

"I'm really sorry," she sputtered against me.

"We all are."

Chase patted her back. The falling flakes began to dissipate, shifting the air into a foggy mist that hovered eerily around tombstones, trees and those gathered.

A figure moving out the corner of my eye drew my attention to an imposing older man in a long, black dress coat. His sable hair was slicked back, baring a sharp face that reminded me of a raven. Next to me, Chase shifted.

"Krissy!" the man barked.

Krissy jerked from my arms and turned. The shock in her body that she'd felt hearing her name, rang through mine as if I'd been shoved.

"I'm coming." Her tone was meek.

The man stopped when he was ten feet away. He glared at Chase, then slid his onyx eyes to mine in a patronizing acknowledgement that annoyed me. Krissy stepped his direction and I said, "I'm Zoe Dodd. And you are?"

He tilted his head, not amused. "I'm Krissy's father." He snatched Krissy's elbow and turned. My stomach clenched. Slithering up and down his back was a pack of black spirits so dense, I couldn't see where one ended and another began. I'd never seen so many, so tightly entwined, like sinewy black snakes in constant motion circulating from his ankles to his head. Nausea tickled my throat. As disgusted as I was, I couldn't take my eyes from the crawling infestation.

I shuddered and Chase inched closer. "You want my coat?" He started taking off his suit jacket, but I shook my head.

"Thanks, but I'm going back to Weston. Do you know Krissy's parents at all?"

We started across the grass, weaving in and out of headstones.

"Not really. She just told me her parents were really mad that she'd had the party and, of course they're furious now that they've been in the papers." He shrugged. "Why?"

"He gave me the creeps."

"He was pretty austere, I agree."

Should I tell Chase about the black spirits? We stopped next to the police vehicle. Weston still sat inside, head back, eyes closed.

"How's he doing?" Chase's gaze lit on Weston.

"He's pretty traumatized."

"I imagine so." Chase glanced around. "Well, I'm going to go. I hope none of these guys recognizes me from the party bust, or I'm really in trouble. My parents will think I'm jinxed or something."

"No they won't," I slugged his bicep lightly. "I wonder what will happen with Brady." My gaze shifted to the lone casket, still straddled over the open earth.

"It stinks his own mother won't be able to see him go down," Chase said.

"I doubt she'll miss that," I said. "I mean, the finality of it would break her, you know?"

"She's already broken," Chase said.

TWENTY-NINE

After the police escorted Weston and me to his truck—out of range from the nosy press—Weston drove me home. The casket still suspended over the grave forever embedded in my mind. A horrific sadness refused to leave my thoughts. Brady's body would be laid to rest eventually. I wasn't sure who would be around to see it happen.

The air in Weston's truck was thick with gloom. He seemed to be drowning in it, his face still pale and his general energy level barely above comatose. We didn't speak. The CD player was off. Only the heater made a low hum.

I'd called my parents after the police officer had finished asking me questions. They hadn't heard anything on the news yet. Both were shocked and saddened at what had happened, and were relieved I was coming home.

Weston parked his truck by the curb in front of the house and killed the engine. I didn't see Luke's Samurai. I hoped he wasn't somewhere getting high. With addicts, there was always the chance he was back to using. Stresses were a trigger, and today had been one stress after another.

"Zoe," Weston's tone cut through the air like a blade. Mourning had vanished from his brown eyes, and now they locked on mine incisively. "What happened at the funeral?"

"What are you really asking?"

He paused. "Matthias was there."

"Yes."

The silence between us suddenly grew cold.

My palms began to sweat. Something in his eyes made my heart pound with uncertainty. Weston's head tilted back, he blew out a breath. "Zoe. You... you forced him to intervene?"

"I didn't think about it, Weston." My tone was defensive. "I saw the gun and stepped in front of you. What was I supposed to do? Stand there and let her shoot you?"

"So you honestly didn't do it thinking Matthias would show up?"

"Of course not. I followed my gut reaction." Why was he so upset Matthias had saved him? Or was I the one not looking at things clearly. Had I done something wrong? Maybe the fact that I hadn't seen Matthias since the shot meant I had broken the final rule. Dread sunk in my stomach.

Weston scrubbed his jaw. More quiet, cold and brittle, filled the air. He shot me a censuring glare. "I don't know." He shook his head. "This whole thing... you, him, me... it's freaking me out."

"You've had a shock today, you can't judge your feelings by—"

"The bullet dissolved. It dissolved."

The knot resurfaced in my throat. "Yes."

"Man." More silence. "How can... I can't..." His hands gripped the steering wheel as if for strength to continue. "I can't compete with that."

"Who's asking you to compete?" I slid closer and rested my hand on his tight shoulder. The contact didn't seem to ease the frustration raging through him. He stared at his whitening knuckles.

"You don't get it." His voice was a thready whisper. "He's this being who will always be there, in the background, vying for a piece of you. Like some superhero. And I'm..." His eyes shifted to mine and held.

"You're human." Fear and sadness ached through me. What was he trying to tell me? Though my feelings for him weren't as ripe as his were for me, I cared about him. Enjoyed being with him. Loved that he loved me so much. Losing that would create a hole inside, and I wanted to be with him. Here. Now.

I leaned over and kissed his cheek. "I'm sorry," I murmured against his skin. My hand wrapped around his neck to keep us close. "I didn't want anything to happen to you."

He closed his eyes. I hoped my words convinced him that I hadn't premeditated anything, only acted on instinct. "You'd have done the same for me, right?" I whispered, moving my lips along his jaw, toward his mouth.

He nodded again, jaw tensing beneath my lips. Desire dripped in slow drops of heat from my mouth to my belly. Knowing he was vulnerable at that moment made me want him even more.

Maybe he sensed that I wanted him, because he let go of the steering wheel and wrapped his arms around me, his mouth crushing mine in another needy kiss. My arm slipped around his neck.

The day and its horrors vanished, replaced by the fervent beat of our hearts, reaching out against our breathless chests for each other. Desperation heated the cloistered air.

"Zoe." Weston broke the hot contact of our lips and he slid his words across my cheek. "This... we shouldn't... not today."

"You're... probably... right."

He nodded, his forehead fused with mine. "My head fogs when you kiss me like that. I can't think," he murmured.

"It does?" I grinned. "I like making your head fog." I kissed him again.

The crack of surrender in his chuckle made us both laugh. He sat back, creating more distance between us, and let out a sigh. I hoped he felt better, that whatever had bothered him was gone with the kiss. I hoped he still wanted to be with me.

The sober paleness I'd seen occupying his countenance all day crept back. My heart sunk. He grasped the wheel with one hand, his focus out the front window in a blankness that threatened me. "As much as I love you, I need some time to think about all of this."

I took a deep breath. "Okay." Familiar insecurities stood ready to jump into the emptiness Weston's absence would create. But I had to respect his feelings. "I understand. If you want to talk about anything, I'll talk. If you need time, take it. I'm not going anywhere." I opened my door and got out.

His eyes met mine. He remained inside the car. "I'm just not sure I can share you with... an angel."

I couldn't—and wouldn't—change my relationship with Matthias, not for anyone. And yet, it seemed the closer Matthias and I became, the more vast the canyons that separated me from other opportunities.

Weston and I held the last moments together with our gaze. How long should I stand and wait for more words? Would anymore be said? Would they change anything? Time ticking on was my answer.

I shut the door and walked toward the house. The rumble of Weston's truck finally got further and further away, and emptiness followed me through the door.

"Zoe?" Dad's voice came at me from the family room. I kicked off my shoes, dropped my purse on the floor and headed that way. He and Mom met me in the hall; their faces fraught with bridled concern.

"Are you okay?" Mom's arms wove around me and I sunk into the comfort she offered.

I nodded.

"What happened?" Dad pressed. "Where's Luke?"

"He's fine. I thought he'd be here. He's not?"

Mom shook her head and shot Dad a worried look.

The three of us walked into the family room. "Mrs. Wilcox... she tried to shoot Weston."

I fell onto the couch, the day's events catching up and throwing themselves over me with the force of a cement wall toppling over, with me caught beneath it. Dad sat on my right, Mom on my left.

Silence.

"I was standing next to him while he was speaking. Mrs. Wilcox was on the other side of the grave. She was totally inconsolable. A wreck. I saw her pull the gun out of her hand muff and aim it at Weston. The police said she fired a blank."

Mom's face paled. She leaned back into the couch pillows and closed her eyes, tears streaming from the corners. I wrapped around her and her grip locked. "You were so close. I don't think I could have… I couldn't… if anything had happened."

"I'm fine Mom." In my head, the moment the gun fired played over and over with Matthias appearing, his hand causing the bullet to disintegrate. "It's a miracle," I murmured.

Mom was too emotional to speak, she only nodded, dabbing at her eyes with a tissue she'd pulled from somewhere. Dad laid his hand on my back. "Was anyone hurt?"

"No. Mr. Wilcox grabbed the gun from his wife. It was crazy after that. I don't remember anything." Nothing I could share with them, not at this moment anyway. Mom hugged me closer.

"Mom. I'm okay."

"You're right. You're here and by some miracle, no one was hurt." Her fingers skimmed my cheek. "I can't imagine that poor woman's anguish. Losing her child and then this… what a horrible thing."

I nodded, the sight of Brady's casket over the open grave still fresh in my head.

"How's Weston?" Dad asked.

"A good as can be expected. He was devastated that Mrs. Wilcox set him up to kill him. He's taking it pretty hard. I don't want to talk about it right now, if you don't mind." Tears sprung behind my eyes, the building emotions of the day finally bursting. Mom hugged me, then released me.

"Of course, honey."

I stood. "I'm going upstairs."

Their silence behind me told me they were curious and concerned about Weston and I, but I appreciated that they didn't press for more information.

I passed Luke's open bedroom door and looked in, catching sight of his boogie boards and the faint scent of incense. Abria's room was on my right. Empty. She was still at school.

Once in my room I shut the door, went to the window and looked out. Loneliness crept into my heart. I had two men in my life, both were out of reach at the moment. My future with Weston looked as hopeless as my future with Matthias.

My cell phone vibrated and I pulled it out of my pocket. I hoped it was Weston. Chase.

"Hey."

"You home now?" he asked.

"Yeah. You?"

"Yeah. Man, what a day, huh?"

"Yeah." I sunk to the bed.

"So, Weston looked terrible. Like he'd eaten something putrid."

"It's hard for him, you know? His best friend's mom tried to kill him."

"And his girlfriend saved the day. He should be kissing your feet, Zoe."

The word girlfriend caused my stomach to flutter. "Honestly? He's... he said the whole thing is too much for him and he's taking a break."

Silence.

"Did you tell him about Matthias?"

I took a deep breath. "Yes, he knows."

"No wonder he's freaking out. Why did you tell him?"

"Why are you getting mad?"

"Because. Just because."

"Because that was our secret?"

"Well... yeah."

"It's still our secret, Chase. He hasn't seen Matthias like you and I have."

"Did he believe you?"

"Yes, he did. I think that made it worse. He feels overwhelmed. Like, this angel intervened because I stepped in. I forced the issue."

"I never thought of it that way. Wow. He may be right."

The idea bugged me.

"What did Matthias say?"

"I... haven't seen him since it happened."

"Uh-oh."

"Quit jumping to conclusions. I did what I had to do. What was the alternative? To stand there and watch Weston, and maybe somebody else get shot?"

"I'm not trying to be annoying, Zoe. I'm sorry."

I let out a sigh. "I know. It's okay. I'm sorry, I didn't mean to bite your head off."

"Well, speaking of drinks." Chase grinned. "Maybe you and I should meet at Starbucks tonight?"

Eating was the last thing I felt like doing. "Another night, 'kay?"

"Oh, sure. No prob. If Matthias shows up, be sure to call me. I wanna know what he says about you jumping in front of Weston."

"I didn't jump. I stepped. Forget it. I'm cranky and I need to be alone."

"Sure. Okay. You take care, Zoe."

"Yeah, you too." I flipped my phone closed, fell back on the bed and stared up at the ceiling. I'd like nothing more than for Matthias to come, but the quiet surrounding me left me sure I wouldn't have my questions answered today.

I soaked in a hot bubble bath, the floral fragrance bringing to mind the flowers that had bathed Brady's dark wood casket—a pretty scent unable to mask the ugliness of what had happened.

Krissy. The poor girl's tormented face came into my mind. I closed my eyes. The shock that she'd egged Brady on in a deadly game that had cost him his life added a morbid twist to the tragedy. Was it my responsibility to tell someone? The thought pressed heaviness into my chest. I'd talk to her about that later.

Seeing her dad's back infested with black spirits, I realized she probably had a lot happening none of us really knew about. My mind wandered dark, disgusting roads contemplating the possibilities. I truly hoped Krissy was not the victim of the grotesque visions of incest and sexual abuse passing through my mind. I hoped her dad's issues with temptation and evil were his and had nothing to do with Krissy. Maybe he was just one super angry guy.

I stepped out of the tub and the gurgle of water draining ate up the silence in the bathroom as I toweled off.

In the mirror, my eye caught the scar on my breast. Light purple lines remained. Disgust rumbled through my empty stomach. Would any guy ever be able to look beyond the scar and still find my body acceptable? I closed my eyes, holding back tears and no longer able to look at the disfigurement. *Whatever. I can't worry about that now.* If the shoe was on the other foot, how would I feel?

Not surprisingly, Matthias' beautiful body came into my mind. Though I hadn't seen him naked, I wouldn't care if he had kept his scar. I loved him. I opened my eyes and faced myself again. The imperfection would only be with me in mortality, unless I chose to keep it as a reminder, like Matthias had kept the scar over his eye. Though the truth offered me some relief, no one knew better than I that mortality could last a long, long time.

I wrapped a towel around myself and opened the door to my bedroom. A cold whoosh of air sent a flurry of goosebumps across my exposed skin. Was the window open? I looked, but it was closed. Had Mom and Dad turned the heat off?

I quickly crossed to my dresser and pulled out clean underwear. The oddest sensation whispered down the nape of my neck—like I was being watched. My heart pounded. I whirled around. The room was empty.

Knowing what I knew about evil spirits, I hoped none were watching me. I hadn't invited them, I hadn't even had an evil thought—unless my brief thought of Matthias naked had gotten me in trouble.

Sorry! I swallowed. A cold sweat broke out on my skin. My eyes roved every inch of my bedroom, my heart thudding against my ribs. I inched backwards into the bathroom, seeking the protection of the small confinement, then realized that if I were truly in any danger, Matthias would be here.

I slipped on my panties and bra, then slapped my forehead, wishing I'd remembered to grab clothes. *Duh, idiot.* My fluffy robe hung on the back of the bathroom door and I slowly opened the door, eyes darting. Nothing.

Still cold, but no black spirits. I snatched the robe, shut the door and let out a rapid breath.

Why did I feel... watched? Matthias wouldn't hide from me. So, what was the big deal? Why did I feel like I wasn't alone?

I slipped on the soft robe. The thick fabric helped warm me a little before I counted to three and yanked open the door. Bitter, icy air shoved a bone-wracking shudder through me and I braced myself in the door jamb.

Matthias.

Joy swept through my body from head to toe. "Hey."

He smiled. "Hey yourself."

My naked flesh tingled beneath the terry cloth. I wrapped my arms around myself. "I was hoping I'd see you."

His hands slid in his front pockets. Had I done something wrong when I stepped in front of Weston? I waited for an answer, for comfort, but nothing even remotely comforting washed over me and panic trickled into my stomach.

"Thank you for what you did for Weston," I said.

He nodded, his head still lowered. Why wouldn't he look at me? "I didn't mean to—"

"You didn't." His blue gaze lifted. "Don't worry about it. It's okay."

He wasn't convincing. I longed to feel safe, comforted and spiritually embraced. He was mad at me, had to be, or he wouldn't deny me the solace that automatically accompanied his visits.

"I'd never jeopardize—"

"I said don't worry about it, didn't I?"

Silenced, I jerked my head back in shock. His taut features softened and he stepped closer. "I didn't mean to snap." He smiled and then his gaze swept me from head to toe, lingering at the openings of my robe. Goosebumps erupted all over my skin. "You look fantastic." His voice had an unfamiliar gravelly tone that took me aback.

"Thanks. I think."

He chuckled, inched closer. "Did you just get out of the bath?" His eyes wandered languorously along the edges of my face and fastened at my lips, before continuing a lusty journey down my throat to the crevasse of my covered bosom.

He'd never looked at me with lust in his eyes and where a low murmur of desire began to build in my blood, the surprise of his advance took the edge off. "Um. Yeah, actually, I did."

He brought himself closer. His blue eyes smiled into mine, peering, probing as if he saw right through my robe to flesh. "I want to eat you up."

I swallowed. "Excuse me?"

"Start at those luscious lips of yours and work my way down. Right now."

My mouth opened. *What the?*

His head dipped close, and for some reason, fear raced out of control through my blood. Was he serious? Had he been drinking at the juice joint in the sky? What had gotten into him?

"Let me taste," he whispered, but I was too stunned to feel his breath. All I felt was an arctic cold emanating from him. Not the usual warm serenity I was accustomed to. My spine flattened against the bathroom door. One of his arms lifted, and he grabbed the doorjamb. Then the other until he'd caged me in. "I'm going to give you the most exquisite pleasure on earth."

"Leave." Matthias' voice.

I jerked my head left. Matthias' identical image stood three feet away, aglow in fiery eminence. *What?* I stared at the Matthias inches from my face, his lips curled in a flirtatious grin. He pressed closer.

My heart swooped in fear and confusion.

The Matthias to my left stepped closer, his hand extended. In a flash of angry black vapor, the Matthias standing in front of me disintegrated into countless whirling fragments, the vortex then sucked out of the room until there was nothing.

Silence.

My body trembled, the fear, shock and deception that had been so close—drained me. Matthias wrapped around me before I could crumple to the floor in a useless heap.

My fingers clung to the fabric of his shirt. "I thought it was you. He looked so much—exactly—like you. How did Albert do that? How can he?"

"Evil takes on any form it can to deceive."

"I should have known it wasn't you. It didn't feel the same. I felt cold. Weird. Watched." I shuddered. In need of his reassuring protection, I snuggled against him. *Don't leave me, please. That creeped me out big time.*

I'm here.

His gentle hand stroked my hair. "Why did he do that? What did he expect to accomplish?"

"I imagine he wanted to seduce you."

"That's just sick." I shook again, and held on tighter. "I'd never let him touch me."

"He couldn't even if he wanted to. He doesn't have a body. A mortal who has chosen evil can't have flesh and bone in the afterlife."

"How can he think he does if he doesn't?"

"He's being deceived, Zoe. He thinks he can have what he will never have, be what he will never be."

"But he said I smelled good."

"Whatever he thought he smelled was an echo of his past, something he smelled in life and stored in his memory."

I couldn't shake the deep fear that now resided inside of me. Fear at Albert's deprivation. It was inconceivable to me that a father could be so driven to destroy their own child.

An ache of grief tingled around my heart. Vivid images—Matthias' memories—flashed through my mind.

"Zoe, my father had me killed to pay a debt."

Shock caused my mouth to fall open. This day. This horrible day, had taken another tragic turn.

"I want to know everything. Please."

The ache in his eyes passes through me, and in my mind, his memories flash fresh, vibrant moments of his life—lush rooms decorated in rich velvets and tapestries, dark woods and golden lights. Women dressed in sheer gowns, their faces painted, smiling, laughing, their lithe jeweled bodies hanging on Matthias—*on me*— as I slip into his life, living his memory. The women flirtatiously touch my face, chatting, drinking. The pungent scent of alcohol fills the air, mixing with cedar cologne and musky perfume. As Matthias, I move through a dark room, heading for the bar where I lay eyes on a young, handsome, white-suited Albert, a long dark cigar hanging from his smiling lips.

"My boy." Albert moves away from the women thronging him and his head comes in close. I smell cigar on his breath, feel his arm wrap around my shoulder. "I'm expecting a delivery from the Cracciola family. I need you to meet Junior out back."

I nod, feel a pat on my back and dodge a handful of eager women as I walk through clouds of smoke and clusters of drunks hanging at the bar, engaged in necking and arguing and talking. One woman catches my eye. Her doe-like brown eyes hold me for a moment before her gaze slides away.

I walk down a wood-paneled hall. Open a door. Dark, narrow stairs. I take them up and am on the street, in an alley. I look around. Empty. Rainwater from a storm drips from the dirty rain gutter to my left. A white cat darts across the wet street, back arched, frightened eyes golden in reflected light. My heart races. Matthias' heart. Unsure. Nervous. *Go back inside!* But I'm shouting a warning to a ghost, and my words come decades too late.

A shiny black car slowly drives through the alley, stopping where I stand. Doors open and six men wearing black suits and fedoras hop out. One has a cigar tipped on his lips. Their faces are hidden in the shadows of their hats. They approach me and my heart bangs with fear.

"The package?" I hear Matthias' voice—the same voice I've heard when he speaks in his angelic form to me.

One of the men nods, two in the back look around and I know something is wrong. "Run Matthias! Run!" I shout, but Matthias doesn't move. He trusts. He trusts the man he knows as his father, sure his fearful thoughts are just figments of his imagination.

⮡ ✦ ⮢

"There is no package." Junior spits out his cigar. It lands in a filthy puddle of water and dies. A gleam of sliver catches my eye but I see it too late. The men come down on me like animals. A sharp piercing gouge fires from my groin, up my stomach, my chest and lodges in my heart.

Theirs are the last faces I see in this life, six men I thought I knew and trusted. They loom over me, watching me take my last breath, waiting for my pumping heart to stop.

I gasped, started to breathe again, my gaze locked with Matthias'. He stared beyond my eyes, searching my reaction to his death. Tears streaked my cheeks.

"Zoe."

"How could he do that to you?"

Matthias closed his eyes and for a long moment anguish straddled the taut silence. *I'm sorry. I shouldn't have asked for you to share with me something painful. I'm so sorry.* I longed to wrap real comfort around him, comfort I doubted he never received in the arms of his own flesh and blood.

"I don't want you to think I dwell on my past. Or that my life was one miserable event after another. Don't be angry or feel sorry for something that no longer hurts me."

"But there's still hurt in your eyes. I feel it go through me."

"The hurt is not like it was. When you feel my pain, it combines with your mortal emotion and feels much worse than it is."

"How could he ... I'm sorry... but parents don't try to kill their children. That's just wrong."

Matthias let out a breath and looked away, as if he didn't want to talk about it anymore.

His Adam's apple shifted and he studied me a moment. "He wasn't always like that, Zoe. My mother left him when I was young and hurt him deeply. He never said, but I gathered enough on my own to know that many of his decisions were made in revenge and anger at her."

"Neglecting you? Then having you killed? How could that hurt her? She wasn't even around to see it. That's the most absurd thing I've ever heard."

"Sassy bearcat."

"I want to wring that woman's neck. And your father taking it all out on you—is just so unfair."

"I've forgiven him." He set his palms on my shoulders. "You mustn't let anger canker your soul."

"Okay, okay. Just... I won't be responsible for my actions if that loser shows up again. He makes me so mad."

"Just what he wants. You must never give into him, Zoe."

"I wouldn't. Ever. My anger is my own." I grinned. He tossed back his head in a heartwarming chuckle.

"I love you," he said.

Hold me.

Gladly.

His gentle embrace sealed his words in a tender expression of certainty.

Matthias eased back his thumb sliding over my chin. "Know this, Zoe, truth never changes."

His words settled me. Still, I was haunted by his past and bugged about Albert. "Does refinement take *all* the pain away? I mean, you're so..." amazing. Everything I wanted to be someday.

"I see life's events in a broader perspective. In my heart, I have forgiven my father." His fingertips tightened on my shoulders, and a beam of gravity rang through my limbs.

"What?"

He remained silent. I wrapped my hands around his and squeezed. "Tell me."

"One day, our memories will be our judge. There will be no denying, no excuses, nothing to hide behind."

The truth of his words sunk deep. My grip tightened around his hands. "So revenge will be sweet then—for you."

He shook his head, a flash of sorrow in his eyes. "Unless my father's heart changes, that will be the most heartbreaking day for us both."

I marveled that, after everything—including his father's attempts to steal *my* soul—Matthias still loved him. "How can you love him still?"

"Zoe, it wouldn't matter what you did, I'd love you."

"I don't think I could love someone like your father, especially after everything he's done."

His blue eyes skimmed my face. "What does your heart tell you?"

"That I want you to hold me again."

He chuckled. "About forgiveness."

I allowed my relaxed state of mind to journey to my peaceful center. Serenity. "Forgiving brings peace."

"Yes. You forgave the truck driver and Weston and Brady."

But Albert... hurting you... I can't take the thought.

Because you love me, and I thank you for that. The comforting aura surrounding him submerged my troubled thoughts of Albert for the time being.

"How much longer do you think it will be?" I asked.

"I don't know. Don't dwell on it. Enjoy mortality. Do everything you have dreamed of doing."

"But everything pales in comparison to being with you."

"We'll be together. Someday."

"You're already where I want to be, while I'm stuck."

"I hardly think your gift of life qualifies as being stuck." He traced my face. *Maybe my presence makes it too hard for you.*

No. No. Forget I said that. I wrapped my arms around him.

"You're a feisty sheba who can kick the blithers out of any piker."

"If I have to, yes. It's settled then, you're with me forever."

"With a few untimely exceptions." Matthias kissed the top of my head and withdrew, holding my hands as he stood back.

Now?

He nodded.

What if I refuse to let you go? I'll keep hold of your hands.

His teeth glittered in a grin. I linked our fingers and gripped hard, laughing. His contagious laugh joined mine. Light beamed down through the ceiling, as if Heaven reached out for him. He disappeared before my eyes, but his laugh echoed off the walls of my empty room.

I stared up at the ceiling in awe, my arms extended as though I still held his. How long I stood wondering, wishing, waiting for him to return, I don't know. But when I finally realized the drywall was not going to give way and life was my own to live—just like he'd said—I let out a sigh.

I dressed in jeans and my red hoodie. I could use a night out. A Starbucks. My horrid day had ended with a glorious visit from the one I loved. I didn't need to hang with anyone, not tonight. Matthias was tucked in my heart and that was enough.

My cell phone vibrated as I grabbed my purse and walked out my bedroom door. Chase.

krissy texted me
and?
she's in trouble can u meet me at her house in 10?
My heart tripped. **b right there.**

ABSOLUTION

My lungs burned with the frigid air. My mind raced with images of Matthias suffering. Paying for being with me. Punished for loving me. I couldn't bear the unfairness. Heaven was cruel. God was unjust.

I kept running. Harder. Faster. The trees grew thicker. More dense, becoming fuzzy, dark spindles towering over me. Spines scratched, tearing the fabric of my tee shirt. Through the padding of my booted slippers, the soles of my feet hit rocks, sending sharp pain up my calves.

Unable to suck in air fast enough, I slowed. Gasping. I stopped. Fell to the forest floor. And wept uncontrollably.

My sobs filled silent air. I rolled onto my stomach, fallen pine needles sticking to my tear-ravaged face.

I'm so sorry, so sorry Matthias.

"You can't outrun me, Zoe." Albert.

I opened my eyes. Could barely catch my breath. I sat up and futilely backed away on my hands, the sharp pine needles slivering into my cold hands but the close distance between Albert and me was unbreachable.

"Give yourself to me."

ABOUT THE AUTHOR

Jennifer Laurens is the mother of six children,
one of whom has autism. She lives in Utah with her family,
at the base of the Wasatch Mountains.

Other Titles:

Falling for Romeo

Magic Hands

Nailed

Heavenly

Visit the website: www.heavenlythebook.com

9 781933 963839